THE LADY
FROM ZAGREB

Also by Philip Kerr

THE LADY
FROM ZAGREB

A BERNIE GUNTHER NOVEL

PHILIP KERR

A MARIAN WOOD BOOK
Published by G. P. Putnam's Sons
a member of Penguin Group (USA)
New York

G. P. Putnam's Sons
Publishers Since 1838
Published by the Penguin Group
Penguin Group (USA) LLC
375 Hudson Street
New York, New York 10014

USA · Canada · UK · Ireland · Australia
New Zealand · India · South Africa · China

penguin.com
A Penguin Random House Company

Library of Congress Cataloging-in-Publication Data
Kerr, Philip.
The lady from Zagreb / Philip Kerr.
p.   cm. — (Bernie Gunther ; 10)
"A Marian Wood Book."
ISBN 978-0-399-16764-5
1. Gunther, Bernhard (Fictitious character)—Fiction.   2. Private
investigators—Germany—Fiction.   3. Germany—History—1933–1945—Fiction.
I. Title.
PR6061.E784L33   2015   2015002935
823'.914—dc23

International edition ISBN: 978-0-399-17650-0

Printed in the United States of America
1   3   5   7   9   10   8   6   4   2

BOOK DESIGN BY AMANDA DEWEY

THIS BOOK IS FOR IVAN HELD,
WITHOUT WHOSE ENCOURAGEMENT
IT WOULD NEVER HAVE EXISTED.

And if you ask again whether there is any justice in the world, you'll have to be satisfied with the reply: Not for the time being; at any rate, not up to this Friday.

—ALFRED DOBLIN

I had come to Yugoslavia to see what history meant in flesh and blood.

—REBECCA WEST

It was written I should be loyal to the nightmare of my choice.

—JOSEPH CONRAD

Prologue

French Riviera, 1956

Wolves are usually born with deep blue eyes. These lighten and then gradually fade to their adult color, which is most often yellow. Huskies, on the other hand, have blue eyes and because of this, people think that there must be blue-eyed wolves, too, but, strictly speaking, there aren't any; if you ever meet a wolf with blue eyes, then it is very likely not a pure-blooded wolf but a hybrid. Dalia Dresner had the most strikingly blue eyes of any woman I ever saw; but I'll bet that there was a small part of her that was wolf.

Dresner had been a star of German cinema back in the thirties and forties, which was when I'd been involved with her, albeit briefly. She is almost forty now but even in unforgiving Technicolor she is still astonishingly beautiful, especially those slow-blinking, ray-gun blue eyes that look as if they might have destroyed a few buildings with a careless glance or a particularly wide-eyed stare. They certainly managed to burn a hole through my heart.

Like the pain of parting, you never really forget the face of a woman you've loved, especially when it's the face of a woman the press had called the German Garbo. Not to mention the way they make love;

somehow that tends to remain in the memory, also. Perhaps this is just as well when the memory of making love is pretty much all you've got.

"Don't stop," she would whimper on the few occasions when I was trying to please her in bed. As if I had any intention of stopping, ever; I'd happily have continued making love to Dalia until the end of time.

I was seeing her again in the Eden Cinema in La Ciotat, near Marseilles, reputed to be the world's oldest and possibly smallest movie theater. It's where the Lumière brothers showed their first film, in 1895, and sits right on the seaside, facing a marina where lots of expensive boats and yachts are moored all year and just around the corner from the crummy apartment I'd been living in since leaving Berlin. La Ciotat is an old fishing village enlivened by an important French naval shipbuilding yard—if you can use words like important in the same sentence as the French Navy. There's a nice beach and several hotels, in one of which I work.

I lit a cigarette and as I watched the film I tried to recall all of the circumstances that had led up to our first meeting. When was it exactly? 1942? 1943? Actually, I never thought Dalia looked much like Garbo. For me the actress she most resembled was Lauren Bacall. Germany's Garbo was Josef Goebbels's idea. He told me that the solitary Swede was one of Hitler's preferred actresses and *Camille* one of the Führer's favorite films. It's a little hard to think of Hitler having a favorite film, especially one that's as romantic as *Camille*, but Goebbels said that whenever the Führer saw this film there were tears in his eyes and he was glowing for hours afterward. For Goebbels, I don't doubt that relaunching Dalia as German cinema's answer to Greta Garbo had been another way of currying favor with Hitler, and of course with Dalia herself; Goebbels was always trying to make up to some actress or other. Not that I could blame him for trying to make up to Dalia Dresner. Lots of men did.

She'd spent much of her life living in Switzerland but she was born in Pula, Istria, which, after 1918 and the dissolution of Austria-Hungary, was ceded to Italy; but this peninsula was always a natural part of Yugoslavia—indeed all of Dalia's ancestors had been Croatian—and, in order to escape forced Italianization and the cultural suppression of Mussolini's fascists, she was taken to live in Zagreb from a very early age. Her real name was Sofia Branković.

After the war was over she'd decided to leave her home near Zurich and go back to Zagreb to find what remained, if anything, of her family. In 1947, she'd been arrested by the Yugoslavian government on suspicion of collaborating with the Nazis during the war, but Tito—who it was generally held was infatuated with her—intervened personally and arranged for Dalia's release from custody. Back in Germany she attempted a comeback career but circumstances stalled her return. Fortunately for Dalia she was offered work in Italy and appeared in several well-received films. When Cecil B. DeMille was looking to cast *Samson and Delilah* in 1949 he considered Dalia Dresner before choosing to cast the more politically acceptable Hedy Lamarr. Hedy was good—she was certainly very beautiful—but I strongly believe Dalia would have been convincing. Hedy played the part like a thirty-five-year-old schoolgirl. Dalia would have played it like the real thing. As a seductive woman with brains that were as big as Samson's muscles. By 1955 she was again working in German film when she won the Volpi Cup for best actress at the Venice Film Festival in a film called *The Devil's General*, where she played opposite Curd Jürgens. But it was the English who gave Dalia her most successful roles and, in particular, British Lion Films, which cast her in two films alongside Dirk Bogarde.

I got all of this information from the program I bought in the Eden's tiny foyer before the film started, just so as I could bring myself up to date with the details of Dalia's life. Although less interesting than mine—and for the same reason—it also looked a lot more fun.

The film I was watching her in now was a comedy with Rex Harrison called, in French, *Le Mari Constante*. It was curious—hearing a voice that wasn't hers and speaking French, too. Dalia's German had always been layered with honey and cigarettes. Maybe the film worked in English but it didn't work in French, and I don't think it was anything to do with the fact that it was dubbed or that it brought a lump to my throat to see her again. It was just a bad film and, gradually, my eyes closed in the warm Riviera darkness, and it seemed like it was the summer of 1942. . . .

One

I awoke from a long but agitated sleep to a world that was black and white but mostly black, with silver piping. I'd stolen some Luminal from General Heydrich's country house outside Prague to help me sleep. He didn't need it for the simple reason that he was dead, and I certainly wouldn't have stolen it from him otherwise. But pills were even harder to get than booze, which, like everything else, was in short supply, and I needed them because as an officer in the SD I was a part of the horror now, much more than Heydrich. He was dead, buried the month before with full military honors with a clove of garlic in his mouth and a stake through his heart. He was well out of it, his last thoughts of revenge upon his Czech assassins still suspended inside his elongated El Greco head like so much frozen gray mud, and there was no more harm he could do anyone. But in my wretched efforts to stay alive at almost any cost I could still hurt and be hurt in my turn, and as long as death's black barrel organ was playing it seemed I would have to dance to the cheerless, doom-filled tune that was turning inexorably on the drum, like some liveried monkey with a terrified rictus on its face and a tin cup in its hand. That didn't make me unusual; just German.

Berlin had a haunted look that summer, as if behind every tree and around each street corner was a screaming skull or some wide-eyed and shape-shifting *alp*. Sometimes when I woke in my bed at the flat in Fasanenstrasse, soaked with sweat, it was as if I'd had some demon sitting on my chest, crushing the breath out of me, and in my rush to draw a breath and check that I was still alive, I often heard myself cry out and reach to grab at the sour air I had exhaled during the day, which was when I slept. And usually I lit a cigarette with the alacrity of someone who needed the tobacco smoke to breathe a little more comfortably and to help overcome the omnipresent taste of mass murder and human decay that stayed in my mouth like an old and rotten tooth.

The summer sunshine brought no joy. It seemed to exercise a sinister effect, making Berliners irritable with the broiling heat because there was nothing but water to drink, and reminding them always of how much hotter it probably was on the dry steppes of Russia and Ukraine, where our boys were now fighting a battle that already looked like much more than we had bargained for. The late afternoon sun cast long shadows in the tenement streets around Alexanderplatz and played tricks on your eyes, so that the phosphenes on your retinas— the aftereffects of the mercilessly bright light—seemed to become the greenish auras of so many dead men. It was in the shadows where I belonged and where I felt comfortable, like an old spider that simply wants to be left alone. Only there wasn't much chance of that. It always paid to be careful what you were good at in Germany. Once I'd been a good detective in Kripo, but that was a while ago, before the criminals wore smart gray uniforms and nearly everyone locked up was innocent. Being a Berlin cop in 1942 was a little like putting down mousetraps in a cage full of tigers.

On Heydrich's orders I'd been working nights at the Police Praesidium on Alexanderplatz, which suited me just fine. There was no proper police work to speak of but I had little or no appetite for the company of my Nazi colleagues or their callous conversation. The Murder Commission, what remained of it—which existed to investigate homicides—left me to my own devices, like a forgotten prisoner whose face meant death for anyone unwise enough to catch a glimpse of it. I was none too fond of it myself. Unlike Hamburg and Bremen, there were no nighttime air raids to speak of, which left the city sepulchrally quiet, so very different from the Berlin of the Weimar years, when it had been the noisiest and most exciting city on earth. All that neon, all that jazz, and more especially all that freedom when nothing was hidden and nobody had to hide who or what they were—it was hard to believe things had ever been like that. But Weimar Berlin had suited me better. The Weimar Republic had been the most democratic of democracies and yet, like all great democracies, it had been a little out of control. Prior to 1933, anything was permitted, since, as Socrates learned to his cost, the true nature of democracy is to encourage corruption and excess in all its forms. But the corruption and excesses of Weimar were still preferable to the biblical abominations now perpetrated in the name of the Nuremberg Laws. I don't think I ever knew what mortal sin really meant until I lived in Nazi Germany.

Sometimes when I stared out my office window at night I caught sight of my own reflection staring back at me—the same but different, like another ill-defined version of myself, a darker alter ego, my evil twin or perhaps a harbinger of death. Now and then I heard this ghostly, etiolated double speak sneeringly to me: "Tell me, Gunther, just what will you have to do and whose arse will you kiss to save your miserable skin today?"

It was a good question.

From my office aerie in the east corner tower of police headquarters I could more often hear the sound of steam trains pulling in and out of the station on Alexanderplatz. You could just see the roof—what was left of it—of the old orthodox synagogue on Kaiser-Strasse, which I think had been there since before the Franco-Prussian war and was one of the largest synagogues in Germany, with as many as eighteen

hundred worshippers. Which is to say, Jews. The Kaiser-Strasse synagogue was on a beat I'd patrolled as a young *Schupo* in the early twenties. Sometimes I would chat to some of the boys who attended the
Jewish Boys' School and who used to go trainspotting at the station.
Once, another uniformed copper saw me talking to those boys and
asked, "What do you find to talk about with these Jews, anyway?" And
I'd replied that they were just children and that we had talked about
what you talk about with any other children. Of course, all that was
before I found out that I had a trickle of Jew blood myself. Still, maybe
it explains why I was nice to them. But I prefer to think it doesn't
explain very much at all.

It had been a while since I'd seen any Jewish boys on Kaiser-Strasse.
Since the beginning of June they'd been deporting Berlin's Jews from
a transit camp at Grosse Hamburger Strasse to destinations somewhere
in the east, although it was becoming better known that the destinations were more final than some nebulous compass point. Mostly the
deportations were made at night, when there was no one around to see
it done, but one morning, at about five a.m., when I was checking out
a petty theft at Anhalter Station, I saw about fifty elderly Jews being
loaded into closed cars on an impatient train. They looked like something Pieter Bruegel might have painted back in a time when Europe
was a much more barbarous place than it is now—when kings and
emperors committed their black crimes in the open light of day, and
not at a time when no one was yet out of bed to see them. The cars
didn't seem so bad but by then I had a pretty good idea of what was
going to happen to those Jews, which I expect was more than they did,
otherwise I can't imagine they'd ever have boarded those trains.

I was on the point of being moved along by an old Berlin *Schupo*
until I flashed him my beer-token and told him to go and fuck
himself.

"Sorry, sir," he said, touching his leather shako smartly, "I didn't know you was RSHA."

"Where's this lot headed?" I asked.

"Somewhere in Bohemia. Theresienstadt, I think they said it's called. You feel almost sorry for them, don't you? But I reckon it's better for them and for us, really. I mean, us Germans. They'll have a better life there, living among their own in a new town, won't they?"

"Not in Theresienstadt they won't," I told him. "I've just got back from Bohemia." And then I told him all I knew about the place and a bit more besides, about what was happening in Russia and Ukraine. The look of horror on the man's florid face was almost worth the risk I took in telling him the unvarnished and unpalatable truth.

"You can't be serious," he said.

"Oh, but I am. It's fact that we're systematically murdering people by the thousands out there, in the swamps east of Poland. I know. I've seen it for myself. And by 'we' I mean us, the police. The RSHA. It's us that's doing the murdering."

The *Schupo* blinked hard and looked as if I'd said something incomprehensible. "It can't be true, what you just said, sir. Surely you're joking."

"I'm not joking. What I just told you is the one true thing you'll probably hear today. Just ask around, only try to do it discreetly. People don't like talking about this, for obvious reasons. You could get into trouble. We both could. I'm telling you, those Jews are on a slow train to hell. And so are we."

I walked away smiling sadistically to myself; in Nazi Germany truth makes a powerful weapon.

But it was one of those RSHA murderers who brought me in from the cold. An Austrian, Ernst Kaltenbrunner, was rumored to be the next chief of the Reich Main Office for Security—the RSHA—but the same rumor said that his appointment could not be approved by Hitler until the man had finished drying out at a sanatorium in Chur, Switzerland. This left Kripo in the forensically capable if thoroughly murderous hands of General Arthur Nebe, who, until the previous November, had commanded SS Operation Group B in Byelorussia. Group B was now commanded by someone else, but if what was bruited about the Alex was correct—and I had good reason to think it probably was—Nebe's men had killed more than forty-five thousand people before he finally earned his ticket back to Berlin.

Forty-five thousand. A number like that was hard to comprehend in the context of murder. Berlin's Sportpalast, where the Nazis held some of their rallies, had a capacity of fourteen thousand. Three whole Sportpalasts full of people who were there to cheer a speech by Goebbels. That's what forty-five thousand looked like. Except none of those murdered had cheered, of course.

I wondered what Nebe told his wife, Elise, and his daughter, Gisela, about what he'd been doing out in Ivan's swamps. Gisela was a beautiful young woman of sixteen now, and I knew Arthur doted on her. She was intelligent, too. Did she ever ask him about his work in the SS? Or did she see something elusive in her father's fox-like eyes and then just talk about something else, the way people used to do when the subject of the Great War had come up in conversation. I never knew anyone who was comfortable talking about that, certainly not me. If you hadn't been in the trenches there was no point in expecting anyone even to imagine what it was like. Not that Arthur Nebe had anything to feel ashamed about back then; as a young lieutenant in his pioneer battalion with the 17th Army (1st West Prussian) Corps on the Eastern Front, he'd been gassed twice and won a first-class Iron Cross. Nebe was none too fond of the Russians as a result but it was unthinkable that he would ever have told his family that he'd spent the summer of 1941 murdering forty-five thousand Jews. But Nebe knew that I knew and somehow he could still look me in the eye; and while we didn't talk about it, what was surprising to me more than him was the fact that I could tolerate his company, just about. I figured that if I could work for Heydrich, I could work for anyone. I wouldn't say we were ever friends, Nebe and me. We got along all right, although I never understood how someone who had plotted against Hitler as early as 1938 could have become a mass murderer with such apparent equanimity. Nebe had tried to explain this, when we were in Minsk. He'd told me that he needed to keep his remarkable nose clean long enough for him and his friends to get another opportunity to kill Hitler; I just didn't see how that justified the murders of forty-five thousand Jews. I didn't understand it then and I don't understand it now.

At Nebe's suggestion we met for Sunday lunch in a private room at Wirtshaus Moorlake, a little southwest of Pfaueninsel, on the Wannsee. With an attractive beer garden and an orchestra, it looked more Bavarian than Prussian and was very popular with Berliners in the summer. This summer was no exception. It was a beautiful day and neither of us was wearing a uniform. Nebe was dressed in a three-piece, belt-back Knickerbocker suit made of light gray houndstooth tweed, with button pockets and peak lapels. With his light gray stockings and polished brown brogues, he looked like he was planning to shoot something with feathers, which would certainly have made a welcome change. I was wearing my summer suit, which was the same three-piece, pin-striped navy suit I wore in winter except that I had neglected to wear the vest as a concession to the warmer weather; I looked as sharp as a seagull's feather and I didn't care who knew it.

We ate lake trout with potatoes and strawberries with cream, and enjoyed two bottles of good Mosel. After lunch we took a longish sort of boat or shell on the water. Because of my extensive naval experience Nebe let me row, of course, although it might have had as much to do with me being a captain and him a general; and while I applied myself to the oars he smoked a large Havana cigar and stared up at an unblemished Prussian blue sky as if he didn't have a care in the world. Perhaps he didn't. Conscience was a luxury that few officers in the SS and SD could afford. The Wannsee looked like an impressionist painting of some idyllic scene on the River Seine at the turn of the century, the kind that looks like the picture is suffering from a severe case of spots. There were canoes and outrigged shells, sailing boats, and sloops, but no boats that required petrol: petrol was even harder to get than pills and booze. There were plenty of young women around, too—which was one of the reasons Nebe liked it there—but no young men; they were all in uniform and probably fighting for their lives in some Russian shell hole. The women in the long narrow shells wore white singlets and the briefest of shorts, which were an improvement on corsets and French bustles because they showed off their breasts and behinds to anyone like me who was interested in that kind of thing; they were tanned and vigorous and sometimes flirtatious, too; they were only human, after all, and craved male attention almost as much as I craved the chance to give it to them. Some of them rowed alongside us for a while and made conversation until they realized just how old we were; I was in my forties and I think Nebe must have been almost fifty. But there was one girl who took my eye. I recognized her as someone who lived not so far away from me. I knew her name was Kirsten and she was a schoolteacher at the Fichte Gymnasium on Emser Strasse. Seeing her row, I resolved to see a little more of Emser Strasse and perhaps, by some happy accident, her. After she and her lithe companions pushed off I kept an eye on their boat, just in case; you never know when a beautiful girl is going to fall in the water and need rescuing.

Another reason Nebe liked it on the Wannsee was because you could be absolutely sure that no one was eavesdropping on your conversation. Ever since September '38 and the failed Oster coup, of which he'd been an important part, Nebe had suspected that he was suspected, of something; but he always spoke very freely with me, if only because he knew I was held in even greater suspicion than he was. I was the best kind of friend anyone like Nebe could ever have had; the kind of friend you could and would give up to the Gestapo without a second's thought if it meant saving your own skin.

"Thanks for lunch," I said. "It's been a while since I bent the elbow for something as decent as that Mosel."

"What's the point in being head of Kripo if you can't get an extra supply of food and drink coupons?" he said.

Coupons were needed for Germany's rationing system, which seemed increasingly draconian, especially if you were a Jew.

"Mind you, what we ate, it was all local stuff," he said. "Lake trout, potatoes, strawberries. If you can't get that in Berlin during the summer then we might as well surrender now. Life wouldn't be worth living." He sighed and puffed a cloud of cigar smoke into the sky above his silver-gray head. "You know, sometimes I come here and take a boat out on my own, slip the mooring and then just drift across the lake without a thought to where I'm going."

"There is nowhere to go. Not on this lake."

"You make it sound like there's something wrong with that, Bernie. But this is the nature of lakes. They're for looking at and enjoying, not for anything as practical as what you imply."

I shrugged, lifted the oars and looked over the side of the boat into the warm water. "Whenever I'm on a lake, like this one, it's not long before I start to wonder what's underneath the surface. What undiscovered crimes lie hidden in the depths? Who's down there at the bottom wearing a pair of iron jackboots? If there's a Jewish U-boat hiding from the Nazis, perhaps. Or some lefty who got put there by the Freikorps back in the twenties."

Nebe laughed. "Ever the detective. And you wonder why you continue to be useful to our masters."

"Is that why we're here? So you can flatter me with an assurance of my utility?"

"It might be."

"I fear my days of being useful to anyone are long past, Arthur."

"As usual, you underestimate yourself, Bernie. You know, I always think of you as a bit like one of those people's cars designed by Dr. Porsche. A little blunt, perhaps, but cheap to run and very effective. Built to last, as well, to the point of being almost indestructible."

"Right now, my engine could use some air-cooling," I said, resting on the oars. "It's hot."

Nebe puffed his cigar and then allowed one hand to drag in the water. "What do you do, Bernie? When you want to get away from it all? When you want to forget about everything?"

"It takes a while to forget everything, Arthur. Especially in Berlin. Believe me, I've tried. I've got an awful feeling it's going to take the rest of my life to forget as much as that."

Nebe nodded. "You're wrong, you know. It's easy to forget if you put your mind to it."

"How do *you* manage it?"

"By having a certain view of the world. That's a concept that's familiar to all Germans, surely. My father was a teacher and he used to say, 'Find out what you believe in, Arthur, what your place in it is, and then stick to that. Use that view of the world to order your life, no matter what.' And what I've concluded is this: life is all a matter of chance. That's the way I look at things. If it hadn't been me out there in Minsk, in charge of Group B, it would have been someone else. That bastard Erich Naumann, probably. He's the swine who took over from me. But sometimes I think that I was never really there. At least not the real me. I have very little memory of it. No, I don't.

"You know, back in 1919, I tried to get a job at Siemens selling Osram lightbulbs. I even tried to become a fireman. Well, you know what it was like back then. Any kind of a job looked like it was worth having. But it wasn't meant to be. The only place that would have me after I left the army was Kripo. That's what I'm talking about. What is it about life that takes a man one way, selling lightbulbs or putting out fires, or that takes the same man in quite another way so that he becomes a state executioner?"

"Is that what you call it?"

"Why not? I didn't wear a tall hat, it's true, but the job was the same. The fact of the matter is that quite often these things have very little to do with the man himself. I didn't end up in Minsk because I'm a bad man, Bernie. I sincerely believe that. It was an accident that I was ever there at all. That's the way I look at it. I'm the same man I always was. It's just fate that took me into the police instead of the Berlin fire department. The same fate that killed all those Jews. Life is nothing but a random series of events. There's no logic to anything that happens, Bernie. Sometimes I think that's your real problem. You keep looking for some sort of meaning in things, but there isn't any. Never was. All of that was a simple category mistake. And trying to solve things doesn't solve anything at all. After what you've seen, surely you know that by now."

"Thanks for the philosophy seminar. I think I'm beginning to."

"You should thank me. I'm here to do you a favor."

"You don't look like a man who's carrying a gun, Arthur."

"No really, I am. I've got you a job with the War Crimes Bureau at the Bendlerblock, starting in September."

I laughed. "Is that a joke?"

"Yes, it is rather amusing, when you think about it," admitted Nebe. "Me, finding a job for you there, of all places. But I'm perfectly serious, Bernie. This is a good deal for you. It gets you out of the Alex and into somewhere your skills will be properly appreciated. You're still SD, there's not much I can do about that. But according to Judge Goldsche, to whom you will report, your uniform and investigative experience will open a few investigative doors that remain closed to the people who currently work there. *Von* this and *von* that, lawyers most of them, the wing-collar kind whose scars were earned in university societies rather than on the battlefield. Hell, you'll even make more money." He laughed. "Well, don't you see? I'm trying to make you respectable again, my friend. Semi-respectable, anyway. Who knows, you might even make enough to afford a new suit."

"You're serious, aren't you?"

"Of course. You don't think I'd waste my time lunching you without a damn good reason. I'd have brought a nice girl here, or even a girl who isn't so nice, not a stinger like you. You can say thank you now."

"Thank you."

"So, now that I've done you a favor, I want you to do something for me in return."

"In return? Perhaps you've forgotten our dirty weekend in Prague, Arthur. It was you who asked me to investigate Heydrich's death, wasn't it? Less than a month ago? You didn't like my conclusions. When we met and had a conversation at the Esplanade Hotel, you told me we never had that conversation. I never did collect on that favor."

"That was a favor to us both, Bernie. You and me." Nebe started to scratch the eczema on the backs of his hands; it was a sign he was beginning to get irritable. "This is different. This is something that even you can do without causing trouble."

"Which makes me wonder if I'm the right person to do it."

He put the cigar in his mouth and scratched some more, as if there might be a better solution to his problem under the skin. The boat turned slowly in a circle so that we were pointing in the direction we had just come; I was used to that feeling. My whole life had been going in a circle since 1939.

"Is this something personal, Arthur? Or is this what we detectives laughingly call 'work'?"

"I'll tell you if you'll just shut your beer hole for a minute. I don't know. How did someone with a mouth like yours manage to stay alive for so long?"

"I've asked myself the same question."

"It's work, all right? Something for which you're uniquely qualified, as it happens."

"You know me, I'm uniquely qualified for all sorts of jobs it seems most other men wouldn't touch with a pair of oily pliers."

"You'll remember the International Criminal Police Commission," he said.

"You don't mean to say that it still exists?"

"I'm the acting president," Nebe said bitterly. "And if you make a joke about making a gardener out of a billy goat, I will shoot you."

"I'm just a little surprised, that's all."

"As you may know, it was based in Vienna until 1940, when Heydrich decided that it should be headquartered here, in Berlin."

Nebe pointed west, across the lake to a bridge across the Havel that was just a little way south of the Swedish Pavilion.

"Over there, as a matter of fact. With him in charge, of course. It was just another neon-lit showcase for the Reinhard Heydrich Show, and I had hoped that now the bastard's dead, we might use that as an excuse to wind up the IKPK, which has outlived any usefulness it ever might have had. But Himmler is of a different opinion and wants the conference to go ahead. Yes, that's right—there's a conference in a week or two's time. The invitations to all the various European police chiefs had already gone out before Heydrich was murdered. So we're stuck with it."

"But there's a war on," I objected. "Who the hell is going to come, Arthur?"

"You'd be surprised. The French Sûreté, of course. They love a good feast and any chance to air their opinions. The Swedes. The Danes. The Spanish. The Italians. The Romanians. Even the Swiss are coming. And the Gestapo, of course. We mustn't forget them. Frankly, it's almost everyone except the British. Oh, there's no shortage of delegates, I can assure you. The trouble is that I've been given the task of organizing a program of speakers. And I'm scratching around for some names."

"Oh, no. You don't mean—"

"I do mean. It's all hands on deck for this one, I'm afraid. I thought you might talk about how you caught Gormann, the strangler. Even outside Germany that's a famous case. Forty minutes, if you can manage it."

"That's not scratching, Arthur. That's scraping. Gormann was almost fifteen years ago. Look, there must be someone else in your new police building on Werderscher Markt."

"Of course there is. Commissioner Lüdtke is already drafted in. And before you suggest them, so are Kurt Daluege and Bernhard Wehner. But we're still a couple of speakers short for a conference that lasts for two whole days."

"What about Otto Steinäusl? He used to be the IKPK president, didn't he?"

"Died of TB, in Vienna, year before last."

"That other fellow in Prague. Heinz Pannwitz."

"He's a thug, Bernie. I doubt he could speak for five minutes before he used a swearword or started beating the lectern with a cosh."

"Schellenberg."

"Too secretive. And much too aloof."

"All right, what about that fellow who caught Ogorzow—the S-Bahn murderer? That was only last year. Heuser, Georg. That's the fellow you should get."

"Heuser is the head of Gestapo, in Minsk," said Nebe. "Besides, since Heuser caught Ogorzow, Lüdtke is terribly jealous of him. That's why he's going to stay in Minsk for the time being. No, you're it, I'm afraid."

"Stopgap Lüdtke's not exactly fond of me, either. You are aware of that."

"He'll damn well do what I tell him. Besides, there's no one who's jealous of you, Bernie. Least of all Lüdtke. You're no threat to anyone. Not anymore. Your career is going nowhere. You could have been a general now, like me, if you'd played your cards right."

I shrugged. "Believe me, I'm a disappointment to myself most of all. But I'm not a speaker, Arthur. Sure, I've handled a few press conferences in my time, however, they were nothing like what you're asking. I'll be terrible. My idea of public speaking is to shout for a beer from the back of the bar."

Nebe grinned and tried to puff his Havana back into life; it took a bit of doing but he finally managed to get the cigar going. I could tell he was thinking of me while he went about it.

"I'm counting on you being crap," he said. "In fact, I expect every one of our speakers will be bloody awful. I'm hoping the whole IKPK conference is so fucking boring that we'll never have to do another one again. It's ridiculous talking about international crime while the Nazis are busy committing the international crime of the century."

"First time I've ever heard you call it that, Arthur."

"I said it to you, so it doesn't count."

"Suppose I say something out of turn? Something to embarrass you. I mean, just think who'll be there. The last time I met Himmler, he kicked me on the shin."

"I remember that." Nebe grinned. "It was priceless." He shook his head. "No, you needn't worry about putting your foot in the German butter. When you've written your speech you'll have to submit the

whole text to the Ministry for Propaganda and National Enlightenment. They'll put it into proper, politically correct German. State Secretary Gutterer has agreed to cast his eye over everyone's speeches. He's
SS anyway so there shouldn't be a problem between our departments.
It's in his interest if everyone sounds even duller than him."

"I feel reassured already. Jesus, what a farce. Is Chaplin speaking, too?"

Nebe shook his head. "You know, one day I think someone really
will shoot you. And that will be goodbye, Bernie Gunther."

"Nothing says goodbye quite like a bullet from a nine-millimeter
Walther."

In the distance, at the shimmering edge of the lake, I could just
about make out the schoolteacher, Kirsten. She and her shapely friends
were now disembarking at the jetty in front of the Swedish Pavilion. I
collected the oars and started to row again, only this time I was putting
my back into it. Nebe hadn't asked and I didn't tell him, but I like pretty
girls. That's my worldview.

Two

Ever since the Second Reich, Berlin's city architects have been trying to make its citizens feel small and insignificant, and the new wing of the Reich Ministry of Propaganda and National Enlightenment was no exception. Located on Wilhelmplatz, and just a stone's throw from the Reich Chancellery, it looked very much like the Ministry of Aviation on the corner of Leipziger Strasse. Looking at them side by side it would have been easy to imagine that the architect, Albert Speer, had managed to mix up his drawings of these two gray stone buildings, so closely did they resemble each other. Since February, Speer was the minister of Armaments and War, and I hoped he was going to make a better job of doing that than he had of being Hitler's court architect. It's said that Giotto could draw a perfect circle with just one turn of his hand; Speer could draw a perfectly straight line—at least he could with a ruler—and not much else. Straight lines were what he was obviously good at drawing. I used to sketch quite a good elephant, myself, but there's not much call for that when you're an architect. Unless the elephant is white, of course.

I'd read in the *Volkischer Beobachter* that the Nazis didn't much like German modernism—buildings like the technical university in Weimar, and a trade union building in Bernau. They thought modernism was un-German and cosmopolitan, whatever that meant. Actually,

I think it probably meant that the Nazis didn't feel comfortable living and working in city offices designed by Jews that were mostly made of glass, in case they suddenly had to fight off a revolution. It would have been a lot easier defending a stone building like the Ministry of Propaganda and National Enlightenment than it would have been defending the Bauhaus in Dessau. A German art historian—probably another Jew—once said that God was in the details. I like details, but for the Nazis a soldier positioned in a high window with a loaded machine gun looked like it offered more comfort than anything as capricious and unreliable as a god. From any one of the new ministry's small, regular windows a man with an MP40 commanded a clear field of fire across the whole of Wilhelmplatz and could comfortably have held an intoxicated Berlin mob at bay for as long as our handsome new minister of Armaments and War could keep him supplied with ammunition. All the same, it was a contest I should have enjoyed watching. There's nothing quite like a Berlin mob at play.

Inside the ministry things were a little less rusticated and more like a sleek, modern ocean liner; everything was burred walnut, cream walls, and thick fawn carpets. In the ballroom-sized entrance hall, underneath an enormous portrait of Hitler—without which no German ministry could possibly do its work—was an outsized scalloped vase of white gardenias that perfumed the whole building and doubtless helped conceal the prevailing smell of billy goat shit that's an inevitable corollary of national enlightenment in Nazi Germany, and which otherwise might have offended the nostrils of our glorious leader.

"Good morning, gentlemen," I said as I turned right through the heavy doors and entered what I assumed was the old Leopold Palace.

Behind a solid oak reception desk they could have used as a redoubt to provide a second line of defense against a mob, a couple of silent clerks with soft collars and softer hands regarded my slow progress across their floor with a well-practiced show of indifference. But I wel-comed it: the only pleasure I ever get from wearing the uniform of an SD officer is the knowledge that if I wasn't wearing it I might have to take a lot more humiliation from the kind of stone-faced bureaucrats that run this country. Sometimes I even get the chance to hand out a little humiliation of my own. It's a very sadistic, Berlin sort of game and one I never seem to get tired of playing.

The two clerks were a low pair of clubs and didn't look particularly busy but they still went through a comedy routine they had perfected that was supposed to make me feel as if they were. It was several min-utes before one of the men looked like he was paying me some attention.

And then another minute.

"You ready now?" I asked.

"Heil Hitler," he said.

I touched my cap with a finger and nodded. Paradoxically, without any storm troopers around to kick your backside, not giving the Hitler salute was safe enough in a place like a Reich ministry.

"Heil Hitler," I said, because there is only so much resistance that can safely be given at any one time. I glanced up at the painted ceiling and nodded my appreciation. "Beautiful. This is the old ceremonial palace, isn't it? It must be fine working here. Tell me, have you still got the throne room? Where the Kaiser used to hand out the important decorations and medals? Not that my own Iron Cross would count as anything like that. It was given to me in the trenches, and my com-manding officer had to find a space on my tunic that wasn't covered in mud and shit to pin it onto my chest."

"Fascinating, I'm sure," said the man who was the taller of the two. "But this has been the government press building since 1919."

He wore pince-nez and lifted himself up on his toes as he spoke, like a policeman giving directions. I was tempted to give him some directions of my own. The white carnation he wore in the buttonhole of his summer-weight, double-breasted black jacket was a friendly touch but the waxed mustache and the pocket handkerchief were pure Wilhelmstrasse. His mouth looked like someone had poured vinegar in his coffee that morning; his wife, supposing he had one, would surely have chosen something a little more fatal.

"If you could come to the point, please. We're very busy."

I felt the smile drying on my face like yesterday's shit. "I don't doubt it. Did you two characters come with the building, or did they have you installed with the telephones?"

"How can we help you, Captain?" asked the shorter man, who was no less stiff than his colleague and had the look of a man who came out of his mother's womb wearing pin-striped trousers and spats.

"Police commissar Bernhard Gunther," I said. "From the presidium at Alexanderplatz. I have an appointment with State Secretary Gutterer."

The first official was already checking off my name on a clipboard and lifting a cream-colored telephone to his pink rose of an ear. He repeated my name to the person on the other end of the line and then nodded.

"You're to go up to the state secretary's office right away," he said as he replaced the phone in its cradle.

"Thank you for helping."

He pointed at a flight of stairs that could have staged its own "Lullaby of Broadway."

"Someone will meet you up there, on the first landing," he said.

"Let's hope so," I said. "I'd hate to have to come down here and be ignored again."

I went up the stairs two at a time, which was a lot more energy than they'd seen around that palace since Kaiser Wilhelm II lifted his last Blue Max off a silk cushion, and came to a halt on the enormous landing. No one was there to meet me but without a pair of binoculars to see across to the other side of the floor I couldn't be sure. I glanced over the marble balustrade, and rejected the idea of whistling at the two tailor's dummies downstairs. So I lit my last cigarette and parked my behind on a gilt French sofa that was a little too low, even for a Frenchman; but after a moment or two I stood up and walked toward a tall open door that led into what I assumed was the old Blue Gallery. It had frescoes and chandeliers and looked like the perfect spot if they ever needed somewhere to dry-dock a submarine for repairs. The frescoes covering the walls were mostly naked people doing things with lyres and bows, or standing around on pedestals waiting for someone to hand them a bath towel; they all looked bored and wishing they could be out on the nude beach enjoying the sun at Strandbad Wannsee instead of posing in a government ministry. I had the same feeling myself.

A slim young woman in a dark pencil skirt and white blouse appeared at my shoulder.

"I was just admiring the graffiti," I said.

"They're called frescoes, actually," said the secretary.

"Is that so?" I shrugged. "Sounds Italian."

"Yes. It means fresh."

"It figures. Personally, I think there's only so many naked people you can have getting fresh with each other on one wall before the place starts to look like a Moroccan bathhouse. What do you think?"

"It's classical art," she said. "And you must be Captain Gunther."

"Is it that obvious?"

"It is in here."

"Good point. I guess I should have taken off my clothes if I'd wanted to blend in a bit."

"This way," she said without a flicker of a smile. "State Secretary Gutterer is waiting for you."

She turned away in a haze of Mystikum and I followed on an invisible dog leash. I watched her arse and gave it careful appraisal as we walked. It was a little too skinny for my taste but it moved well enough; I expect she got a lot of exercise just getting around that building. For such a small minister as Joey the Crip it was a very big ministry.

"Believe it or not," I said, "I'm enjoying myself."

She stopped momentarily, colored a little, and then started walking again. I was starting to like her.

"Really, I don't know what you mean, Captain," she said.

"Sure you do. But I'll certainly try to enlighten you if you care to meet me for a drink after work. That's what people do around here, isn't it? Enlighten each other? Look, it's all right. I got my Abitur. I know what a fresco is. I was making a little joke. And the scary black badge on my sleeve is just for show. I'm really a very friendly fellow. We could go to the Adlon and share a glass of champagne. I used to work there so I've got some pull with the barman."

She didn't say anything. She just kept walking. That's just what women do when they don't want to tell you no: they ignore you and hope you'll go away right up until the moment you don't and then they find an excuse to say yes. Hegel got it all wrong; relations between the sexes, there's nothing complicated about it—it's child's play. That's what makes it such fun. Kids wouldn't do it if it wasn't.

Blushing now, she led me through what looked like the Herrenklub library into the presence of a heavyset, clean-shaven man of about forty. He had a full head of longish gray hair, sharp brown eyes, and a mouth like a bow that no ordinary man could draw into a smile. I resolved not to try. The air of self-importance was all his but the cologne with which it was alloyed was Scherk's Tarr pomade and must have been battering on the panes of the double-height windows there was so much of it. He wore a wedding band on his left hand and plenty of cauliflower on the lapel badges of his SS tunic, not to mention a gold party badge on his left breast pocket; but the ribbon bar above the pocket was the kind you bought like sticks of candy from Holter's, where they made the uniform. On such a warm day the brilliantly white shirt around his neck was perhaps a little snug for comfort but it was perfectly pressed and encouraged me to believe that he might be happily married. To be well fed with all laundry found is really all that most German men are looking for. I know I was. There was a large gold pen in his fingers and some red ink on a sheet of paper in front of him; the handwriting was neater than the typing, which was mine. I hadn't seen that much red ink on my homework since leaving school.

He pointed to a seat in front of him; at the same time he consulted a gold hunter watch that was on his desk as if he had already decided for how long I was going to waste his time. He smiled a smile that wasn't like any smile I'd seen outside a reptile house and leaned back in his chair while he waited for me to get comfortable. I didn't, but that hardly mattered to someone as important as him. He fixed me with a look of almost comic pity and shook his head.

"You're not much of a writer, are you, Captain Gunther?"

"The Nobel Prize Committee won't be calling me anytime soon, if that's what you mean. But Pearl Buck thinks I can improve."

"Does she, now?"

"If she can win, anyone can, right?"

"Perhaps. From what General Nebe has told me, this is to be your first time on your hind legs at the lectern in front of an audience."

"My first, and hopefully my last." I nodded at the silver box on the desk in front of me. "Besides, I usually do all my best talking with a cigarette in my mouth."

He flipped open the box. "Help yourself."

I took one, latched it onto my lip, and lit myself quickly.

"Tell me, how many delegates are expected at this IKPK conference?"

I shrugged and took a puff at the nail in my mouth. Lately I'd been going for a double pull on my cigarettes before inhaling; that way I got more of a hit from the shitty tobacco when the smoke hit my lungs. But this was a good cigarette; good enough to enjoy; much too good to waste talking about something as trivial as what he had in mind.

"From what I've been told by General Nebe, some senior government officials will be present," he said.

"I wouldn't know about that, sir."

"Don't get me wrong, what you've written, it's all fascinating stuff, I'm sure, and you're an interesting fellow right enough, but from what's written here, you've certainly a lot to learn about public speaking."

"I've cheerfully avoided it until this present moment. Like the saying goes, it's hard to press olive oil out of a stone. If it was down to me, Brutus and Cassius would have gotten away with it, and the First Crusade would never have happened. Not to mention Portia in *The Merchant of Venice*."

"What about her?"

"With my speaking skills I'd never have gotten Antonio off the hook with Shylock. No, not even in Germany."

"Then let us be grateful that you don't work for this ministry," said Gutterer. "Shylock and his tribe are something of a specialty in our department."

"So I believe."

"And yours, too."

I tugged some more on his nail; that's the great thing about a cigarette—it lets you off the hook sometimes; the only thing that need come out of your mouth is smoke, and they can't arrest you for that; at least not yet. These are the freedoms that are important.

Gutterer gathered the sheets of laboriously typed paper in a neat stack and pushed them across the desk as if they were a dangerous species of bacillus. They'd damn near killed me anyway; I was a lousy typist.

"Your speech has been rewritten by me and retyped by my secretary," he explained.

"That's enormously kind of her," I said. "Did you really do that for me?"

I turned in my chair and smiled warmly at the woman who had brought me to Gutterer. Positioned behind a shiny black Continental Silenta as big as a tank turret, she did her exasperated best to ignore me but a touch of color appearing on her cheek told me that she was losing the battle.

"You didn't have to."

"It's her job," said Gutterer. "And I told her to do it."

"Even so. Thanks a lot, Miss—?"

"Ballack."

"Miss Ballack. Right."

"If we could get on, please," said Gutterer. "Here's your original back, so you can compare the two versions and see where I've improved or censored what you wrote, Captain. There were several places where you allowed yourself to become a little sentimental about how things were in the old Weimar Republic. Not to say flippant." He frowned. "Did Charlie Chaplin really visit the Police Praesidium on Alexanderplatz?"

"Yes. Yes he did. March 1931. I remember it well."

"But why?"

"You'd have to ask him that. I think he may even have been doing what the Americans call 'research.' After all, the Murder Commission used to be famous. As famous as Scotland Yard."

"Anyway, you can't mention him."

"May I ask why?" But I knew very well why not: Chaplin had just made a film called *The Great Dictator,* playing an Adolf Hitler looka-like who was named after our own minister of culture, Hinkel, whose high life at the Hotel Bogota was the subject of intense gossip.

"Because you can't mention him without mentioning your old boss, the former head of Kripo. The Jew, Bernard Weiss. They had dinner together, did they not?"

"Ah yes. I'm afraid that slipped my mind. His being a Jew."

Gutterer looked pained for a moment. "You know, it puzzled me. This country had twenty different governments in fourteen years. People lost respect for all the normal standards of public decency. There was an inflation that destroyed our currency. We were in very real danger from Communism. And yet you almost seem to imply that things were better then. I don't say that you say it; merely that you seem to imply it."

"As you said yourself, Herr State Secretary, I was being sentimental. In the early years of the Weimar Republic my wife was still alive. I expect that would help to explain it, if not to excuse it."

"Yes, that would explain it. Anyway, we can't have you even suggesting as much to the likes of Himmler and Müller. You'd soon find yourself in trouble."

"I'm relying on you to save me from the Gestapo, sir. And I'm sure your version will be a great improvement on mine, Herr State Secretary."

"Yes. It is. And in case you are in any doubt about that, let me remind you that I've spoken at a great many Party rallies. Indeed Adolf Hitler himself has told me that, after Dr. Goebbels, he considers me to be the most rhetorically gifted man in Germany."

I let out a small whistle that managed to sound as if I was lost for words and impertinent at the same time, which is a specialty of mine. "Impressive. And I'm absolutely certain the leader couldn't be wrong—not about that kind of thing, anyway. I'll bet you treasure a compliment like that almost as much as you do all of those medals put together. I would if I were you."

He nodded and tried to look through the veneer of a smile that was on my face as if searching for some sign that I was absolutely sincere. He was wasting his time. Hitler might have held Gutterer to be one of the most rhetorically gifted men in Germany but I was a grand master at faking sincerity. After all, I'd been doing it since 1933.

"I expect you'd like a few tips on public speaking," he said without a trace of embarrassment.

"Now you come to mention it, yes, I would. If you feel like sharing any."

"Give up now, before you make a complete fool of yourself." Gutterer let out a loud guffaw that they could have smelled back at the Alex.

I smiled back, patiently. "I don't think General Nebe would be too happy with me if I told him I couldn't do this speech, sir. This conference is very important to the general. And to Reichsführer Himmler, of course. I should hate to disappoint him most of all."

"Yes, I can see that."

It wasn't much of a joke, which was probably why he didn't laugh very much. But at the mention of Himmler's name Gutterer started to sound just a little more cooperative.

"Tell you what," he said. "Let's go along to the cinema theater and you can give me a read-through. I'll explain where you're going wrong." He glanced around at Miss Ballack. "Is the theater free at this present moment, Miss Ballack?"

Poor Miss Ballack snatched a diary off her desk, found the relevant date, and then nodded back at him. "Yes, Herr State Secretary."

"Excellent." Gutterer pushed back his chair and stood up; he was shorter than me by a head, but walked like he was a meter taller. "Come with us, Miss Ballack. You can help make up an audience for the captain."

We walked toward the door of the vast, uncultivated acreage he called an office.

"Is that wise?" I asked. "After all, my speech—there are some details about the murders committed by Gormann that might be unpleasant for a lady to hear."

"That's very gallant, I'm sure, but it's a little late to be thinking about sparing poor Miss Ballack's feelings, Captain. After all, it was she who typed your speech, wasn't it?"

"Yes, I suppose so." I looked at Gutterer's secretary as we walked. "I'm sorry you had to read some of that stuff, Miss Ballack. I'm a little old-fashioned that way. I still think murder is a subject best left to murderers."

"And the police, of course," said Gutterer without turning around.

I thought it best to let that one go. The very idea of policemen who'd killed more people than any lust murderer I'd ever come across was as challenging as watching a hopped-up Achilles failing to over-take the world's slowest tortoise.

"Oh, that's all right," said Miss Ballack. "But those poor girls." She glanced at Gutterer for just long enough for me to know that her next remark was aimed right between her boss's shoulder blades. "It strikes me that murder is a little like winning the German State Lottery. It always seems to happen to the wrong people."

"I know what you mean."

"Where are you going to make this speech, anyway?" asked Gutterer.

"There's a villa in Wannsee that the SS use as a guesthouse. It's close to the IKPK."

"Yes, I know it. Heydrich invited me to a breakfast meeting he held there in January. But I couldn't go, for some reason. Why was that, Miss Ballack? I forget."

"That's the conference that was supposed to be held back in December, sir," she said. "At the IKPK. You couldn't go because of what happened at Pearl Harbor. And there was already something in the diary for the date they supplied in January."

"You see how well she looks after me, Captain."

"I can see a lot of things if I put my mind to it. That's my trouble."

We went along the corridor to a handsomely appointed cinema theater with seats for two hundred. It had little chandeliers on the walls, elegant moldings near the ceiling, plenty of tall windows with silk curtains, and a strong smell of fresh paint. As well as the screen there was a Telefunken radio as big as a barrel, two loudspeakers, and so many stations to choose from they looked like a list of lagers in a beer garden.

"Nice room," I said. "A bit too nice for Mickey Mouse, I'd have thought."

"We do not show Mickey Mouse films in here," said Gutterer. "Although it would certainly interest you to know that the leader loves Mickey Mouse. Indeed, I don't think he would mind me telling you that Dr. Goebbels once gave the leader eighteen Mickey Mouse films as a Christmas present."

"It certainly beats the pair of socks I got."

Gutterer glanced around the cinema theater proudly.

"But it is a wonderful space, as you say. Which reminds me. Tip number one. Try to acquaint yourself with the room where you're to make your speech, so that you will feel comfortable there. That's a trick I learned from the leader himself."

"Is that so?"

"You know, if I'd thought about it, we could have filmed this," said Gutterer, giggling stupidly, "as a sort of training film for how not to be a public speaker."

I smiled, took a long hit on another cigarette, and blew some smoke his way, although I would have much preferred a hot round from a tank gun.

"Hey, Professor? I know I'm just a stupid cop but I think I've got a good idea. How about giving me an even chance to succeed before I fall flat on my face? After all, you said yourself, I've got the third best public speaker in Germany to teach me."

Three

I took the S-Bahn train to Wannsee. The RAF had dropped a few token bombs near the station at Halensee, where there was now a large gang of railwaymen working on the track to keep the west of Berlin moving smoothly. The men stood back as the little red-and-yellow train passed slowly by, and as they did so a small boy in the carriage I was in gravely gave them the Hitler salute. When one of the track workers returned the salute, as if he had been saluting the leader himself, there was much mirth on and off the train. In Berlin a subversive sense of humor was never very far beneath the patriotic sham and counterfeit postures of everyday German life. Especially when there was a child to cover yourself; after all, it was disloyal to the leader not to return the Hitler salute, wasn't it?

It was the same journey I'd made when I'd had lunch with Arthur Nebe at the Swedish Pavilion, except that this time I was wearing a uniform. There was a line of cream-colored taxis parked in front of the Märklin train-set station but none of them were doing much business and about the only traffic around was on two wheels. A huge bicycle rack stood next to the entrance looking like a rest stop for the Tour de France. Some of the cabbies and the local florist were staring up at a man on a ladder who was painting one of the station's church-shaped windows. In Wannsee, where nothing much ever happens, I suppose that was a performance of sorts. Maybe they were waiting for him to fall off.

I crossed a wide bridge over the Havel onto Königstrasse and, ignoring Am Kleinen Wannsee to the south, which would have taken me to the offices of the International Criminal Police Commission at number 16, I walked along the northwest shore of the largest of Berlin's lakes, onto Am Grossen Wannsee, past several yacht and boating clubs and elegant villas, to the address of the SS guesthouse Nebe had given me: numbers 56–58. In a road as exclusive as that it was easy enough to find. There was an SS armored car parked in front of a large set of wrought-iron gates and a guardhouse with a flag, otherwise everything was as quiet and respectable as a family of retired honeybees. If there was any trouble around there it certainly wasn't going to come from the villa's moss-backed neighbors. Trouble in Wannsee means your lawn mower has stopped working, or the maid didn't turn up on time. Stationing an armored car in Am Grossen Wannsee was like ensuring a Vienna choirboy to sing Christmas carols.

Inside a largish landscaped park was a Greek Revival–style villa with thirty or forty windows. It wasn't the biggest villa on the lake but the bigger houses had bigger walls and were only ever seen by bank presidents and millionaires. The address had seemed familiar to me, and as soon as I saw the place I knew why. I'd been there before. The house had previously belonged to a client of mine. In the mid-thirties, before I got frog-marched back into Kripo by Heydrich, I tried my hand at being a private investigator, and for a while I'd been engaged by a wealthy German industrialist called Friedrich Minoux. A major shareholder in a number of prominent oil and gas companies, Minoux had hired me to subcontract an operative in Garmisch-Partenkirchen—where he owned another equally grand house—to keep an eye on his much younger wife, Lilly, who had chosen to live there, ostensibly for reasons of health. Maybe there was something insalubrious about the entitled air in Wannsee. It was too rich for her, perhaps, or maybe she just didn't like all that blue sky and water. I didn't know since I never met her and wasn't able to ask her, but understandably, perhaps, Herr Minoux doubted the reasons she'd given him for not living in Wannsee, and once a month for most of 1935, I'd driven out to this villa in order to report on his wife's otherwise blameless conduct. They're the best kind of clients any detective can have, the ones with money enough to spend finding out something that just isn't true, and it was the easiest two hundred marks a week I ever earned in my life. Previously Minoux had been a keen supporter of Adolf Hitler; but that hadn't been enough to keep him out of jail when it was discovered he'd defrauded the Berlin Gas Company of at least 7.4 million reichsmarks. Friedrich Minoux was now doing five years in the cement. From what I'd read in the newspapers, his house in Wannsee had been sold to pay for his defense but until then I hadn't realized that the buyer was the SS.

The guard on the gate saluted smartly and, having checked his list, admitted me into the finely manicured grounds. I walked around to the front of the house and down to the lakeside, where I smoked a cigarette and pictured myself back in 1935, smartly dressed, with a car of my own, making a decent living and no one to tell me what to do. No one but the Nazis, that is. Back then I'd told myself I could ignore them. I'd been wrong, of course, but then so were a lot of other people smarter than me, Chamberlain and Daladier included. The Nazis were like syphilis; ignoring them and hoping everything would get better by itself had never been a realistic option.

When I finished my cigarette I went into the one-and-a-half-story hallway at the center of the house. There everything was the same but different. At one end of the house was a library with a bay window and a table with plenty of copies of *Das Schwarze Korps*, but these days even the most fanatical Nazis avoided the SS newspaper as it was full

of the death notices of dearest sons—SS men and officers who had
fallen "in the east" or "in the struggle against Bolshevism." At the
other end of the house was a conservatory with an indoor fountain
made of greenish marble. The fountain had been switched off; possibly
the sound of something as clear and pure as Berlin water was distract-
ing to the types who stayed there. In between the library and the fountain were several salons and drawing rooms, two of them with
magnificent fireplaces. The best of the furniture and a rare Gobelin
tapestry were gone but there were still a few pieces I recognized,
including a large silver cigarette box from which I grabbed a fistful of
nails to fill my empty case.

They had three senior SS officers from Budapest, Bratislava, and
Krakow staying at the villa and it seemed I was just in time to get some
veal and potatoes and some coffee before they finished serving lunch.
Very soon I regretted giving in to my hunger when these three engaged
me in conversation. I told them I was not long back from Prague, and
they announced that Berlin's former chief of police, Kurt Daluege, was
now the acting Protector of Bohemia and Moravia and that a whole
month after Heydrich's death the effort to find all of his assassins was
still continuing. I already knew that Lidice, a village suspected of having harbored the killers, had been destroyed and its population executed. But these three officers now told me that, not content with this
stupid act of reprisal, a second village called Ležáky had also been
leveled—just a couple of weeks before—and the thirty-three men and
women who lived there had been massacred, too.

"They say Hitler ordered the deaths of ten thousand randomly
chosen Czechos," explained the colonel from Krakow, who was an Austrian, "but that General Frank talked him out of it, thank God. I mean,
what's the point of reprisal if you end up shooting yourself in the
foot? Bohemian industry is much too important to Germany now to piss
the Czechos off. Which is all you'd succeed in doing if you slaughtered

that many. So they had to content themselves with Lidice and Ležáky. As far as I know, there's nothing important in Lidice and Ležáky."

"Not anymore," laughed one of the others.

I excused myself and went to find a lavatory.

Arthur Nebe had told me that the speeches to the IKPK delegates would all be given in the central hall and it was there I now went to see where my ordeal was to occur. I felt a little sick with nerves just thinking about it, although that might as easily have been something to do with what I'd just been told about Ležáky; besides, I knew that what I was facing wasn't much compared to the ordeal that Friedrich Minoux now found himself subjected to. Five years in Brandenburg is certainly no weekend at the Adlon when you're a career pen-and-desk man.

One of the officers offered me a lift back into Berlin in his Mercedes, which I declined for all the reasons that I hoped weren't obvious. I told him that there was a concert in the Botanic Garden in Zehlendorf I wanted to attend. I wasn't in a hurry to enjoy the joke about Ležáky again. I walked back down to Königstrasse and headed back to the station, where, under the octagonal ceiling of the entrance hall, I met a man wearing olive-green lederhosen that I hadn't seen for seven years.

"Herr Gunther, isn't it?"

"That's right."

The man was in his fifties with fair hair; the sleeves of his collarless blue shirt were rolled up to reveal forearms that were as big as fire hydrants. He looked tough enough so I was glad to see he was smiling.

"Gantner," said the man. "I used to drive the Daimler for Herr Minoux."

"Yes, I remember. What a coincidence. I've just been up at the villa."

"I figured as much, you being SD n'all. There's plenty of your lot round that way now."

I felt myself smart at the idea that the SD was "my lot."

"Really, I'm still just a policeman," I said, keen to distance myself from the kind of SS who had destroyed Lidice and Ležáky. "I got called back onto the force in 'thirty-eight. And they put us all in uniform when we invaded Russia. There wasn't much I could do about it."

The number of times I'd heard myself utter this excuse. Did anyone believe it? And did it really matter to anyone but me? The sooner I was part of something worthwhile like the War Crimes Bureau the better.

"Anyway, they've got me on nights at the Alex, so I don't offend anyone with my choice of cologne. What are you doing here anyway?"

"I live around here, sir. Königstrasse. Matter of fact, there's several of us who used to work for Herr Minoux who are there now. Number 58, if you're ever in the area again. Nice place. Owned by the local coal merchant. Fellow called Schulze, who used to know the boss."

"I was very sorry to read about what happened to Herr Minoux. He was a good client. How is he dealing with bed and breakfast at German Michael's?"

"He's just started a stretch at Brandenburg at the age of sixty-five, so, not well. The bed's a little hard, as you might expect. But the food? I mean, we're all on short rations because of the war, right? But what they call food in there, I wouldn't give it to a dog. So I drive out to Brandenburg every morning to take him breakfast. Not the Daimler, of course. I'm afraid that went south a long time ago. I've got a Horch now."

"It's allowed? You bringing in breakfast?"

"It's not just allowed, it's actively encouraged. Excuses the government from having to feed the prisoners. About the only food he'll eat is what I take him in the car. Just some boiled eggs, and some bread and jam. Matter of fact, I was just in town to fetch some of his favorite jam from someone who makes it especially for him. I take the S-Bahn to save petrol. Frau Minoux, she's still in Garmisch, although she also rents a house in Dahlem. And Monika, Herr Minoux's daughter, she lives on Hagenstrasse, in Grunewald. I'll tell the boss you said hello if you like."

"You do that."

"By the way, what are you doing over at the villa? Are you part of this conference they're planning?"

"Yes, I am. Unfortunately. My boss, Arthur Nebe, the head of Kripo, he wants me to make a speech about being a Berlin detective."

"That should be easy," said Gantner. "Since you are a detective."

"I suppose so. He's ordered me to go to Wannsee and tell a lot of important foreign cops what a great detective I was. Bernie Gunther, the Berlin policeman who apprehended Gormann, the strangler."

State Secretary Gutterer had exaggerated all that, of course, which was his job, I suppose. I rather doubted that any one man could ever have been the omniscient sleuth my speech now said I was. But you didn't have to be Charlie Chan to figure out that it was this little speech of mine that was behind much of what happened in the summer of 1942, not to mention the summer of 1943.

Four

Outside the Kripo offices at the Alex was a giant pigeonhole cabinet where they left your mail, just like in a hotel. The first thing I did whenever I came on duty was check my pigeonhole. Usually it was just Party propaganda, or Prussian Police Union stuff that no one paid any attention to—the more important case correspondence was brought straight to your desk by one of two uniformed policemen, two ferociously ill-tempered old men who were universally known as the Brothers Grimm, for obvious reasons. You wouldn't have dreamed of having anyone leave something valuable in your pigeonhole, or anywhere else, for that matter—not at police headquarters. A few senior coppers like me still remembered Berlin's master burglars, Emil and Erich Krauss, who stole back their own tools from our own museum of crime. But it wasn't just our clients who were long-fingered; some of the coppers around the place were just as bent. You left a cigarette case lying around at your peril, especially if you were lucky enough to have cigarettes in it, and things like soap and toilet paper in the lavatories were always going missing. Once, someone even stole all of the electric lightbulbs in the police canteen, which meant that for several days we had to eat in the dark, although that did at least mean the food tasted better. (There used to be an electrician on Elsasser Strasse who would pay six marks for secondhand bulbs, no questions asked.) Imagine my surprise, then, when late one night, I went to my pigeonhole and opened an envelope to find five new pictures of Albrecht Dürer; I think I even turned them over just to check that the Brandenburg Gate was on the back of them, where it usually was. There was a lawyer's letter, too, but it was a while before enough of the novelty of having a hundred marks in my pocket had worn off for me to look at it.

The envelope had a little brown Hitler on the corner. It was odd how he was on the stamps but not on the banknotes. That could have been a precaution against him being associated with another hyperinflation. Or maybe he wanted people to think he was above things like money, which, in retrospect, was a pretty good reason not to trust him. Anyone who thinks he's too good for our money is never going to succeed in Germany. The postmark was Berlin and the letter paper was as thick as a starched pillowcase. On the sender's letterhead was a drawing of Justitia, wearing a blindfold and holding up a set of scales, which almost made me smile. It had been a long time since justice had been quite so objective and impartial as that in Germany. I took the letter—which wasn't dated—back to my desk to read it in a better light. And as soon as I'd done so I put it in the pocket of my jacket and went out of the Alex. I went across the road to the station to use the pay phones. The author said he suspected his telephone was being monitored and perhaps it was, but I was more concerned about the phone lines at the Alex, which had certainly been tapped since the days when Göring had been in charge of the Prussian State Police.

Although it was almost ten o'clock, the sky was still light and the station on Alexanderplatz—full of people arriving back after an afternoon stolen on the beach, their faces red from the sun, their hair messed up, their clothes peppered with white sand—buzzed with life like a huge hollowed-out tree colonized by a swarm of bees. Mercifully the station had, so far, escaped the bombs and remained my favorite place in the world. All human life was here in this glass Noah's Ark, which was full of the things that I loved about the old Berlin. I picked up a phone and made the call.

"Herr Doctor Heckholz?"

"This is he."

"I'm the man with five twenty-reichsmark notes and one pressing question."

"Which is?"

"What do I have to do for them?"

"Come and see me at my office tomorrow morning. I have a proposition for you. I might even say, a handsome proposition."

"Would you care to give me a clue as to what this is all about? I might be wasting your time."

"I think it's best I don't. I have a strong suspicion that the Gestapo are listening in to my telephone calls."

"If someone's listening it's certainly not the Gestapo," I told him. "The German Signals Intelligence—the FA—is run by Göring's Aviation Ministry and Hermann keeps a pretty jealous hold on it. Any information obtained by the FA is seldom shared with anyone in the RSHA. As long as you don't say anything rude about Hitler or Göring, my professional opinion is that you've nothing to worry about."

"If that's the case then you've already earned your money. But do please come anyway. In fact, why not come for breakfast? Do you like pancakes?"

His accent sounded Austrian; the way he said "pancakes" was very different from the way a German would have said it and something a little closer to Hungarian. But I wasn't about to hold that against him with his Albrechts in my pocket, not to mention the prospect of fresh-made pancakes.

"Sure, I like pancakes."

"What time do you finish your shift?"

"Nine o'clock."

"Then I'll see you at nine-thirty."

I hung up and went back across the road to the Alex.

It was a quiet night. I had some urgent paperwork but now that I was soon to be on my way to the War Crimes Bureau I wasn't much inclined to do it; that's the thing about urgent paperwork: the longer you leave it the less urgent it becomes. So I just sat around and read the newspaper and smoked a couple of the cigarettes I'd stolen from the Wannsee villa. Once, I went to check on the blackout blinds just to stretch my legs; and another time I tried the crossword in the *Illustrierter Beobachter*. Mostly I waited for the phone to ring. It didn't. When you're working nights for the Murder Commission, you don't really exist unless there's a murder, of course. Nobody cares what you look like or what your opinions are. All that is asked of you is that you're there until it's time to go home.

At nine o'clock I signed off and went back to the station, where I caught an S-Bahn train to Zoo Station and then walked a few blocks north, across Knie onto Bismarckstrasse. Bedeuten Strasse was off Wallstrasse, behind the German Opera House. In a solid, five-story redbrick building a short series of steps led up to an arched door and a large round skylight. I mounted the stairs and looked around. There was an older man in a cheap gray suit on the other side of the street reading the *Beobachter*. He wasn't Gestapo; then again he wasn't really reading the newspaper, either. Nobody leans on a lamppost to read a newspaper, especially one as dull and boring as the *Völkischer Beobachter*, unless he's on a stakeout. Above the number on the wall was a mosaic of brass plaques for German doctors, German dentists, German architects, and German lawyers. Since there were hardly any Jews left in Berlin, and certainly none in these noble professions, their Aryan character seemed hardly worth mentioning. Everyone was Aryan now, whether he liked it or not.

Five

I tugged on a brass bellpull as big as a butcher's weight, heard the door spring open, and climbed a white marble staircase to the third floor, where, at the end of a well-polished landing, I found a frosted-glass door open and a smallish, thickly bearded man standing with his hand outstretched toward me. He was smiling broadly and there was a touch of the fairy king about him. We shook hands. He was wearing a tailored, cream-colored linen suit and a pair of horn-rimmed glasses that were on a length of gold chain around his neck. In a waiting room behind him was a luscious-looking redhead who was draped in a beige, wraparound summer dress, and on her head was a wide-brimmed straw hat you could have used as a beach parasol. She was reading a magazine and smoking with a little amber holder that was the same incandescent shade as her hair. There was a full set of Malle Courier luggage with leather and brass trim by her chair, and I supposed she was traveling somewhere; she looked much too fresh to have come from somewhere else. The man was as friendly as a kitten but the redhead stayed put on the leather chesterfield and she was not introduced nor did she look at me. It was as if she didn't exist. Perhaps she was another client for another lawyer. Either way, she was keeping herself to herself, which suited her a lot better than it suited me.

"I'm Gunther," I said.

Heckholz brought his heels together silently and he bowed.

"Herr Gunther," he said, "it's good of you to come here at such short notice. I am Heinrich Heckholz."

"There were five good reasons to come, Herr Doctor. Or perhaps a hundred, depending on how you look at it."

"Surely you're forgetting the pancakes. Will you join me?"

"I've been thinking about nothing else since midnight."

We went along a corridor floored with white boards and lined with law books and box files, all of which carried the same little drawing of Justitia that appeared on his letterhead. He led me into a small kitchen where the mixture was already made, and immediately he put on a clean white apron and set about making the pancakes, but I felt him sizing me up out of the corner of his eye.

"Have you just finished your shift?"

"Yes. I came straight here."

"Somehow I thought you'd be wearing your uniform," he said.

"Only in the field," I said, "or on ceremonial occasions."

"In which case I wonder how you ever find the time to take it off. Berlin has more ceremonial occasions than imperial Rome, I fancy. The Nazis do like a good show."

"You've got that right."

He'd heated some cherry sauce in a small copper saucepan that he poured generously onto the finished pancakes and we carried Meissen plates into a meeting room. There was a round Biedermeier table and four matching chairs; on the yellow-papered wall was a portrait of Hitler, and on a sideboard in the window a large pot of white orchids. Through another open door on a white-wood floor was a partners desk, a large filing cabinet, and a safe. On the desk I spied a bronze head of the leader. Heckholz didn't look like he was taking any chances with appearances. A third door was partly open, and I had half an idea that behind it was a room and that there was someone in that room; someone wearing the same perfume as the redhead in the waiting room.

Heckholz handed me a napkin and we ate the pancakes in silence. They were predictably delicious.

"I'd offer you an excellent schnapps with that but it's a little early, even for me."

I nodded, but it was just as well he didn't twist my arm as it's never too early for a glass of schnapps, especially when you've just finished work for the day.

He saw me looking at the picture on the wall and shrugged. "That's good for business," he said. "If not necessarily good for the digestion." He shook his head. "Our leader has a very hungry look. Doubtless a result of his many years of struggle in my hometown of Vienna. Poor man. He almost looks as if he has been forbidden any pancakes and sent to bed early, don't you think?"

"I really couldn't say."

"Still, his is an inspiring story. To come so far, from nothing. I've been to Braunau-on-the-Inn where he was born. It's completely unremarkable. Which makes his story all the more remarkable when you think about it. Although, to be quite frank with you, as an Austrian I prefer not to think about it at all. It's true that we Austrians will have to take the blame for giving the world Hitler. But I'm afraid it's you Germans who must take the blame for giving him absolute power."

I said nothing.

"Oh, come now," said Heckholz, "there's no need to be so coy, Herr Gunther. We both know you're no more a Nazi than I am. Despite all the evidence to the contrary. I was a member of the Christian Social Party, but never a Nazi. The Nazis are all about show, and a show of loyalty to the leader is usually enough to deflect suspicion.

How else can you explain the fact that so many Austrians and Germans who hate the Nazis give the Hitler salute with such alacrity?"

"I usually find that the safer explanation is to believe that they're Nazis, too."

Heckholz chuckled. "Yes, I suppose it is. Which probably explains why you've stayed alive for so long. You'll remember Herr Gantner, who used to drive for Friedrich Minoux—he said that when you were working for Herr Minoux, as a private investigator, all those years ago, you told him you'd been a dedicated Social Democrat, right up until the moment that the Nazis gained power in 1933, when you had to leave the police."

"So, it was him who recommended me to you."

"Indeed it was. Only, now you're in the SD." Dr. Heckholz smiled. "How is that possible? I mean, how does someone who supported the SPD end up as a captain of SD?"

"People change," I said. "Especially in Germany. If they know what's good for them."

"Some people. But not you, I think. Gantner told me what you said to him. In Wannsee. He told me that you virtually apologized for wearing the uniform. Like you were ashamed of it."

"People see the scary SD badge on my sleeve and become alarmed. It's a bad habit of mine, that's all. Trying to put people at their ease."

"That's certainly unusual in Germany."

Heckholz cleared away the plates, removed the apron, and then sat down; it was obvious he didn't believe a word of what I'd said.

"All the same, Herr Gantner thought your remarks noteworthy enough to mention you to me in the hope that you might be able to provide us with some assistance."

"What kind of assistance?"

"With a problem that results from what happened to Herr Minoux."

"You mean the Berlin Gas Company fraud."

"The Berlin Gas Company fraud. I do mean that, yes."

"Thank you for the pancakes," I said, standing up. I tossed the five Albrechts back onto his table. "But whatever you're selling, I'm not interested."

"Please don't go just yet," he said. "You haven't heard about my handsome proposition."

"I'm beginning to believe your handsome proposition is about to turn into a rather ugly frog. Besides, I'm all out of kisses."

"How would you like to make ten thousand reichsmarks?"

"I'd like it fine just as long as I was able to live to spend it. But if I've stayed alive for so long it's because I've learned not to have conversations like this with strangers, especially when it's next to an open door. If you want me to stay and hear you out, Herr Doctor Heckholz, then you'd better ask your friend wearing the Arabian Nights perfume to come in here and join us."

Heckholz grinned and stood up. "I should have realized the difficulty of trying to trick a famous detective from the Alex."

"No, that's remarkably easy. You just send them a hundred marks in an envelope."

"Lilly, darling, will you please come in here?"

A minute later the redhead was in the meeting room. She was taller than I had supposed, with larger breasts, and as Heckholz made the introductions she took my hand as if she'd been handing alms to Lazarus.

"Herr Gunther, this is Frau Minoux."

"That's a bad habit, Frau Minoux. Listening outside doors like that."

"I wanted to see what kind of man you are before I made my mind up about you."

"And what's the conclusion?"

"I still haven't decided."

"You're not alone there."

"Anyway, it's a bad habit I learned from you, Herr Gunther. It was you my husband paid to spy on me at my home in Garmisch-Partenkirchen, wasn't it? When was that exactly?"

I nodded. "Nineteen thirty-five."

"Nineteen thirty-five." Frau Minoux rolled her eyes and sighed. "So much has happened since then."

"Well, I guess he didn't find anything," Heckholz told her, "otherwise you'd hardly be here now, would you? Still married to Friedrich."

"You'd have to ask Herr Gunther that," said Frau Minoux.

"I didn't find anything, no. But strictly speaking, Frau Minoux, I never actually listened outside your door. As it happens, I subcontracted the job in Garmisch to a local detective—an Austrian named Max Ahrweiler. He was the one who was looking through your keyhole, not me."

Frau Minoux sat down, and as she crossed her legs the wraparound dress she was wearing fell from her thigh to reveal a lilac-colored garter; I turned politely away to give her time to fix this but when I looked again, I could still see the garter. I told myself that if she didn't mind me looking then I didn't mind, either. It was a nice garter. But the length of smooth, creamy white thigh over which it was stretched was better. She screwed a cigarette into her holder and allowed Heckholz to light her.

"Is it Arabian Nights?" he asked. "The perfume you're wearing, Lilly? Just out of interest."

"Yes," she said.

Heckholz put away his lighter and looked at me. "I'm impressed. You have a good nose, Herr Gunther."

"Don't be. My nose for perfume is the same as the one I use for trouble. And right now I'm getting a strong scent of it from both of you."

But I sat down anyway. It wasn't like I had very much to do at home except stare at the walls and sleep, and I'd already done quite enough of that at work.

"Please," she said. "Put the money back in your pocket and at least hear us out."

I nodded and then did as she had asked.

"First," said Heckholz, "I should explain that my main offices are in Austria, which is where Frau Minoux is still primarily a resident. However, she also rents a house here in Berlin-Dahlem. I act for both her and for Herr Minoux, who is of course currently languishing in Brandenburg Prison. I take it that you're familiar with the basic facts of the Berlin Gas Company case."

"He and two others defrauded the company of seven and a half million reichsmarks and now he's doing five years." I shrugged. "But before that he helped steal a company—the Okriftel Paper Company— from a family of Jews in Frankfurt."

"That company had already been Aryanized by the Frankfurt Chamber of Commerce," said Frau Minoux. "All Friedrich did was buy a company the owners were legally obliged to sell."

"Maybe. But if you ask me, he had it coming. That's what I know about Herr Friedrich Minoux."

Frau Minoux didn't flinch. Clearly she was made of stronger stuff than her husband. For a minute I let my imagination play around in her pants; maybe they smell something in the air, but it's surprising how often women guess what I'm up to; it's a technique I use some-times to let them know that I'm a man. But she finally woke up to the fact that she was showing a garter and tugged the dress back over her thigh.

"The rights and wrongs of the Berlin Gas Company case are not in dispute," said Heckholz. "And it might interest you to know that several million reichsmarks have already been repaid by the three convicted men. No, it's what happened afterwards that is a matter of some concern to the Minouxes. Are you perhaps acquainted with a Berlin private detective by the name of Arthur Müller?"

"I know him."

"Tell me about him, if you would."

"He's efficient. A little lacking in imagination. Used to be a cop at the Police Praesidium here in Charlottenburg, but he's from Bremen, I think. He got stabbed in the neck by an SA man once, so he has no great love for the Nazis. Getting stabbed—sometimes it just works that way. Why?"

"Herr Müller's currently engaged by the Berlin Gas Company to find out if Herr Minoux has any hidden assets in the hope that even more money can be recovered from him. And more pertinently, Frau Minoux also. To this end he and his own operatives have been keeping Frau Minoux and her daughter Monika under surveillance at her home here in Berlin and at Frau Minoux's home in Garmisch. And very likely this office, as well."

"There's a man watching your front door. But it's certainly not Arthur Müller. This fellow looks like he learned the job from reading *Emil and the Detectives*. My guess is that he's keeping a mark on you while Arthur gets some sleep."

"We assumed the Gestapo might also be involved until you explained the position with regard to telephone tapping. So then. The plain fact of the matter is that Frau Minoux has substantial works of art and furnishings of her own that were in the matrimonial home in Wannsee that she has been obliged to hide at a warehouse in Lichtenberg, for fear that these would also be confiscated by the government."

"I begin to see your problem."

"Would you say that Herr Müller was honest?"

"I know what it used to mean. To be honest. But I've got no idea what it means today. At least not in Germany."

"Could he be bribed, perhaps?"

"Maybe. I guess it would depend on the bribe. If it was ten thousand reichsmarks then the answer would almost certainly be yes, possibly. Who wouldn't? But it makes me wonder why it's my nose you're riffling these bills in front of and not his."

"Because he's only half the problem, Herr Gunther. Have you heard of a company called Stiftung Nordhav?"

"No."

"Are you sure?"

"I don't hang around the Börse Berlin. I was never much interested in the financial pages. And the only figures I'm interested in are wearing swimsuits right now. Or not. Depending on which end of the beach they like."

Heckholz lit a small cigar and, smiling, puffed it lightly, as if he liked the taste more than the sensation it delivered.

"This isn't the kind of company that has a listing. It's a so-called charitable foundation that was set up by your old boss, Reinhard Heydrich, in 1939, ostensibly to build rest-and-recreation centers for members of the RSHA. In fact, it's a very powerful company that makes all kinds of business deals designed to profit the directors, of whom Heydrich was the chairman. Since his death there are five directors left: Walter Schellenberg, Werner Best, Herbert Mehlhorn, Karl Wilhelm Albert, and Kurt Pomme. It was the Stiftung Nordhav that bought Herr Minoux's Wannsee villa in November 1940 for 1.95 million reichsmarks, which was a great deal less than what it was worth. Most of that money was used by Herr Minoux to pay fines, compensation, and legal fees. Since then the Nordhav Foundation has bought several properties including Heydrich's own summer home, in Fehmarn, using money stolen from disenfranchised and murdered Jews. It's our strong suspicion that none of this money goes to the government and that all of it is used to benefit the remaining five directors."

"In other words," said Frau Minoux, "these men are guilty of the very same crime for which my husband is now doing five years in prison."

"We believe the Wannsee villa was earmarked to become Heydrich's new home here in Berlin," explained Heckholz. "It isn't so very far away from his old home, on Augustastrasse, in Schlachtensee. Of course, now that he's dead it has little real use to the Foundation other than as a venue for the IKPK conference that's about to take place. Which is the day after tomorrow, isn't it?"

I nodded. "You're well informed."

"Herr Gantner lives with Katrin, a maid who still works at the villa."

"Yes, I think he mentioned her."

"After that's over it's hard to see what they can do with it, the Berlin property market being what it is."

"Our aim is simple," said Frau Minoux. "To find evidence of malfeasance and wrongdoing against any of the five remaining directors of the Nordhav Foundation. Once we have that we shall attempt to recover the house, at a fraction of what we paid for it. But if the existing directors fail to cooperate, we shall have no alternative but to put what we know before State Secretary Wilhelm Stuckart at the Ministry of the Interior. And if that fails, to get the story into the international press."

"This is where you come in," said Heckholz. "As a captain in the SD, with access to the villa, and the higher echelons of the SS, it's possible you will perhaps overhear some information pertinent to the sale of the villa and by extension our case. Perhaps you could even be persuaded to conduct a search of the place while you're staying there. At the very least we are asking only that you keep your ears and eyes open. We would put you on a cash retainer; say, a hundred marks a week. However, there is a ten-thousand-reichsmark bonus if you do find something significant."

"Something that can get us justice," she added.

I lit one of my own cigarettes and smiled sadly. I almost pitied them for thinking that they still lived in a world where ideas like justice were even possible. I thought there was probably less chance of him bringing prosecutions against the directors of the Nordhav Foundation than there was of him winning the Nobel Peace Prize and then donating all of the prize money to the World Jewish Congress.

"We should also very much welcome your assistance in handling Arthur Müller," added Frau Minoux.

"Now that you've told me what you've got in mind I think it even less likely I could live to spend that bonus. These people you're up against—they're dangerous. Albert is currently the chief of police in Litzmannstadt, in Poland. There's a ghetto in Litzmannstadt with more than a hundred thousand Jews in it. Have you any idea what happens in a place like that?"

When I saw them look at each other and look blank I wanted to bang their heads together.

"No, I thought not. Best and Schellenberg aren't exactly shy flowers, either. Most of their friends are dangerous, too: Himmler, Gestapo Müller, Kaltenbrunner. Not to mention extremely powerful. Maybe the directors of this Nordhav Foundation do have some sort of racket going but then so does everyone else in the RSHA. Everyone except me, that is. My advice is that you should give this up. Forget this idea of taking on Nordhav. It's much too dangerous. If you're not careful you'll end up in the cement alongside Herr Minoux. Or worse."

Frau Minoux took out a tiny square of cotton that was laughingly called a handkerchief and dabbed either side of her perfect nose. "Please, Herr Gunther," she said with a sniff. "You simply have to help us. I don't know what else to do. Who else to turn to."

Heckholz sat beside her for a moment and put his arm around her in an attempt to stop her from crying any more. It was a job I wouldn't have minded having myself.

"At least say you'll keep your ears and eyes open while you're at the conference," said Frau Minoux. "My hundred reichsmarks ought to buy me that much. And there's another two hundred in it if you just come back here and tell Dr. Heckholz about anything you've learned about the sale of the villa. Anything at all. I won't be here, myself. I'm going back to Austria this afternoon."

It was the tears, I suppose. A woman cries and it cracks something open inside me, like Rapunzel's tears, only they were supposed to restore her handsome prince's sight, not blind him to the risks of snooping around a villa owned by the SS. I should have laughed and told them both to go to hell and walked straight out the door. Instead I thought about it for a moment, which was a mistake; you should always trust your first instincts in these matters. Anyway, I told myself there seemed little risk involved in just poking around a bit when I was at Wannsee and that was all I intended to do. Besides, Frau Minoux looked like she could afford to lose another hundred marks. So what did it matter? I'd make my speech, drink my coffee, steal a few cigarettes, and then leave and neither Frau Minoux nor Dr. Heckholz would be any the wiser.

"All right. I'll do it."

"Thank you," she said.

I stood up and walked to the door.

"And Arthur Müller?" asked Heckholz. "The private detective? What about him?"

"You want him to lay off, right?"

They nodded.

"Just long enough for me to get my property out of the country," she said. "Across the border into Switzerland."

"Let me take care of it." I shrugged. "But I get ten percent of what-ever payoff I can negotiate."

"That's fair," said Heckholz.

I couldn't help but laugh.

"What's so funny?" asked Heckholz.

"Because fair's got nothing to do with it," I said. "That's a word for children. When are people going to wake up and realize what's happen-ing in Germany? People like you. Worse than that, what's happening in the east. In the so-called swamps. In places like Litzmannstadt. Believe me, fair's got absolutely nothing to do with anything. Not anymore."

Six

arly on the first morning of the conference I took the S-Bahn back
to Wannsee and walked to the villa. It was another warm day and
by the time I arrived there my white shirt was sticking to my back
and I almost wished I had my own staff Mercedes. I was certainly the
only officer arriving at the villa who seemed not to have one. Well-
polished cars played tag in the driveway, delivering their self-important
passengers while, at the back of the house, on a terrace that faced the
lake, thirty or forty officers wearing lounge suits and a variety of foreign bandbox uniforms were smoking cigarettes, talking, and drinking
cups of coffee. It was all very clubbable and you'd hardly have believed
there was a war on.

In front of the Greek Revival entrance there were flower beds full of
blue geraniums. In the conservatory the fountain had been turned
back on but someone had thoughtfully removed all copies of *Das
Schwarze Korps* from the library, as even a cursory glance through its
morbid pages might have encouraged any reader to doubt that Germany was winning the war in the east, as Dr. Goebbels insisted it was.

On display underneath the curving staircase in the main hall was a
bronze of Heydrich's death mask, which made him seem oddly benign.
With eyes closed, his head looked as if it had been on display at the old
panopticum in Lindenpassage, or perhaps recovered from the basket

under the guillotine at Brandenburg, for display in a glass case at the police museum. On an easel next to the death mask was a large facsimile of the sixty-pfennig stamp featuring a photograph of the death mask that the occupation government planned to use on letters in Bohemia and Moravia, which was a bit like hanging a portrait of Bluebeard in a girls' school dormitory.

Staring critically at the mask and the giant stamp was a very tall man and next to him was a junior officer; from the monkey swing on his shoulder I took him to be the taller man's aide-de-camp. I advanced a short way up the staircase until I was standing immediately above them and, in the vague hope of hearing something interesting about Stiftung Nordhav, I started to eavesdrop on their conversation. My conscience might be getting a bit dull these days, but there's nothing wrong with my hearing. Their wisecracks were all taken from the SS joke book, which—take my word for it—only the SS think is funny.

"That's one stamp I won't be putting on my fucking Christmas cards," said the senior officer. I guessed him to be almost two meters in height.

"Not if you want the card to get there in time for Christmas," said the aide.

"Hardly matters, does it? We've made Christmas illegal in Bohemia."

Both men laughed unpleasantly.

"They were going to put a picture of Lidice on the ten-pfennig stamp," said the aide, "until someone told them that there was nothing actually left to photograph. Just a lost shoe and a lot of empty brass cartridges."

"I just wish he was here to see it," said the senior officer. "Just so I could see the look on his goat's face. Strange-looking bugger, Heydrich. Didn't you think so? He looks like a Paris perfumer, inhaling some rare scent."

"Death, probably. The scent which fills that long nose. His death, thank God."

The senior officer laughed. "Very good, Werner," he said. "Very good."

"Do you think he really was a Jew, sir? Like they say?"

"No, it was Himmler who put that rumor into circulation. To deflect attention from his own very questionable origins."

"Really?"

"Keep it under your hat, Werner, but his real name is Heymann, and he's half Jew."

"Christ."

"Heydrich knew that. He had a whole file on the Heymann family. The slippery bastard. Still, anyone could be forgiven for thinking Heydrich was a Jew. I mean, look at that fucking nose. It's straight out of *Der Stürmer.*"

I'd never liked Heydrich, but I'd certainly feared him. It was impossible not to fear a man like Heydrich. And I wondered if these two would have made such openly critical remarks about the former Protector of Bohemia if the general had still been alive. I rather doubted it. At least I did until the senior officer looked around and I realized exactly who he was. I'd only ever seen a picture of him but he was a hard man to forget: there were so many scars on the bedrock of his craggy face that they might almost have been left there by a glacier retreating from the moraine of his forbidding personality. It was Ernst Kaltenbrunner, the man rumored to be the next head of the RSHA. The Swiss clinic had dried him out sooner than anyone would have supposed possible.

I went up to the next floor to have a nose-around. There was a long narrow corridor of doors and on one of them were painted the words STIFTUNG NORDHAV and EXPORT DRIVES G.M.B.H. PRIVATE. I was just about to try the handle when an SS major came out the door. He was accompanied by a tall foreign-looking officer who, from the kepi under his arm, I thought might have been French, until I saw the little crosses on his buttons. I guessed he might be Swiss.

"As before, we'll do the deal through Export Drives," the major was saying. "That was the company we used for the purchase of the machine guns."

"I remember," said the Swiss.

Their conversation stopped abruptly when they saw me.

"Can I help you?" asked the SS major.

"No. I was just looking for somewhere quiet to gather my thoughts. I'm the morning's first speaker, worse luck."

"Good luck," he said, and locked the door behind him.

The two men went downstairs and out onto the terrace and, at a distance, I followed.

Half a kilometer away to the east and across the lake, at Strandbad Wannsee, hundreds of Berliners were arriving at the city's favorite lido for a day on the beach, reserving their wicker beach chairs, or spreading their towels on eighty meters of pristine white sand. There was a light breeze that stirred the blue flags on top of the two-story clinker-brick promenade and which carried the sound of the PA system already announcing a lost child to the unconcerned ears of those who were present at the villa: Frenchmen, Italians, Danes, Croatians, Romanians, Swedes, and Swiss. What was happening on the beach seemed a very long way from what I was there to talk about.

"Feeling nervous?" Arthur Nebe smiled and clapped me on the shoulder.

"Yes. I was just wishing I was over there, on that beach talking to some pretty girl."

"Did you get anywhere with that schoolteacher we saw at the Swedish Pavilion? What was her name?"

"Kirsten? Yes. A little. I know where she works. And more importantly, where she lives. In Krumme Strasse. I even know that she goes swimming two nights a week at the local bathhouse."

"As always you make romance sound like a murder inquiry." Nebe shook his head and smiled. "If you'll permit me. You have a piece of toilet paper stuck to your chin." He picked it off my face and let it flutter to the ground.

"I wondered why people were looking at me so strangely on the S-Bahn. They were thinking, 'Nobody else in this city seems to have any toilet paper, how come he does?'"

"You need a cognac," said Nebe, and took me back into the villa, where he found a drink for us both. "We both do. It's a little early, I know, even for me. But the truth is I'm feeling a little nervous myself. I'll be glad when this is over and I get back to some real work."

I wondered what that would amount to for a man like Arthur Nebe.

"Strange, isn't it?" he said. "After all we went through in Minsk. Crazy Ivans all over the place trying to kill you and it's something like this that really squeezes your guts."

I glanced out the window where Reichsführer Himmler was now speaking to State Secretary Gutterer. Walter Schellenberg was talking to Kaltenbrunner and Gestapo Müller.

"That's hardly a surprise when you consider the guest list."

I took a large sip of the brandy.

"Relax," insisted Nebe. "If your speech goes down like shit we'll just blame the whole thing on Leo Gutterer. It's about time someone took that awful man down a peg."

"I thought you wanted me to fuck up, Arthur."

"Whatever gave you that idea?"

"You did."

"I was joking, of course. Look, all I really want is never to be IKPK

president again. Next year this is all going to be Kaltenbrunner's problem. Not mine and not yours. You'll be safely out of the way in the War
Crimes Bureau and I'll just be safely out of the way, I hope. Switzerland, if they'll have me. Or Spain. I always wanted to go to Spain.
Admiral Canaris loves it there. And by the way, just in case you were
wondering, I'm still joking."

"A sense of humor. That's nice. I think we need that just to get up
in the morning."

Nebe threw back his cognac and then pulled a face. "Anyway,
you'll be fine. I've every confidence that you're going to be the most
interesting speaker of the day."

I nodded and glanced around. "It's a beautiful house."

"Designed by Hitler's favorite architect. Paul Baumgarten."

"I thought that was Speer."

"So did Speer, I think. But it seems he was wrong about that, too."

"Who owns it now?"

"We do. The SS does. Although God knows why. We've got several
houses around here. The Havel Institute. The Horticultural School."

"Since when were the SS interested in horticulture?"

"I think it's a home, for Jews," said Nebe. "The forced laborers who
work on the gardens round here."

"That sounds almost benign. And the Havel Institute?"

"A radio HQ that directs spy and sabotage operations against the
Soviet Union." Nebe shrugged. "There are probably more houses that
even I don't know about. Frankly, the state has so many houses coming
into public ownership that the Ministry of the Interior could open its
own sales and lettings agency. Maybe I'll do that instead of being a
policeman."

"So it's not the Nordhav Foundation that owns this house."

"What do you know about the Nordhav Foundation?"

"Not much. There's an office upstairs with that name on the door. Apart from that, not much. That's why I asked." I shrugged.

"Where Nordhav is concerned, nothing is always the best thing to know. Take my advice, Bernie. Stick to homicide. It's a lot safer." Nebe glanced around as the delegates started to file into the central hall where the speeches were to be given. "Come on. Let's get it over with."

Seven

The irony of being introduced to the audience at an international crime commission conference by a man who had not long finished murdering forty-five thousand people did not escape me, or indeed Nebe himself. Arthur Nebe, who was ex–political police, when such men had still existed, had never been much of a detective. He colored a little around the ears as he talked, a little, about the Murder Commission, almost as if he recognized that the commission of murder was something in which he was rather more expert. I don't think there was anyone in that room who could have looked death in the face more often than Arthur Nebe. Not even Himmler and Kaltenbrunner. I still remembered something Nebe had told me back in Minsk, about experimenting with blowing people up in the search for a more efficient and "humane" method of mass killing. I wondered what some of the Swedes and Swiss in our audience would have said if they'd known anything of the crimes that were being committed by German police in Eastern Europe and Russia, even as we spoke. Would they have cared? Maybe not. You could never quite predict how people would react to the so-called Jewish question.

When he finished his introduction there was a ripple of polite applause and then it was my turn. The bare wooden floorboards creaked like an old leather coat as I walked on jelly legs to the lectern, although that might have been the sound of my nerves pulling at the muscles of my heart and lungs.

I've seen a few tough-looking crowds in my time but this was the toughest. At least five or six of them only had to raise a finger to have me face a firing squad before morning coffee was over. Galileo had an easier job with the Inquisition, trying to persuade them that the algebra in the Bible doesn't add up to a month of Sundays. The audience at the Café Dalles on Neue Schönhauser Strasse used to throw chairs at the piano player when they were bored. And I once saw a tiger get a bit rough with a clown at the Busch Circus. Now, that was funny. But the faces I was looking at would have given Jack Dempsey pause for thought. Anita Berber was wont to piss on the customers when she decided that she didn't like them, and much as I should like to have taken a leaf out of her book, I thought it best if I just read what was written on the pages I'd spread on the lectern in front of me, although a lot of what I said had been added onto my speech by Leo Gutterer and stuck in my throat like an S-hook from a burglar's cigar box.

"Heil Hitler. Gentlemen, criminologists, distinguished foreign guests, colleagues, if the last ten years have proved anything at all it is that many of the frustrations the German police experienced under the Weimar Republic have diminished to the extent that they no longer exist. Street fights and the threat of communist insurrection that characterized the time before the election of a National Socialist government are a thing of the past. Police manpower has been increased, our equipment modernized, and, as a corollary, the institutions of state security are considerably more efficient.

"From a time when Germany, and Berlin in particular, was virtually run by criminal gangs and cursed by one ineffective government after another, a strong centralized, classless state now exists where factionalized politics ensured that only anarchy existed before. When the National Socialists came to power, one or two policemen such as myself remained mildly skeptical of the party and its intentions; but that was then. Things are very different now. A healthy respect for the law and its institutions are now the natural inheritance of every true German."

As I spoke, Himmler—who moments earlier had removed his glasses to polish the lenses with a neatly folded handkerchief—smiled and put a mint in his mouth. He showed no signs of having remembered our first and only meeting, at Wewelsburg Castle, in November 1938, when he kicked me on the shin for being the bearer of some unwelcome news about one of his SS colleagues. Even wearing boots, it was not an experience I was keen to repeat. Meanwhile, Kaltenbrunner scowled and inspected his manicure; he had the look of a man who was already craving a drink. I put my head down, and pushed on.

"My name is Bernhard Gunther and I've been a Berlin policeman since 1920. For more than fifteen years I've been a member of Berlin's Murder Commission, which as General Nebe has explained is a group of detectives assisted by experts such as a medical jurisprudent and a photographer. The cornerstone of the commission is the criminal commissars, several of whom are also German lawyers. Under each commissar is a staff of about eight men, who do all the work, of course. The commission is controlled by Commissioner Friedrich-Wilhelm Ludtke, whom many of you will know. Anyone who wishes to discover more about the Berlin police and in particular its famous Murder Commission, should perhaps read a book called *Continental Crimes* by Erich Liebermann von Sonnenberg—who was himself the director of Kripo until his death last year—and criminal director Otto Trettin. Writing about the stories that appear in this book, George Dilnot, the celebrated English crime reporter, said, 'There is enough drama and excitement in these tales to satisfy the most voracious appetite.'"

(This was a lie, of course: the truth was that Dilnot hated the book, considering it clichéd and naïve. The book's many failings were

perhaps hardly surprising given that it had been subject to the censor-
ship of the Ministry of Truth and Propaganda, and many of the more
interesting cases the commission had investigated, including the Fritz
Ulbrich case, were deemed to be too sensationalist for public consump-
tion. But Dilnot, an Englishman, wasn't exactly around to contradict
me, or more accurately, Gutterer.)

"I'm afraid I can't promise to provide much in the way of drama
and excitement. The fact is that Liebermann von Sonnenberg or Otto
Trettin would almost certainly do a better job of speaking to you, today;
as would Commissioner Ludtke or Inspector Georg Heuser, who
recently and cleverly apprehended Ogorzow, the S-Bahn murderer,
here in Berlin. The fact is that, even by the blunt standards of this city,
I'm a plain speaker. But I've always believed that a certain amount of
straight talk comes with the job, so if you'll forgive my lack of rhetorical
flourish, I will do my best to describe one particular crime which, at
the time I took over its investigation, had become a cold case and was
generally symptomatic of the devastating lack of morale that affected
the Berlin police under the previous government.

"Indeed, back in 1928, five years after the events I'm about to
describe to you, the case was almost forgotten, and when it was assigned
to me by the then Berlin police commissioner, Ernst Engelbrecht, at
the Police Praesidium on Alexanderplatz, it was with the expectation
that I would come up empty-handed. In truth, this case had almost
become a means of putting arrogant young detectives like me firmly in
their place, as more experienced policemen are wont to do. And the
fact that I eventually apprehended the perpetrator owes as much to my
own good luck as to any forensic judgment on my part. Luck is not
something that should ever be discounted in a criminal investigation.
Most detectives rely on good luck a lot more than they would have you
believe—including Engelbrecht, who was something of a hero and a
mentor to me. Engelbrecht once told me that a good detective has to

believe in luck; he said that it's the only explanation why criminals ever get away with anything."

(My speech neglected to mention that Ernst Engelbrecht had been obliged to leave the Berlin police force because of some things he'd said about the SA in his nonfiction book, *In the Footsteps of Criminality*, published in 1931.)

"Beyond a few bare facts that appeared in the newspapers at the time, the full details of this case have never been made known to the public. So soon after the sensational case of Fritz Haarmann, the Düsseldorf Vampire, it was held by the government of the day that the details of the Gormann case were much too unpleasant and salacious to lay before the general public, although some might legitimately say that these murders were the inevitable corollary of carelessly liberal policies pursued by a whole series of ineffectual Weimar governments.

"Fritz Gormann worked as a bank clerk agent for the Dresdner Bank on Behrenstrasse. He was a quiet, unassuming sort of man who lived with his wife of fifteen years and three children in Berlin West. Highly thought of by his employers, and well paid to boot, he appeared to be a respectable member of the community and was a regular worshipper at his local Lutheran church. He was never late for work, he didn't drink alcohol, he didn't even smoke. There are detectives I know—myself included—who could not have measured up to the apparently high moral standard of Fritz Gormann.

"Gormann's uncle was an amateur cinematographer and when he died in 1920, he left his nephew his film studio and camera equipment in Lichterfelde. Gormann knew nothing at all about filmmaking but he was interested enough to take some night classes in the craft, and before very long he was making short, silent films. Having cut his teeth filming and editing harmless little movies, Gormann now turned his attention to his real interest, which was making erotic films. To this end, in 1921, Gormann placed an advertisement in the *Berliner*

Morgenpost inviting aspiring models to tea at the Café Palmenhaus on Hardenbergstrasse.

"His first applicant was Amalie Ziethen, aged twenty-five, recently arrived in Berlin from Cottbus; she had a good job at Treu and Nuglisch's perfume shop on Werderstrasse and was considered an excellent employee. But like a lot of young women of her age, she entertained ambitions of becoming a film actress. Gormann appeared to be benign, even avuncular, and explained that studios like UFA-Babelsberg were looking for girls all the time but because the competition was so intense, it was necessary that she arrange her own screen test. He explained that this same screen test should attempt to answer as many questions as possible, including what a girl looked like naked and when she was enjoying ecstasy. Cleverly, he added that this was why he always met girls at the café, instead of at the studio, so they would feel no pressure and had time to properly think things over. Amalie didn't really need to think twice about what Gormann was proposing. She'd wanted to be in pictures all her life and had already done some nude modeling for a couple of magazines, including the cover of a naked culture magazine called *Die Schönheit*.

"She and Gormann left the café in Gormann's car and drove to Lichterfelde, where, after appearing in Gormann's pornographic film, she was strangled with a length of electrician's wire. The body was subsequently dumped in the Grunewald Forest, not very far north from where we are now. If this was all that had happened to poor Fräulein Ziethen that would have been bad enough. It was only much later on, after we had finally arrested Gormann, that a viewing of his film collection revealed just what agonies Amalie and several other girls had endured before Gormann took their lives. Suffice it to say that he was a modern Torquemada.

"As is typical of the lust murderer, with each girl the script was horribly the same; Gormann would film her in the studio at Lichterfelde until she had gone as far as her own sense of modesty allowed, at which point he would drug her and then subject her to a pedal-operated sex machine which he had manufactured especially for him in Dresden. Then he would torture the girl for some hours, before finally having sex with her, and it was during the very act of intercourse that finally he strangled her with a ligature made of Kuhlo wire. He even devised an ingenious clockwork device to enable him to crank the camera and which allowed him to appear in front of the lens so that he could film himself in the very act of committing murder—a device which he later patented and sold to a German movie company.

"At least nine girls disappeared in this way between 1921 and 1923, and their strangled bodies were found dumped in sites as far afield as Treptow and Falkensee. The Murder Commission knew that all the dead girls shared one thing in common: they were all strangled with Kuhlo wire, which was why at the Police Praesidium on Alexanderplatz, for a long time these murders were known as the Kuhlo killings.

"Several good detectives—Tegtmeyer, Ernst Gennat, Nasse, Trettin—all tried to solve the Kuhlo killings. Without putting too many details before the public, the Murder Commission sought to enlist the huge public interest there was in this case. On one celebrated occasion a couple of Berlin furniture shops—Gebruder-Bauer on Bellevuestrasse, and J. C. Pfaff on Kurfürstendamm—each donated a window where various exhibits from the murders could be displayed in the hope that a member of the public might recognize them: clothes, a length of curtain material one of the bodies had been wrapped in, the wire used to strangle the girls, and photographs of the places where the bodies had been found. But the displays caused huge crowds to collect in front of the windows and the police were obliged to intervene with the result that the shop owners requested that the articles be removed, as they were interfering with their businesses. Other appeals for information were no more successful. Detectives were even invited from

Scotland Yard in England and from the Sûreté in Paris to help, all to
no avail.

"Meanwhile the particular batch of wire used to strangle the girls
was tracked down to UFA film studios, Babelsberg; this and the fact
that two of the murdered girls had told friends they were going to meet
a Rudolf Meinert for a casting session caused the Murder Commission
to focus for a time on the film industry. In order to meet some of his
victims, Gormann had used this name, knowing that there was a real
Rudolf Meinert who was head of production at UFA. Meinert was in
fact interviewed by detectives several times. As were other producers
and directors at UFA film studios. After a while, anyone who had anything to do with German cinema was interviewed. Detectives even saw
Gormann's advertisement in the newspaper and spoke to him; but he
seemed like no one's idea of a suspect in a murder case. He was a
church elder; a man who had won the Iron Cross and been wounded
during the war; he even gave money to the Prussian Police Benevolent
Fund.

"Gormann also showed detectives some of the movies he had
made—innocuous casting films that were a million kilometers away
from the kind of film he preferred to make; and he directed detectives
to some of the girls he had filmed who testified to his kindness and
generosity. Those girls he hadn't strangled, that is. But what no one
thought to check was Gormann's relationship with the film studio;
there was no relationship. As far as the studio was concerned, Gormann was just another supplicant in a long line of supplicants that
were, more often than not, ignored.

"Then, in 1923, even as Gormann was being rejected as a suspect,
the murders stopped completely. At least, those murders that bore Gormann's trademarks. Any detective will tell you that the most terrible
thing about investigating a series of lust murders is that the murderer
stops killing before he is caught. It's the most appalling feeling on earth

to find yourself wishing another murder will be committed in the hope that it might yield up the one vital clue that will crack the case. It's moral paradoxes like this that make the job so difficult sometimes and which cause homicide detectives many sleepless nights. In circumstances like these I've even known detectives to blame themselves for a victim's death. As paradoxes go, to desire a death in the hope that you might save a life is about as acute a dilemma as you'll find outside of wartime. It's no good telling a cop how the philosopher Kant argues that to act in the morally right way people must act from duty. Or— again, according to Kant—that it is not the consequences of actions that make them right or wrong but the motives of the person who carries out the action. Most cops I've ever met couldn't even spell 'categorical imperative.' And I know I myself fall short of his morally absolute standard every day I go to work.

"But back to Fritz Gormann. When the Kuhlo killings case came my way in 1928, I took the files home with me and spent several nights reading them through in their entirety. And then I read them again. You see, it's almost invariably the case that when eventually you make an arrest, the evidence was staring you in the face all along; and with this in mind, sometimes the best thing you can do is to arrange a review of all the available evidence in the hope that you may see something that wasn't seen the first time. You see, a cold case is nothing but all of the false and misleading evidence that, over a period of years, has come to be accepted as true. In other words, you start by patiently challenging almost everything you think you know; even the identity of the victims.

"You might reasonably think that it would be impossible to mistake the identity of a murdered girl. You would be wrong. It turned out that one of the nine murdered girls was someone else: the girl we thought she was had, after a year living in Hannover, turned up safe and well. Meanwhile I was struck by how much work had gone into the investigation and how many people the detectives in the Murder Commission had managed to interview. But by the time I finished I knew the case as well as any detective who'd been in on the case since the beginning.

"Now, before joining the Murder Commission I had been a sergeant working in Vice. Consequently many of my informants were to be found in some less than salubrious places, including a place called the Hundegustav Bar. Previously known as the Borsig Cellar, this was a real dive. At the Hundegustav they had some private rooms where they used to show what were called Minette movies—movies that explicitly featured naked girls on film. Not only were such pornographic films tolerated under the Weimar Republic, incredibly they were actively encouraged as a way of asserting the complete freedom that characterized a modern society—one that had left behind outmoded concepts like morals and accepted standards of behavior. This is one of the reasons why Germany demanded a Nazi revolution in the first place.

"Anyway, I was in there on police business—well, I would say that, wouldn't I?—and I happened to see one of these films and something about the girl in the film struck me as familiar. I'd seen her before somewhere. But it was several days before I thought to check the Kuhlo case files, and when I did, it turned out that the girl in the film was none other than Amalie Ziethen, the very first girl that Gormann had strangled.

"I went back to the club with my commissar to interview a thief called Gustave the Dog, who owned the Hundegustav Bar. We checked the film and were astonished to find the girl's name scratched on the film's leader and also the actual date of her death. Gustave told us he'd paid cash for the film; the man who'd sold it to him hadn't left a name, of course, but he described him well enough. A respectable man with a bow tie, stiff collar, a limp, perhaps an injured arm, a bowler hat, and an Iron Cross on his lapel. I had an artist friend draw a likeness of the man to Gustave's exact instructions. Then I went around to some of the other clubs looking for a man like this who might have sold them a Minette movie. But I always drew a blank.

"Doubtless many of you are familiar with the phrase *Media vita in morte sumus*. I think all homicide detectives have this written on the inside of their hats. And you can hear that sentiment in a poem by the great German poet Rilke, of whom I am fond, which goes, 'Death stands great before us, We all are his, Even our most carefree laughter to him belongs, and in the midst of the joy that life is, Mortal tears are most immortal songs.'"*

I glanced up as Heinrich "Gestapo" Müller took out a notebook and started to make notes with a silver pen. Was he—I wondered—a fan like me of Rilke? Or was there another, more sinister reason why he was making a note? Was he reminding himself to have some of his thugs come to my flat on Fasanenstrasse in the early hours and arrest me? That was the thing about Müller; as a policeman he was a real wire brush: it was hard to think of him having anything but sinister reasons for doing anything at all.

"Since detectives on the Murder Commission live with death as much as anyone, it's perhaps natural that they should often believe that murderers stop only because they get caught or because they are dead. Nearly all of the detectives in the Murder Commission who were on the original investigation believed what they wanted to believe: that the killer had been stricken with remorse and committed suicide. But given the fact that the murderer might have been the man in the bowler hat who'd sold Gustave the Minette film, it was now equally possible that this earlier explanation as to why the killer had simply stopped after the last Kuhlo killing—that of Lieschen Ulbrich—was

---

*Author's own translation of Rilke's poem *Schlussstück*.

wrong. So I asked myself what other reason might have accounted for the strangler giving up an activity he seemed to very much enjoy? Had something else happened to the Kuhlo killer? Something that had made him stop killing? If he wasn't dead, had he perhaps left Berlin? Returning to a lengthy list of witnesses who'd been interviewed, I started to investigate what dramatic life events had occurred to any of these men five years ago that might have put a stick in the spokes of a lust murderer's career. And finally I came up with a list of possible suspects, at the head of which was the name of Fritz Gormann.

"Gormann had been awarded a second-class Iron Cross in 1917, having served as a train transport commander with a field artillery regiment. He had a limp, which was the result of an injury sustained in 1916. As I mentioned, Gormann had been a suspect until detectives rejected him on the grounds that the bank clerk—now a bank manager— was perceived to be much too mild-mannered ever to kill someone. This was nonsense as his military record clearly demonstrated that Gormann's medal had been awarded for courage under fire.

"Further research revealed that on the day before his wife's fortieth birthday in the summer of 1923, Fritz Gormann visited Braun's jewelry shop at 74 Alte Jakobstrasse. The shop had been robbed twice before— in January 1912 and again in August 1919. Unknown to Gormann when he visited the shop to buy his wife a brooch, the shop was in the process of being robbed a third time. Gormann entered the store to find Herr Braun, the proprietor, lying dead on the floor and a man advancing upon him from a back room with a gun in his hand, demanding the cash that Gormann had brought with him to buy the brooch. Gormann refused and was shot, but not before he managed to hit the murderer with the lead-filled cosh that Braun had kept for self-defense. The robber was subsequently captured and executed while Gormann himself spent six months recovering from his wound in the Charité Hospital.

"But as a result of his wound he lost the use of his right arm, which, I'm sure you will all agree, is a considerable disadvantage for a strangler. And recognizing that his career as a lust murderer was now at an end, Gormann sold his studio in Lichterfelde and went back to being a respectable member of Berlin's banking community. It seems incredible but it was as simple as that.

"Gormann's picture as the hero of Alte Jakobstrasse had appeared in the newspapers at the time. And so I took this picture to the Hundegustav Bar, where Gustave himself confirmed that Gormann was indeed the man who had sold him the pornographic Minette film. But was he the killer? It's one thing selling an erotic film that includes a real murder, but that doesn't necessarily make the vendor a murderer.

"The next day I went to the Dresdner Bank at number 35 on the south side of Behren-Strasse and Friedrichstrasse to take a closer look at my suspect. I was still not entirely satisfied that we had our man, and this feeling was underlined when, after we arrested him, we searched his house and found—nothing. Not one can of film. Not one length of Kuhlo wire. Nor any curtain material that matched the piece we had. Nothing. And of course Gormann himself denied everything. Back at the Police Praesidium on Berlin's Alexanderplatz I was beginning to feel like a bit of a fool. Actually it was worse than that. I felt low enough to think that maybe I wasn't cut out to be a detective, after all. I don't mind telling you that I almost handed in my warrant disc right then and there.

"These are the dark moments that haunt every detective. The shadows of the shadows, as I sometimes think of them, when things can become easily mistaken for something else. When evil masquerades as good and lies appear to be the truth. But sometimes, after the shadows comes the light.

"Experience teaches patience. You learn to rely on routines. On habits. On trusting your own way perforce of doing several things at once. I often think that being a detective is a little like the traffic-control tower that stands in the center of Berlin's Potsdamer Platz: not only do its lights have to control traffic from five different directions, it also tells the time and, in bad weather, provides much needed shelter for a traffic policeman.

"In Gormann's neighborhood of Schlachtensee, I spoke to one of his neighbors who told us that several years before, he'd seen Gormann burying something in his garden. Now, there's nothing unusual about that in Schlachtensee, at least there isn't when the man has two arms. But a one-armed man burying an object in his garden is perhaps more unusual, even in Berlin just ten years after a terrible war that maimed so many. In short it might reasonably be supposed that a one-armed man who buries an object in his garden might have something important to hide. So we got a court order, dug it up, and discovered a tarpaulin-covered box containing several dozen cans of film.

"Gormann still denied everything. At least he did until we discovered that in one of the later movies he actually appeared in several frames; and with this evidence we finally secured a full and detailed confession. He told us everything—every horrible fact. His modus operandi. Even his motive: he blamed a woman for encouraging him to volunteer for the army in 1914, which, he said, scarred him for life. And he'd sold the film to the Hundegustav Bar so that he could see one of his victims whenever he wished. The rest he had planned to destroy. Three months later Gormann was beheaded at Brandenburg Prison. I attended the execution myself, and I take no pleasure in mentioning that he did not die well. Incidentally, if you're so inclined, you can see the death mask they made of his severed head in our police museum at Alexanderplatz.

"The exact number of Gormann's victims cannot be easily calculated. He himself could not actually remember how many he'd killed. He had destroyed much of his film library after the studio was sold.

Also the Weimar decade was a time when so-called lust murders were common, and it was a time when bizarre serial murders regularly occupied the front pages of German newspapers. These cases both engrossed and appalled the German public, and it was this collapse in the moral fiber of the country that led many to call for the restoration of law and order in the form of a National Socialist government. Murder of this kind is much less common today. Indeed, it can honestly be said that it seldom ever occurs; Paul Ogorzow, the S-Bahn murderer whose crimes horrified this city last year, wasn't even a German, he was a Pole, from Masuren."

There was a lot more about Paul Ogorzow's racial inferiority as the reason for his criminality—a simplistically eugenic explanation provided by the state secretary of the kind to which I had no intention of lending my voice; besides, Masuren was part of East Prussia, and Ogorzow, who had grown up speaking German, was no more a Slav than I was. Instead I'd decided to end on a more personal, insightful note—something which, like a tree cake from the famous Café Buchwald, had layers of meaning that were not immediately obvious. I spoke off the cuff, of course, which would certainly have alarmed Gutterer; then again, no one, not even the state secretary of Propaganda, was about to interrupt me now in front of all our distinguished foreign guests.

"Gentlemen, as a detective I can't claim to have learned very much in my twenty years of service. Frankly, the older I get, the less I seem to know and the more I'm aware of it."

A little to my surprise, Himmler started to nod, although I knew for a fact that he wasn't yet forty-two and he didn't look like the type to admit his ignorance about anything. Nebe had told me that in Himmler's briefcase there was always a copy of a Hindu verse scripture called the Bhagavad Gita. I don't read much of that kind of thing myself and I didn't know if I thought this made him a wise man; but I expect he thought so.

"But what I'm sure of is this: that it's the ordinary people like Fritz Gormann who commit the most extraordinary crimes. It's the ladies who play a Schubert impromptu on the piano who poison your tea, the devoted mothers who smother all of their children, the bank clerks and insurance salesmen who rape and strangle their customers, and the scoutmasters who butcher their whole families with an ax. Dockworkers, truck drivers, machine operators, waiters, pharmacists, teachers. Reliable men. Quiet types. Loving fathers and husbands. Pillars of the community. Respectable citizens. These are your modern murderers. If I had five marks for every killer who was a regular Fritz who wouldn't harm a fly, then I'd be a rich man.

"Evil doesn't come wearing evening dress and speaking with a foreign accent. It doesn't have a scar on its face and a sinister smile. It rarely ever owns a castle with a laboratory in the attic, and it doesn't have joined-up eyebrows and gap teeth. The fact is, it's easy to recognize an evil man when you see him: he looks just like you or me. Killers are never monsters, seldom inhuman, and, in my own experience, nearly always commonplace, dull, boring, banal. It's the human factor that's important here. As Adolf Hitler has himself pointed out, we should recognize that Man is as cruel as Nature itself. And so perhaps it's the Man next door who is the beast of whom we had better beware. For that reason it is perhaps also the Man next door who is best equipped to catch him. A very ordinary man like me. Thank you and Heil Hitler."

The men seated in front of me started to clap; they were probably relieved that they could get out of that stifling, smoke-filled room and have a coffee on the terrace. Some of the other speakers who were yet to follow—Albert Widmann, Paul Werner, and Friedrich Panzinger— eyed me with a mixture of envy and contempt. The contempt I was used to, of course. As Nebe had reminded me, my own career was stalled, permanently; I was just air and a threat to no one; but they still had their own speaking ordeals ahead of them, and it wasn't long before I learned that I'd managed to set the bar quite high. As I sat down, Nebe made some long-winded appreciative noises at the lectern and told everyone how I'd modestly neglected to mention the police decoration I'd received for apprehending Gormann and what an asset I was to everyone in Kripo at Werderscher Markt. This was news to me as I hadn't ever been through the door of the smart, new police building on Werderscher Markt and, other than Nebe himself, knew hardly anyone who worked there. It sounded a lot like praise but he might as well have been giving Ebert's eulogy on the steps of the Reichstag. Still, it was nice of him to bother; after all, there were some, like Panzinger and Widmann, who would happily have seen me on my way to Buchenwald concentration camp.

Eight

"General Schellenberg presents his compliments and asks if you might join him outside on the terrace. There's someone very keen to meet you."

I was lurking in the conservatory by the marble fountain, enjoying a quiet cigarette away from all the cauliflower outside; the man who addressed me now was a major, but the majors working for Walter Schellenberg were usually destined for higher things, and I didn't doubt that some cauliflower of his own would soon replace the four pips that were on his gray tunic's collar tabs. He was about thirty and— I later learned—an ex-lawyer from somewhere near Hannover. His name was Hans Wilhelm Eggen and he was the officer I'd seen coming out of the Stiftung Nordhav office on the first floor.

I glanced at the cigarette smoking in my hand. A Manoli, it tasted even better than the ones I'd stolen before. Doubtless someone had thought it important to make a good impression on all our foreign guests and, in my experience, there is no more effective way of doing this in wartime than providing good smokes for the cigarette boxes. My own cigarette case was full again. Things were looking up. At this rate I was going to get my smoker's cough back in no time at all. I took another puff and crushed the end onto a slab of crystal that passed for an ashtray.

"Of course, sir," I lied. "I'd be delighted."

As I followed Major Eggen onto the villa terrace I prayed I wasn't
about to be introduced to one of what were jokingly known as the big
three: Himmler, Kaltenbrunner, and Müller. I didn't think my nerves
were up to the task of a conversation with any of them, not without a
silver crucifix in my pocket. But I needn't have worried. When I got
outside I saw that Schellenberg was with the same Swiss army officer
I'd seen coming out of the Nordhav office with Major Eggen. I'd met
Schellenberg before at Prinz Albrechtstrasse when he'd been working
closely with Heydrich. He was good-looking and as smooth as an
English butler's silk underwear and, since Heydrich's demise, in charge
of the SD's Foreign Intelligence department. Most people had believed
Schellenberg would take over from Heydrich when he was assassinated, including Schellenberg himself. He was able enough. But the
splash in the RSHA's men's room was that Himmler thought Schellenberg was too smart for Heydrich's job; and if the Reichsführer had preferred Kaltenbrunner it was only because he wanted someone who was
easier to control, especially with good brandy in such short supply.

The Swiss was taller by a head than the shortish Schellenberg and
as handsome as he was self-assured. From his manner I thought maybe
he owned a small bank but, as things transpired, it was just a large castle. Generally speaking, something like that produces the same over-
privileged, nothing-can-touch-me effect. The boots he was wearing
looked as if they'd been polished by Carl Zeiss, while the thighs of his
pegged riding breeches were so flared he might have got clearance for
a takeoff from Tempelhof. His hand was inside his gray tunic,
Napoleon-style, although it might just have been holding the broom
handle that was doubling as a backbone. But his smile was genuine
enough; he was pleased to see me, I guess.

"This is Captain Paul Meyer-Schwertenbach," said Schellenberg.
"From the Swiss military police."

The Swiss bowed stiffly. "Captain Gunther," he said. "It's an honor, sir."

"Captain Meyer is a famous Swiss novelist," explained Schellenberg. "He writes adventure and detective stories under his pen name, Wolf Schwertenbach."

"I don't read many detective stories," I admitted. "Or anything else very much. It's my eyes, you understand. They don't see as well as they used to. But I knew a Swiss detective once. At least, I spoke to him several times on the telephone. Fellow called Heinrich Rothmund."

"Rothmund's now the head of the Swiss Federal Police," said Meyer.

"Then I wonder why he's not here," I said, glancing around.

"He was going to come," said Schellenberg. "But I'm afraid his visa didn't arrive in time."

"That would explain it," I said, although it hardly explained why a mere captain had been granted a visa to visit Germany ahead of a detective of the caliber of Heinrich Rothmund. "Pity. I should like to have talked to him again."

"I must confess that I'm a great admirer of yours," said Meyer.

"That's quite a confession these days."

"Both as an author of detective fiction and as a criminologist. Before I was a writer I was a lawyer. Every lawyer in Zurich remembers reading about the famous Gormann case."

"Like I said, I was lucky. Well, almost. You know, it might just be that I'm the only Fritz here who was never a lawyer." I glanced at Schellenberg. "How about it, General?"

"Yes, I studied law."

"Major Eggen?"

Eggen nodded. "Guilty as charged," he said.

"I enjoyed your talk," said Meyer. "While I am in Berlin I should like very much to speak with you in private, Captain Gunther. Perhaps you would indulge the questions of an enthusiastic amateur. For the purposes of my research, you understand."

"You're writing another novel?"

"I'm always writing another novel," he said.

"That's good. In Germany there's always room for another novel, so long as we keep burning them."

Schellenberg smiled. "Captain Gunther is that rare thing in the Reich Security Office. A man who is a very poor Nazi. Which sometimes makes him quite entertaining to the rest of us."

"Does that include you, General?" I had long suspected that, like Arthur Nebe, Walter Schellenberg was a lukewarm Nazi and more interested in his own profit and advancement than anything.

"It might do. But it's not my entertainment with which we're concerned right now. It's Captain Meyer's."

"He's quite right," Meyer told me. "As an author it's not very often that I get the chance to find out where a real detective's inspiration starts and stops."

I was thinking of a few questions I might have for the captain myself; questions about Stiftung Nordhav, perhaps, or Export Drives GMBH.

"I don't know much about inspiration, Captain Meyer. But I'd be glad to help you in any way I can. Are you staying here at the Villa Minoux?"

"No, at the Adlon Hotel."

"Then you're in very good hands."

"Why don't you meet there for drinks?" suggested Schellenberg. "This evening? I'm sure you can spare some time for the captain, Gunther."

"Actually I have tickets for the German Opera," said Meyer. "Weber's *The Marksman*. But before might be possible. Or after."

"There is no after in German opera," I said. "There's only the eternal present. Besides, the opera's a little too far from the Adlon to be comfortable for the curtain-up. Perhaps we'd better meet at the Grand Hotel on the Knie."

"Gunther's right," agreed Schellenberg. "The Grand would be more convenient for you, Paul."

"Shall we say six p.m.?" asked Captain Meyer.

I nodded; men were drifting back into the villa for the next lecture, but before that happened, Major Eggen took me aside.

"The general would like you to take special care of Captain Meyer and Lieutenant Leuthard."

"Is he Swiss, too?"

"Yes. That's him over there." Eggen nodded at a tall young man with a hard, unsmiling face that could easily have found a home in the Gestapo. "Go to the general's office on Berkaerstrasse and borrow a car. I'll telephone ahead so they'll be expecting you. Come back here. Drive them to the Grand Hotel for drinks, to the opera, and then wherever they want to go. Show them a good time."

"At the German Opera?" I smiled. "I'm not sure something like that's even possible."

"Before. During the interval. After. Then take them back to the Adlon. Just make sure they're happy, all right?"

"That's asking rather a lot, don't you think? They're Swiss. Especially that young one. He looks very Swiss indeed. I could make a wristwatch happier than him."

"Maybe so. But right now, you're Captain Meyer's enthusiasm, and whatever Captain Meyer wants, Captain Meyer gets. Understood?"

He handed me a fistful of banknotes and some food and drink coupons.

"I'll bet you're the man who made sure the cigarette boxes were full today," I said.

"I beg your pardon?"

"You'll forgive me for asking, sir, but who the hell are you? I'm not under your command. Exactly who do you work for? Foreign Intelligence? Stiftung Nordhav? With that manicure I know you're not police. It was General Nebe who asked me to be here today. I'm sure he wouldn't like it very much if I went off the farm before we've finished making hay here and slipped away into town like you're asking. It's not good manners to make a speech and then quit before some of my colleagues have had a turn at the lectern."

"I work for the Reich Ministry of Economic Affairs," he explained. "And if I square it with Nebe, will you do as General Schellenberg asks?"

"Well, I hate to drag myself away from this crime conference. Usually I'm very good at concealing my boredom. But if it's all right with Nebe, it's all right with me. Frankly I've already heard enough billy goat shit for one day. I know. I could take him to a couple of shops to see if we can find some of his books. Marga Schoeller's Bookshop, perhaps. I expect he'd like it there, being an author."

Marga Schoeller's, on the Ku'damm, was the only bookshop in Berlin that still refused to sell Nazi literature.

"I don't care where you take him, as long as he has a good time. Understood?"

Half an hour later I was walking down Am Grosser Wannsee again, only this time with a bit of a spring in my step. Frankly I was glad to be away from the Villa Minoux, even though it meant missing out on a lunch of mustard eggs and a pig knuckle with pea puree, not to mention more free cigarettes. The thought of meeting Himmler a second time was much too daunting; my shins couldn't have taken it. The smile on my face lasted for precisely a hundred meters, at least until I came past the SS Horticultural School, where three undernourished young men were toiling in the sun with rakes and hoes. I walked up to the wrought-iron gate and watched them work. I'm good at that, too. But I never did like gardening very much, not even when there was a well-stocked window box on the sarcophagus-sized balcony outside my living room. I have green fingers only when I dip them in a Berliner Weisse with woodruff syrup—the champagne of the North. The three didn't look up. Not even to wipe their brows, and the blue sky might as well have been gray for all the interest they had in looking at it.

There didn't seem to be anyone in a uniform keeping guard so I whistled to one of the men and, seeing my uniform, he came running over to the gate, snatched off his cap, and then bowed his head, like someone in the SS had taught him that little show of respect with the toe of a boot and the end of a quirt. Now that he was near I could see that he wasn't much more than a boy; perhaps fifteen or sixteen years old.

"Jewish?"

"Yes, sir."

"From Berlin?"

"Yes, sir."

"What were you, son? I mean, before they got you doing such vital war work for your country?"

"I was studying for my Abitur," he said.

"Which school?"

"The Jewish School, on Kaiser-Strasse."

"I know it. I used to know it well." I swallowed uncomfortably, and removing a fist from my breeches pocket, I pushed it through the bars of the wrought-iron gate. "Take it quickly," I said. "Before someone sees you."

He looked at the banknotes and the cigarettes I'd dropped into his hand with astonishment and then pocketed them swiftly. Too surprised to say thank you, he just stood there with his cap in his bony hand, sweating uncomfortably, with eyes that were as hollow as a half-empty catacomb.

"An Abitur isn't much good these days if you end up wearing a uniform like this one. Take my word for it, my boy. At least you have the scent of those nice flowers in your nostrils. Not like me. I get to smell shit all day long. And sometimes I even have to eat it, too."

Nine

caught the S-Bahn north to Grunewald Station and walked south-west, along Fontanestrasse onto Hohenzollerndamm. Department Six of the RSHA was located in a modern, four-story building on Berkaerstrasse that looked more like apartments than the headquarters of the Foreign Intelligence Service, with only a flagpole on the flat roof and a few official cars parked in front of the curving façade to suggest that it was any different from the sleepy residential bricks-and-mortar surrounding it. Short of having the SD's Foreign Intelligence conducted from a back room in a small suburban theater, number 22 couldn't have been more anonymous and out of the way, and was quite a contrast to the kinds of grand, intimidating buildings that Schellenberg's sinister masters preferred. Just looking at it now told me a lot about Schellenberg. A German who cares nothing for show is someone with a lot to hide, and as I approached the modest, unguarded entrance I wondered just how it was that Schellenberg had also avoided service in one of Heydrich's murderous operation groups. That was clever, too. I had to hand it to Walter Schellenberg; it seemed that he'd made a much better job of pretending to be a Nazi than I had.

An SD captain called Horst Janssen came down to the reception area to hand me a set of keys for one of the cars parked outside.

"Nice place you have here," I observed as I followed him outside.

"It used to be a Jewish old people's home," he said without a trace of embarrassment; then again he was just back from Kiev, where he'd probably done something even more dreadful than kick a few old people onto the streets—you could see it in his blue eyes—the kind of thing that people like me and Schellenberg had so neatly sidestepped. An international crime conference can sharpen up your instincts like that.

"That explains why it's so quiet around here," I said.

"It is now they're all in the Lublin Ghetto," Janssen said, and tossed me the keys. "That one there," he said, pointing to a Mercedes 170.

"Has it got petrol?"

"Sure we've got petrol. That's why we invaded the Caucasus."

"Comedian. What's he like to work for? Schellenberg."

"He's all right."

"Where does he live? Round here, I suppose. In some fancy big villa. Like Heydrich's place in Schlachtensee."

"Not at all. He's a very modest man, our general. Listen, can you give me a lift as far as the West End?"

"Sure. Where in particular?"

"The military court in Charlottenburg," he said. "I'm a witness in a trial."

"Oh?"

"An SS man accused of cowardice."

"That shouldn't take long."

But Janssen wasn't the talkative type. He said nothing on the way to the court and short of asking him a question directly about Schellenberg and the Stiftung Nordhav, I figured that was it with him.

I dropped Janssen off outside the court on Witzlebenstrasse, just a couple of blocks south of the German Opera House, and spent the rest of the morning and the larger part of the afternoon just driving in Berlin. It had been a while since I'd had a chance to motor around the city with no particular place to go, even though I did have somewhere I was supposed to be; then again that's the best way to see any city—I mean when you should be doing something else. Stolen pleasure beats anything.

Around five I drove back to the villa. In the main hall they were busy listening to someone else performing a long solo about modern policing and I took advantage of this diversion to go upstairs again to check out the Stiftung Nordhav office. The door was still locked, of course, but a quick glance outside revealed that if I stepped out onto the curving balcony that occupied the space above the Greek Revival entrance I might get in there through the third-floor window. A couple of minutes later I was sitting at a little wooden desk and going through the drawers looking for some useful tasty mouthful concerning the sale of the Villa Minoux I might feed to Dr. Heckholz and his charming client, Frau Minoux.

There were lots of files about the IKPK, which mostly I ignored, except to note that the International Criminal Police Commission* was now an active part of the Gestapo. And there was plenty of correspondence between Export Drives GMBH—which turned out to be owned by Major Eggen—and a Zurich-based company called the Swiss Wood Syndicate, some of which had been signed by Paul Meyer. There were also lots of documents about a deal, brokered by the Ministry of Economic Affairs, between a government-owned company called German War and Munitions AG and the Luchsinger Company of Zurich to supply the Swiss with 275 submachine guns and two hundred thousand rounds of ammunition. But there was no sign of any documents regarding the sale of the Villa Minoux to Stiftung Nordhav. Not even a mildewed title deed.

Looking back on it now it seems incredible that I had so much

---

*After 1956, the ICPC became better known as INTERPOL.

important information in my hands but that I didn't think to do anything with it because none of it was about the villa. But that was my
brief from Heckholz and Frau Minoux, after all. How was I to know
that, much later on, the Swiss Wood Syndicate would turn out to be
important? Of course, that's detective work for you. If I had to give that
stupid lecture again I might add that sometimes the work is a bit like
dealing with a beautiful woman you're in love with: you never know
what you've got until she's gone.

I went downstairs, helped myself to some more cigarettes and a
large schnapps from a bottle on a silver tray in the library—the best
kind, made from the best fruit, which in this case was pears, and probably Austrian, as the finest schnapps usually is, and like eating the most
delicious pear you've ever eaten only to discover that it was a wonderful, magic pear and that the effect extends far beyond the mouth into
every corner of the human body like a benign witch's spell. I quickly
poured another and felt a smile spread on my face like a cloud shifting
away from the sun. The bottle was too good to leave lying around in a
place like that. If ever anything needed rescuing from the Nazis, it was
that bottle.

The last lecture of the day was now over and the delegates were
starting to drift out of the main hall. I swallowed the schnapps and,
after a certain amount of talk was splashed about, I ushered Captain
Meyer and his somber companion out to the car.

"I'm afraid it was all downhill after you left," declared Meyer. "Very
dull indeed."

"I'm sorry."

"I don't mind telling you that I've been looking forward to meeting
you again all day."

I'd been working on my smile and quickly deployed it as I opened
the car door.

"But it's always nice to be back in Berlin," he added politely.

"How about you, Lieutenant—?"

"Leuthard," said the man dully.

"Are you enjoying Berlin?"

"No," he said. "I never liked it here much before. And I like it even less now."

Captain Meyer laughed. "Ueli says what's on his mind, generally."

"That's not recommended in Berlin."

We drove north, straight up the old AVUS speedway and then east onto Bismarckstrasse where, outside the Grand Hotel am Knie, I parked the car and gestured the two Swiss inside.

"Shall we?"

Lieutenant Leuthard stared sourly up at the hotel's tall façade with its twin bell towers and steep Dutch gable, lit a cigarette, and then checked his watch. I made a mental note of the size of his hands and his shoulders and resolved not to have any kind of disagreement with him. He might have been Swiss but he didn't look like the kind of man whose neutrality you could depend on.

"Is this a better hotel than the Adlon?" he asked.

"No. Not in my opinion."

"What makes you say so?"

"Before the war, I worked at the Adlon," I said.

"My father's in the hotel business," he said. "I thought I might go into that myself. After the war."

"With your skill for diplomacy, it's a sure thing you'd be successful."

Leuthard smiled a patient sort of smile.

"If you'll forgive me," he said, "I've heard enough waffle for one day. I'm going for a walk. To stretch my legs. I'll see you in the opera house foyer in one hour, Captain. Sir." Then he fixed his kepi on his head and walked east on Berliner Strasse, in the direction of the Tiergarten.

"Sorry about that," said Meyer. "Ueli is a difficult character, at the best of times. A bit hotheaded, frankly. But I think he's a good policeman."

We sat down outside the hotel entrance under the large awning that covered the open-air bar and ordered some beers, for which I felt obliged to apologize in advance.

"The best beer is in short supply," I said.

"Believe me, things are just as bad in Switzerland. We're a land-locked country, as you know, and totally dependent on Germany's goodwill for our survival. Which isn't easy to maintain, given certain recent events."

I shrugged, unaware of what recent events he might have been referring to.

"I'm talking about Maurice Bavaud," explained Meyer. "The Swiss theology student who tried to shoot Hitler in 1938. He was executed last year."

I shrugged. "Speaking for myself, I'm not about to hold a little thing like that against you all."

Meyer chuckled. "Schellenberg was right. You are an excellent detective, but a very poor Nazi. I wonder how you've stayed alive for so long."

"This is Berlin. Most of the time people don't notice when you call a child nasty names. It's not just Lieutenant Leuthard who hates us. It's our masters, too. Been that way since Bismarck's time. We're constitu-tionally ungovernable. A bit like the Paris mob, but with uglier women."

He laughed. "You're a most amusing man. I'm sure my wife, Patri-zia, would love to meet you. If you're ever in Switzerland, you must look us up."

He gave me a stiff little card that had more names and more addresses than a Maltese confidence man.

"Sure. I'm often in your neck of the woods. Actually, my bankers in Zurich think I should move there permanently. But I like it here.

There's our famous air, for one thing. I'd miss that. Not to mention all our hard-won freedoms."

"Seriously, though," he said. "There's an old murder case I've long been fascinated with. Happened in a place called Rapperswil. A woman was found dead in a boat. The local detective is a friend of mine. I'm sure he'd love to have the benefit of your insight. We both would."

"The only insight I can offer you at the present moment is that hosting an international crime conference in Germany is like the Goths and the Vandals offering suggestions on new ways of tackling crimes against property during the sack of Rome. But it would certainly seem like a shame to go to Switzerland just to tell you this."

The beers came and they were better than I had expected. But very expensive.

"Are you really a writer?" I asked.

"Of course. Why do you ask?"

"I never met a writer before. Especially one who was a policeman."

Meyer shrugged. "I'm more on the intelligence side of things," he explained.

"That explains why you know Schellenberg. He's got a lot of intelligence. Maybe just enough to survive the war. We'll see."

"I like him. And he seems to like me."

"How did you two meet?"

"In Bucharest. At the 1938 IKPK General Assembly, where it was proposed the IKPK headquarters be moved from Vienna to Geneva. Schellenberg was all for it. At least he was until your General Heydrich changed his mind for him."

"He could be a very persuasive man when he wanted."

"According to Schellenberg, it was Heydrich who brought you back into Kripo, wasn't it? After five years in the cold."

"Yes. But it wasn't so cold. At least I didn't think it was."

"Schelli says there were some more murders he wanted you to solve. In 1938. Of some Jewish girls."

"A lot of Jews have been murdered in this city."

"But you know the ones I'm talking about. These were just before the infamous night of broken glass, weren't they?"

I nodded.

"Would you tell me about them?"

"All right."

From the pocket of his tunic Meyer now produced a notepad and a pencil. "Do you mind?"

"No, go right ahead. Only, you'd better wait until I'm dead before you write about this. Or better still, you'd better wait until another theology student comes along with a gun in his hand."

We talked for about forty minutes and then I walked him along Bismarckstrasse to the German Opera House, where Leuthard was already waiting outside, looking more thuggish than before. You wouldn't have been surprised to have seen him in an opera—Wagner's, full of thugs with swords and wings on their helmets—but attending one was something else again. There was grass on the back of his tunic, as if he'd been lying in the Tiergarten. He walked toward me with a sort of smile on his face and a program in his hand, but I might just as easily have expected him to have been carrying a gun.

"What did you do?" Meyer asked him.

"Nothing much," said Leuthard. "Lay in the sun and slept for a little."

"I'll meet you back at the hotel after the show," I said. "And then we can go to dinner. Or I'll drive you back to the Adlon. Both, if you prefer."

"I'm sure we could get you a ticket," said Meyer.

"One thing you can't knock about the opera is the music; it's just a pity that they take so long to play it."

"What will you do?"

"Don't worry about me. I live not very far from here."

"You know? I'd like to see the home of a real Berlin detective."

"No, you wouldn't. There's no chemistry set, and no Persian slipper where I keep my tobacco. There's not even a violin. The ordinariness of it would horrify a writer. You might never write another word again because of the disappointment. Besides, right now we're not receiving visitors, on account of the fact that we're waiting for a new guest book from Liebmann's."

"Well then. The Alex. I should like to see around the famous Alex."

"Schellenberg will fix that for you. And now I'm going home. I'll see you back here at ten o'clock."

I walked back toward the Grand; but I didn't go home. I had no intention of going home. Just around the corner was the municipal bathhouse where, two nights a week, Kirsten Handlöser—the schoolteacher I'd met in a boat on the Wannsee—went swimming. At least that was what she had told me. You never know with women. What they tell you and what they don't tell you is a very long bridge across a very wide river with all kinds of fish.

The bathhouse was a big redbrick building with ceramic dolphins on the wall. Inside there was a handsome glass roof over a pool about thirty or forty meters long, and above the clock at the north end was a handsome-looking mural of some lakeside idyll: a couple of herons were watching a bearded man in a red toga trying to get the attention of a naked girl who was seated on a little grassy knoll. She looked like she was of two minds about whatever it was he was suggesting, but from where I was sitting it already looked too late for her to change her mind about anything very much except perhaps which bus she caught home.

I took a quick walk around the poolside but Kirsten wasn't there and I certainly didn't have the inclination to swim myself. Getting wet inside seemed like a better bet. I remembered that Dr. Heckholz had boasted of having an excellent schnapps. His office wasn't so far away, on Bedeuten Strasse, and it was still early enough to find a hardworking lawyer in his office. Besides, I had news for him about Stiftung Nordhav, which was that I'd pushed an investigation about as far as it could go without getting myself into trouble.

I walked along Wallstrasse and instinctively looked to see if Heckholz's office lights were on. Not that they needed to be: it was still light; and not that they would have been; if it had been dark there would have been a blackout, but old habits die hard. So I rang the bell and waited, and when nothing happened I rang all of them, which seldom works, only this time it did.

There was an elevator but as before I took the white marble stairs to the third floor and walked along the well-polished landing to the frosted-glass door, which, as before, was slightly ajar, only this time Dr. Heckholz wasn't expecting me. He wasn't expecting anyone. Not anymore. He was lying on the floor as if eavesdropping on the people in the office immediately below. But he wouldn't have heard anyone or anything because he was quite dead. He couldn't have looked more dead if he'd been lying on the side of a trench at Verdun with a bullet through his head.

Ten

The pool of blood on the white floorboards was right under the broken egg that was the dead lawyer's skull, and as big as a bicycle wheel. You could see his brains under the blood and the bone, and it was clear to me that someone had hit him very hard, several times, with the bronze bust of Hitler that had previously been on the lawyer's desk and which now lay discarded on the floor. There was blood on Hitler's solemn face and tiny strands of Dr. Heckholz's hair on top of the leader's head. I almost laughed as if I could already hear myself telling the cops at the Berlin-Charlottenburg presidium that the victim had been murdered by Hitler. Instead I helped myself to some of the schnapps from a bottle on a silver tray by the window. My fingerprints were all over the door handles and the desktop anyway so it didn't seem to matter that they'd be on a glass, too. Besides, if you can't help yourself to a drink when you're looking at a man with his head bashed in then I can't see why the stuff was ever invented. And Heckholz had been right; it was an excellent schnapps, at least as good as the one I'd had at the Villa Minoux. I poured another. So much schnapps, only this time, so little to smile about.

I took another, closer look at the body. There was such a lot of blood. You always forget just how much there is inside a fully grown man, especially his head. You never forget the first time you ever see a man shot in the head, especially when you do it yourself. Sometimes it seems that there's a natural spring of red that comes out of a person; and there is, of course, only that natural spring is called his life. And once that's tapped it's very hard to stop. Heckholz's right hand, lying by his face, was surrounded with the stuff and it looked as if he'd dipped his finger in his own blood and used that to try to write something— perhaps the identity of his killer—but whatever it was I couldn't make it out. I bent down to touch the pool of blood and rubbed it experimentally between my fingers; it was still quite viscous, as if poor Heckholz hadn't been dead for very long.

I fetched his handkerchief from the breast pocket of his suit and wiped my hands. A key chain led out of his trouser pocket on the floor like the body of a golden snake but there was no key on the end; that was in the safe, which was wide open like Ali Baba's sesame, and immediately I saw that the motive for the murder hadn't been robbery. Whatever was missing from the safe, it wasn't money because there were several bundles of banknotes on the top shelf, just like the ones he'd sent to me at the Alex. I helped myself to the two hundred marks I'd been promised and left the rest for the murder boys at the local presidium. It was just around the corner on Bismarckstrasse. They'd probably built it there in case they had any trouble with the crowd at the German Opera. They were a rough lot, opera and ballet fans, as Nijinsky could probably have testified.

After a while I sat down in the meeting room where, just a few days before, I'd eaten those delicious pancakes. I had a lot to think about. I was going to have to tell the police, of course. The question was whether or not I was going to involve Frau Minoux in any of this. If I did, then it might come out that I'd been involved in paying off Arthur Müller, the private detective who'd been employed by the Berlin Gas Company to spy on her and see if she was hanging on to any of her husband's property they could make a claim against. If that happened, Müller would go to prison, and so would I; Frau Minoux, too, if either one of us chose to give evidence against her. I didn't see any reason to do any of that. Besides, I figured she had enough to deal with: a husband in the cement at Brandenburg. Saying very little looked like it was by far the best option; that was always the best option, with the Nazis in charge of things.

I went around the corner to the presidium on Kaiser-Strasse—a smaller version of the Alex—and then returned about half an hour later with a couple of plainclothes detectives, only one of whom I knew. Criminal commissar Friedrich Heimenz was an older man with a pipe and a manner as deliberate as a chess move, which he used to conceal the fact that he knew almost nothing about detective work, least of all how to investigate a murder. Before taking the promotion at Charlottenburg he'd been an inspector at the Grunewald Station, and the last time I'd seen him had been when we were both investigating the death of the air ace Ernst Udet. I figured the promotion was a reward for agreeing to the fiction that Udet's death had been suicide and not murder. A small man with small hands, he looked like he'd just finished drying the dishes. And right away he let it be known that he was looking for a free ride from me, hoping that I'd whitewash his curbstone so that he wouldn't trip over his own feet in the blackout that was his mind.

"I suppose you'll be wanting to take this case yourself, Herr Commissar," he said.

"Me? Whatever gave you that idea? This is your jurisdiction, not mine. I'm not even on duty."

"All the same, you're the more experienced man."

"I may have found this body but I'm still not welcome with the murder boys at Werderscher Markt. Besides, it wouldn't be right. I couldn't say I knew the man, exactly. But he sent me this letter inviting me to his office. And we spoke on the telephone. That was yesterday, and now here I am. A potential witness."

I handed over the undated letter Heckholz had sent me at the Alex and five of the Albrechts I'd taken from his safe. But I kept back the envelope with the postmark.

"Who knows?" I added provocatively. "Maybe even a suspect."

Heimenz read the letter and then nodded. "Did he say what he wanted to talk to you about?"

"He said he had a proposition for me and that there would be another hundred in it for me if I showed up."

"That's all?"

"That's all."

Heimenz nodded and brandished the money I'd given him. "I shall have to keep this for a while," he said. "As evidence."

"Be my guest."

"You'll get a receipt, of course."

It was beginning to get dark. The other detective, an equally old sergeant—all the younger cops were in uniform—switched on a light, absently in the vain hope that it might illuminate their pedestrian thoughts.

"I wouldn't do that if I were you," I said. "You'll have the RLB on your back."

The RLB was the Air Raid Protection Squadron.

"Of course," he said, and switched the light off again.

Heimenz looked down at the body with obvious distaste before finding his own handkerchief and pressing it to his mouth, as if he were going to vomit. Then he turned away and opened a window. "Horrible," he whispered. "You wouldn't think there would be so much blood."

"No," I said. "From the sheer quantity of the stuff I expect it's gone through the floorboards. Tomorrow morning the ceiling in the office below is going to look like the ace of diamonds. Or the ace of hearts."

"It's a dentist's waiting room," said the sergeant.

"That will give them something to think about while they're waiting to have their teeth pulled," I said.

Heimenz didn't mention the possibility that Heckholz had been trying to write something with his own blood and neither did I. He asked me some more questions and after a while I looked at my watch and told him I had to be going.

"I'll be at the Alex if you need me," I said. "On the graveyard shift."

The *Schupos* had cordoned off the entrance to the building on Bedeuten Strasse and some of the neighbors had come out of their burrows to see what the fuss was all about. It's only a dead body, I wanted to tell them; there are tens of thousands of those around if you know where to look for them.

I walked back down to the opera house. Inside I could hear the sound of applause. People started to come out of the auditorium. They looked pleased that the opera was over but none more so than Lieutenant Leuthard. He was holding the small of his back and yawning.

"Did you enjoy that?" I asked.

"Not in the least," he said. "To be quite frank with you, I can't remember ever being so bored."

"He slept all the way through act three," said Meyer.

"Christ, I need a drink," said Leuthard.

"Me too," I said. "Come on. As it happens, I know the best bar in the Tiergarten."

I drove them to a little spot on the Neuer See where there was an open-air café and lots of boats.

"I was here earlier," said Lieutenant Leuthard. "They had nothing to drink. Not even with a coupon."

"I've already thought of that," I said, and from the glove box I took out the bottle of pear schnapps and three glasses.

We sat down at a table and I filled three glasses. Meyer lifted one and looked at the SS etching on the glass and grinned.

"You stole this? From the Villa Minoux?"

"Of course I stole it. Which reminds me of another valuable little aperçu for your notebook, Captain Meyer. A good detective should always be honest, but not too honest. Not too honest for his own good. And not too inquisitive, either. There are some things it's best not to know. This I know for sure. And you can put that in your next book."

Eleven

That was good advice and in most circumstances I would have heeded it. What did it matter to me who killed Dr. Heckholz? I'd only met him once and I felt quite sure I'd never see Frau Minoux again. She was safe in Vienna, and as soon as she heard that her lawyer was dead, I figured she'd probably stay there for a while, at least until she judged it safe to come and shift her belongings from the warehouse in Lichtenberg. That's what I would have done if I'd been her. The trouble was that I had liked Dr. Heckholz. How can you not like a man who cooks you pancakes? I liked her, too, but in a different way, of course. What was more, I'd taken their money, and maybe I felt that while I still had a car at my disposal it could hardly matter if I took a drive out to Brandenburg Prison, so long as I was armed with some breakfast. And very early the next morning I drove to number 58 Königstrasse, in Wannsee, where Herr Minoux's driver, Herr Gantner, had told me that he was living with Katrin, who was a maid at the villa. By now I'd formed the strong impression that for all his apparent avarice, Minoux must have been a decent sort of employer to have encouraged such loyalty, which just goes to show that no man is all bad.

There was all that and then there was this: sometimes you have to know something because that's just how you are made, and what really matters is what you do about it afterward. Or don't do about it. It depends on what it is you end up knowing. And if that sounds like having the bread roll and the five pfennigs that paid for it then I'll just say this. We Germans are used to that. Since 1933 our lives have been about having two incompatible things: peace and German pride.

Wannsee is on the way to Brandenburg and in a decent car, alone on the AVUS speedway, I put my foot down as if the sensation of speed might erase the disquiet I was feeling about visiting the biggest and most secure prison in Europe. For a long time I had often felt that one day it would be offering me room and board, too.

The coal merchant's house on Königstrasse was a modest little villa between an apothecary and a gas station, with shutters and a little wooden balcony. There was a Horch parked out front and a dog lying on a small patch of lawn in the front garden. The dog regarded me suspiciously out of the corner of one eye and growled quietly as I approached the front door. I didn't blame the animal. If I'd seen a man wearing a field-gray SD uniform anywhere near my front door I'd probably have bitten him, especially at that hour. I knocked and waited and eventually the door opened to reveal a woman of about thirty-five wearing a dressing gown and a whole heap of blond hair on top of her head. A bit blowsy, but nice. She yawned in my face and scratched a little; I could still smell the sex on her, which smelled just fine to me. I like the smell of sex in the morning.

"I'm sorry to disturb you so early," I said. "But I need to speak with Herr Gantner. Is he here?"

"You'd be Gunther," she said.

I nodded.

"Then you had better come in."

I walked into a parlor as neat as a Swiss banker's drawer and waited while she went to fetch Gantner. The dog had followed me in and went into the kitchen to look for something to drink; at least that's what it sounded like. Either that or they had a very loud goldfish. I lit a cigarette and walked around the room, which took about two seconds. There was a sideboard that looked like a cathedral altarpiece and beside it a nicely carved tavern chair that was a lot more interesting to admire than to sit on. The wall was home to a large aquarelle of a corner bouncer leaning on his local beer house. It was hard to tell if he was waiting to go in the beer house or if he had already come out, which, given the shortage of beer in Berlin, is a problem most of us have these days. After a while I heard footsteps on the stairs and then Gantner was standing in front of me wearing just his trousers and climbing into his braces. It must have been earlier than I had imagined.

"What's up?" He rubbed a face that was as rough as the scales on a coelacanth and just as ugly and then explored his mouth with a big yellow tongue.

"Dr. Heckholz is dead," I said. "Murdered. I went to see him around eight o'clock last night and found him lying on the floor of his office with his head stove in. It wasn't about money. His safe was open and there was plenty of cash in there. So I figure it was to do with business. Maybe the same business that made him and Frau Minoux ask me to see what I could find out about the sale of the villa to Stiftung Nordhav. In which case you might be in danger yourself." I paused, awaiting some sort of reaction. "Sure. Don't mention it."

He sighed. "You want some coffee, Herr Gunther?"

"No, thanks. I thought I'd take a drive out to Brandenburg and speak with Herr Minoux. Get it all from the authorized mouth, so to speak. And maybe save you a journey in the Horch with the bread and jam."

He nodded at the cigarette in my hand. "You got another nail like that one?"

I gave him one from my case and lit it. He smoked it with more interest than seemed appropriate in the circumstances. Then again maybe he was just looking for the right words.

"He was a good man, Dr. Heckholz," said Gantner.

A little underwhelmed by this reaction, I shrugged. "I liked him."

"Any idea who did it?"

"I have a couple of ideas. Stiftung Nordhav is, as I'm sure you know, a company which has five senior figures from the SS on the board of directors. So I don't think we're going to run short of suspects here. I warned him and Frau Minoux that this was probably something best left alone. I'm just sorry to have been proved right. I get that a lot these days. Anyway, it might just be that Herr Minoux can shed some more light on what happened to Dr. Heckholz. In any event, someone needs to tell him the news and it might as well be me because there's my own position to consider here."

"What position is that?"

"It might sound a bit late given that the cat is already down the drain here but I'd like to know just a little more how it got there. In short, I want to understand a bit more about what you got me into so that I'll know the best way to get out of it."

"Fair enough."

"That goes for you, too, by the way, Herr Gantner. Anything you can tell me. When you see the danger you can flee the danger, right?"

"There's not much I can tell you. Me, I'm just the driver. When I saw you again outside the station the other day I thought you were the right man to help them. You being in the SD n'all, and knowing the boss and everything. He always liked you, Herr Gunther. Look, the details I don't know, beyond the name of the company you mentioned. The Nordhav Foundation. Plus the fact that Minoux is spending time with his German Michael for something that there are plenty of others doing, only worse, if you ask me."

"What, you expect honesty from these people? That's how the world works these days, you dumb Fritz. The Nazi world we've made for ourselves. In case you hadn't noticed, we've got hypocrisy running

out of every orifice in this golem we call a country. Wake up." I shook
my head. "Better still, get me the bread and jam and then go back to
bed. That's a nice-looking girl you've got there, son. Go back and enjoy
her. Hell, I wish I could."

Five minutes later I was heading west alongside the Havel with
Minoux's breakfast on my passenger seat.

There are three buildings of note for tourists visiting Brandenburg:
the cathedral, the Catherine Church, and the old state town hall with
its famous statue of Charlemagne's nephew, Roland, who according to
the Baedeker is a symbol of civic liberty. But these days the only reason
anyone came down from Berlin to Brandenburg was to visit one of the
four thousand people who were locked up in the most notorious prison
in Nazi Germany. So much for Roland. There's been a prison in the
Görden quarter of Brandenburg since 1820, but it wasn't until 1931
that a new building was erected and a couple of years after that before
it became what it is now: a so-called house of discipline and an execution site, with as many as two people a day going to the guillotine,
which, by all accounts, is housed in the old garage, alongside an equally
busy gallows. I'm not sure how it's decided who gets topped and who
gets a haircut. It's the kind of nice detail that they could probably
explain better in the People's Court on Elssholzstrasse, in Schöneberg,
and very probably do. It's said that the court president, Roland Freisler—
himself a former Bolshie—screams out the death sentences at the top of
his voice, no doubt to escape any suspicions regarding his own loyalty.

A gray stone Noah's Ark of a building, Brandenburg-Görden is full
of creatures every bit as desperate. Surrounded with forests and poorly
maintained lakes, there are plenty of mosquitoes around in summer to
add to a prisoner's daily torments. And if that wasn't enough, there's the
airport just a couple of miles to the north where German bombers and
supply planes come and go at all hours of the night. It's as if the local
air was ruled by Beelzebub.

I parked my car and walked to the head of the visitors' line. The uniform was good for that, at least. A prison guard took me to a gloomy room with a nice view of the prison yard. After about ten minutes, Friedrich Minoux was brought in. A smallish man with a hatchet face and a small mustache, he'd always been slim, but now he looked emaciated, and my first thought on seeing him was that even with someone bringing him breakfast every day, he wasn't going to make it; the combination of poor diet and hard labor was going to kill him just as surely as any guillotine.

"Oh, it's you," he said, as if we'd seen each other only the day before. In fact it had been all of six years.

"You look well, Herr Minoux."

Minoux snorted. "I'm afraid that even a witch with good eyes would think this particular Hansel was much too thin to eat. But it's kind of you to say so. However, I shouldn't complain. There are some here—" He paused and seemed momentarily choked with emotion. "They're executing Siegfried Gohl this morning. A Christadelphian conscientious objector." He shook his head. "We live with that kind of thing every day."

Minoux took a deep breath and then a cigarette from the case I'd pushed across the table. He lit one and inhaled it gratefully. I didn't like to tell him that the cigarette he was smoking had been stolen from his own silver cigarette box at Villa Minoux.

"I brought you breakfast," I said, handing him a paper bag that had already been searched by the guard. "Since I was coming here to see you I thought I'd save Herr Gantner a trip."

"Thanks. I'll save this for later, when I can take the time to enjoy it. You've no idea how long I can make breakfast last. Sometimes until supper."

"But the main reason I came to see you today was to tell you that

Dr. Heckholz is dead. Someone went to his office last night and bashed his head in."

"I'm very sorry to hear that."

"It was me who found him, actually. I was hoping you might shed some more light on exactly what he was up to. I mean, I have a rough idea, but I assumed you could tell me more than I already know, which isn't much, really. In the circumstances I'd rather not contact your wife. The police don't know of her involvement and I think it's best we keep it that way. Wouldn't you agree?"

Friedrich Minoux shrugged. "Why ask me?"

"Have I missed something here? I'd somehow formed the impression that their efforts were directed to getting you out of this place. In which case anything you can tell me—"

"I don't know what you expect from me. I certainly never hired Heckholz. How could I? I have no money. Everything I had has been swallowed up in fines and legal bills and compensating Berlin Gas."

"Really? He told me that you did hire him."

"Then I'm also sorry to say that he lied."

"And is your wife a liar, too?"

"I'm afraid that's for you to decide. Whatever my wife might have hired him for was done entirely without my knowledge. But that shouldn't be a surprise to you, of all people, given our history together. Lilly and I were never very close, as I'm sure you will remember. She's her own woman, with her own money and her own selfish agenda. It's fine for her to stir these things up while she lives in luxury in Garmisch. But she gave absolutely no thought to how her actions might impact upon me while I remain in prison. None whatsoever. Nor did I in any way sanction bringing you into this matter. That was as unwise as it was precipitate. Look here, I'm sorry you've had a wasted journey from Berlin but let me make something quite clear to you, Herr

Gunther. I have absolutely no interest in contesting the verdict of the court. Or for that matter in disputing the terms of sale of the Villa Minoux at Wannsee to the Nordhav Foundation. I was properly convicted of defrauding the Berlin Gas Company and the sentence could have been a lot heavier. And I received a very fair price for the Villa Minoux. Now, is all that absolutely clear to you?"

He was trying to sound tough but his hands were shaking and the cigarette he had been smoking was now lying neglected in the little tinfoil ashtray. No one ever leaves a cigarette unfinished when they're in the cement.

"Crystal clear, Herr Minoux."

He stood up and knocked on the door to summon the guard.

"And please. Without meaning to sound rude, I'd appreciate it if you didn't come here again. Not ever. You being here, stirring things up that don't need to be stirred up, might count against my chance of parole. The governor is obliged to keep a record of all my visitors, even the ones I didn't invite."

I collected my cigarette case off the table, dropped it into my pocket, and nodded my dumb assent. And then without another word he was gone into the echoing gray void that was Brandenburg-Görden. I couldn't find it within me to feel angry with him. He was scared, I could see that. In a place like that, I'd have been scared myself.

Twelve

The deputy prison governor was an ex-cop from the Alex named Ernst Kracauer. He'd been a lawyer and then a *Schupo* commissar for twenty years, and although he was a die-hard Nazi, he had the reputation of being hard but fair, if such a thing is possible in a place like that. I went to see him in his office and waited alone for him to return from one of his many duties. A rolltop was up against the yellow wall and a partners desk by the window; on this was an oak and brass inkwell set that looked more like a Habsburg coffin, and hanging on the wall, a Tiergarten scene of a Wilhelmine family by a bandstand; in my mind's eye they were probably listening to "The Song of Krumme Lanke." The dusty office window was as big as a church triptych but the room still needed the piano desk lamp to see through the gloom. Outside, some prisoners were tending a large vegetable patch, which boasted a scarecrow but that might have been another prisoner.

When Kracauer returned I greeted him affably, but he said nothing; instead he removed his pince-nez, fetched a bottle from a cupboard in the rolltop, poured two glasses of brandy and handed me one, silently. The jacket of his gray suit looked more like the curtain in front of a crime scene than anything a tailor might have made. He was overweight and clearly under pressure but not as much as the mahogany chair behind the partners desk that creaked ominously when he sat down.

"I need this," he said, and tossed the brandy down his throat like it was a fruit cordial.

"I can tell."

"Part of my duties here are to attend executions. Right now that's one every day. Sometimes more. You'd think I'd be used to it by now. But I don't think one can ever get used to it."

"Siegfried Gohl."

"My nerves are as tight as the strings on a zither. What the hell is a Christadelphian, anyway?"

"Brothers in Christ, I imagine. I think they don't believe in the immortality of the soul." I sipped the brandy. It tasted better than my breakfast.

"Then in that respect they're just like the Nazis." He shook his head. "I mean if the Nazis believed in the immortality of a soul—in a heaven and in a hell—then—" He shrugged.

"They couldn't do what they do," I offered.

"Yes." He poured another for himself as if the idea of meeting his maker was troubling him.

We talked old times for several minutes and he even managed a smile when he told me that for obvious reasons the prisoners called him "the Pole," but I wasn't fooled; clearly the man had learned to hate his job.

"You see that telephone," he said, pointing to one of two telephones that stood on his desk. "It's connected to Franz Schlegelberger's office."

Schlegelberger was the latest Reich Minister of Justice.

"He's going to retire soon, I believe. Otto Thierack is to be the new minister. Not that Schlegelberger's been in the job for very long. Anyway, that telephone is supposed to ring if a death sentence is ever commuted to life imprisonment. But in all the years I've been here it's rung just once, and that was someone who thought this was the Schwarzer Adler Hotel." He laughed. "Christ, I wish it was."

"You're not alone in that wish, I shouldn't wonder."

"What can I do for you, Bernie?"

"I was just visiting one of your prisoners. Friedrich Minoux."

"The Gas Company fraudster. I know. I'm supposed to write your name down in the log of people who've been to see him." He opened a file. "This log, here."

"Minoux is not doing so well."

"Better than his partners. Max Kessler and Hans Tiemessen are both doing a five stretch in Luckau, and from what I hear, they're having a tough time."

"He's sixty-five years old, Ernst. I'm not sure I could do five years in this place."

"There's nothing I can do, Bernie. I can't make his time any easier. A lot of people on the outside are watching to make sure he doesn't get any special treatment because of his wife's wealth. Perhaps, when the attention on him dies down a bit, I'll see what I can do, but until then, my hands are tied."

"Thanks, Ernst." I shrugged. "One more thing. When I saw him just now, he seemed nervous about something. Scared, even."

"Scared?"

"Is he being bullied, do you think?"

Kracauer shook his head. "Discipline in this place is good. If he was being bullied, believe me I'd know about it. The punishment for that kind of thing is harsh, to say the least."

"What about pressure from the outside? Has he had any visitors— apart from his driver, Gantner, the one who brings him his breakfast every day? Someone who might have threatened him, perhaps?"

"Is this official?"

"No."

"Then you know I'm not allowed to tell you. But I tell you what. I won't write your name down in this file. How's that?"

"Thanks, Ernst. I appreciate it." I smiled. "How are the wife and kids?"

"Fine. Fine. My eldest has just joined the Luftwaffe."

"You must be very proud of him."

"I am. Look, would you excuse me for just a minute? I have to use the men's room. Help yourself to another drink if you want it." He pointed vaguely at the bottle on the desk. It was beside Friedrich Minoux's still-open file.

"Thanks," I said. "I think I will."

I waited until he was out of the room and poured myself another brandy and, while I was doing so, I took a look at Minoux's file, as Kracauer had meant me to, of course. There wasn't time to do much more than check the visitor's log. The previous morning, Minoux had received two visitors: Gantner, bringing him his breakfast, and then Captain Horst Janssen, of the RSHA.

I sat down and lit a cigarette, and a few minutes later, Ernst Kracauer returned.

"Well, I must get on," he said, rubbing his hands. "I trust your visit here has been satisfactory?"

"Yes, Ernst. Thanks. And look after yourself."

With much to think about, I drove slowly back to Berlin and the offices of the RSHA's Foreign Intelligence section, on Berkaerstrasse. Janssen, who was probably already a mass murderer, worked for Schellenberg, who was a director of Stiftung Nordhav. Had Janssen put the *Schreck* on Minoux? It seemed highly likely. Not only that, but hadn't I dropped him off at the military court in Charlottenburg the very same day? There was that to consider, too. Witzlebenstrasse was a fifteen-minute walk from Heckholz's office on Bedeuten Strasse. He could have given evidence in a trial and then murdered Heckholz on his way home for the day. All in a day's work for a man like Janssen. I certainly liked him better for Heckholz's murder than my only other suspect, who was Lieutenant Leuthard. I liked Janssen better for it because, in spite of himself, I liked Leuthard. Any man who could fall asleep during an opera was all right by me. Besides, if you've just killed a man in cold blood it's not easy to take a nap, even at the German Opera House. It spoke of a clear conscience. By contrast it was all too easy to see Captain Janssen murdering Dr. Heckholz on Schellenberg's orders. I knew a bit about doing someone else's dirty work myself. I'd done my fair share of it for Heydrich and Nebe.

I walked the keys into the office and met Janssen coming down the stairs.

"You finished taking those two Swiss around Berlin with my car?" he said.

"Finished."

"What did you do with them anyway?"

"Took them to the German Opera."

"The opera? That's nice."

"It might have been but there was a murder around the corner on Bedeuten Strasse and the police sirens got in the way of the music. At least I think it did. I'm never too sure with modern opera. Some lawyer got his head bashed in with a length of lead pipe. I mean, for real. This wasn't in the opera."

I was never much of a card player but I can bluff a bit, and I can tell when, just for a second, a man checks his mouth.

"Is that so?" Janssen frowned. "Only, the way I heard the splash this morning, the killer used a bust of Hitler to smash the man's head in. Kind of funny when you think about it. Killed by Hitler like that. And the victim wasn't even a Jew."

"Hilarious, when you put it like that." I smiled.

"Are you the investigating officer?"

"No. As it happens I'm leaving Kripo and the RSHA. I have a new job. I'm joining the War Crimes Bureau next week."

"You surprise me. I didn't know there was such a thing."

"You mean such a thing as a war crime? Or a bureau that investigates them?"

"Both."

"I've a feeling it's going to be more important than you think." I smiled patiently. "Anyway, thanks for the car."

"Can I give you a lift somewhere?"

"No, I'll walk. Around this time of day I generally need some air. Especially when I'm in uniform."

"It is rather warm today," he said.

I walked back to Grunewald Station. I told myself that I'd gone as far as I could with my inquiries without ending up like Friedrich Minoux or even Dr. Heckholz, and I felt an enormous sense of relief that I could just walk away from it all. What did I care who was profiting from Stiftung Nordhav? Or Export Drives GMBH? It certainly wasn't any of my business. I wouldn't have minded a little taste of some real money myself. And as it happened there was even less chance of State Secretary Wilhelm Stuckart at the Ministry of the Interior listening to their evidence of malfeasance and wrongdoing than even I had imagined. For I had since discovered Stuckart was also an honorary general in the SS.

Like so much of what happened with the Nazis, the whole thing was best left well alone. Life was already too short to go sticking my nose into the affairs of people like Walter Schellenberg and Werner Best. With any luck, no one would know that I'd ever been involved. All that mattered now was that I was away from the Alex and out of the RSHA and working for men to whom honor wasn't just a word on a ceremonial belt. It wasn't like the Murder Commission—at least not the one that used to exist when Bernhard Weiss was in charge of Kripo; and I didn't honestly think that any of the cases I might be asked to handle would matter for very much in Justitia's scales, but it would do for now.

INTERLUDE

French Riviera, 1956

U p on the screen Dalia unzipped her beautiful red mouth to reveal a row of perfect teeth, laughed, and stared into the camera with those big blue eyes, and I was in love all over again. After more than ten years it was as if we had never been parted. Well, almost. Cinema is cruel like that. So cruel that it must have been invented by a German, or at least imagined by one. Nietzsche, perhaps, with his idea of eternal recurrence; I can't think of a more cinematic idea than that because, to be honest, it's highly probable that, for obvious reasons, I'll see this film more than once. Well, why not? I could almost smell her.

And yet, tantalizingly, I could not touch her, nor would I touch her ever again, in all likelihood. Just the thought of that made me suddenly feel so weak and sick it was as if I'd lost the will to live. You never quite succeed in filling the space of a woman you have loved. But did she even remember me? Was there ever a moment in a day when something crossed her mind to remind her of Gunther and what had happened to us both? I rather doubted that, just as in the final analysis she had certainly doubted me. She could never have believed that I would assume some of the guilt that was hers. Probably she didn't believe it until she was safely back home. Frankly I surprised myself at the time, and I fully expected to die for what I'd done; perhaps, without her, that was even what I wanted most in the world. To die. After I came back from Belarus I'd grown tired of survival at any cost. Usually, of course, I'm not quite so noble, but love does funny things to a man. Looking at her now, on screen opposite Rex Harrison, a man who represented everything I hate most about the English—smug, self-satisfied, snobbish, only vaguely heterosexual—I formed the conclusion that, most likely, I was just a small footnote to her more notorious relationship with Josef Goebbels, which, to be fair to her, Dalia had always denied but which continued to dog her footsteps. To the Yugoslavian authorities she had steadfastly maintained that, while Hitler's propaganda chief had certainly pursued her, she had never succumbed and in evidence argued the fact that she'd seen out the last years of the war in Switzerland in preference to accepting the film roles that Goebbels had offered her in his capacity as the head of the UFA film studio at Babelsberg.

Did I believe those denials? I'd like to have done. Even at the time I had my doubts, although you could hardly blame Dalia for the priapic doctor's interest in her. Not entirely. A woman can only choose who she tries to make fall in love with her, not who actually does. And I certainly didn't blame Goebbels for being besotted with her, for, in many respects, he was no different from me. We both had an eye for a pretty face—two for a very beautiful one—and it was easy to find yourself obsessed with a woman like Dalia Dresner. An hour in the woman's company was enough to make you fall for her. That sounds like an exaggeration and perhaps it is for some but not for me. I fell in love with her almost the moment I saw her, which is perhaps hardly surprising as she was completely naked in her Griebnitzsee garden at the time. But I'm getting ahead of myself. Stories should have a beginning, they should even have a middle, but I'm never sure that ones like this ever really have an end; not while I can still feel like this about a woman I haven't seen, or touched, or spoken to in a thousand years.

Thirteen

I t was almost exactly a year after the crime conference at the Villa Minoux when I found myself summoned once more to the Ministry of Truth and Propaganda. This time, it was not to see State Secretary Leo Gutterer but to meet with the minister himself. The Mahatma Propagandhi. In truth we'd met once or twice before. I'd recently returned from Belarus where, at his personal request, I'd been his eyes and ears during the Katyn Forest investigation. The bodies of four thousand Polish officers and NCOs had been discovered in a mass grave near Smolensk and, as an officer working for the German War Crimes Bureau, I'd helped facilitate the international investigation, the propaganda value of which Goebbels was still busy exploiting in the hope that it might drive some sort of wedge between the Soviets— who had murdered the Poles—and their embarrassed British and American allies. It was a faint hope but, on the whole, Goebbels was pleased with what I'd helped to achieve. Me, less so, although that was becoming something of an occupational hazard. After working for Heydrich, on and off, over the course of three years, I had grown used to the feeling of being used to good advantage by people who were themselves not good. If I'd been a little more imaginative, perhaps I might have worked out a way of withdrawing my labor, or even disappearing; after all, there were plenty of other people in Nazi Germany who disappeared. The trick was discovering how not to do this permanently.

I'd been in Joey's office before but I'd forgotten how large it was. Henry Morton Stanley would have thought twice about mounting an expedition to try to find the washroom. And in that vast expanse of thick carpet and dense soft furnishings it would have been easy to miss completely the diminutive minister who occupied a small corner of a country-sized sofa like some malign and understandably abandoned child. Goebbels was wearing an immaculate, summer-weight, three-piece suit with lapels as wide as a Swiss guard's halberd; his white shirt was brighter than a sunrise from Mount Sapo, and instead of a tie he was wearing a striped ascot with a pearl pin. It made him look like a pimp. Then again maybe the knot in a tie felt too much like a noose. He put down the novel by Knut Hamsun he'd been reading and stood up. The minister might have lacked stature but he didn't lack charm or manners. He was all smiles and compliments and gratitude for a job well done. He even shook my hand with one that was smaller and some-what clammier than my own.

"Sit down and make yourself comfortable."

I sat at the opposite end of the sofa but I couldn't have felt less comfortable in that vast office if there had been a Gaboon viper coiled on one of the silk cushions.

"Relax. Help yourself to a cigarette. To some coffee. I'll fetch some-thing to drink if you like."

"Coffee's fine, thank you."

There was a silver pot with a saucepan handle and some Meissen cups on a small tray; I poured myself a black one but didn't drink it. My bladder was already playing games with me and coffee wasn't what it needed. I took a cigarette but just rolled it between my fingers. Relax-ing was never so stressful. But then, my host was a man who counted himself an intimate of Adolf Hitler; not only that, but a clever man, too; a man who could have talked a flock of rock penguins into a sauna bath.

"When I gave you the job in Katyn I knew it wouldn't be pleasant."

It seemed that the doctor had a gift for understatement as well as for exaggeration. Every morning I woke up I could still smell those four thousand Polish corpses.

"And if you remember, I promised you that in return I would offer you an opportunity to work for me in a private capacity. Something that would be very much to your profit and advantage. This is why I asked you to come here and see me today. To offer you just such an opportunity."

"Thank you, Herr Doctor. And don't think I'm not grateful. Only, since I got back to Berlin from Smolensk my duties at the War Crimes Bureau have been keeping me very busy. I have a mountain of paperwork to complete and a couple of urgent investigations to undertake."

This was true; it seemed that some top secret plans had gone miss- • ing from the army's Strategic Planning Section in the Bendlerblock and, reluctant to involve the Gestapo, my boss, Judge Goldsche—who was friendly with the top *bonzen*—had asked me if I'd look into the matter. But the planning section had been hit by an RAF bomb and it was probable that these missing plans had been very likely destroyed.

"Nonsense. I'm sure they can spare you at the Bendlerblock for a few days on my account. I'll speak to Judge Goldsche and ask him to lend you to me. There will be plenty of time to catch up with paperwork when you've performed this service for me. The job will not be without its pleasures but it's a task that also requires some very special skills. In short, it requires the services of a real detective. No, it's rather more than that. It requires the services of a detective with a proven reputation."

By now I was starting to guess which one of the two people in the room to whose advantage this job really was; and it didn't look like it was going to be me.

"It's been a while since anyone described me like that."

"Really? As I recall, it was only last year that you were being offered up to the various guests at an international criminal police conference as Berlin's answer to Sherlock Holmes. Or had you forgotten that speech you gave at the Villa Minoux? The one State Secretary Gutterer helped you to write."

"As a matter of fact I had forgotten about that. I'd also formed the impression that that would be the last place Dr. Gutterer's exaggerations regarding my abilities as a policeman would actually be taken seriously."

"Did you, by God?" Goebbels laughed harshly. "Well, you'd be wrong. Any lingering doubts we might have had about your unique talents were removed when you managed to unfuck things so well at Katyn. I wasn't wrong about you, Gunther. I realize we might have had one or two differences back there. I may even have left you in an awkward situation. But you're a good man in a tight spot. And that's what I'm in right now."

"I'm sorry to hear that," I said with very little sincerity. Too little for a man with ears that were so carefully tuned to meaning, like the Mahatma's.

He picked a tiny piece of thread off the trouser of his suit and dropped it onto the thick carpet, as if it had been me.

"Oh, I know you're not a Nazi. I've read your Gestapo file—which, by the way, is as thick as a DeMille screenplay and probably just as entertaining. Frankly, if you were a Nazi you'd be held in rather better odor at RSHA headquarters and then you'd be no fucking good to me. The fact is I want this matter handled off the books. Which means to say I certainly don't want bastards like Himmler and Kaltenbrunner finding out about it. This is a private matter. Do I make myself clear?"

"Quite clear."

"Nevertheless they will try to find out what we're doing. They can tell themselves all they like that it's in the country's best interests to know the private affairs of everyone in government. But it's not. It's in their best interest to get the dirt on everyone so they can use that to cement their own positions with the leader. Not that there's any actual wrongdoing here, you understand. It's just that they might easily imply that there is. Insinuation. Rumor. Gossip. Blackmail. That's second nature to people like Müller and Kaltenbrunner. You may not be able to tell them to go to hell, exactly, but I'm confident that you're the kind of fellow who can outfox them. With total discretion. Which is also why I'm prepared to pay you, out of my own pocket. How does a hundred reichsmarks a day sound?"

"Frankly? It sounds much too good to be true. Which is a habit of yours, after all."

Goebbels frowned, as if he were unable to decide if I was being insolent or not. "What did you say?"

"You heard me. You'll forgive me, sir, but in the event that I do end up working for you, then I have to be straight. Believe me, if this job does require the discretion you say it does, then you wouldn't want it any other way. I never yet met a client who wanted me to put some syrup on top of a piece of hard cheese."

"Yes," he said uncertainly. And then with greater certainty, he added, "Yes, you're right. I'm not used to people being straight with me, that's all. Truth is in rather short supply in this day and age—when you have to rely on German civil servants. But then even the British have become experts in twisting the facts. Their reports of a night raid on the city of Dresden were a triumph of lies and obfuscation. You would think that there had been not one civilian casualty, that they bombed this city without a single civilian casualty. But that's another matter. Thank you for the lesson in pragmatism. And since they do say that money talks, then perhaps it might be best if I were to pay you in advance."

Goebbels put his hand inside his jacket and removed a soft leather wallet from which he proceeded to count five one-hundred-mark notes onto the table in front of us. I left the money there, for the moment. I was going to take the money, of course, but I still had my pride to take care of first; this residual feeling of my own dignity—which was not much more than a small shard of self-respect—was going to need some careful last-minute handling.

"Why don't you tell me what the problem is and then I'll tell you what can be done?"

Goebbels shrugged. "As you wish." He paused and then lit a ciga-rette. "I take it you've heard of Dalia Dresner."

I nodded. Everyone in Germany had heard of Dalia Dresner. And if they hadn't they'd certainly heard of *The Saint That Never Was*, one of the more sensational films in which she'd starred. Dalia Dresner was one of UFA-Babelsberg's biggest film stars.

"I want her to be in *Siebenkäs*, my next picture for UFA. Based on the classic novel by Jean Paul, *Married Life, Death, and Wedding of Siebenkäs, Poor Man's Lawyer*. Have you read it?"

"I haven't, no. But I can see why you felt you had to change the title."

"She's perfect for the leading role of Natalie. I know it, she knows it, the director—Veit Harlan—knows it. The trouble is she won't do it. At least she won't until her mind has been put at rest about her father, with whom she appears to have lost contact. I believe they've been estranged for a long time, but her mother died quite recently and she's decided she wants to make contact with him again. It's a fairly typical story of our age, really. Anyway, she insists she needs a detective to help her find him. And since it's Dalia Dresner, it can't be just any detec-tive. He has to be the best. And until she speaks to such a man and he does whatever it is that she wants him to do, it's clear that her mind is going to be on other things than the making of this motion picture."

"And you don't want the Gestapo doing it."

"Correct."

"May I ask why?"

"I really don't see that it's any of your damn business."

"And it can certainly stay that way. Frankly the less I know about your personal affairs the better I'll feel. I certainly didn't ask for this job. I didn't ask to come here and be offered an opportunity for profit and advantage. If I was interested in either of those things, then by your own admission I wouldn't be sitting beside you on this sofa. But I won't work for you with a patch over one eye and one hand tied behind my back. If I am going to outfox the likes of Kaltenbrunner and Müller, then I can't be treated like your poodle, Herr Doctor. That's not how foxes operate."

"You're right. And I have to trust someone. Recent events have taken their toll on my health and I was obliged to cancel a badly needed holiday. This whole affair isn't helping me, either. I should get myself in shape but I can see no possibility of that happening. Frankly it's all left me feeling rather depressed."

He crossed his legs and then nervously hugged his right knee toward him so that I had a good view of his famously deformed right foot.

"Do you have a sweetheart, Herr Gunther?"

"There's a girl I see, sometimes."

"Tell me about her."

"Her name is Kirsten Handlöser and she's a schoolteacher at the Fichte Gymnasium on Emser Strasse."

"And are you in love with her?"

"No. I don't think so. But lately we've become quite close."

"But you've been in love, Herr Gunther?"

"Oh, yes."

"And what was your opinion of being in love?"

"Being in love is like being on a cruise, I think. It's not so bad if you're sailing on a smooth sea. But when things start to get rough, it's easy to start feeling lousy. In fact it's amazing how quickly that can happen."

Goebbels nodded. "You put it very well. Most of the policemen I've met have been blunt instruments. But I see you have a subtler side. I like that. The fact is, I am in love. This is not an unusual situation for me. I like women. Always have. And they seem to like me. I'm married, of course, with several children. Sometimes I forget how many. But, before the war, there was another actress. Her name was Lída Baarová. You've probably heard of her, too."

I nodded and finally lit the cigarette in my fingers. It's not every day that the Reich Minister of Propaganda opens up to you about his love life, and I wanted to give this my full concentration.

"I wanted to leave my wife and live with her but the leader wouldn't hear of it. Lída is a Slav, you see, and considered to be racially inferior. So is Dalia Dresner." He nodded. "For Dalia's sake, I have tried not to become too involved with her. Himmler and Kaltenbrunner would dearly love to cause trouble for me by being able to tell the leader that I'm involved with another Slavic woman. And of course he'd be furious. The leader takes a very dim view of anything but total monogamy. So I've tried to keep a distance. But I am in love with her. And the plain fact of the matter is that she very much reminds me of Lída."

"Now you come to mention it, there is a certain similarity."

"Exactly. I've even tried to sell her as the German Garbo just to make Hitler forget about that. The similarity between her and Baarová, I mean. Just to deflect any hint of suspicion that this is why I'm advancing Dalia's career."

"And are you? Is that the reason you're building her up into a star?"

"Perhaps a little, yes. You see, when I'm with Dalia I find that I don't really need a holiday. And right now all I want to do is to make her happy."

"I can understand something like that."

"Good. Because you should also understand that I would take a very dim view of anything that happened to embarrass her, or me."

"I can keep my mouth shut, if that's what you mean, Herr Doctor."

"It is. I want this case handled as quietly as possible."

"That's just the way I was planning to handle it."

"So then. What I want you to do is meet with her, find out what the problem is, and put a smile back on her face. I need that smile. And the picture needs it, too. We need it so that we can start production on this picture before the summer is over. I've got Veit Harlan and Werner Krauss under contract and it's costing the studio a fortune. Not only that but this good weather is perfect for us, only we can't shoot a damn thing until she's got what she wants."

I shook my head. "There's still something you're not telling me. Which really doesn't surprise me."

Goebbels laughed. "My God, but you're an impudent fellow."

"I expect that's in my file, too. So why act so surprised about it? Like you said yourself, if I was a good national socialist I'd have already made something of myself in the RSHA and then I'd be no good to you."

Goebbels nodded patiently. I'd pushed him just about as far as I could go and then a bit further. That's the one thing I know about people with power and money; when you've got something they want, they'll take almost anything in the ear in order to make sure they get it.

"You're right. But I'd rather she told you herself. So, will you please go and see her? At least listen to what she's got to say?"

I picked up his money off the table. It seemed the least I could do was see his girl. Like I said, it's not every day the Reich Minister of Propaganda opens his heart and, more importantly, his wallet to you. And it's not every day you get a chance to meet a film star.

"All right. Where can I find her?"

"In Potsdam. On Griebnitzsee, close to the film studios. There's a house that's recently come into my possession on Kaiser-Strasse. My secretary will give you all of the details. Address, telephone number, everything. When shall I tell her that you're coming?"

I shrugged and glanced at my watch. "This afternoon? I don't know. Is there an S-Bahn station near there? I don't know Potsdam all that well."

"Neu-Babelsberg," said Goebbels. "I believe it's quite a hike from the station. But you could go now and be there before lunch if you were to borrow my car."

"Sure."

He tossed me a set of keys. "One thing about the car," he added, as if he already regretted letting me borrow it. "The supercharger whines a bit on start-up. And you have to let the oil heat up before you let out the clutch."

I walked toward the door. "I'm trusting you with the two things I love most in this life. My car. And my leading lady. I hope that's clear enough."

"Crystal clear, Herr Doctor. Crystal clear."

Fourteen

I ought to have been in a better mood. I was driving a bright red Mercedes-Benz 540K Special Roadster, the one with the streamlined body and the boot-mounted spare wheel. I had the top down, the wind in my hair, and my foot hard on the gas. I liked driving—especially on the AVUS speedway—and I should have been smiling from one earlobe to the other, but until Goebbels had asked me the question in his office, I hadn't realized that I wasn't in love with Kirsten, and wasn't likely to be, either. Which made me wonder if I was doing the right thing in going out with her at all. Even a car as beautiful as the 540K wasn't enough to compensate for that kind of feeling. After all, love is rare, and to find that you aren't in love is almost as upsetting to the human mind as finding that you are.

I'd started seeing her regularly on my return from Smolensk after she'd spoken sharply to me in the line for bread, because of the uniform I was wearing. She'd accused me of jumping the line, which wasn't true. Later on the same day, I saw her at the swimming baths on Schlacht-Strasse and she'd apologized. She explained that she was upset because the SD had come to her school asking questions in an effort to find out why none of the children in her school had chosen to be evacuated from Berlin to a KLV camp, because of the bombing. She'd told the SD that everyone in Berlin knew the poor reputation of these camps—that parents didn't want their daughters taken advantage of by the Hitler Youth boys who were also at these camps. Kirsten was worried she'd said too much, and in truth she probably had, but I advised her not to worry and that, if she found herself in trouble, then I'd speak up for her, although in truth that would hardly have helped her cause.

I realized that when I was through with whatever service it was that Goebbels and Dalia Dresner wanted me to do for them, I was going to have to have a quiet word with Kirsten and tell her the bad news. It was only bad news for me, of course; she was an attractive girl and it wasn't going to be hard for her to find another man, perhaps even one nearer her own age, assuming that after the war was over there would be any of those still left.

I came off the AVUS and slowed down to drive through Wannsee. A few people turned and stared at the red car; they must have thought I was Tazio Nuvolari. I know I did.

Until the 540K arrived there, Potsdam was a quiet town of about eighty-five thousand just thirty miles southwest of Berlin, although it might as well have been located on Rome's Palatine Hill. Most of Prussia's kings had made the place their summer residence, which is a bit like saying that Louis XIII used to own a hunting lodge at Versailles. With several beautiful parks and palaces, and surrounded by the Havel and its lakes, Potsdam is now home to some of the richest people in Germany. Of these the richest probably live on the edge by the Griebnitzsee in the so-called villa colony on Kaiser-Strasse, where the houses are a little smaller than the average palace, but rather more private, which is what real money buys these days. That and twenty-five rooms and entranceways like the Parthenon and enough garden to park a squadron of Dorniers.

The finials on the wrought-iron fence in front of the address I'd been given looked like oak trees; there were smaller ones in the front garden. I hadn't ever seen the Alhambra, but I imagine there were parts of it—the guesthouse perhaps—that resembled the place I was looking at now. Built of cream-colored stone, with redbrick details and church windows, it even had towers and castellations, not to mention a car parked on the gravel driveway that was the exact twin of the one I'd just left on the street. It was exactly the kind of house where you expected to meet a movie star, so the little lozenge-sized scar on the right-hand side of the doorpost from where a *mezuzah* had once been fixed to the doorframe brought me up short. You didn't have to be the local rabbi or see a bar mitzvah party in the garden to know that this large eccentric house had once belonged to a family of Jews.

I cranked the old-fashioned silver doorbell handle and heard it ring loudly in the hall. I waited and cranked it again, and when nothing happened I peered through the glass in the door for a while but, seeing nothing but a hall tree and bench with a mirror as big as a cinema screen, I walked around to the back where the lawn rolled gently down to the side of the lake. Several orange marker buoys had been deployed in the water to remind any unwelcome visitors with boats that the residents of the house weren't ever home to visitors. But I wasn't looking at the water, I was looking at the green baize lawn and what was on the lawn, because it was there, lying on a large white linen spread, that I first laid eyes on Dalia Dresner in the flesh, of which there was rather more on show than I'd been expecting. She was as naked as a Potsdam Giant's bayonet and every bit as hazardous to men, as I was about to discover. Tiresias at least had the good grace to cover his eyes when he accidentally walked in on Athena taking a shower. I did not. Eventually my own natural good manners persuaded me that—certainly after five minutes—I should have announced myself or at least cleared my throat.

"When Dr. Goebbels asked me to come and see you I had no idea that this is what he meant."

She sat up quickly and covered herself with the linen spread, but not before she'd made sure I had seen everything.

"Oh," was all she said.

"I'm sorry," I said, although I wasn't sorry at all. "I rang the bell but no one answered."

"I gave the maid the day off today."

"If she doesn't come back, I'll take the job."

"You're Gunther, of course. The detective. Josef said you were coming."

"I'm Gunther."

"The studio makes us lie in the sun like this. To get a tan. I can't imagine it's very good for my skin but Josef insists that this is what the public wants."

"I've got no argument with that."

She smiled shyly.

"Perhaps I ought to wait in the house."

"It's all right. You stay here. I'll go and put on some clothes. I won't be long."

She got up and went into the house. "Help yourself to some lemonade," she said without looking back.

It was only now that I noticed the garden chairs and table and the jug of lemonade that was standing on it. If there'd been a pink elephant in the garden I probably wouldn't have noticed that, either. I unbuttoned my tunic and sat down and lit a cigarette and put my face in the warm July sunshine. There was a smile on it now although really there shouldn't have been. After all, I'd seen Dalia Dresner naked before. Millions had seen her naked. It was the only high spot of *The Saint That Never Was*, a *Jud Süss*–in–reverse movie about a woman called Hypatia who was a fourth-century Greek philosopher. At the end of the movie, also directed by Veit Harlan, Hypatia, played by Dalia Dresner, is stripped naked and stoned to death by the Jews of

Alexandria. Until that moment it had been a very boring film and there were some women I knew who said that Hypatia had it coming—that Dresner's was not a great performance. Others, less critical of actors and acting and mostly men such as myself, enjoyed the film for what it was—a good excuse to see a beautiful woman taking off her clothes. Goebbels knew half of his audience, anyway. The smile on my face persisted; but instead of rerunning a sequence of shots inside my mind's eye of Fräulein Dresner's naked body, I ought to have asked myself how, if she knew I was coming to the house on Kaiser-Strasse, she'd prepared so carefully for my arrival—after all, there were two glasses on the table next to the lemonade jug—by being splinter-naked in her garden.

A few minutes later she came back wearing a dark blue floral dress. The brown cowboy boots were an eccentric, individual touch. I'd never seen a German woman wearing cowboy boots, least of all with bare legs. I liked her legs. They were long and brown and muscular and they were attached to her backside, which had seemed just right, for me. Her golden-blond hair was now gathered into a bunch. On her strong wrist was a gold Rolex and on her ring finger a sapphire as big as a five-pfennig piece. Her nails were nicely manicured and varnished with pink, like the perfectly formed petals of little geraniums. She sat down and stared at me with the most direct stare I'd ever received from a woman; when she looked at me it was like facing down a cat with blue eyes. The kind of cat that plays with a mouse until the mouse can't stand the game for another minute, and then some more.

"Josef said that you're a famous detective." Her voice was low and soft, like an eiderdown pillow. "I always thought they'd be men with waxed mustaches and pipes."

"Oh, I'll smoke a pipe when I can get the tobacco. And you're the famous one, Fräulein Dresner. Not me."

"But you *are* a detective."

I showed her my beer-token—my little brass warrant disc.

"Tell me about yourself," she said.

"The important stuff?"

"Of course."

I shrugged. "I'm forty-seven. I smoke too much. I drink too much. When I can."

"I'm afraid all I have out here is some lemonade."

"Lemonade will be fine, thanks."

She poured two glasses and handed one to me.

"Why do you drink too much?"

"I've got no wife and I've got no children. I work for the army right now because the police—the real police—they don't want me anymore. You see, there's no room in this country for people who want to know the truth, about anything. People like me, that is. I have one good suit and a pair of shoes that I have to stuff with newspaper in the winter. I have a bed with a broken leg. That's in a tiny apartment in Fasanen-strasse. I hate the Nazis and I hate myself, but not always in that order. That's why." I smiled ruefully. "I'll tell you a secret, fräulein. I don't know why but I will. There are times when I think I'd like to be some-one else."

She smiled to reveal a row of perfect teeth. Everything about this woman looked perfect. I was beginning to appreciate her.

"That's something I know a little about. Who? Who do you wish you were?"

"It doesn't really matter who. The important thing is what."

"What, then?"

"Dead."

"That must be easy enough to fix in Germany."

"You would think so, wouldn't you? But you see, there's two kinds of dead. There's ordinary dead and then there's Nazi dead. The worst kind is Nazi dead. I don't want to die until I've seen the last Nazi do it first."

"You don't sound like a detective. You sound like a man who's lost all his faith. Who's full of doubt, about everything."

"That's what makes me a good detective. That and a certain romantic charm I might have."

"You're a romantic, then. You begin to interest me, Herr Gunther."

"Sure. I'm a regular hero with a sentimental yearning for old times. Almost eleven years ago, to be precise. You should see me walking around on the seashore. I can get quite sensitive about a lot of things. The dawn, a storm, the price of fish. But mostly I specialize in helping damsels in distress."

"You're making fun of me now."

"No, I meant what I said. Especially the part about the damsels in distress. The minister of Truth told me you were in trouble and that you needed my help. So here I am."

"Did he, now? What else did he say about me?"

"That he was in love with you. Of course, he could have been lying. It wouldn't be the first time. That he's been in love, I think. I imagine he always tells the truth, at least about that sort of thing. And now that I've met you, it's easy to see anyone might feel that way."

"Did he also tell you I'm married?"

"He left out that particular detail. But then men in love often do. I think it's what the poets call a pathetic fallacy."

"Are you speaking from experience?"

"Yes. I was a private detective for about five years. I did a lot of missing persons, husbands mostly. For one reason or another."

"Then you sound like the one man who might be able to help me."

"I bet you said exactly the same thing to—to Josef."

"He warned me that you were a tough guy."

"Only when I'm standing next to the doctor."

She smiled. "You know, I don't think he's a real doctor."

"I wouldn't get undressed in front of him if that's what you mean. But he's a real doctor, all right. At least, he has a PhD from Heidelberg University on nineteenth-century literature. I guess that's why they put him in charge of the book burning. There's nothing like a university education to make you hate literature."

"What book burning?"

I smiled. "Before your time, I guess. Suddenly I feel my age. Do you mind me asking how old you are, Fräulein Dresner?"

"Twenty-six. And I don't mind at all."

"That's because you're twenty-six. In ten years' time you'll start to think differently. Anyway, back in 1933, when you'd have been sixteen, I guess, the good doctor helped organize an action against the un-German spirit. That's what they called it, anyway. They burned a whole load of books right here in Berlin, on Opernplatz. Books written by Jews and more or less anyone who was opposed to the Nazis, but mostly people who could just write. People like Heinrich Mann."

She looked horrified. "I wasn't living in Germany at the time so I had no idea. They really did that? They burned books?"

"Sure. And it wasn't because it was the end of Lent or because the public libraries were looking to make some space, or even because of the tough winter we were having. This was in May. They put on quite a show. Lit up the whole city. I had to draw my curtains early that night."

Dalia shook her head. "You say the strangest things. I wonder how Josef even knows someone like you, Herr Gunther."

"I've asked myself the very same question."

"I mean, wearing that uniform you look like a Nazi. But you make it quite clear, to me at least, that you disapprove of them."

"Obviously I didn't make myself clear enough. It's a lot more than disapproval. I hate them."

"You know, I think you did, only I've learned to be one of the wise monkeys when I hear that kind of subversive talk. After all, if you're a good citizen you're supposed to do something about it, aren't you? Call the Gestapo, or something."

"Be my guest."

"But then you wouldn't be able to help me. And then where would I be? Still in distress."

"I wouldn't get your hopes up, Fräulein Dresner. Not yet. After all, you haven't told me what the problem is. I have a habit of disappointing people."

"Maybe I'd better tell you all about it."

"Maybe you should and then we'll know if I can help you."

I waited for a moment but she said nothing, as if she wasn't yet quite ready to talk. That happens a lot. Generally you just have to wait until they're good and ready to open up.

"Josef said he was certain that you could," she said uncertainly.

"Josef is the minister of Propaganda. Not the minister for Pragmatism. It's up to me to decide if I'm going to stick my neck out for you. It's my neck, after all."

"I'm not asking you to stick your neck out for me."

"Josef was."

"I don't see how."

I told her about Kaltenbrunner and Müller and how they were keen to find some scandal about the little doctor that would embarrass him in front of the leader.

"That's what I mean by sticking my neck out. Those people have a tendency to play rough."

"I've done nothing for which either one of us need feel embarrassed," she insisted.

"I'm sure it's none of my business if you have."

"I haven't slept with him, if that's what you mean," she said indignantly, and then shuddered.

"He does have a reputation as a ladies' man."

"And I'm supposed to be a saint, after that awful film I was in about Hypatia. But it doesn't mean I am any more than he is a ladies' man, as you put it, or the devil."

I let that one go.

"I wonder that you can even think such a thing. He's not my type at all. And as I said, I'm married."

"And that usually prevents this kind of thing from happening."

She relaxed a little and smiled again. "What, you don't believe people can be happily married?"

"Sure I do. It's just that history shows how, from time to time, people decide they want to be happily married to someone else."

"You're such a cynic," she laughed. "I like that."

"I think maybe that's the real reason the doctor seems to like me."

"Maybe it is."

"Only, he seems to like you more."

"You can't blame me for that."

"Speaking as a cop, I couldn't blame you for anything. Not even if you were alone in a locked room with a body on the floor and the murder weapon in your bloodstained hand."

"Why do you say that?"

"I told you. I'm a romantic. The worst kind."

"An incurable case?"

"Terminal."

Dalia Dresner lit a cigarette and crossed her legs. She watched me watching them for a while and then smiled. "You're a strange man."

"I imagine you make a lot of men feel that way."

"Oh, I'm used to that. No, what I mean is that you almost make me feel like a normal person. That's a rare thing for me, Herr Gunther. For anyone in the movie business. I don't have many friends. How could I? Just look at this mausoleum of a house. The king of Siam would feel just a little overawed by this place. When they meet me, most Fritzes go all tongue-tied and bashful and fall over their own feet in an effort to light my cigarette or find me a chair. But you're something else. For one thing, you know just what to say to keep me interested. And for another, you know how to make me laugh. Any man can open a door for me, or pay me a handsome compliment. But there are very few men who know how to make me feel comfortable in their company. I like that about you. Maybe it's because you're a little older than most of the men I know."

"All right. No need to spoil it. I'm a regular Dietrich of Verona. So maybe now you're feeling comfortable enough to tell me what it is that stops you from going to work in the morning."

"Yes, I think I'm ready now."

Fifteen

My real name is Dragica Djurkovic and I was born in what rather romantically used to be called the Kingdom of Serbs, Croats, and Slovenes. That was a bit of a mouthful, even for Serbs and Croats, so, in 1929 we started calling ourselves the Kingdom of Yugoslavia, which was probably a death knell for the poor king. My father was a former Roman Catholic priest from a little Serbian town called Banja Luka. After the war he lost his faith and left the Church and married my mother, who was an actress and a German-speaking Croat. I went to school in a place called Novi Sad. But he and my mother didn't get along and she went back to her hometown of Zagreb, where I went to school, while my father, regretting his decision to abandon his faith and leave the Church, went to live at a Franciscan monastery back in his hometown of Banja Luka. Politics in Yugoslavia were always fractious to say the least. King Alexander was assassinated in Marseilles, during a state visit to France, by a Macedonian, in October 1934."

I nodded. I remembered seeing the newsreel of his assassination. Everyone did. It was probably the first time anything like that had ever been seen in German cinemas. The king had been shot in his limousine, just like Archduke Ferdinand. Which just goes to show: when you're a king or an archduke, it pays to rent a car with a hardtop.

"Following the assassination of King Alexander, my mother decided the writing was on the wall for Yugoslavia, and soon after that we left the country for good to live with her brother in Zurich, where I enrolled at the Girls' High School. I passed my Matura exam with top marks and won a place at the polytechnic to study mathematics, which I think is where my real talents lie. I've always been more interested in science and maths than anything. In another life I think I should have liked to have been an inventor. Maybe I still will be when people get tired of seeing my face up on the screen. However, because of my mother I was always being pushed toward the theater, and I started acting as a hobby, only to discover that people thought I was actually good at it. I played Cordelia in *King Lear* at Zurich's famous Theater am Neumarkt; and, in 1936, I was Lena in Büchner's *Leonce and Lena*, which is when I was discovered, as they say in cinema, by Carl Froelich, who's a big noise at UFA studios and second only in importance to Josef himself. Carl arranged for me to have a screen test in Berlin, as a result of which I was offered a seven-year contract. At his suggestion I changed my name to Dalia Dresner—because it sounded more German—and had all sorts of acting and deportment lessons and was generally groomed for stardom, although frankly I was more interested in going to the polytechnic and completing my education. I don't know whether you are aware of it, but Albert Einstein was a student at Zurich Polytechnic; and he was always a bit of a hero of mine. Anyway, there's nothing complicated or clever about acting. It's a job. A dog could do it. In fact dogs often do. One of the biggest stars in Hollywood used to be a German shepherd called Rin Tin Tin.

"Of course, my mother wanted the contract with UFA more than I did, and so we both moved to Berlin, in 1937. My mother generally got what she wanted. She was always a rather overbearing figure in my life, and when you met her it was easy to see why she'd driven my father back into the arms of the priesthood. Which is probably why I married my own husband, Stefan. He's a Swiss-Serbian lawyer who lives and works in Zurich. He's much older than me, but he loves me very dearly and helped me to break the hold my mother had over me. When I'm not working, I live there, with him. But mostly I'm here in Babelsberg, making three or four indifferent pictures a year."

She shook her head. "If I'm as frank about this as you were earlier, Herr Gunther, indifferent is putting it mildly. Let's face it, anything directed by Veit Harlan is not going to be without controversy, to say the least. I only narrowly avoided being cast as Dorothea in *Jud Süss*. Fortunately Harlan gave that part to his wife. But *The Saint That Never Was* had its anti-Semitic side. It wasn't the Jews who stoned Hypatia but Christians. At least that's what the history books say, although it's perfectly possible that many of those Christians were Jews first."

She paused.

"Anyway, my mother died recently."

"I'm sorry."

"Don't be. She was a difficult woman. But even so, I did miss her. And suddenly feeling very alone, in spite of my husband, I realized that I simply had to try to get in contact with my father again. When you've lost one parent, the one that survives, no matter how distant he or she has become, starts to look more important. Of course, since I left Yugoslavia the political situation has deteriorated badly, and to cut a long story short, my country was invaded by German, Italian, and Hungarian forces in April of 1941. The Independent State of Croatia was established as a Nazi state, ruled by a fascist militia known as the Ustaše. On the other side are two factions: the communist-led Yugoslav partisans and the royalist Chetniks. The partisans are probably the largest resistance army in occupied Western Europe. And it's probably no exaggeration to say that outside of Croatia, and away from the influence of the Axis powers, Yugoslavia is now in total chaos. All of which probably explains why I've been unable to make contact with my father. I've sent several letters, without reply. I've met with the foreign minister, von

Ribbentrop, to see if he can help. I've even been to see Cardinal Frings in Cologne, in secret, to see if he could help."

"Why in secret?"

"Because Josef would not approve. In fact he'd be furious. He's very much against the Roman Catholic clergy in Germany. Or anywhere else, for that matter. But the cardinal couldn't help, either. Frankly, I'd go back to Yugoslavia and look for my father myself but Josef simply won't hear of it. He says it's much too dangerous."

"He's probably right about that," I said. "Beautiful movie stars are in short supply these days."

"All he really wants is for me to start this stupid picture as soon as possible."

"I'm just guessing, but somehow I don't think it's all that he wants."

"No, perhaps it isn't. But trust me, I can handle him easily enough. If the leader ever heard about what Josef's wife, Magda, gets up to—her 'retaliatory affairs'—there would be hell to pay."

"Do you mean you'd tell him?"

"If I had to, I would. Indirectly, anyway. I've no wish to become another of Josef's many conquests."

"It almost makes me glad I'm not married myself."

"If I could just know for sure that my father was alive. If he could only read a letter I've written to him. I'm sure I'd feel I'd done everything possible. But until then, my mind is elsewhere. I simply can't concentrate on something as frivolous as a movie like *Siebenkäs*. I mean, have you read the novel?"

"No," I said. "And somehow I don't think I'm going to."

She shook her head, as if the book were beneath contempt. "I know it's a lot to ask of anyone—to go to Yugoslavia on my account—but if I could just know that everything that could be done to find him has been done, then I'd feel a whole lot better. Do you understand? Then I might actually be able to do this stupid picture."

I nodded. "Let me get this straight, Fräulein Dresner. You want me to be your postman. To travel to Yugoslavia and deliver a letter, in person, to your father, if I can find him."

"That's right, Herr Gunther. To remind him he has a daughter who would like to see him again. I was thinking that Josef might be able to organize a visa for him to travel to Germany, and I could meet with him here in Berlin. It would mean so much to me."

"And the minister's prepared to do that? To facilitate my going there and your father coming here?"

"Yes."

"This monastery in Banja Luka. Is that your father's last known address?"

She nodded.

"Tell me about it."

"Banja Luka is in Bosnia-Herzegovina, about two hundred kilometers south of Zagreb. It's a largish town in the hands of the Ustaše. So quite safe for Germans, I think. You could probably drive there in a day, depending on the condition of the roads. The Petrićevac Monastery of the Most Holy Trinity is run by Franciscans. I've only been there once, when I was a small child. It's probably the biggest building in Banja Luka so I don't think you could miss it."

"What's his name?"

"Antun Djurkovic. When he joined the order he took Ladislaus as his religious name. After the saint. He calls himself Father Ladislaus now. I have some pictures of him in the house, if you'd care to look at them."

"Sure. But I might need to take them with me if I'm going to look for him."

"Does that mean you'll do it? That you'll go to Yugoslavia?"

"Don't rush me, Fräulein Dresner. It's considered normal practice when you're going to stick your head in a lion's mouth to think about it first, even in the circus. Not least to check out the lion. See if he's been fed. What his breath is like. That kind of thing."

"Meaning what, exactly?"

"Meaning I shall probably go and speak to some of our people in Foreign Intelligence this afternoon. The kind of people who know the country and who can tell me how things are down there. And there's a judge from my own department—Judge Dorfmüller—who's handled many investigations in Yugoslavia. I expect he'll have something useful to say, too. After that I'll come back here and tell you what I propose to do. How does that sound?"

"It sounds fine if you let me cook you dinner at the same time. I'm an excellent cook considering that I'm never allowed to cook. Shall we say eight o'clock?"

I thought for a minute. On my way to the War Crimes Bureau offices on Blumeshof I could stop by Berkaerstrasse and speak to whoever it was in Schellenberg's Foreign Intelligence department who knew anything about Yugoslavia. Of course, I'd have to return Joey's car and come back to her house on the S-Bahn, but that would be all right. Then again maybe I could persuade Joey to let me keep the car for the night. Besides, it had been ages since a pretty girl had made me so much as a cup of coffee.

"Don't say yes too soon," she said. "I'll get to thinking you actually like me."

"Oh, I like you all right. I was just trying to work out if I could do what I need to do—that is, speak to the right people—and then be back here wearing a clean shirt having learned something useful."

"And what's the conclusion?"

"That I should leave. But I'll be back here at eight. If your cooking is as good as you say it is, then I wouldn't miss it for the world, a bit like your bathing costume. I'd certainly like to see that again sometime."

Sixteen

took the 540K back into Berlin. It was like driving a shiny new Messerschmitt. And Joey was right; the supercharger did whine when you started it. But once it was going, the car was magnificent. The ultimate driving machine.

At Department Six in Berkaerstrasse I asked to talk to one of Schellenberg's people about the situation in Yugoslavia and found myself ushered upstairs into the presence of the little general himself. It wasn't a large office like the minister's. And the view from the window seemed relentlessly suburban. But it was easy to see why he preferred being here to somewhere closer to Prinz Albrechtstrasse; a man could be left alone out here in the sticks, with no one like Himmler to bother him. He stood up and came around his modern-looking desk. There was some gray in his neatly combed hair. He looked thinner than when last I'd seen him—his uniform was at least a size too big—and he confessed that he was suffering from problems with his liver and his gallbladder.

"These days I only seem to gain weight," I said. "Although I think it's mostly on my conscience, not my waistline."

Schellenberg liked that one. We were off to a good start.

"This will be the second time this year I'm obliged to go back to Holter's and have my suits and uniforms altered," he said. "I'm even seeing Himmler's masseur. He's the only one who seems to make me feel better. But there's nothing he seems to be able to do about my weight loss."

From a man like Schellenberg this was quite a confession. In a department full of murderers, any one of whom would have wanted his job as the SD's chief of Foreign Intelligence, what he'd told me almost counted as an admission of weakness and, but for knowledge that his offices had once been an old people's home and the strong suspicion that he must have had a hand in the murder of Dr. Heckholz the previous summer, I might even have felt sorry for him. Of Horst Janssen, the man I presumed had done the actual killing, there was no sign, and when I asked Schellenberg about him, he said, "Safely back in Kiev, for the moment."

"Doing what?"

Schellenberg shook his head as if he didn't want to discuss it and rubbed the blue stone on his gold signet ring as if he hoped it might make the man disappear for good. And perhaps it wouldn't be long before that came true: rumor had it that the Battle of Kursk wasn't going well for the German forces; if we lost that front, Kiev would certainly be next.

"So what's this war crime you're investigating in Zagreb?" he asked. "You must be spoiled for choice in a place like Croatia."

It suited me very well for Schellenberg to believe that my business in Zagreb was on behalf of the German Army's War Crimes Bureau; but at the same time, I hardly wanted to tell him an outright lie. I was still an officer of SD, after all.

"I'm sorry, sir, but I can't say what that is."

"I respect that. I like a man who can keep his mouth shut. Pity there aren't more like you, Gunther. I used to think you were Heydrich's man. But I think I know different now. He was a master of case-based reasoning and mental reservation. Rather like a Jesuit. For him the end always justified the means. I don't expect you ever had much choice but to work for him. But I have a different approach. I couldn't ever trust a man I'd coerced to work for me."

"I'll remember you said that, General."

"Please do. You know, your lecture at last year's IKPK conference impressed me. As a matter of fact, there was something you said that I even wrote down. About how being a detective is a little like the traffic-control tower that stands in the center of Berlin's Potsdamer Platz: not only do its lights have to control traffic from five different directions, it also tells the time and, in bad weather, provides much needed shelter for a traffic policeman. That's a pretty good analogy for what I do in this office, too."

"Have you seen Potsdamer Platz lately? There's hardly any traffic at all. No one has petrol to waste driving around Berlin."

No one except Goebbels, it seemed.

"You impress me, Gunther. As a matter of fact, you also made an impression on Captain Meyer-Schwertenbach. You remember? The Swiss fellow you met at the conference? He said he thought you were a man who could be trusted. And so do I. It occurs to me now that you can do me a small service when you're in Zagreb."

"I was afraid of that."

"Oh, it's nothing much. And you don't have to do this if you don't want to. You can call it a favor, if you like. I just need a man to deliver something—someone I can rely on. Believe me, that's in rather short supply around here, what with Kaltenbrunner's spies everywhere. You wouldn't believe how paranoid that man is. But before I tell you what I want you to do, let me first tell you about the situation in Zagreb, which is what you came here to ask about. The situation is bloody awful, and likely to get even worse if—as seems likely—the fucking Italians capitulate this side of Christmas. As usual it'll be us who has to go and tidy up after them. Just like in Greece. But I think you'll be all right to go there for the present. With regard to going anywhere else, like Banja Luka, it's really impossible to say from here how safe it will be. You could seek advice from the Grand Mufti of Jerusalem, of course—Haj Amin al-Husseini. He's living just up the road from here in a very nice house on Goethestrasse that's costing von Ribbentrop seventy-five thousand reichsmarks a month."

"What's he got to do with Yugoslavia?"

"There are lots of Muslims in Yugoslavia. Himmler's made Haj Amin a general in the SS, so that he can organize the establishment of a Bosnian Islamic Waffen-SS division. There's a whole bunch of them undergoing training right now in France and Brandenburg. And Goebbels has had him give several radio broadcasts in Arab countries calling on Muslims to kill Jews."

"From Radio House? On Masurenallee?"

"No, he's got his own transmitter in the house. It all sounds insane, I know."

"I sometimes wonder just how insane things are going to get before it all ends."

"More insane than I hope you can know. But as far as Yugoslavia is concerned, you'd probably do better to get an appraisal of the situation in the country at large from my man on the ground down there, a fellow named Koob. Sturmbannführer Emil Koob. He's more of a Bulgarian expert, really, but good on the Balkans in general. I want you to take some American dollars to him, that's all. We're in the process of setting up a wireless communication system in Zagreb: called I-Netz, it can communicate with the Wannsee Institute. In the event of the Balkans being overrun by the Allies, we want some people who will be able to function behind enemy lines. I'll send Koob a signal to expect you. You'll find him at the Esplanade Hotel. It's the only decent place to stay in Zagreb. Now, that's some foreign intelligence which is really worth having. Think you can handle that?"

"No problem. And thanks for the tip about the hotel."

"Look, come and speak to me when you're back in Berlin. I'd like an appraisal of the latest situation in Croatia myself. Will you do that?"

"Certainly, sir."

Before I left, Schellenberg gave me a briefcase in which was a small parcel he informed me was full of money. And then I was on my way again.

At the Bendlerblock I went to find Eugen Dorfmüller, a judge who, like me, was one of the temporaries recruited to the War Crimes Bureau. Dorfmüller had considerable experience investigating war crimes in Yugoslavia. He was about the same age as me and perhaps just as cynical.

"It's a simple missing persons inquiry," I told him. "With any luck, I can be there and back in no time at all. I just want some advice on how far I'm sticking my neck out by going there. I don't like sticking it out unless I have to. On account of the fact that my head's attached to it. Which is important when I nod."

"Advice? My advice is this. If you go to Croatia, try and keep away from the Ustaše. Nasty lot. Cruel."

"I'm looking for a priest, so hopefully I won't need to have too much contact with them."

"A priest, eh? You'll find plenty of those in Croatia. It's a very Catholic country." He shook his head. "I don't know much about Banja Luka. But it's mostly SS who are down there now. A volunteer Waffen-SS division called the Prinz Eugen commanded by a highly decorated Romanian-German general called Artur Phleps. He's a bit of a bastard, quite frankly, even by the standards of the SS. You'd do well to stay away from them, too. But I don't have to tell you about that, of course. You were in Smolensk, weren't you? The Katyn Forest massacre, wasn't it? Christ, investigating a Russian mass murder down there—well, that was like the donkey calling the ass 'big ears.'"

"It was kind of ridiculous."

"Actually, it's good you're going down there to Croatia," he said. "I want you to confirm a decision the bureau made at the beginning of the year, which is to stop investigating war crimes in Yugoslavia."

"Why did we stop?"

"Because there were so many it hardly seemed to matter. By the way, here's an interesting thing I discovered only just the other day. All the bureau's files on war crimes in Yugoslavia have gone missing. All the depositions I took, all my case notes, all my observations, everything. Hundreds of pages of documents, all gone. It's like I was never there. Be careful. It's not just files that can go missing in Yugoslavia, Bernie. It's men, too. Especially men like you. My advice to you when you're down there is this: to say nothing at all about the fact that you are currently on attachment to the War Crimes Bureau. Do this job for the Ministry of Truth—whatever it is—and get yourself back here as quickly as possible and then forget you even heard the name of Croatia."

My last port of call was the ministry, to return Joey's magnificent car and to make a bid to hang on to it for the evening. I liked having a car again. Having a car makes it so easy to get around. You just turn the engine over and then aim the sights at the end of the bonnet where you want to go.

At the Ministry of Truth a secretary told me that Joey had gone to his city mansion, at the corner of Hermann-Göring-Strasse. It was a short drive away from Wilhelmplatz and anyone from Berlin could have found the place with his eyes closed: formerly the palace of the marshals of the Prussian royal court, the old building had been demolished and replaced with an expensive new house designed by Albert Speer. I was thinking of having Speer around myself to see what he could do with my place on Fasanenstrasse. Goebbels had the whole of the Tiergarten round his town house and quite a bit of it on the walls; I've never seen so much oak paneling. A butler with a face like a melted elephant led me to a cozy little room with a tapestry as big as a battle-field and an uninterrupted view of prelapsarian Berlin; just grass and above the trees in the distance, the golden lady on top of the Victory Column. A lot of people said she was the only girl in Berlin who Goebbels hadn't been able to get his leg over.

He was on the telephone and in a bad mood. From what I could gather, Hitler had decided to award a posthumous Knight's Cross with Oak-Leaf Cluster and Swords to the chief of the Japanese Navy; the only trouble was that it seemed the Japanese emperor had raised some objections to the idea of a Japanese officer being decorated by "barbarians," by which I assume he meant us.

"But it's a great honor," Goebbels said. "The first time a foreign military officer has been awarded this decoration. Please impress upon Tōjō and his Imperial Majesty that the leader merely wishes to acknowledge the respect in which the admiral was held by him and that this is in no way intended as a way of trumping your own Order of the Chrysanthemum. Yes. I understand. Thank you."

Goebbels banged down the telephone receiver and stared at me balefully.

"Well? What do you want?"

"I can come back if you like, Herr Doctor," I said.

Goebbels shook his head. "No, no. Tell me what you think." He pointed to a chair and I sat down.

Finally he smiled. "Beautiful, isn't she?"

"Yes, I suppose she is," I said with teasing skepticism; and then: "Astonishingly so. She's beautiful in a fantastic, unearthly, in-your-dreams sort of way."

"That's right. And her face. Did you notice how it has a very luminous quality? Like it has its own key light." Seeing me look baffled, Goebbels added, "That's a technical, film-lighting name for a stage light that shines only on one person. Usually the star of the picture."

"Yes, I did." Under the circumstances I thought it best not to say anything more about how attractive I thought Dalia Dresner was. I'd already said too much. "I can go to Yugoslavia as soon as you like, provided I can get into the Esplanade Hotel," I said. "But first I'd like to take a run out to Brandenburg and speak to a detachment of Bosnian Muslim SS about the situation in their country. If I'm going to travel to Banja Luka, I want to make sure that I'm fully aware of the local situation. Which, by all accounts I've had so far, is uncertain, to say the least. From what I've heard, I'm going to earn every pfennig of what you've paid me, Herr Doctor."

"Yes, yes, of course. Well, please do that. And I'll have someone make the arrangements for you to travel down to Zagreb on the next available plane."

"It's just that Brandenburg is sixty kilometers away and I'm going to need a car to get me there and back."

"Of course. And yes, you may borrow the roadster until tomorrow. Just have it back here before ten. I'm planning a picnic at Schwanenwerder tomorrow."

I got up to leave and began the long journey toward the door.

Halfway there, he said, "What you were saying just now about Fräulein Dresner. I liked it. I liked it very much. She is, as you say, beautiful in a fantastic, unearthly, in-your-dreams sort of way. But that's all it can ever be for someone like you, Gunther. She can exist only in your dreams, Herr Gunther. And only ever in your dreams. Do we understand each other?"

"As always, Herr Doctor, you make your meaning very clear."

Seventeen

It wasn't unusual for Germans to have the words of Dr. Goebbels ringing in their ears as they went about their daily business. He was often on the radio, of course, making some important speech from the Sportpalast or the Radio House. Everyone still remembered with a shudder the speech he'd made in February when he called for "total war," which somehow managed to seem even more frightening than the war with which we had already become wearily familiar. Mostly we'd learned not to pay much attention to what Joey said. But the speech he'd made as I left his city mansion was different; this particular speech was just for me. A speech that ought to have scared me as much as the one about total war.

After I'd been home and put on a clean shirt and my best lounge suit I jumped back in the car, shooed away some boys who were staring at it as if it had arrived from another planet, and started the engine. And now thinking it best that Goebbels didn't know I wasn't going to Brandenburg at all but to dinner with the woman he loved, I decided to take a few detours along the way, just in case I was being followed. But mostly I just put my foot on the gas when I had my ticket for the AVUS speedway because the 540K could outrun almost any other car on the road.

I got back to the house on Griebnitzsee just a little before eight and parked the car several streets away, just in case anyone noticed that there were two identical red roadsters on the driveway. I checked the street for cars but it was empty; if Goebbels was having her watched it could only have been from the window of one of those other enormous houses. Without those pips on the lapel of my uniform I figured I was harder to identify but I pulled the brim of my hat down over my eyes anyway, just in case. When you're trying your best to steal the minister's girl it's as well to be a little careful. I'd bought some flowers from Harry Lehmann's on Friedrichstrasse and, holding these like some lovesick young suitor, I cranked the doorbell again. This time the maid answered. She gave me a slow up-and-down like I was something the cat had brought to the door, and then pulled a face.

"So you're it," she said. "The reason my day off had to be cut short in order that her royal highness can play Arsène Avignon in the kitchen."

"Who's he?" I asked, advancing into the hall.

"You wouldn't know him. He's a French chef. Cooks at the Ritz. That's an expensive hotel, in case you didn't know that, either. What's this you're holding? Some kind of cheap umbrella?"

"*Pour votre maîtresse,*" I said.

"I thought all the cemeteries were closed at this time of night. Kind of small, aren't they?"

Dalia appeared behind her maid's shoulder. She was wearing an iridescent navy taffeta evening gown with a quilted collar and hem, cut very close to the line of her hips, which was where my eyes lingered for more than a moment or two.

"Are those for me?" she asked. "Oh, Harry Lehmann. How lovely. And how thoughtful."

"I'd have brought a nice juicy bone if I'd known you had such a fierce dog looking out for you."

Dalia took the flowers from me and handed them to her maid.

"Agnes, put these in some water, will you please?"

"I thought you said he was handsome," Agnes said sourly. "And an officer, to boot. Did you check his teeth? This one looks kind of old for that beef you've cooked, princess."

I took Dalia's hand and kissed it.

"Take my advice with this one, princess," said Agnes. "Look before you leap. For snakes among sweet flowers do creep."

Agnes went one way along the corridor, Dalia and I went the other.

"Is she always this friendly?"

"As a matter of fact, she likes you."

"How can you tell?"

"Telepathy. I warned you I was clever, didn't I? You should hear her when Joey turns up at the door. You would think she was talking to the coal man."

"I'd like a front seat for the next time that happens."

"She told Veit Harlan that he should write a suicide scene with himself as the star."

There were lots of suicides in Harlan's movies; his wife, the Swedish actress Kristina Söderbaum, was always taking her life in his films, which must have made her wonder if he was trying to tell her something.

"I'm beginning to see why you keep her around. She doesn't just growl. She bites, too."

"Yes, she does. But not as much as I do."

In the drawing room was a Swan Biedermeier living room set upholstered in white leather, several elegant tables, and a tall chest of drawers, only you didn't notice the furniture much because of the paintings on the wall. Brightly colored, they were also recognizable, which is how I like my modern art. She told me they were by the German artist Emil Nolde and had been hanging on the walls of Joey's city mansion until Hitler had seen them.

"He told Josef they were degenerate and to get rid of them, so now they're here. I rather like them, don't you?"

"I do now you've told me that story. In fact, Emil Nolde just became my favorite German artist."

There was a black lyre-shaped clock on the mantelpiece and a mahogany grand piano, which couldn't have been played much because there were as many photographs of Dalia on the lid as there were winged horses on the rug. In most of the photographs she was with someone famous like Emil Jannings, Werner Krauss, Viktoria von Ballasko, or Leni Riefenstahl. She pointed me toward an ice bucket and a bottle of Pol Roger and I managed to open it without scaring the pet white rabbit that was hopping around the floor.

"If that's dinner, it's looking a little undercooked for my taste."

She pretended to scold me and then made me sit beside her on the sofa, which suited me nicely. It was quite a small sofa.

"So, what did you discover this afternoon?" she asked.

"About Yugoslavia? Only that a lot of people have advised me not to go there, Fräulein Dresner. And to be careful if I do. I thought Germany could teach the world something about hatred but it seems your countrymen know a thing or two about hate themselves. About all that I've learned to my advantage has been the name of the best hotel in Zagreb—the Esplanade. Which is where I'm staying, I think."

"So you are going?"

"Yes, I'm going. Just as soon as Joey can get me on a plane."

"Thank you," she said quietly. "I'm so grateful to you, Herr Gunther. But please call me Dalia. And if I'm going to sit next to you on this sofa I can hardly call you Herr Gunther. I used to know a butcher in Zurich called Herr Gunther and if we're not careful I shall ask you for some sausage. And that wouldn't do at all."

"Bernie," I said. "It's Bernie."

We talked for a while—the kind of fast and elegant talk that passes for conversation but is really just dueling with short swords, with a man and a woman making gentle attacks and parries and ripostes. No scars are given and the vital organs are always left well alone. A very pleasant hour was spent like this before we moved into a dining room that was no less elegant than the drawing room, with a ceiling high enough to accommodate a chandelier as big as a Christmas tree. The wood grain on the table was so perfect it looked like one of those inkblot tests designed to test your imagination. Mine was doing just fine thanks to the scent Dalia was wearing, the sibilance of her stockings, the curve of her neck, and the frequency of her dazzling white smiles. A couple of times we bowed our heads and cigarettes toward the same match and, once, she let me touch her blond hair, which was so fine it was like a child's. Meanwhile Agnes served a dinner that Dalia assured me she'd cooked herself, although I hardly cared if she had or hadn't. I wasn't there for a good meal—although it had been at least a year since I'd eaten as well—any more than I was there because I was a fan of her pictures: I wasn't. I don't go to the cinema much these days because I don't like being told that Jews are like rats, that great folk songs are not made but fall out of the sky, and that Frederick the Great was the best king who ever lived. Besides, there are the newsreels to cope with: all that relentlessly positive news about how well our troops are doing in Russia. No, I was there, eating Dalia Dresner's food and drinking her Pol Roger champagne, because Goebbels had been right: this siren woman's face was permanently illuminated, not by anything so crude as an electrical bulb placed on a stage by a clever cameraman but by her own special light—the sun or the moon or whatever star was shooting through the sky at the time. Every time she looked into my eyes the effect was devastating, as if my heart had been stopped by some beautiful Medusa.

Dalia herself hardly ate anything; mostly she just smoked and sipped champagne and watched me making a pig of myself, which wasn't difficult. But I guess I must have made conversation because I know she laughed a lot at some of my jokes. Some of them were pretty feeble, too, which ought to have put me on my guard against whatever it was she wanted. Maybe it was me, after all; then again, I'm no catch, and in retrospect I figure she just hoped to make sure that I did my best to find her father when I got to Yugoslavia. What you might call an incentive. But as incentives go, what happened next, when we went back into the drawing room for coffee—real coffee—and brandies—real brandy—would take some beating.

"Well, Bernie Gunther, I think if you don't kiss me soon, I shall die. You've been sitting there wondering if you should and I've been sitting here wishing that you would. Look, whatever it was that Josef told you, I'm a free agent and not his possession. Thanks to him it's been a while since any man had the guts to kiss me. I think you're just the man to fix that, don't you?"

I slid toward her on the white sofa and pressed my lips to hers and she gave herself up to me. It wasn't long before my lips were anticipating more intimate ones and the exquisite secret sweet-and-sour taste of the other sex that only men can know.

"An abominable mystery," she said breathily.

"What is?"

"Sexual behavior. That's what Darwin called it. An abominable mystery. I rather like that, don't you? It implies that there's very little control we can exert about what's happening to us."

"That's certainly the way I feel about it right now."

She kissed me again and then began to gently chew at my earlobe while I set about feasting on her perfumed neck, and I remembered that there's nothing quite like the feel of skin and flesh younger than your own. Newly picked fresh fruit as opposed to the kind that's been on the shelf for rather longer, like mine.

"I've often thought," she said, "that there's some important scientific work to be done concerning the mathematics of fatal attraction. The male and female gametophytes. The pollen grain. The embryo sac. The irresistible attraction to the ovule. The altruistic self-sacrifice of the pollen tube cell exploding to deliver the sperm cells to the embryo sac."

"I bet you say that to all the Fritzes you know."

"It's just pure organic chemistry, of course, and where there's chemistry, there's mathematics, too."

"I was never very good at maths. Or chemistry."

"Oh, I don't know. I think you're pretty good at it, Bernie. In fact, I think you're getting better at it by the minute."

I kissed her again, warming to my appointed task, and why not? She was easy to kiss. The fact is, you never really forget how to do it. After a while she pushed me gently away and, taking me by the hand, led me out of the drawing room toward a curving iron staircase. "Shall we?"

"Are you sure?"

"No," she said simply. "But that's what makes it exciting, isn't it? No one can ever be sure. Being truly human is all about risk, not certainty. At least that's the way I always look at it."

She put one hand on the polished wooden handrail and led me slowly up to the second-floor landing.

"Besides, I already told you, Bernie Gunther—I do like saying your name—I'm a clever girl. You don't need to worry that you're taking advantage of me."

"Maybe it's the other way around," I heard myself say.

"Let me know when you want me to call you a taxi," she said. "I'd hate to feel that I made you spend the night with me against your will."

I felt my heart leap a little as she said this. But now that she had I knew that there was no going back. About halfway up the stairs I thought of Goebbels and the warning he'd given me. It didn't work. Life seemed too short to care very much about tomorrow; if I ended up facing a military firing squad on a hill in Murellenberge—where all the death sentences of the Reich War Court were carried out—then it would have been worth it. If you're going to die, you might as well die with a sweet memory of a woman like Dalia Dresner in your head.

At the door of her bedroom we met Agnes, who said nothing and didn't even meet my eye, but it was clear she'd been in there to prepare for our arrival. The heavy curtains had been drawn; there was quiet band music coming out of the radio and the lights were low; the enormous bed had been turned down; a negligee lay on the top sheet; the flowers I'd bought were now in a vase on the dressing table; there was a drinks tray with several decanters and two brandy glasses; the cigarette box beside the bed was open; there was an armchair with a newspaper lying on the cushion; and in the en suite bathroom, a bath had been drawn. I realized that all of this had been planned in advance—not that I cared, particularly. There's only so much blood a man has in his body—and clearly not nearly enough for his brain and what makes him a man. Which is probably just as well as I can't see how the human race is going to survive in any other way. I just hoped that she wouldn't eat me after it was all over like a praying mantis. Then again, it was probably a good way to go.

Dalia picked up her negligee. She didn't need my help, it wasn't very heavy. "Help yourself to a drink and to a cigarette," she said. "Relax. I won't be long."

She went into the bathroom. I poured myself a drink, lit a cigarette, and then sat down in the armchair to look at the newspaper. I couldn't have felt less relaxed if Goebbels had been sitting up in bed looking at me. I didn't read the paper because I was too busy listening to the sound of her as she got into the bath and splashed around. It was certainly better than anything I could hear on the radio. After a while I noticed that there was a picture on the dressing table that had been laid facedown and, being a nosy sort of fellow, I picked it up. I didn't recognize the man in the picture though I guessed he was Dalia's husband because she and he were cutting a wedding cake. He was older and grayer than me, which pleased me enormously. In all the talk about Goebbels, she hadn't mentioned her husband and I certainly wasn't about to bring him up now. I replaced the picture facedown and went back to my newspaper. It was probably best that he didn't see what I still hardly believed was going to happen.

When she came out of the bathroom she was wearing the negligee. At least I think she was. Frankly it was so thin and transparent it might have been the brandy I was seeing through. But I wasn't worried the alcohol I'd consumed was going to stop me from making love to her. Goebbels and her husband—Stefan?—could have hit me on the head with a sledgehammer and I wouldn't have noticed it. Nothing was going to stop me now.

"Like it?" she said, turning around a couple of times so that I could appreciate her almost-there garment and the very shapely contents.

"I like it and I like you," I said. "Very much. I like any girl who knows what she wants. You go out after it and nothing stops you from getting it. I have the most wonderful feeling that you've been planning for this to happen since I left here this morning."

"Oh, I knew it was going to happen as soon as I saw you," she said matter-of-factly. "This morning, when you caught me sunbathing in the nude, I knew that if you'd taken me right then and there I'd have let you do whatever you wanted. In fact that's what I wanted myself. Couldn't you tell? I was sure you could."

"You know, in Byelorussia, there were these women in the Russian Army. Marksmen and snipers. Rifle *babushkas*, we used to call them. Dead shots all of them. Once they had you in their sights, you'd had it because they seldom ever missed. They always got their man, is what we used to say. That's what you remind me of. I feel like I just got one in the head."

This was only partly true; when these women were caught, the German Army called them "rifle sluts" and hanged them, but under the circumstances, I didn't think she needed that amount of detail. No one did.

She smiled. "I guess that answers a question I was going to ask you," she said.

"Which was?"

"Where you got those big sad-looking blue eyes of yours."

"You want to know why they're sad? Because they haven't seen you in years."

She sat on my lap and kissed my eyelids.

"Besides," I added. "My eyes. They're not so sad right now. As a matter of fact, I was just thinking how this is the first time in a very long time that I've felt as if life was actually worth the candle. That I can actually manage a smile that isn't oiled with sarcasm."

"I'm glad about that," she said.

"I could get to like it here, with you."

"Good. I hope you'll come again. By the way, I ran you a bath just in case you wanted one. Would you like me to wash you?"

"Back in Berlin they have several words for girls like you."

She frowned. "Oh? Such as?"

"Astonishing. Amazing. Astounding."

She smiled. "It was a simple question, Bernie Gunther. Would you like me to bathe you?"

"Do you think I need bathing?"

"Need has got absolutely nothing to do with it," she purred. "Want is all that matters now. What you want me to do for you, what will bring you delight."

Dalia took my head in her perfumed hands and started to cover it with tiny kisses as small as her pink fingernails. Through the negligee I could see and feel every part of her delicious body. I ran my hand over her breast and onto her bottom; now that I actually had it in my hand it was even more perfect than I'd realized. She shifted and parted her thighs slightly so that my fingers could pleasure her a little.

"That's all that matters when you're with me, Bernie Gunther." Each word she spoke was punctuated with a kiss now. "All you've ever wanted from a woman is exactly what you're going to get. So, please. Try to relax and get it through your beautiful big head that when you're here, in this room, giving you pleasure is what I'm for. More pleasure than you've ever had from a woman before."

"You know something? I think that, all things considered, I'd really like to have a bath."

Eighteen

The Fieseler Fi-156 Storch liaison aircraft dropped through the warm air toward Borongaj airfield, east of Zagreb. The three-seater Storch was well named; with its long legs and big wings the aircraft resembled a stork, only this one wasn't delivering babies, just myself and a bad-tempered Austrian SS police general named August Meyszner. The general was arriving in Yugoslavia after a week's leave in Berlin, to take command of an anti-partisan offensive in Bosnia, and regarded my mission—whatever it was—as of little or no consequence, and during the flight he made it quite clear that I should not speak to him unless addressed directly. This suited me very well since it inhibited me from mentioning that it was well known in Berlin police circles that Meyszner—a notorious anti-Semite—had a brother, Rudolf, who just happened to be married to the famously Jewish stepdaughter of the famous composer and conductor Johann Strauss II.

From the air the countryside surrounding Zagreb was mostly woodland with large fields that were divided into long, narrow strips, as if the land were still farmed according to feudal principles of agriculture. This wasn't so far from the truth. As the Storch neared the ground, General Meyszner forgot that he was trying to ignore me and explained that most Yugoslavians were "Swabian peasants" and had "no more idea of enclosures and crop rotation than they did of single variable calculus." I said nothing. Inside the cabin I took hold of the seat in front of me and closed my eyes as a gust of wind caught the wings and the plane wobbled uncertainly, which did nothing for my nerves or my underwear. A few trips in a plane had given me a grudging respect for Heydrich, who, in the months leading up to his death, had seen some active service with the Luftwaffe, first as a rear gunner in a Dornier and then as a trainee fighter pilot, until a crash and then Himmler had obliged him to quit. I could no more have served in our air force than I could have gone over the Reichenbach Falls in a beer barrel.

We landed and I let out a breath that steamed up the whole window next to me. After a minute or two I climbed unsteadily out of the plane just in time to see the general disappear in the only transport that seemed to have been provided—a Horch driven by the local field police, who were easily identifiable from the silver dog collar warrants that hung around their necks. I picked up my bag and walked toward the airport building where, after waiting almost half an hour, I was able to get a lift into town from the Storch's suddenly garrulous German pilot, who proceeded to give me a tour guide's explanation for how things were in modern Yugoslavia.

The Hotel Esplanade on Mihanoviceva had been built during the previous century as a railway hotel for the Vienna-Zagreb stage of the Orient Express. It contained a quarryful of black-and-white marble, several art deco ceilings, a ballroom as big as a circus tent, and a formal courtesy that seemed better suited to Vienna and absurdly excessive for a city of just one hundred thousand people. It was like finding a tram driver wearing a white tuxedo. Come to think of it, these days that kind of old-world formality seems inappropriate for Vienna, too. But that Austro-Hungarian imperial past died hard in Zagreb; indeed it was perhaps what the Ustaše mistakenly imagined they were fighting for.

And yet—according to my driver—the old enmity between Croat and Serb could not simply be dismissed as a conflict of two defunct empires. If Croats hated their Serbian near-neighbors it wasn't entirely because of their Ottoman past. Croats might have been anti-Semites but they were tolerant of Islam. Why else would they have built a mosque in one of their main squares?

Once I'd checked in, I went to find Schellenberg's local SD officer, Sturmbannführer Emil Koob, but he was out so I left a message for him at the hotel's reception. Then I looked for the local army liaison officer, who also had an office in the Esplanade. He was a lieutenant in the Wehrmacht and, like Meyszner, another Austrian. His name was Kurt Waldheim. Very lean and tall, with a nose like a billhook, I guessed he was probably in his mid-twenties, and he reminded me more than a little of Heydrich. I showed him my credentials—which were of course impeccable—and explained my mission.

"I need to make contact with the local SD and then to travel to a place in Bosnia called Banja Luka," I said. "I'm looking for this man." I showed him a photograph of Father Ladislaus given to me by Dalia Dresner. "He was last heard of at the Petrićevac Monastery of the Most Holy Trinity, which is run by the Franciscans. Dr. Goebbels wishes me to give an important message to him and, if he wishes it, to facilitate his coming to Berlin at some future stage. I'd appreciate any help or advice you can give me."

"I'm not wholly familiar with that part of the country, and as a matter of fact this is my last week as army group liaison with the Italian Ninth Army here in Yugoslavia. After a bit of leave I'm off to Greece to take up a position with Army Group South as the liaison officer with the Italian Eleventh Army. But what I can tell you is that the roads between here and Sarajevo aren't too bad, especially now, with the temperatures in the high twenties and thirties. Bombed about a bit, of course. In winter it's a very different story. It's almost two hundred kilometers down to Banja Luka. I should think you could make it there in a day. Most of the partisans are operating to the southeast of there, in the Zelengora Mountains. But they're pretty tenacious and move around the country with frightening speed so it's best to be on your guard at all times. At least it is in Bosnia. You'll find the SD at Gestapo headquarters on King Peter Kresmira Street. They'll probably be able to arrange some transport down south for you. Some sort of a car or field wagon, I expect. I could drive you over there myself, if you like. It's a little far to walk there in this heat."

"Thank you, Lieutenant, I'd appreciate that."

Waldheim wasn't a bad sort of fellow. He'd been in Yugoslavia since the previous summer, after being wounded on the Eastern Front and discharged from combat service; since then he'd seen service only as a liaison officer with the Italians because he spoke the language. But he held a dim view of the prospects for our main ally in the Axis.

"Anyone can see that now the Allies have invaded Sicily, the writing is on the wall for Mussolini. I'd be very surprised if he manages to cling onto power until the end of the month. Not without German help, anyway."

"They're sending you, aren't they?" I said.

Waldheim grinned uncertainly as we drove past the new city mosque. With three tall minarets still under construction, it seemed an improbable building to find in one of the most Catholic countries in Europe. Waldheim explained that the mosque was due to open the following summer, always assuming that Ante Pavelić—the leader of the fascist Ustaše—lasted as long as that, since the mosque had been his own initiative.

"Tell me, Lieutenant Waldheim, is Italian the only language you speak or do you speak whatever it is they speak here? Croat, I suppose. Because when I get to Banja Luka I think I'm going to need a translator."

"I speak Czech and a bit of Croat. But like I said, I'm off on leave quite soon. And then bound for Greece, I'm afraid."

"And like you also said, it's only a day's drive down from Zagreb to Banja Luka. And a day's drive back again. That's plenty of time before you leave for Greece. Besides, unless I'm very much mistaken, the Italian Ninth Army no longer exists in this theater. On account of the fact that they've all gone back to defend their homeland against the Allies. Or more likely to surrender as quickly as possible. And who could blame them?"

Waldheim frowned. "It's very flattering of you to ask, but my commanding officer, General Löhr, couldn't possibly spare me right now."

Waldheim pulled up in front of a huge modern building. The street, lined with maple trees that were shedding their bark, was closed to all traffic except those on Gestapo business. A rank of camouflaged German cars stood in front of the main entrance. Behind them was a quaint little park with a rose garden and the bronze statue of a naked dancing girl, which made a very pleasant change from the equestrian statues of forgotten Croat kings that seemed to be all over the city like so many giant dog turds.

"Here we are, sir. Gestapo headquarters."

"I could ask him, if you like? General Löhr. I could ask him to let you come with me to Banja Luka. After all, this mission is a high priority for the Ministry of Truth and Propaganda. I'm sure your general would want to make sure that I have everything I need to make sure it's a success. Dr. Goebbels is not a man who likes failure."

Waldheim was looking very awkward and probably wishing he'd never set eyes on me.

"Look," he said, "what if I was to find you someone else? Someone who speaks much better Croat than me?"

"Is that possible?"

"Oh yes. My Croat isn't that good at all." He saluted. "Leave it to me, sir. And I'll see what I can do."

I watched Lieutenant Waldheim drive quickly away with a smile on my face; there aren't many jobs that come close to being God's representative on earth, but arriving in a place like Zagreb with Joey's letter in the pocket of my tunic was one of them. It read:

> To Whom It May Concern: The bearer of this letter, Captain Bernhard Gunther, a Police commissar with the RSHA in Berlin, is to be extended every cooperation and courtesy. He is my personal envoy in Zagreb and should be always treated as if he were me and his mission is of the utmost importance to my ministry. Signed, Dr. Josef Goebbels, Reich Minister of Truth and Propaganda.

With a letter like that I was going to have some fun in Yugoslavia. Or so I thought.

Gestapo headquarters was mercifully cool after the searing heat of the street. The pictures of Hitler and Himmler and Ante Pavelić on the wall of the entrance hall were hardly a surprise, nor indeed was the giant map of Yugoslavia, but, in the circumstances, the portrait of Benito Mussolini—the one with him wearing a black helmet and looking more than a little like a circus daredevil about to be shot out of a cannon, which, perhaps, wasn't so far away from the truth—already seemed out of place in that company.

And yet it was a picture that gave me hope—hope that one day soon people like young Lieutenant Kurt Waldheim would be predicting the imminent demise of Adolf Hitler.

Nineteen

The next morning, after a disturbed night due to the many trams that passed in an almost steady stream of light blue beneath the open window of my stiflingly hot second-floor room, I was up early and waiting outside the hotel, ready to leave Zagreb in the open-top Mercedes 190 that SD Sturmbannführer Emil Koob had lent to me with some alacrity after I gave him the parcel of money from Schellenberg. Waldheim was also there, to introduce me to the two SS officers who were recently returned from Germany and heading for Sarajevo and then Savnik, to rejoin their division. Banja Luka is almost halfway from Zagreb to Sarajevo and the two officers had been assured that there would be transport waiting for them at this ancient Bosnian city's Ustaše headquarters. I could have wished for more congenial companions than the SS but Waldheim assured me that both men were ethnic volunteers—Croatian Germans who knew the country as well as the language. Besides, he added, there were rumors that the partisans had broken out of southeastern Bosnia and were headed toward the Dalmatian coast across the very region to which we were traveling. All of which meant that three armed men in a car were certainly better than just one.

Of the two officers, the sergeant was the first to arrive. He gave a casual sort of salute and said his name was Oehl. The left side of his face had been badly burned, which probably explained the Iron Cross 2nd Class he wore on his tunic and his taciturn manner; I'd have been a bit taciturn myself if half of my face looked like a plantation shutter. The hair on top of his head was short and gray and exactly matched the short gray hair on his enormous chin; his narrow blue eyes looked more like murder holes in the walls of an impregnable castle. Looking at him I felt as if I had just met a powerful gorilla while at the same time being in possession of the world's last banana.

"Where is Captain Geiger?" Waldheim looked at his watch.

"We're going to pick the boss up on the way out of town."

"Where is he now?"

"You don't want to know."

"All right."

I shook hands with Waldheim and wished him luck in Greece as the sergeant threw his kit into the back of the car and, nursing a daddy under his arm, climbed into the front seat and lit a cigarette.

"You'd best drive, sir," he told me. "If we run into any trouble I might need to sweep the road with this."

A daddy was a Russian-made Tokarev PPSh—the Papasha, which is Ivan for "daddy." Oehl's daddy had a drum magazine, the kind that holds seventy-one rounds as opposed to half as many in a box mag.

I started the car and drove off with Oehl giving me directions.

"Is that at all likely?" I asked.

"I reckon we'll be all right until we get over the Sava River. After that, anything's fucking possible. The First Proletarian Brigade has broken out of the encirclement. And there are Chetniks in the same area. Proles are the communists. Tito's men. Chetniks are royalists. Some of them are friendly. Some are not. Some Chetniks are really Proles pretending to be friendly Chetniks so they can kill you. The only way you can be sure which they are is if they start shooting at you."

His voice sounded vaguely irritable and tired. I recognized that sound; it's what you sound like after people have been trying to kill you for a while.

"Have you seen much fighting down here?"

He let out a sigh that was almost as loud as the engine of the car I was driving and grinned patiently as if trying not to obey his first instinct which was to shove his daddy's polished wooden butt in my face. The submachine gun was the only really clean thing about him.

"There is no fighting down here," he said. "They kill us when we're not expecting it, and we kill them when they're not expecting it. That's how it works with partisans. It's just killing. And more killing. Except there's more of them than us. Twenty thousand in the partisans. Probably more. It certainly seems that way to those of us who have to do the killing."

At his request we stopped in front of a building near the new mosque on Franje Rackog Street; at the opposite end of the street could be seen the twin spires of Zagreb's Catholic cathedral. The entrance of the building was busy with men wearing black uniforms and forage caps. Oehl said they were Ustaše and that our stuff would be safe enough in the car while we went to fetch Captain Geiger.

"We?"

"I might need your help getting him out."

"Are you sure about our stuff? The gun?"

"No one would fucking dare to steal from a German car outside Ustaše headquarters," he said. "That's why we're leaving it here. The banging hut's only a minute away."

We walked around the corner to a cream-colored building with a mock Doric entrance and, above the door, a double-width buttressed balcony as big as an armored car where several semi-clad girls were already enjoying the hot Croatian sun. We went up to the second floor and entered a warren of rooms. A soldier wearing just his pants was sitting at a little harmonium and having a go at playing *"Bolle Lied"*—a traditional Berlin song about a fellow called Bolle from Pankow who goes to the fair, loses his child, gets drunk, kills five people with a knife, comes home with a broken nose, torn clothes, and a missing eye and, after his wife has polished his skull with a rolling pin, chokes to death on his own vomit. It's a jolly little number that every Berliner knows and loves but which seemed oddly appropriate for Croatia.

I followed Oehl through a warren of rooms that were busy with more half-naked girls and several soldiers until we finally found a tall, cadaverous man seated in an armchair smoking a cigarette. He was fully clad in an SS uniform but clearly drunk. By his leg was a bottle of cloudy spirit and all his kit, including another daddy. He looked at us through half-closed eyes and then nodded.

"Where the fuck have you been, Sergeant?"

"This is Captain Gunther," said Oehl. "He's going to drive us to Banja Luka."

"Is he now? That's very decent of him."

"I told you last night. That lieutenant at the Esplanade fixed it for us to travel south with him. He's from Berlin."

"We were in Berlin, last week," said the captain. "Or was it the week before? We only went because we thought there'd be women. Well, everyone knows about Berlin women. We thought there'd be nightclubs. But it wasn't like that at all. Anyway, we stayed at some boring SS villa at a place called Wannsee. Do you know it?"

"The Villa Minoux? Yes, I know it."

"It was very boring. There's more nightlife in Zagreb than there is in Berlin."

"On the evidence of this place, that's probably true."

Geiger smiled affably and proffered the bottle, and hardly wishing to start what I hoped would be our short association on the wrong foot, I took it and swigged at the contents: it was raki, or the milk of the brave, and believe me, you had to be brave to drink that stuff.

"I can tell that this is your first time in Croatia," he said. "The way you drank the raki."

"First time." Thinking I'd better let them know I wasn't a complete green beak, I added something about having just come from Smolensk.

"Smolensk, eh? This is better than Smolensk. Not as many Wehrmacht around to get in the way, with their sense of honor and fair play and all that shit."

"I love it already."

"You grab his kit," Oehl told me, "and I'll get him onto his feet."

I returned Geiger's bottle, hoisted his pack onto my back, and then picked up the daddy.

"Watch that," said Geiger. "Trigger's a bit light. You wouldn't want to shoot anyone, would you? At least not until we're across the border into Bosnia. Then it really doesn't matter who you fucking shoot." He laughed as if he were joking, and it was later on that day before I discovered that this was not a joke.

Oehl maneuvred Captain Geiger down the stairs behind me, with the captain still giving advice on how things were in Yugoslavia.

"The important thing to remember is that you shoot them before they shoot you. Or worse. Believe me, you wouldn't want to be captured by these First Proletarian bastards. Not unless you want to find out what your own dick tastes like. They like to cut it off, you see, and make you eat it before you bleed out. Balls, too, if they're in a mood to be generous with your provisions."

"Good meat's in short supply everywhere," I said.

Geiger laughed loudly as we emerged onto the street. "I like him, Sergeant. Gunther, did you say? Well, Captain Gunther, you're not as much of a cunt as you look. What do you think, Sergeant?"

"Whatever you say, boss."

"Does this fellow Tito have a Second Proletarian Brigade?" I asked.

"Good point," said Geiger. "I don't know. But it makes you think, eh? Even when you're a fucking Prole there's some sort of class division. Marx *would be* disappointed."

It wasn't yet nine o'clock but already it was so hot my tunic was sticking to my back, and when we reached the Mercedes I dumped Geiger's kit on the backseat and took off my tunic. Geiger removed his, too, and I caught sight of an enormous thick scar on his chest, as if someone had drawn a knife across it. His hooded, hollow eyes caught mine looking at it and he smiled a thin smile without feeling the need to offer any explanation as to how he had come by it. But I knew he hadn't got it from helping old ladies across busy roads. Tall, thin, blond, distinguished even—in another life he might have been a student prince, or an actor; but now he had such a disappointed, corrupted look that he reminded me most of a fallen angel. He brushed off Oehl's hands, swayed a little, vomited copiously into the gutter, and then climbed into the back of the car, where he uttered a loud groan and then closed his eyes.

"That way," said Oehl, pointing around the windscreen. "Drive past the fucking mosque and then down past Gestapo HQ."

We quickly left the city behind. The sun was strong, the land seemed to cower underneath its fierce effect. With the hood of the car folded down behind us like the bellows of an accordion we drove southeast from Zagreb, into Slavonia. The land was very flat and very fertile as a result of the Pannonian Sea, which had existed here about half a million years ago. Apparently, the sea lasted for nine million years, which was probably going to put what happened over the course of the next couple of days into some sort of perspective; but I knew that the sooner I was away from this place and safely back in Berlin, the better. And all I could think about was sleeping with Dalia Dresner again. Especially now that I'd met my two traveling companions. Every time I looked at them I had a bad feeling about this particular road trip. Geiger's sergeant kept the machine gun over the edge of the door like a rear gunner in a Dornier and looked like he was keen to use it. After half an hour, Geiger opened his eyes and lit one cigarette after another as though the clean country air was an affront to his lungs. The machine gun on his lap might have been a briefcase, he looked so relaxed with it. The smile on his face was not a happy smile. It was more like Bolle's smile, just like in the Berlin song, because, for all the terrible things that he does and that happen to him, Bolle still has a bloody marvelous time.

Twenty

Factories, garages, scrap-metal yards, and lumberyards gave way to houses that were half finished or half destroyed, it was hard to tell which. Villages, centuries old, that were all but deserted. The car jolted along the empty road. I did my best to steer around the potholes and sometimes what were obviously shell holes. After a while the road narrowed and deteriorated in quality so that we were soon making no more than thirty kilometers an hour. We drove on, past small holdings, goats tethered to fences, and men plowing fields or digging ditches. Here and there we saw road signs, all of them punctured with bullet holes, but mostly there was just the dusty road through this godforsaken country. The few people we saw paid us little or no attention. My mission was a universe away from the lives of those who eked out an existence here. Now and then a cart, impossibly laden with grass, or watermelons, or corn, provided a fleeting contact with reality. It was drawn by a knackered horse and steered by men who seemed only vaguely human, their faces covered with ant colonies of stubble and almost expressionless, as if they had been carved from the very oak trees that lined the road. These people wanted no justification for being there, no creed or warped ideology to excuse their unfenced existence in this place. This was their home; it had always been their home and it always would be. Men like me and Geiger and Oehl were just passing through on our way to a private hell that we had created for ourselves. I enjoyed seeing these lean, stoic men; they made me think I belonged in a world where something as straightforward and honest as growing tobacco and sugar beet, and animal husbandry, still existed; but this feeling never lasted long. From time to time Geiger would discharge his daddy at a cow in a field and frighten it off like a rabbit, and once a Focke-Wulf 190 flew low over our heads, ripping open the sky in a great salvo of oil and metal.

Nobody said much until we came across the carcass of a horse lying next to a burned-out Italian tankette. From the look and smell of the dead animal it was days old; but my two companions insisted on taking a closer look, with guns at the ready, of course. While Oehl walked off to scout the road up ahead, Geiger looked at the saddle on the horse and declared it had belonged to a Serb.

"How can you tell?"

"Only a Serb would be stupid enough to put a saddle on like that. Besides, there's something written in Cyrillic on the leather."

"I don't understand why you seem to hate the Serbs so much. It can't just be that they were part of the Ottoman Empire, otherwise why would the Ustaše have built that damn mosque in Zagreb? You even speak the same language."

"Who told you that?"

"Lieutenant Waldheim."

"What the fuck does he know about it?" said Geiger. "The languages are similar. I'll grant you that. But with important differences. Serb is written in Cyrillic and Croatian in the Roman alphabet. And Serb just sounds more fucking stupid than Croat."

"Yes, but why do you hate each other?"

"History. It's the main reason anyone hates anyone, isn't it? History and race. Serbs are stupid and lazy and deserve to be consigned to the racial rubbish heap."

"That's not exactly Hegel."

"You want Hegel, then go back to Berlin. Here there's just killing."

"Believe me, I will, just as soon as I can."

"All right, then, Serbs are backstabbers and assassins. How's that for you? There's Stjepan Radić, a Croat who was shot in the federal parliament by a Serb member—Puniša Račić—in 1928. And before that there was the Archduke Ferdinand, of course. But for the fucking Serbs, we might not have had a Great War. Think about that, Gunther. All of the good fellows you once knew back in Berlin who might still be alive today were it not for one dumb Serb called Gavrilo Princip and his Black Hand. That's right. If you could ask your dead pals what they think about Serbs, I bet you'd get a dusty answer. You see, the Serbs have a habit of starting wars they don't finish. They're always on the wrong side. They were on the Russian side in the last lot and we Croats were on your side. Croats are more like you Germans and some of us *are* Germans, of course. Serbs are just peasants and communists. If you showed a Serb a lavatory he'd probably wash his hands in it. We hate them because they always stick together with the Slovenes regardless of where the interests of the country might lie. Brother Slovene, Brother Serb, that's what we Croats say. You want more reasons why we hate them? Then there's just this: they're double-dealing bastards. You can't trust Serbs any more than you can trust a fucking Jew. You can always rely on a Serb to let you down."

"I'm glad I asked."

He frowned. "What the fuck are you doing down here, anyway, Gunther? Captains in the SD don't normally come out into the field like this. At least not without a special action murder squad at their back. Fritzes and Fridolins like you normally prefer to leave that kind of thing to volunteer SS like me and Sergeant Oehl."

"Murder's got nothing to do with why I'm here, Captain Geiger. I'm on a special mission for the Reich Minister of Truth and Propaganda.

There's a priest in Banja Luka I have to find so I can deliver a letter to him from Dr. Goebbels."

"That gimpy little rat. What does he want with a fucking priest? He hates priests. Everyone knows that. It's why the last Pope issued an encyclical against the Nazis."

"He doesn't tell me why he's hungry, just to bring him breakfast."

"And you aren't just a little bit curious why he's sent you to find a priest in Banja Luka?"

"When I was with the SD back in Smolensk I learned that it's usually best not to question my orders."

"True."

I went back to the car and fetched some of the photographs of Father Ladislaus.

"But since you're interested . . ."

"No," said Geiger. "I don't recognize him. All priests look alike to me. But I'll tell you one thing. If he's a priest in Banja Luka, he's got his work cut out. Things were very bloody there a while back. And that's saying something in this country, believe me."

We drove on, through strangely named villages that were not much more than a couple of ruined houses. Ahead of us the sky was as gray as a dead mackerel. On either side of the road stood tall fields of ripening maize with ears that were longer than beer glasses and almost as thick, piles of still-steaming manure, plum trees, hazels heavy with nuts, then trees and more trees. A flock of starlings swooped up and down above our heads in the shape of a biblical pestilence. A herd of cows was seated so casually by a river I half expected them to have brought a picnic basket. A trio of ponies stood in the shade of an ancient oak. This was rich farming country and yet we might have been in the previous century.

We saw a trail of smoke on the horizon and caught the slight scent of cordite in the air. Then we heard the sound of artillery fire from somewhere up ahead. I slowed to a stop and we listened for a moment.

"Ours?" I asked.

Geiger looked at Oehl, who nodded and said, "Hotchkiss," and then lit a cigarette as if this was all that needed to be said.

A Hotchkiss was a French-made tank and after 1940 we had more than five hundred of them.

We drove on and into a small village close to the Bosnian border and here, in the playground of an empty school, we saw the Hotchkiss and stopped to watch as the two-man Ustaše crew fired the thirty-nine-millimeter gun of the French tank at a semi-ruined building on a distant hillside. A few Ustaše soldiers lay sleeping in a field at the edge of the playground as the tank fired over their heads, which added a touch of madness to what was happening. Others seemed to be taking bets on the marksmanship of the Hotchkiss gunner. They all looked like they were in their teens. None of them paid us the slightest attention.

"Who are they shooting at?" I asked. "Proles? Chetniks?"

Oehl said something to one of the tank's bearded crewmen and, grinning broadly, the man said one word: "*Gađanje.*"

"Target practice," said Oehl.

Geiger handed me some binoculars, and as the tank fired again I looked in horror as an inadequate French-made round whistled feebly through the clear blue sky and hit the building, smashing some of the red-and-yellow brickwork.

"It's a church," I said, horrified.

Worse was the fact that there had been people inside the church; two bodies lay in the rubble. One of the Croats cheered and began to clap and the man sitting next to him handed him a banknote as if he'd won his bet.

"Why the fuck are they using a church for target practice?"

"It must be a Serb Orthodox church," said Geiger. "They certainly wouldn't be shooting at a Catholic one."

"But a church is a church," I insisted.

Oehl laughed cruelly. "Not in Yugoslavia it isn't."

"But can't we order them to stop?"

"That wouldn't be a good idea," said Geiger. "Believe me, you wouldn't want to spoil their fun. Just because we're on their side doesn't mean they couldn't turn nasty. It's only in Zagreb and Sarajevo that your rank makes a halfpenny's worth of difference between you and them. Out here on the black earth of Slavonia it makes no difference at all. Things like the Geneva Convention and the rules of war only mean something back in Berlin. Down here they don't mean shit. The one rule when it comes to dealing with the Ustaše in the field is that you don't get between these lads and their play."

Oehl was asking one of the men on the grass verge a question. Then he turned to us and said, "He says there's a sort of hotel at the end of the street. We might get some coffee there."

Leaving the Ustaše to their amusement, we drove a short way up the street to the Hotel Sunja, where my impression of the place was severely affected by the fact that immediately in front of the hotel, and hanging from the only gas lamp in the village, was the body of a man. At least I thought it must have been a man; there were even more flies on his head than there had been on the dead horse. Geiger and Oehl paid the hanged man no attention at all, as if it were hardly unusual to see a man hanged in front of a hotel, and went inside and, after a minute or two, I followed.

It was dark in the hotel. One of the small windows had been blocked up with a piece of timber. Gradually I made out a few dust-covered tables and chairs and a bar of sorts where Geiger was banging the counter with the flat of his hand and shouting for service. Eventually a man appeared from a back room. He was wearing a black felt hat with a red carnation on the brim, a filthy white shirt, and a black waist-coat. The red carnation struck me as a ludicrous embellishment for an innkeeper to be wearing when there was a hanged man decorating his doorway.

Geiger addressed him three times and on each occasion the man shook his head before finally he said something that Geiger seemed to think was very funny; he was still laughing when he came back to the table where Oehl and I were waiting, and sat down.

"Three times I asked that Slovenian bastard for coffee," he said. "Once in Croatian, *kava*. Then in Bosnian, which is *kahva*, and the third time in Serbian, which is *kafe*. And each time he says no, right? Like you saw? By now I'm thinking he hates Croats, or hates Germans. Maybe that's his fucking brother hanging on the lamppost outside, right? So I said to him, 'What's the problem, why is there no fucking coffee? I've asked you nicely, haven't I, you bastard?' And he said, 'We've got coffee, all right, we just don't have any water with which to make it.'"

Geiger started laughing again as if this were the funniest thing he'd heard in a while; and, judging from his face, maybe it was. I'd never met a more unpredictable man. His smile seemed just as likely to presage something awful as something amusing or pleasant. I lit a cigarette and said nothing. By now I was starting to realize the price that was going to have to be paid for my night with Dalia Dresner. It was the price that Faust pays, perhaps, for a night spent with Helen of Troy.

"See if you can find something to drink, Sergeant," said Geiger. "I'll make some light in this Neanderthal's cave so we can see what we're doing." And while Oehl disappeared into the back of the hotel Geiger stood up, smashed the chair he was sitting on into many pieces, and tossed them into the fireplace alongside some old newspapers. He lit a match and tried to make a fire, but without success. He was still trying to light it when Oehl came back with some bread and cheese, and three tall stoneware bottles.

"Plum rakija," he said. "Homemade."

"You'll never get that fire started," I told Geiger. "Not without smaller sticks or some wood shavings."

Oehl opened one of the bottles and tasted it, let out a gasp and handed it to Geiger. "Fucking hell. This is good stuff. I reckon there's more alcohol in this than was inside my old grandpa on the day he died."

"Nonsense," Geiger told me, "I'll get this going in just a few seconds," and without a moment's hesitation he took a huge mouthful of spirit and then gobbed it all into the fireplace, at which point the whole wall and some of the floor—not just the fireplace—went up in a ball of fire as if a flamethrower had fired blazing oil and petrol into an enemy trench.

I jumped out of the way but not soon enough as I felt my eyebrows scorch, much to Geiger's loud amusement.

"What are you trying to do, you lunatic?" I yelled. "You'll set the whole place ablaze if you're not careful."

"I told you I'd get that fire going, didn't I?"

Oehl smiled and handed me his flask. "Here, Captain," he said, "sit down and have a drink. Welcome to Croatia. This is proper rakija. Not that milky whore's piss we were drinking earlier. Best you've got a real drink inside you when we cross the River Sava."

I took a drink to calm my nerves and stop me from punching Geiger in the mouth.

"You're right, Sergeant," he said, still laughing. "This is the good stuff. Must be eighty proof. You give an army enough of this, you could conquer the world."

"Or just burn it down," I said.

Geiger frowned. "Same thing."

Twenty-one

The River Sava was faster and bigger than I'd expected, at least thirty meters across and as brown as my leather belt. The bridge—the only one for miles that hadn't been destroyed—was a through-truss iron bridge on which a large Ustaše checkpoint had been erected, complete with two 20-millimeter Flak guns and a German-built half-track. From some of the ten or fifteen men lounging in the sun on top of the sandbags surrounding the 20-millimeters, Geiger and Oehl learned that there was a band of Bosnian Muslim partisans operating along the Prijedor Road—which was the more direct, southerly route to Banja Luka—and they strongly advised us to go east, along the road to Gradiška, before turning south.

"Bosnian Muslim partisans," I said as, taking the Ustaše's advice, we drove across and then away from the bridge toward the east. "Shouldn't they be on our side? If they're Muslims?"

"You'd think so, wouldn't you?" said Geiger. "But they're not. You'd think they hated Jews, like us. But they don't. Nothing down here is what it should be."

"Nothing," said Oehl.

"So, if we see any fucking Muslims between here and Banja Luka, we shoot first and ask questions later. Got that?"

I might have argued with them about this until both men opened the bolts on their daddies and pointed them over the side of the Mercedes. When you're a long way from home you get to know when it's best to keep your mouth shut. Even so, Geiger seemed to sense my discomfort and felt obliged to offer an explanation.

"Last week the sergeant and I were in Berlin-Babelsberg, helping to train the Handschar. A Bosnian Muslim SS Division that's supposed to be under the control of the Grand Mufti of Jerusalem. Only it's not. That pie-head couldn't control his own wind. You see, a lot of these Muslim bastards don't even want to be in the SS. And they certainly didn't want to leave their homes in Bosnia. Half of them only volunteered so they could pawn the boots and the uniform. They've gone to France now, most of them, for further training, but in our opinion they're not to be relied on. None of them are. They've got no love for Catholics, and they've got even less for the Ustaše. That mosque you mentioned. It means nothing. The Poglavnik—that's what Ante Pavelić calls himself; it's a bit like your Führer—he made that mosque just for show, really. To try to win the Muslims over and because he and Himmler thought they were pure Aryans, and because they hated Jews. But they're not and they don't. What's more, there aren't any Muslims in the Ustaše administration and there are not likely to be, either. A lot of Ustaše units have burned Muslim villages because some Muslims sided with the Serbs. The Muslims know that. Which is why a lot of them now fight with the partisans."

"Don't trust anyone who's not wearing a uniform," muttered Oehl, "that's what I say."

Geiger patted the submachine gun on his knee. "But we're ready for them if they want us to send them to heaven. That's what they believe, you see, Gunther. If they get killed in action, fighting for Allah, they are ushered immediately into God's presence. Into Paradise. A Paradise with delicious food and drink and seventy-two female companions."

"After that week in Babelsberg I'll be happy to oblige any one of them who wants his ticket upstairs," said Oehl. "And that's the truth."

"Maybe the captain here doesn't believe in heaven," said Geiger. "How about it, Gunther? Do you believe in Paradise?"

I thought for a minute. I couldn't think of a better definition of Paradise than one that involved being given a bath by Dalia Dresner in a negligee.

"Oh yes," I said. "I've been there. As a matter of fact, I was there just the other night. But there was only the one female companion. Frankly one female companion in Paradise is enough for me. And I rather think that if God does exist, he'll look like her. At least he will in my heaven."

"Lucky you," said Oehl. "Me, I've never even been in love. And it sounds like you are."

"He's a typical German," sneered Geiger. "A romantic fool if ever I heard one."

"Right now I think I'm more fool than romantic," I admitted.

"That's fucking Bosnia for you," said Oehl.

Geiger laughed. "We'll see just how romantic you are when you've been here a week. This country is enough to make anyone feel repulsive and uncaring. Just look at Sergeant Oehl. He used to write poetry, didn't you, Sergeant?"

"That's right. I did. Had a gift for it, so my schoolteachers said."

"Hard to believe, I know," said Geiger. "And it seems his gift for killing is even greater than his gift for verse."

Oehl grinned. It was the first time I'd seen him smile, and I was struck with how regular and white his teeth were. In that gray head his pink mouth and white teeth were decidedly lupine.

Going east now, with the River Sava on our left, thick woodland on our right, and the road not much more than a dirt track, our progress slowed again. You would not have thought the road to nowhere could be so flat or so straight. And yet in spite of all that I had seen, I couldn't have felt less cynical. I tried to remind myself that with each kilometer I traveled I wasn't getting farther away from Berlin and Dalia, but nearer her continuing good opinion of me, for wouldn't she be grateful when at last I found her father and gave him his long-lost daughter's letter? Even more grateful than she had been on the night before I had left Berlin to fly to Zagreb? You might even say that I was a little bit in love with her even then, for what else is love but the constant occupation of one person's mind by the thought of another?

It was very quiet now. We seemed to drift through the thick heat like a mote in a beam of bright sunshine. Everything was still. But it was not a stillness that made you feel at peace. It was a preternatural stillness, as if the forest or some hidden creatures were eyeing Hansel and Gretel hungrily. All you could hear was the sound of the car's engine and the occasional curse from one of us as the car's wheel hit another pothole. Which was probably how we ended up with a flat tire. I steered to the side of the road, although there was no other traffic we could have impeded.

"Shit," I said, switching off the engine and glancing around. There was a smell of burning wood in the air that seemed to indicate some human presence thereabouts, but through the thick curtain of trees no one was visible. And not even a breath of wind to cool things down. The leaves on the branches above our heads stayed quite motionless, as if everything around us was holding its breath. Even the birds had grown silent.

"Better make it as fast as we can," said Geiger. "This is not a good place to change a wheel."

"It's never a good place to change a wheel," I said, getting out of the car.

Instead of helping me to remove the spare from its snug place on the lid of the trunk, the other two men walked about thirty paces along

the road in opposite directions, lit a cigarette and, kneeling down on
one leg, kept careful lookout with submachine guns at the ready, leaving me to get on with changing the tire. They didn't need to say anything. It was better that one man changed the wheel and the other two
remained on watch.

I took off my shirt and set quickly to work, hoping that the sound of
the bees might help me to stay as calm as they seemed while they collected pollen. But my heart was thumping in my chest. I knew my
companions were right. This was no place to stop. You could have hidden a whole division of partisans in the trees by the road. Even now I
felt unseen eyes on the small of my bare back.

It had been a while since I'd changed a tire but I managed it in
double-quick time. I was just about to shout out that I'd finished when
I realized that both Geiger and Oehl were gone and that I was alone on
that quiet road. Where were they? In the trees? Down by the river? I
waited for a long moment, hardly daring to call out in case I alerted
any partisans to our presence. But after a while I fetched my pistol and
walked quickly down to the riverbank to wash my hands and fill a canteen. I was almost back at the car when I heard a loud burst of gunfire
up ahead. Whether it meant we were under attack I couldn't tell so I
knelt down by the car and waited. A minute passed and I decided to get
back in the car and start it up in case we needed to make a quick get-
away. After another minute I put the car into gear and crept slowly up
the road, to where the gunfire had come from.

Geiger saw me before I saw him. He and Oehl were standing in a
small forest clearing, staring at something in the bushes.

"It's all right," he said. "False alarm."

I stopped the engine and got out to look. The bodies of two men
lay untidily in a bush, like lost items of laundry drying in the sun.
Large red stains in the center of their chests seemed to be getting bigger by the second. Neither of the two was older than sixteen and both

were extraordinarily handsome, which seemed to make their acciden-
tal killing even worse. It was only gradually that I perceived them to be
identical twins. Next to their bodies a dog was whimpering with grief
and trying to lick one of the twins back to life. An ancient-looking,
single-barreled shotgun lay on the ground a few meters away.

"False alarm?" I said. "What about the gun?"

"Just hunters, I reckon. Out for their pot. Not Muslim partisans,
that's for sure."

I stared at the twins; there was nothing about their dress that distinguished them in any way from the men I'd seen working on the new
minarets in Zagreb.

"How can you tell?"

"The dog," said Oehl. "No Muslim would keep a pet dog."

"Poor bastards were in the wrong place at the wrong time. Probably
fell asleep hiding in the bush, waiting for a pigeon, and then we
happened along. I heard something in the bushes, saw the gun, and
opened fire. Simple as that."

"Pity," observed Oehl. "Nice-looking lads. Twins, I reckon."

Then while we still watched, miraculously one of the twins shifted
and groaned at the same time, as if the dog had worked some kind of
blasphemous miracle. But not for long. Some residually civilized part
of me was just about to suggest that he wasn't beyond help when Geiger killed both man and dog with another short burst from his submachine gun.

"He was just a kid," I said.

"Come on," said Geiger. "There's no time to waste with stupid sentiment. Let's get moving again before the shots bring someone to investigate. With any luck we should make Banja Luka before dusk."

Twenty-two

Occupying some high ground a couple of kilometers north of Banja Luka, the Franciscan monastery in Petrićevac was easy to see. Umbilically attached to an imposing Roman Catholic church whose twin spires soared over the surrounding countryside like the tall hats of two ancient wizards, the monastery itself—with a hip roof and two large dormer windows—was more elegant country mansion than medieval cloister. A couple of old cars were parked on the gravel driveway and the general absence of any agriculture was evidence that these were monks for whom contemplation did not involve looking at a spade or tending a vineyard. The few trees served only to obscure the little road that led up to the monastery, which meant I drove around the place several times before finding an approach to the entrance. No one—not even a chicken or a dog—came to greet us. Perhaps they already knew better than to speak to three SS men.

I sounded the horn and stepped out of the car. Geiger lit a cigarette and leaned back in his car seat to angle his debauched face in the last of the day's sunshine. I looked up at the many windows of the monastery without seeing so much as a single curious head. The place appeared to be deserted. And yet there was a vague smell of cooking in the air.

"Perhaps they're Trappists," said Geiger.

"These are Franciscans," I said. "Not Cistercians."

"What's the difference?"

"Don't ask me, but there's a difference."

"Like the SS and the SD, perhaps," offered Oehl.

"Well, whatever they are," said Geiger, "maybe they've taken a vow of silence."

"Let's hope not," I said. "Otherwise we might be here for some time." I collected the file of photographs of Father Ladislaus and walked toward the main door.

"If all else fails," said Geiger, following me, "I could fire this in the air."

I turned and saw that he was still carrying the daddy.

"For Christ's sake, leave that thing in the car."

"Believe me, when it comes to ending a vow of silence, you can't beat one of these bastards."

"Nevertheless. Please."

Geiger shook his head and handed the daddy to Oehl before following me up a short flight of limestone steps to a set of black wooden double doors with an elliptical transom. On the wall by the doors was a large iron cross and a picture of a sleeping monk holding a skull whom I took to be Saint Francis with a putto playing a lute above his head. I hauled twice on a large bellpull and at the same time peered through some light green sidelights.

"That's not my idea of a vision," said Geiger, looking at the picture. "I don't often doze off with a skull in my hand."

"I think the point might be that we're all going to fall asleep and die one day. Like that kid you shot on the road today."

"While we're here I'll light a candle for him, if it will make you feel any better."

"You do that. But it certainly won't make that boy feel any better."

Seeing movement behind the glass, I added, "We'll want to see the abbot."

The door opened to reveal a muscular-looking man wearing a brown habit with a bald head and a large gray beard. Speaking fluent Shtokavian—which Geiger had explained to me is a dialect of Croatian, Bosnian, Serbian, and Montenegrin—Geiger told him we urgently needed to see the abbot.

The monk bowed politely, asked us to accompany him, and we entered the monastery. This was an uncomfortable, hollow place of long echoes, semidarkness, hidden eyes, tangible silences, and the sour smell of baking bread. We walked the length of a long, uncarpeted corridor—which looked and felt more like a prison than a place where men lived by choice—that ran between damp walls painted two institutional tones of green and beige and past doors of plain wood that were without adornment of any sort. Bare lightbulbs hung from the plain ceiling. Another monk was sweeping the unvarnished floorboards with a rush broom, and somewhere a small bell in a clock was striking the hour. A door in some faraway chamber banged shut, but as Geiger and I marched behind the bearded monk our jackboots were the loudest thing in that building and sounded almost profane. We passed by the open door of a barely furnished refectory where forty or fifty men were silently eating bread and soup, and in a distant room a man began to loudly recite a monotonous prayer in Latin, which felt more superstitious than holy. I did not get the impression I was in a place of retreat and contemplation, more like some cold anteroom of purgatory that was a very long way from heaven. I shouldn't like to have stayed there. Just to be in that place was to feel you were already dead, or in limbo, or worse.

The monk showed us into a plain room with a few comfortable but threadbare armchairs, bowed again, and asked us to wait while he went

to fetch the abbot. He did not return. Geiger sat down and lit a cigarette. I stared out the grimy window at Sergeant Oehl, who appeared to
have gone to sleep in the backseat of the Mercedes. After a while I sat
down beside Geiger and lit one as well. If in doubt, smoke; that's the
soldier's way.

Finally the abbot came to us. He was a largish man in his sixties—
possibly older—with long gray hair, frosted eyebrows that were as big as
fur stoles, a bloodhound's face, and a boxing glove of a black beard.
Keen blue eyes regarded us with justifiable suspicion. The SS may
have been supporters of the Croatian fascist state—which itself supported the Roman Catholic Church—and yet no one who'd given his
life to serving Christ could seriously have believed that serving Adolf
Hitler was a better alternative.

He raised his hand in benediction, crossed the air above our heads,
and said, "God bless all here."

I stood up politely. Geiger stayed smoking in his armchair.

"Thank you for seeing us, Father Abbot. My name is Captain Gunther. And this is Captain Geiger."

"What can our humble order do for you gentlemen?" he asked in
impeccable German. His voice was measured and quiet and lacking
all human emotion, as if he were speaking patiently to children.

"I'm looking for a priest who I believe is one of your order," I said.
"A monk called Father Ladislaus. Also known as Antun Djurkovic. I
have an important letter for him that I have been ordered by my superiors in Berlin to deliver into his hands, personally. We have today
driven all the way from Zagreb just to be here now."

"Zagreb?" He pronounced the name of the city as if it had been
Paris or London. "It's many years since I was in Zagreb."

"It's much the same as ever," said Geiger.

"Really? I heard there was a mosque now in Zagreb. With minarets. And a muezzin who calls the faithful to prayer."

"True," said Geiger.

The Father Abbot shook his head.

"Could I trouble you for a cigarette?" he asked Geiger.

"Certainly," said Geiger.

The abbot puffed a cigarette into life happily and sat down.

"Those pistols you are carrying, gentlemen," he said, clearly enjoying his cigarette very much. "I assume they are loaded."

"There wouldn't be much point in carrying them if they weren't," said Geiger.

The Father Abbot was silent for a minute or two and then said, "Cigarettes and bullets. Both of them so small and yet so efficient. If only we spent more time using one more than the other, life would be so much less complicated, don't you think?"

"It might be less dangerous," said Geiger.

"But. To answer your question. It's true that for a while there was a man here called Father Ladislaus. And I believe his given name is Djurkovic. Happily he is no longer a member of our order and he has not lived in this monastery for several years. Even by the standards of this unhappy country, his views were extreme, to say the least. Most of us in this order practice our Catholic faith with prayer books and a cross. I'm afraid that Djurkovic believed it was necessary to practice it with bullets and bayonets, which is why I asked him to leave this monastery and also why any mail that was received for him here I ordered destroyed. Consequently he is dead, to us. Certainly his life as a priest is over.

"To the best of my knowledge he joined the Ustaše after he left us and his present whereabouts are unknown to me, as is his current occupation. I suggest that your best course would be to inquire after him at their headquarters in Banja Luka. To find the Ustaše building in the center of town you need only look for the Serbian Orthodox Cathedral of the Holy Trinity, which is currently being demolished by a punishment battalion of Jews, Serbs, and Roma using their bare hands."

"Demolished?"

"You did not mishear me, Captain. Race and religion is a vexed issue in this part of the world, to put it mildly. Following some damage that was inflicted on the cathedral by a German fighter aircraft, the Ustaše government decided to finish the job and ordered it to be destroyed, completely. And if that was not bad enough, the bishop of Banja Luka, Platon Jovanović, was taken away and murdered in cold blood. Yes, that is what I said. In this country, a Christian priest was martyred for the way he chose to worship God."

"On the journey here from Zagreb I saw some Ustaše forces shelling a Serbian Orthodox church," I said. "Why?"

The Father Abbot spread his hands as if this question was beyond his understanding.

"At Petrićevac we try to keep ourselves to ourselves and take no interest in politics. But a certain fanatical element in the former Yugoslavia regards the Serbian Orthodox Church and its pro-Russian adherents with unremitting hostility. Doubtless they are partly motivated by the fact that this monastery was itself destroyed by Ottoman Serbs during the middle of the last century. I am myself Croatian but I am not one of those who believe in an eye for eye. As Saint Francis himself reminds us, there are many ways to the Lord, and we pray for all those who are so cruelly oppressed and for their deliverance from bondage. If you have men who will exclude any of God's creatures from the shelter of compassion and pity, you will also have men who will deal likewise with their fellow men."

"Amen to that," I said.

"I'm glad you say so, Captain Gunther. You and your two friends will stay to supper, of course."

"We'd be delighted," I said.

"And if you have driven all the way from Zagreb it may be that you are also seeking a place to sleep. You are welcome to stay the night in our humble quarters. This is the true monk's duty. For the Bible reminds us to 'be not forgetful to entertain strangers: for thereby some have entertained angels unawares.' Hebrews chapter thirteen, verse two."

"I promise you, we're a very long way from being angels," I told him.

"Only God knows the truth of a man, my son," said the Father Abbot.

We stayed for supper at Petrićevac but we did not spend the night there. In spite of the Father Abbot's civilized words, there was something about the place—and him—I didn't like. The man was as forbidding as the north face of the Eiger. He had the world-weary air of a Grand Inquisitor and, in spite of what he had said, I would not have been surprised to have found him in charge of a rack or a set of thumbscrews. Then again, I just don't like priests very much. Most of them are fanatics for a different, less worldly deity than Adolf Hitler but they are fanatics nonetheless.

As soon as we had finished eating we climbed back into the Mercedes and set off for Banja Luka and, as the Father Abbot had promised, we quickly found the Ustaše headquarters building we were looking for. It was a large, cream-colored, square building with Ottoman features—all Corinthian pillars and arched windows—that resembled a theater or an opera house. An Ustaše flag hung limply above a main door that was busy with men wearing black uniforms and even blacker mustaches. On the other side of the main road older men wearing flat caps and carpet slippers were playing chess in a little park that was what you might have found on a summer's evening in almost any provincial European town. But it's not every provincial town that has a punishment battalion of its own citizens tasked with the destruction of a cathedral. At this particular hell on earth an iron cloud of barbedwire fence had been erected around what remained of the cathedral's walls to ensure that the poor people detailed to their slave labor did not escape. Work had not yet ceased for the day, however, and from behind piles of loose rubble the emaciated faces of walking caryatids, drooping under their yellow brick burdens, stared hopelessly back at me as I stepped out of the car. Horrified fascination held me rooted to the spot, and I don't know why but I snatched off my cap as if part of me recognized something about this heap of stones that was still a church. Or perhaps it was the sight of so much human suffering that made me do it—respect for people who were obviously not long for this world. But I did not stay very long to look at what was being done to one church in the name of another in this miserable, godforsaken place; an Ustaše guard advancing on me with a rifle in his hands persuaded me to turn away and go about my business. But man's inhumanity to man had long been a matter of small surprise to me and I might as easily have turned away because I had become callous. I have to confess all I cared about now was finding Father Ladislaus, giving him his daughter's letter, and then getting away from the Independent State of Croatia as quickly as possible.

"I wouldn't get too upset about that if I were you," said Geiger, following me inside the headquarters building. "If you ever saw what their side has done to ours in this war you wouldn't pity them for a minute."

"I expect you're right," I said. "But all the same I do pity them. I rather think that without pity, we might as well be animals."

"It beats me how you ever joined the SD."

"It's a mystery to me, too."

In the headquarters building, which was full of polished marble and crystal chandeliers, I presented my credentials to a sullen Ustaše intelligence officer whose intelligence did not run to speaking any German and who seemed to be more interested in picking his nose and finishing the elaborate doodle on his blotter than in listening to me. Looking at the drawing's Gordian knot complexity, upside down, it seemed like a perfect image for the impossible-to-unravel politics of Yugoslavia.

Having secured transport for himself and Sergeant Oehl, and established the latest whereabouts of the SS Prinz Eugen Division captain, Geiger now came to my aid and further established that the man formerly known as Father Ladislaus was now better known as Colonel Dragan.

"It's a sort of joke, I think," he said. "Colonel Dragan. It means the dear colonel. The joke being that from what this fellow says, the colonel is much feared around these parts and quite notorious. He's currently to be found at a place called Jasenovac, about a hundred kilometers back up the road we were just on. It's a place where they make bricks."

"Bricks? My God, I'd have thought they had plenty of those outside."

"You'd certainly think so."

"How does a Franciscan monk get to be a Ustaše colonel?" I wondered aloud.

Geiger shrugged. "There's only one way in this country," he said. "By being an efficient killer of Serbs."

"Ask him what else he knows about this Colonel Dragan," I said.

Geiger spoke again and gradually the Ustaše officer became more animated.

"This man you're looking for, Gunther, is a great hero," said Geiger, offering me a simultaneous translation. "Adored even and something of a living legend in Bosnia-Herzegovina. He was sick with fever for a while—apparently, the marshes at Jasenovac are full of mosquitoes—and it was feared he would die. But lots of good Catholics prayed to God and lit many candles, so now he is back to full health again and, if anything, stronger than before and more feared than ever. But even the Ustaše fear the colonel and for good reason. Because he can't be reasoned with. That's what his men say. Once his mind is made up there's no changing it. His mind is impregnable—that's what this fellow says. But that you can't judge a man like Colonel Dragan the way you would judge an ordinary man. He's anything but ordinary. Perhaps that's because he used to be a priest, like Father Tomislav, who is also attached to the Ustaše troops in Jasenovac. It may be that it is God who gives the colonel the strength to do what he does. Which is to be a man who can do such terrible things. Perhaps it's his special relationship with God that makes him strong. That makes him so resolute and a source of inspiration to his men. To all Ustaše who would see this country free from the threat of Communism and the Jews and Muslims, and the peasant stupidities of the Serbian Orthodox Church."

"And I thought the Nazis had the monopoly on this kind of goat's shit."

Geiger opened his cigarette case and offered me one. Then, taking me by the arm we went outside for a smoke. The summer sun was low behind the clouds now and the sky over Banja Luka was the color of blood. At the Serbian Orthodox cathedral, demolition work had stopped for the day but not the cruelty. I could hear a woman crying. Why had I come to this infernal place?

"You know, it seems to me that I've heard about this fellow, Colonel Dragan, on my first tour of duty down here. About both these men. Your Father Ladislaus and this Father Tomislav. I heard some pretty terrible things. The sort of things that could only happen here in Yugoslavia. This country is full of hate—the Father Abbot was right about that."

"What did you hear, Geiger? What kind of things?"

"Terrible things. Something about two monks who were working with the Ustaše. Just a name, really. They used to call them Ante Pavelić's twin priests of death. That's right. The priests of death. I heard they killed a lot of people. Not just in battle. And not just partisans—people who need killing—but women and children, too."

"Because they were Serbs?"

"Because they were Serbs. Look, Gunther, it's none of my business what you do. But in this country, you're a fish out of water. In Berlin you probably know what you're doing, but down here, wearing that uniform, you're just another target. My advice to you is to stay away from this Colonel Dragan, and from Jasenovac. Leave the minister's letter here with this fellow, drive back to Zagreb, and get on the next plane home."

"I've thought about that. Don't think I haven't. But I've a personal reason for making sure the letter gets into his hands. Besides, the minister won't be too pleased with me if I tell him I could have met this fellow and then funked it. He might not sign my expenses, and then where will I be?"

"Alive. Look, I'm not kidding you. This colonel is a real monster. The fact is that even the SS don't go to Jasenovac if we can possibly avoid it. The place used to be a brickworks, before the war, but now it's a concentration camp. For Serbs. I believe there were some Jews in Jasenovac, at the beginning of the war, but they're all dead now. Murdered by the Ustaše."

After Smolensk, I wondered how bad things could be in Jasenovac. And after all, I was only delivering a letter. Surely I could do that in next to no time. Besides, I'd met the devil before; in fact I was pretty certain I used to work for him. Heydrich was my best guess as to what the devil was really like. And I could not conceive that Croatian mass murderers could be any worse than German mass murderers like him, or Arthur Nebe. But what was I going to tell Dalia Dresner? That her father was a monster? I didn't think she was going to be pleased to hear something like that.

"Don't worry about me," I said. "I'm tougher than I look."

"No, you look tough enough. That's not the problem. The problem is that I've seen inside your soul, Gunther. There's still a sliver of decency left in there. There's your fucking problem. What does Nietzsche say? A man might think he can stare into the abyss without falling in but sometimes the abyss stares back. Sometimes the abyss exerts a strange effect on your sense of balance. Take it from one who knows."

I shrugged. "I'm still going to Jasenovac. Besides, like you said, it's on the way back to Zagreb."

"I like you, Gunther," said Geiger. "I don't know why, but I do. Maybe it's that sliver of decency in you. I envy you that. Me, I'm up to my elbows in blood. But you. You're different. I don't know how you've managed it in the SD but you have and I admire that. So, you give me no alternative but to go to Jasenovac with you. Think about it. You don't speak Croatian. Or Bosnian-Serb. Besides, suppose you run into some Proles? Or some hostile musclemen?"

Musclemen was what Oehl was in the habit of calling Muslims.

"I told you. These bastards like to make you suck your own dick. You need me and the sergeant riding shotgun on the road with you. Besides, we've got another car now. With a driver. So you'll be even safer than you were before."

I had to admit he had a point.

"What about rejoining your SS unit?" I said.

Geiger shrugged. "There's plenty of time to do that. Besides, now we're here in Banja Luka, I know a good place to eat and to stay. Tonight you're my guest. And we'll leave first thing in the morning."

Twenty-three

I t was a beautiful warm day and we made excellent progress back along the narrow road to Jasenovac. I'd managed to persuade myself that once there I would be halfway back to Zagreb and then Germany, which would somehow make everything all right. You can stand to see almost anything provided you know it isn't going to be for very long. Reeking of alcohol, Geiger dozed in the passenger seat beside me, while Oehl and another SS man followed in the car behind. A couple of times we saw Ustaše trucks heading the other way but the men inside them paid us little regard. Once or twice we heard the sound of small-arms fire in the distance and as a precaution stopped for a while and had a smoke. But if it was Proles, we didn't see them. Our new companion, a Croatian SS corporal called Schwörer, was a boy not much older than the one Geiger had shot the previous day. His hair looked like fine gold thread and his complexion was as fair as a schoolgirl's. He didn't say much. It wasn't a place for conversation. He tried to match us smoke for smoke but ended up puking at the side of the road after turning himself green with tobacco, which Geiger thought was very funny. We set off again and, after a couple of hours, we slowed to cross a wooden bridge near the confluence of the Sava and Una rivers. Underneath the light mist that hung above the water like the breath of some foul underwater creature, something caught my eye. I stopped the car and got out to take a look and quickly lit a cigarette when I heard the whine of a mosquito. I never did take to being bitten by anything very much, even if it was female. For a brief moment I thought the object in the water was someone swimming. But as I was about to discover, we were a long way from Wannsee and the Havel and anything as innocent as swimming.

"What is it?" asked Geiger.

"I'm not sure."

I pointed at the river and waited for the slow, mud-brown water to bring the object nearer but I already had a strong suspicion about what it was. It was a woman's body, still wearing a floral dress, and it floated right under the bridge we were standing on—close enough to see that her hands were tied behind her back, her eyes had been gouged out, and a large piece of her head was missing. A second body and then a third were in the water not far behind her and these were women, too, also mutilated. Schwörer stared impassively at these bodies and I got the strong impression that despite his innocent-looking face he was already familiar with such sights as this.

"This river goes right through Jasenovac before it gets here," said Geiger.

"On its way to Hades, perhaps. And meaning you think that's where they were killed. In Jasenovac."

"Probably."

"Shit."

"I did warn you it wasn't a place for us. I believe there used to be an SS office at Jasenovac until they closed it a year ago, after the last Jews there were killed. That's the official reason. No more Jews, no more German interest. What the UNS do with Serbs is their own affair. But from what I heard, the five Germans who had stayed on there couldn't take it anymore and left, without permission. So it must have been bad. As bad as this, I guess."

"UNS?"

"The Ustaše Supervisory Service. The special police force that guards these camps. And that reminds me, Gunther. When we get to the brickworks, it would be very advisable if you kept your very obvious disgust under control. It's not just Serbs, Jews, and Roma who disappear in this part of the world. It's anyone who the UNS decide they've taken a dislike to. And that could easily stretch to include me and you. For all I know, those five Germans who were stationed there didn't disappear at all, but were murdered. You see, these UNS bastards are killing not for ideological reasons like me and the sergeant but because they like to kill and because they take pleasure in cruelty, and you don't want to piss them off with any of your Berlin airs and graces. Me, I might enjoy the company of a civilized man like you occasionally, but these boys don't think like that. Out here the better angels of our nature simply don't exist. Out here there's just the beast, and the beast is insatiable. Back in Banja Luka that intelligence officer said something about your evil friend Colonel Dragan that I failed to mention. A couple of times he referred to him as Maestrovich, and once he even called him the maestro, which, as I'm sure you know, is an honorific title of respect. Well, you can imagine the sort of thing that commands respect down here. And it isn't playing the bloody cello. So, please try to remember that when you deliver your fucking letter."

I nodded silently.

"Serb or not, I can't see the point of killing a woman unless she's a Prole rifle slut, and she's had a pop at you," said Oehl. "And even then, not until you've had some fun with her."

"You mean raped her," I said.

"It's not rape," said Oehl. "I've never fucked a rifle slut who didn't want me to fuck her. Really. Even a Prole will try and get you to fuck her if she thinks she's going to be shot. That's not rape. They want you to fuck them. Sometimes they want you to fuck them even when they know you're going to kill them immediately afterward. It's like they want to die with some life still wriggling inside of them, if you know what I mean. But these girls don't look like they've even been touched."

Reflecting that the legal niceties of what constitutes consent were likely to be lost on a man like Oehl, I lit a cigarette with the butt of the other. "Camps," I said. "You said camps, Geiger."

"The brickworks at Jasenovac is just the largest of at least five or six concentration camps in this area. But there could be more. Out here, in this swamp, who knows? I heard tell that they've got a special camp just for Roma where all the usual cruelties have been refined to a hellish level." He shrugged. "But you hear all kinds of things in this country. Not all of them can be true."

"I don't think the Ustaše can teach the SS very much when it comes to cruelty," I said. "Not after what I saw in Smolensk."

"Don't you now? From what I hear, the SS in Poland is killing Jews with poison gas now, for humane reasons." Geiger laughed grimly. "No one gets gassed in Yugoslavia. As you can see for yourself."

While we were standing there, at least nine or ten bodies floated by like driftwood. Most had their heads bashed in or their throats cut.

"They smash their heads in with big mallets," said Geiger. "Like they were knocking in tent pegs. So much for humanity."

I sighed and took a double drag on my cigarette and shook my head. "To save bullets, I suppose," I heard myself say.

"No," said Geiger. "I think the UNS just likes cracking Serb skulls."

"Why do they throw them in the river like that?" I asked, as if I actually expected an answer that would count as even vaguely reasonable. And the fact was, it wasn't really a question at all, but an observation born of an infinite sadness and the absolute certainty that I didn't belong here. I took off my cap, tossed it into the car, and rubbed my head furiously with the flat of my hand as if that might enable me to understand something. It didn't.

"Saves the effort of burying them," said Schwörer. "I expect they think the fish will tidy things up. They're right about that, too. There's asp in this river that grow to be at least a meter long. I've fished a bit so I know. Had a friend once who caught an asp in the Sava that was twelve kilos. You mark my words, in a month or two you won't ever know those bodies were here." It was as much as he'd said since leaving Banja Luka.

"Why didn't you join the Ustaše?" I asked him.

"Me, sir? I'm not Croatian. I'm ethnic German, I am. And damned proud of it."

In the light of what I'd already seen, I wasn't feeling proud of being human let alone German so I let that one go.

We got back into the cars and drove through a thick, dark forest and onto a large marshy plain, where we caught our first sight of the camp, and soon after that we stopped at a checkpoint and were obliged to explain our business to the guards. In the distance, running parallel with the river, we could see a train heading for the camp. The guard picked up a telephone, spoke a few words, and then waved us on.

"You're in luck," said Geiger. "It seems that Colonel Dragan is here. He wasn't yesterday." He laughed. "Apparently he was in Zagreb."

"That certainly sounds like my sort of luck," I said. "I wouldn't have missed this for the world."

Finally we arrived at the main entrance to what described itself as Camp III. It was easy to see why this was a brickworks; the whole place was enclosed by an enormous brick wall about three meters high, perfectly built, and hundreds of meters in circumference. There was an entrance arch also made of bricks, with a big sign and, on top, an Ustaše shield featuring a *U* and a Croatian red-and-white flag. Inside the arch was a curiously ornate wrought-iron coaching lamp. Leaving Oehl and Schwörer and the two cars, Geiger and I walked up to the entrance. The Croatian guard escorted us through and it was only now that I perceived the true size of the camp, which was spread across a huge flat plain. The humid, swampy air was thick with the corrupt smell of death and the infernal whine of mosquitoes and I breathed it with more than a little distaste. When the very air contains human decay, it catches on the throat. Running parallel to the Sava River to the east was a single railway track where even now the black steam train we'd seen earlier was making its slow and laborious way to the end of the line.

In front of us to the northwest were the camp buildings dominated by a single-story barracks that was fifty or sixty meters long; behind these were several tall chimneys and some watchtowers. In the distance we could just about see a lake where even now hundreds of prisoners were at work retrieving clay to make bricks. Everything seemed preternaturally calm, but already my eyes had taken in the body hanging from a nail on a telegraph pole, and then a proper gallows on which were hanging two more bodies. But all that was nothing compared with the sight that awaited us in a little picket-fenced garden out front of the brick-built villa to which we were now escorted. Where someone in Germany might have chosen to display some plants in terra-cotta pots, a rockery, or even a series of ceramic garden gnomes, here there was a virtual palisade of severed human heads. As I mounted the steps to the front door I counted at least fifteen. The guard went to fetch the colonel while, waiting for him inside the villa, we discovered the true horror of exactly how the heads in the garden had been obtained. Surrounding the near mandatory portrait of Mussolini on the neatly papered wall were framed photographs of decapitations—men and women, presumably Serbs, having their heads cut off with knives, axes, and, in one particularly nauseating picture, a two-man crosscut saw. This was bad enough but it was the smiling faces on the large team of Ustaše men inflicting these cruelties that disturbed me most of all.

These pictures made Goya's disasters of war look like a set of illustrated place mats. I sat down on a poorly sprung sofa and stared unhappily at the toes of my boots.

"Try to remember what I told you," said Geiger. "You need to keep your mouth shut if we're going to get out of here alive. This is none of our fucking business. None of our fucking business. Just bear that in mind. Here. Have a drink."

Geiger produced a silver flask. It was filled with rakija from the Hotel Sunja. Gratefully I took a bite of it and enjoyed letting the stuff burn the coating off my insides; it was the drink I deserved—a drink from the ninth circle of hell—and just to swallow it was enough to leave you silent for several minutes, as if some infernal imp had poured liquid fire down your throat.

We waited half an hour. I tried not to look at the photographs on the wall but my eyes kept on being dragged back there. What was it like to kneel in front of a man who was about to cut your head off with a knife? I could hardly imagine a worse fate than that.

"Where is this bastard anyway?" I asked.

"The guard said he was on the other side of the river. In Donja Gradina. A little island called the place of sighs." He shrugged. "It sounds nice. Almost relaxing, really. But I have the awful feeling it's nothing of the sort."

Finally we heard voices and a tall, dark-haired man wearing a smart gray uniform, black boots, and a Sam Browne entered the room.

"I'm Colonel Dragan," he said. "I understand that you wanted to see me."

He spoke perfect German, with a near-Austrian accent, like most ethnic Germans. It was easy to see where Dalia had got her good looks. Colonel Dragan was unsmiling but film-star handsome. His tunic lapels and forage cap had a gold letter *U* on them but I could have wished that he'd had a letter *U* branded on his forehead. After the war, I hoped that someone else would think of this and take it upon themselves to mark him out for ostracism and then death.

Geiger and I stood and introduced ourselves; he was, after all, a colonel.

"Might I ask if you were previously known as Father Ladislaus, at the Petrićevac Monastery in Banja Luka, and before that, as Antun Djurkovic?"

"It's been a while since anyone called me that," said the colonel. "But yes. I'm he."

"Then," I said, "I have a letter to you from your daughter," and opening my briefcase, I gave him Dalia's letter.

He glanced at the handwritten name and address on the back of the envelope with some incredulity, as if it had been posted on Venus. He even lifted it to his nose and sniffed it, suspiciously.

"My daughter? You say you know my daughter, Dragica?"

"I know her. I'm sure her letter will explain any questions you might have."

"The last time I saw her she was but a child," he said. "She must be a young woman now."

"She is," I said. "A very beautiful one."

"But how is it in the middle of the war that Dragica has two errand boys from the SS? Is she so very important? Frau Hitler, perhaps? The last I heard she was living in Switzerland. In Zurich, I think. Or are the Swiss no longer neutral? Has the temptation to invade that ridiculous place become too much for your Hitler?"

"She's a movie star in Germany," I told him. "At UFA-Babelsberg in Berlin. As well as being the minister of Truth and Propaganda, Dr. Goebbels is head of the film studio. It's on his direct authority that I'm here. I'm to wait until you've read that letter and see if there's a reply."

"I had no idea. She was always beautiful. Like her mother. But a movie star, you say?"

I nodded. I thought it best not to mention that his former wife was dead. That was best left to Dalia's letter.

"I was a boy the last time I went to the cinema," said the colonel. "Must have been. It was a silent film." He frowned. "How did you find me?"

"Your old Father Abbot at Petrićevac in Banja Luka. That was your last known address, apparently."

"Father Marko? I can't believe that someone hasn't killed that man. He's much too outspoken for his own good. Even for a Catholic priest. There are others who were less fortunate than him."

"I rather liked him," I lied.

"He pointed us in the direction of the Ustaše headquarters in the town," explained Geiger. "And there they told us you were most likely here. In Jasenovac. Making bricks."

"Forgive me, gentlemen, you've come a long way. Would you like some lunch, perhaps? Some beer? Some rakija? Some bread and sausage?"

I was about to decline when Geiger answered. "That would be very kind of you, Colonel Dragan."

The colonel went off to order his men to bring us something and, presumably, to read his letter. I sat on the sofa again. And when, another twenty minutes later, the food and drink arrived, Geiger fell on it hungrily. I watched him eat with something close to contempt but I said nothing. I didn't need to. My face must have looked like a letter from Émile Zola.

"Not eating?" asked Geiger. He grinned horribly as he ate.

"Strangely enough I don't seem to have brought my appetite with me."

"A soldier learns not to pay much attention to appetite. You eat when there's food, hungry or not. But as it happens, I am hungry. And nothing gets in the way of me and my grub." With his mouth full of bread and sausage, he got up to inspect the photographs. "Not even those heads and this little wall of Ustaše heroes. Never seen a man having his head sawn off before. You know, lumberjack-style. I've seen some terrible things in this war. Done one or two, as well. But I've never seen anything like that."

He turned and stared out the window.

"Why don't you ask Colonel Dragan if you can have a demonstration?"

"You know, I just might do that, Gunther. Should be easy enough. I don't suppose those people who were on the train have anything better to do than provide me with some amusement. After all, I imagine they're all going to die anyway."

"You mean there are people in those wagons?"

I went to the window and looked out. As Geiger had said, the goods wagons were now open and several hundred people were climbing down from the train and were being herded toward the river and a barge that was already coming to ferry them to their most likely fate.

"Serbs?" I said.

"Probably. Like I said, all the Jews in this part of the world are dead. But there are still plenty of Serbs left to kill."

From his tone it was hard to determine if Geiger approved of what was happening at Jasenovac or not.

I picked up the bottle of rakija the Ustaše guard had brought and helped myself to a brimful glass. It wasn't nearly as strong as the stuff in Geiger's hip flask but that hardly mattered.

"The sooner we're away from this godforsaken place, the better," I said.

"I tend to agree with you, Gunther. Although I rather think God might disagree. It's not God who forsakes us but man who forsakes

God. His presence would be more obvious here, of course, if instead of a high wall to imprison and then torture human beings, they'd built a great cathedral. As a celebration of God's glory and the dignity of man. Just as other men like these men—perhaps their great-great-grandfathers—created a fine cathedral from bricks in Zagreb. On this occasion, however, they built this place to mark where and what man has been. To testify to what we all have within us—that capacity for death and destruction which all men possess. You see, for every Sistine Chapel there are a hundred places like this one, Gunther. And let me ask you this: Truly, is one any less valid as an expression of human endeavor than the other? No, of course not. Personally, I think God's never far away, even from this shameful horror. Perhaps, ultimately, that's what makes horror truly horrible. The knowledge that God sees it all, and does nothing."

A couple of days later, with Colonel Dragan's letter to his daughter, Dalia, in my tunic pocket, and Geiger's cynical words still ringing in my ears, I was back at the Esplanade in Zagreb and, with nothing better to do with myself until I could fly gratefully back to Berlin, I became a German tourist. I might just as easily have stayed in my room at the Esplanade and drunk myself into oblivion with the flask of rakija I had brought back with me. It's what I felt like doing. I would have done it, too, except for the fear that once I'd started to drink like that I would never stop. Among so many others who were intoxicated with cruelty, who would have noticed one man intoxicated with drink? So, I begged the loan of a map from the concierge and went to explore the city.

In Zagreb it seemed there were more Roman Catholic churches squeezed into one small space than in the Vatican telephone directory. One of these, St. Mark's, had a fairy-story roof that was seemingly made of thousands of Haribo candies. On the façade of every other

building were Atlantes, as if the place were weighed down with its own
history. It was. Between them, the Habsburgs and the Roman Catholic
Church had crushed all the tomorrows out of this place so that all that
remained was the past and, for most people, a very uncertain future. It
was the kind of place you expected to find a Dr. Frankenstein listed in
the telephone book, although the last time the scrofulous citizenry had
rioted it wasn't to burn some mad scientist's castle but the shops and
homes of innocent Serbs. Most of the swivel-eyed locals still looked as
if they kept a burning torch and a pitchfork behind the kitchen door. I
walked along uneven cobbled streets lined with mustard-colored
houses, up and down vertiginous wooden stairways and past steep garden terraces with urban vineyards, through open squares the size of
Russian steppes with public buildings, many of these a forgotten shade
of yellow, like old icing sugar. Approaching the old city gate, I heard a
low, human sound, and when I turned the corner I found myself in a
vaulted archway where a hundred or so hawk-faced women and potbel-
lied unshaven men stood mumbling their adoration of a shrine to the
Virgin Mary, which occupied a place behind a baroque iron fence. But
to me it looked and sounded like a satanic mass. Later on I saw a gang
of loud young men approaching. It gave me pause for thought when I
saw they were all dressed in black. I thought they were Ustaše thugs
until I saw their collars and realized they were all priests; and then I
asked myself, "What's the difference?" After what I had seen at Jasenovac, Catholicism didn't seem like a faith so much as a kind of curse.
Fascism and Nazism were bad enough but this more ancient cult
seemed almost as wicked.

I walked along to the city's cathedral and found other German soldiers already there seeking respite against the heat of the day, or perhaps, like me, they were looking for something spiritual. As he came in
through the door, one soldier crossed himself reverently and genu-
flected in the direction of the altar. A pinch-faced nun told him sternly

to roll down his shirtsleeves out of respect for God, and meekly he obeyed, as if God actually cared about such observance in a country where, less than a hundred kilometers away, his priests were butchering women and children. Having delivered her rebuke, the nun took herself off into a chapel that was a little Gethsemane of twinkling candles and set about cleaning Christ on the cross with a long feather duster. He didn't bat an eyelid. I expect it made a welcome change from a Roman spear in his side. I wondered what either one of them— Christ, or the nun—would have made of what I'd seen at Jasenovac. For all their pagan cruelty, I doubt the Romans could have devised anything more bloodthirsty than the scenes I'd seen in that swamp. Then again, maybe the Ustaše belonged in a much older tradition of persecution than I had imagined.

Before we'd left the malarial insanity of Jasenovac, Colonel Dragan had proudly shown me his special glove—more of a leather mitt, really, and properly used for cutting wheat sheaves—with a razor-sharp, curving blade sewn onto the underside so that he might cut throats with greater speed and efficiency. With this *Srbosjek*—his Serb cutter— the unspeakable colonel had boasted to us of having cut more than thirteen hundred Serbian throats in a single day.

But I could restrain myself no longer and to this I replied: "That such a beautiful woman as Dragica could have a father like you simply beggars belief."

At which point Geiger hustled me back to the car and we drove quickly away before the mad Croatian colonel could say or do anything.

Now, as I sat there in the cathedral, the confessional door opened and a young officer of the SS stepped out of the booth, and I wondered to what it was he had just confessed. Murder, perhaps? And could absolution ever be given for what we Germans had set into motion in that country? The Roman Catholics probably thought it could. That was the belief they lived by. Me, I rather doubted it. Later on, I walked to a jewel of a park, lay down, and stared numbly at the shiny grass and thought the ants and the bees were more deserving of God's mercy than me. For was I not German? And had not we Germans put dreadful monsters like the Ustaše and Colonel Dragan into power? Then again, maybe Geiger was right after all. Maybe all men were somehow at fault. The Belgians had done some dreadful things in the Congo, as had the British in India and Australia. The Spanish had little to feel proud of in the way they had raped South America. Would the Armenians ever forgive the Turks? And the Russians—well, you could hardly leave them out of the evil equation, either. How many millions of deaths had Lenin and Stalin ordered? I had seen the evidence of that at Katyn. Were the Germans so very different from everyone else? And would an apology ever be enough? Only time would tell. One day in the future the dead would speak from the past about what was being done here in the present.

Twenty-four

Goebbels listened carefully to what I was saying.

It was just the two of us, in his vast office at the ministry again. Given who he was, it was hard to imagine me talking and him just listening, but that's how it was. The monkey instructing the organ-grinder. I wondered if anyone had ever told him of some of the terrible things that were being done in Germany's name. While I seemed to be talking only about what was happening in the former Yugoslavia, I was also indirectly referring to what was happening on our Eastern Front. I certainly wouldn't and couldn't have mentioned this in any more of a direct way. And Goebbels was much too intelligent not to realize this. If anyone knew when words could mean more than they appeared to mean, it was him. With a PhD from Heidelberg, Goebbels was perhaps the most intelligent Nazi I'd ever met; certainly more intelligent than Heydrich, and that was saying something. I suppose he must have let me talk like this for ten or fifteen minutes without interruption. The head of the film studio had given me this supporting role, and now he was obliged to see and hear what I'd made of it. But finally he sat forward on the sofa and lifted one of his delicate, womanly hands to say something:

"There's no doubt that some terrible things are being done in this war, on both sides. Let's be clear about that. Last night there was an exceptionally heavy raid on Hamburg with most serious consequences for the civilian population. Five hundred British planes attacked and bombed the city indiscriminately. For the moment no one can estimate how many German women and children were killed. But I can tell you it's hundreds, perhaps thousands. Not only that, but almost two hundred thousand people have just been made homeless, and I don't know how we're going to solve that problem. Altona was especially hard hit. That's a real catastrophe, just as what's happening in Croatia is a catastrophe, too. I'll admit that. But this stupid historic enmity between Slavs is a complete sideshow to the real war. Germany's war. So our first thoughts have to be about what's happening here, at home. If our people ever lose their will to resist, I don't have to tell you what will happen. The most serious crisis this country has ever faced. The Russians will do to this country and to our people what the Ustaše are doing now in Croatia. There can be no doubt about that. I know you don't want that, Gunther. No one does."

As Goebbels moved his head in an avian sort of way I realized that with his black hair and beaky nose he reminded me most of a carrion crow.

"I agree with you," he continued. "This fellow Colonel Dragan sounds like an absolute monster. A murderous beast from the deepest pit in hell. I must confess I had no idea that something like this might happen. He used to be a priest, after all. You don't expect priests to become murderers, do you? Although of course Stalin trained for the priesthood before becoming a bank robber. No, if I'd known that such a thing was even possible, I'd never have sent you down there. And I can see you've had an awful time of it, Gunther. I'm sorry about that. But you're back home now and the present question is, what are we going to tell poor Dalia? After all, we—you, probably—will have to tell her something. But what? Like most actresses, she's sensitive. Temperamental. Emotional. Well, you know that already. By the way, she spoke very highly of you. Very highly indeed. You seem to have made quite an impression on her. Considering yours was such a short acquaintance."

I lit a cigarette and wondered how much Goebbels knew about what had happened between his star and me. I didn't for a minute think that Dalia would have told him that we'd slept together; but he was smart, and even a suspicion on his part that there was something between us would have been disastrous for me. Just because there weren't any thugs in the ministry didn't mean Goebbels couldn't pick up the phone to Prinz Albrechtstrasse and have me in a Gestapo cell in the time it took for him to unlace his surgical boot.

"I thought that you wanted me to impress her, sir. Someone with special skills, you said. A detective with a proven reputation, you said."

"Did I say that?"

"You're not someone who's in the habit of being vague about what he says. Or not remembering it. I think we both know that the lady needs a lot of very careful handling. I had the idea that you wanted me to make her believe that I wasn't just some ministry stooge sent by you to smooth things over so you could get her back to work on this picture. That I really was a proper detective and that I stood a genuine chance of tracing this fellow. Which I did. Against considerable odds, and no small danger to myself, I might add."

"The garden was actually decorated with human heads?"

"Like it was landscaped by Salome and Bluebeard. Just to be there made my neck itch."

"I don't think there can be any possibility of inviting such a man here to Berlin. That's the substance of his letter to her, apparently. He wants to come and visit her at the studio."

"You've read it?"

"I had it translated from Croat. Yes, I've read it. Colonel Dragan says he wants to come and visit her as soon as possible. Well, you can

hardly blame a man for wanting to see his estranged daughter, I suppose. Especially when she's a famous movie actress."

I pulled a face.

"What?" he asked.

"The man is a homicidal maniac. I don't think that I would welcome the news that my father was the most unspeakable war criminal
who takes pleasure in cutting hundreds of throats in one day. Let alone
him turning up on my doorstep."

"No," said Goebbels. "Neither would I. There's also the publicity
value to consider. If it got out that her father was a mass murderer, it
might easily affect her career as an actress, not to mention the current
picture. Germans like their leading ladies to appear virtuous, spotless,
pure. I know I do. They don't want them to have an Igor figure in the
top tower. All of which persuades me that perhaps we shouldn't give
her his letter, either."

"That's up to you. Fortunately I don't have to make that decision.
About his letter or what to tell her."

"Nevertheless, since you're going to see her again—that's the professional thing to do, isn't it? That's what you would do if you were a
private detective? You would go and speak to the client?"

"Yes. I suppose so."

"Then in view of that, your input would be greatly appreciated. We
have to put our heads together and figure out what to do, for her sake.
How we're going to tell her what we're going to tell her without further
jeopardizing this movie."

"All right, then. Try this hat on for size. I went to the monastery in
Banja Luka to look for Antun Djurkovic, also known as Father Ladislaus. Dalia had already sent some letters there before. But they hadn't
been answered. So how about we say they hadn't been answered
because he's dead? The Father Abbot I spoke to said as much. I don't

know what kind of priest he was but Father Ladislaus is now Colonel Dragan. And it might be kinder if she never knew that."

"So, Captain Gunther, your advice is that we lie to the woman, about her own father?" Goebbels laughed. "In case you had forgotten, this is the Ministry of Truth."

I hadn't forgotten, of course; in his white summer suit Goebbels almost looked like someone you could trust; but given the number of lies cooked up in that place I didn't think one more—one meant kindly—could possibly make a difference in the scheme of things. All the same I wasn't about to tell him that. On the whole it's not wise to remind the devil that he's the devil, especially when we were getting on so well.

"And you think you can say this to Dalia without her guessing that it is a lie? It's not everyone who can lie and get away with it. Once you lie you have to stick with it. You have to keep up the lie, even at the risk of looking ridiculous. Just as often you have to lie again to protect the one you told the first time. Lies are like rabbits. One lie gives birth to another. Believe me, Gunther, I know what I'm talking about. And she's a smart woman. Are you sure you can convince her? Are you inventive enough?"

"Can I be honest, sir?"

"You can try."

"The fact is, I've been lying my head off for the last ten years."

Goebbels laughed. "I see what you mean. Since the Nazis came to power. That's what you mean, isn't it?"

"It was easier to stay alive that way. At least it was for someone who used to be a social democrat. But then you must know that. It's why you picked me for this job, after all. Because I'm not a Nazi. Like you said, it's all in my file."

He nodded. "You know, we still have too many philistines in the

Party. I must say, I should prefer to have you on board as a colleague
than some of the others I have to meet with. A little late in the day,
perhaps, but I'm going to get you a membership in the National Socialist Party. Believe me, it will be to your advantage. And you can leave it
all to me. I'm still the Berlin Gauleiter. You won't have to do anything.
Except sign the papers."

"Thank you, sir."

Goebbels laughed again. "Your gratitude overwhelms me. I like
you, Gunther. I don't know why, but I do."

"And I like her, sir," I said, quickly changing the subject. "I like her
a lot. Enough to want to protect her from something like this. Because
the alternative is that I tell her the truth and she has to live with that
knowledge for the rest of her life. There's no telling what that will do to
a person."

For a moment I wondered what Goebbels's several children would
think about their father's crimes when, one day, the Nazis were history.

Goebbels nodded. "You're right. No one should have to go through
life bearing that kind of cross. The lie would certainly be kinder in this
case. And it might be hard for her to play the leading role in this film
knowing her father was a monster like this man you met." He thought
for a moment. "She's in Zurich right now. With her useless fucking
husband. You'll have to go there and speak to her in person."

"What's he like?"

"Dr. Obrenović? Rich. Very rich. Old. At least—much older than
her. He's everything you might expect of a Swiss lawyer, apart from the
fact that he's vaguely related to the former king of Serbia." Goebbels
snapped his fingers. "You know?"

"I know. Alexander the First. The one who got himself assassinated
in Marseille."

"No, actually that was another Alexander. Alexander of Yugoslavia.
I'm talking about Alexander of Serbia. But as it happens, he also

managed to get himself assassinated, by some army officers in 1903. What a people they are for assassinations, eh? Like something out of Italy under the Borgias."

"You want me to go to Zurich?"

"Well, I can hardly go myself. I think the Swiss government might have something to say about that. Besides, it might be a nice break for you after Zagreb. Zurich has some fine hotels. That's one thing the Swiss do very well. In all other respects they're as much of a bloody nuisance as the Serbs and the Croats. But for the Swiss, we could have offered Mussolini and Kesselring our immediate support in the present crisis without a second thought. As it is, we'll have to send troops the long way round through Austria and France."

"I've never been to Switzerland," I said. "But it's got to be better than Croatia."

"I'll speak to the Foreign Ministry," said Goebbels. "Have them fix it up for you to go there immediately. No, wait a minute. There's none of them who strike me as particularly competent. I met the new under-secretary the other day—a man named Steengracht von Moyland. Another damned aristocrat. Utterly mediocre. No, I'll speak to Walter Schellenberg, in SD Foreign Intelligence. After all, you're SD, too. He's smart. He'll know the best way to get you into the country. And the best hotel, too, probably. I'll say one thing for Schellenberg, he's a well-traveled man, considering we're at war."

"Might be nice, at that," I said.

"There's just one problem, as I see it." Goebbels grinned. "You're going to have to get married."

I heard myself swallow. "Married? I don't think I understand."

"Oh, it's quite simple. The only way our government can make absolutely sure that any citizen will come back here from somewhere like Switzerland is if they have family in Germany. Which you don't. At least not yet."

"I don't think that's about to change very soon," I said.

"Don't say that, Gunther. Take it from me, the love of a sweet woman is one of the great pleasures of life."

"Perhaps that's true but there's no woman who's sweet enough to take me on right now."

Goebbels stood up and almost disappeared as he limped behind his desk, where he began to turn the pages of a file. "What about this woman you've been seeing?" He pulled a page out of the folder and came around his desk again. "The schoolteacher at the Fichte Gymnasium on Emser Strasse. Kirsten Handlöser."

"What about her?"

"Couldn't you marry her? She's single."

"There's the small matter of her not being in love with me. And my not being in love with her. Frankly, sir, I don't want to be married."

"Perhaps. But there's this to consider. More importantly. For her, anyway. Which is that you'd be doing her a favor."

"How's that?"

"Quite apart from the fact that as a woman it's her patriotic duty to be married and to have children—like my own wife, Magda—you'd also be keeping her out of trouble."

I stiffened. Whatever was coming around the mountain clearly was going to be something I didn't like. I was beginning to understand that in real life Goebbels operated in the same schizophrenic way he did in his public speaking: seductive and persuasive one minute, intimidating and coercive the next.

"What kind of trouble?" I asked.

Goebbels uttered a harsh sort of laugh.

"There is only one kind of trouble in Germany, Gunther. The serious kind. It seems that a week or two ago some SD men turned up at her school, to conduct a sort of survey. They were asking questions about why none of the girls in her school have chosen to be evacuated from Berlin to a KLV camp. To escape the bombing. The KLVs haven't been as popular as might reasonably have been supposed. Anyway, it seems Fräulein Handlöser was less than complimentary about the sort of boys that are to be found in these camps. She even suggested that any decent parent would avoid sending their girls to a KLV at all costs. I'm afraid that she's going to be questioned again about her whole general attitude. There are some who might regard what she had to say about the Hitler Youth as antisocial behavior, under the 1939 Decree Against National Pests. Under the War Offenders Decree, what she said might even count as undermining the war effort. She could easily find herself doing six months at Brandenburg Prison, to say nothing of losing her job at the school. Of course, it would certainly count in her favor if an SD man and a Party member—albeit a new Party member— were to marry her. Yes, even if the SD man were you, Gunther. It would demonstrate your good faith in her. Especially as I myself would certainly send a letter to the SD to tell them of my confidence in you, as well as to bless your union. Which would count as a reference for you both. And thereby remove any possibility of a prison sentence."

"Suppose she doesn't want to get married? Suppose she sees six months in prison as the lesser of two evils?"

"Did I say six months? It could even be worse than that. The war isn't going so well right now. It might just be that some judge like Roland Freisler decides to make an example of her. He's become rather severe of late. You heard what happened to those idiotic students in Munich. And to Max Sievers."

I nodded.

"So, it's up to you to convince her, isn't it?"

I chose my next words carefully. "It's kind of you to take an interest in my personal affairs. But there's just one problem as far as I can see it. And it's perhaps one reason why I haven't married before. At the risk of a prosecution for antisocial remarks myself, there's this stupid thing called the Bride School, which all SS and SD brides are obliged to attend, to prevent the men from marrying unsuitable women. Quite apart from the fact that unsuitable women are the only ones I'm ever really interested in, there's the fact that the women attending the school have to study childcare, sewing, obedience in marriage, and, at the end of it, there's a certificate issued without which the marriage is deemed invalid. Something like that, anyway. Apparently all that takes several months. I can't see how I can get married in sufficient time to go to Switzerland as quickly as you want."

Goebbels folded his arms and looked thoughtful, the way I'd seen him do when making a speech on the newsreels.

"Yes, I remember now. More of Himmler's mad ideas about blood and matrimony. As always, he makes the master race sound like a matter of getting the right badges in the Boy Scouts. Look, I'll speak to Schellenberg about this, too. I'm sure there's a way around this nonsense." He grinned. "Besides, Dalia's husband—Dr. Obrenović—will feel a lot more comfortable about a handsome fellow like you meeting with his wife knowing that you're a happily married man. And so will I. Yes. I'll make a respectable fellow of you yet, Captain Gunther. Nothing is impossible when you put your mind to it." He laughed. "Nothing is impossible. Try to remember that when you're in Zurich. Just make sure you bring Dalia back. Even if you have to kidnap her."

Twenty-five

The next day I caught the S-Bahn to Berlin West to see Walter Schellenberg. He sat behind his neatly arranged desk, smiling his sardonic smile, stroking his own smooth face or fiddling with the shiny Iron Cross on his breast pocket, and looking like a clever school-boy who'd sneaked in the back door of the SD building on Berkaer-strasse, tried on a discarded uniform and discovered that, while it was very obviously a size too large, no one was about to challenge the general's cauliflower on his lapels. Certainly not in Germany, where it was never much of a handicap to look like you were physically unsuited to high office. Goebbels was the living proof of that and no one looked more ridiculous in military uniform than him, except perhaps Fat Her-mann, although that had more to do with his white peacock uniforms than the man himself. Schellenberg wasn't a lot bigger than Goebbels but as befits a Foreign Intelligence chief, perhaps, much more quietly spoken than the Reich Minister, and handsome with it. Now that I knew him a little better I could see how he was probably just as cynical as Heydrich except that there was something in his character—perhaps it was French upbringing, Schellenberg having spent much of his early life in Luxembourg—that made you call it pragmatism.

Major Eggen was there, too, because of his extensive knowledge of

Switzerland, which must certainly have included the best jewelry stores in Zurich and Geneva, given the presence of a handsome gold Rolex on his wrist. Altogether bigger than the general, Eggen had the look of a successful surgeon or a masseur—the one who treated both Himmler and Schellenberg, perhaps. The two men made a token effort not to enjoy my predicament, but it was no good. They were soon laughing and making jokes at my expense. This was fine by me; I always seemed to have a seemingly endless amount of acute discomfort to go around.

"I've heard of an arranged marriage," Schellenberg said. "I've even heard of a marriage of convenience. But I don't think I've ever heard of a marriage of inconvenience. Have you, Hans?"

"I don't think so, sir."

"You won't say that when you see her," I said, trying to make the best of it. "She's actually quite a beauty. You can ask General Nebe. He's met the girl. Besides, I've every confidence she'll turn me down, and then I won't be able to go to Switzerland on this fool's errand."

"Oh, please don't say that," said Schellenberg. "It turns out that I have an important mission for you in Switzerland, myself."

"You know, Gunther, it's normal for a man to take his bride along on the honeymoon," said Eggen.

"But a lot cheaper if you don't," added Schellenberg. "And in this case, probably advisable. Besides, I've arranged everything. On my personal assurance that there's a mission vital to the SD in Switzerland, the Reichsführer has agreed to waive the usual rigorous requirements for an SD man's marriage. So you're allowed to travel to a neutral country. Just as soon as you are married you're to pick up a new Mercedes from the factory in Genshagen and deliver it to the château of Paul Meyer-Schwertenbach on the Swiss-German border."

"It's a gift," said Eggen. "A sweetener in an important-export contract."

"From Export Drives GMBH, I suppose," I said. "To the Swiss Wood Syndicate, whatever that is."

"What do you know about those two companies?" Eggen's tone had a hard edge.

"Not much. I suspect Captain Meyer must have mentioned those names to me in passing, last summer. You know? When I was keeping him amused after the IKPK conference."

"Of course," said Eggen. "Yes, it must have been then."

"You can deliver the car after you've met with this actress in Zurich," said Schellenberg. "The Reich Minister's mission as a movie-maker must come first. I'm sure we're all dying to see the film version of *Siebenkäs*. But Meyer's very much looking forward to meeting you again. And to talking to you some more about your detective work."

"I'm looking forward to that myself. I'd better make sure I bring my favorite cocktail shaker and my little white dog along for the ride. Not to mention Gunther's famous monograph on shirtfront beer stains. I'm considered something of an expert on that subject."

"The château of Wolfsberg is in Ermatingen," explained Eggen without even acknowledging my attempt at humor. "That's about an hour's drive northeast of Zurich. It's a charming place. Quite delightful. In Zurich you'll stay at the Baur au Lac Hotel. It's the best in the city. You should be very comfortable there. Now then: you'll drive down from Genshagen and cross the border at Fort Reuenthal, in the Aargau canton. You'll be met there by Sergeant Bleiker, a detective from the Zurich City Police, who'll give you your visa and then escort you across the border. You'll be wearing civilian clothes, of course. And please don't take a gun. Not even a small one. The Swiss don't like us carrying guns. In Zurich you'll be met at your hotel by Police Inspector Albert Weisendanger, who will be in charge of your security; he's your first point of contact if you have any problems."

"Yes, I'd keep away from the German Embassy in Zurich if I were you," said Schellenberg. "The foreign office staff there is more or less useless. The rest of them are Gestapo thugs who have nothing better to do than stick their noses in where they're not wanted. But I wouldn't be surprised if you find them on your tail. Them and the Swiss Security Service."

"I thought Meyer worked for Swiss security," I said.

"No, he works for Swiss Army Intelligence. His boss, a fellow called Masson, likes to operate independently of the Swiss Security Service. Doesn't trust them. A bit like us here in Department Six, and the Abwehr." He paused for a moment and then added, with a smile, "And the Gestapo. And the SS. And the people in the Party Chancellery office. Not forgetting Kaltenbrunner. We certainly don't trust him."

Eggen laughed. "You can't trust anyone these days."

"What a coincidence," I said. "That's exactly what I hear, too."

"In fact," said Schellenberg, "the whole of Switzerland is a hotbed of intrigue. A spies' paradise. The Swiss may look harmless enough but they're not to be underestimated. Especially their intelligence services. And let's not forget that as a neutral country there are also the Americans, the Russians, and the British secret services to take into account. They are all highly effective. The Americans in particular. There's a new man in charge. Name of Allen Dulles. He's the OSS station chief in Bern, but he likes to get around. Academic type but highly effective. And he's very fond of luxury hotels when he's not at his home in Herrengasse."

"Yes, Switzerland is fascinating," said Eggen. "Like a very complex watch mechanism. On the surface, everything is quite simple and easy to understand. It's only when you look inside the case that you see how it's beyond any normal understanding. You'll have lots of money, of course. The Ministry of Economic Affairs will be sharing your expenses with the Ministry of Truth. So I want plenty of receipts, Gunther."

"The best hotels. A beautiful actress. A new Mercedes. Plenty of money and no guns. I don't mind telling you, after Yugoslavia, it all sounds delightful."

"Yes, Yugoslavia," said Schellenberg. "You were going to tell me about what happened down there."

But before I could say a word he'd launched into an anecdote that seemed to reveal the younger man's almost naïve ambition—I don't suppose he could have been much more than thirty.

"Three years ago," he said, "I had this idea that not having a doctorate in law might hold me back in my career in the SD. Anyway, I was thinking of trying for my own doctorate in law at the university here in Berlin, and I considered doing my dissertation on the government in Yugoslavia."

"It's lucky you didn't pursue that," I said. "Because there is no government in Yugoslavia. At least none that any German lawyer would recognize by that name." I told him—with several examples—how I thought the country was in total chaos. "The place is one giant killing zone. Like something from the Thirty Years' War."

"Surely it can't be as gloomy as that," Eggen said.

"Actually, I think the situation's probably a lot worse than gloomy. And I certainly don't know what else to compare it to when you have Croatian priests cutting the throats of Serbian children. Babies murdered by the hundreds. For the sheer hell of it."

"But why?" asked Schellenberg. "What's the reason for such ferocity?"

"If you ask me," I said, "it's partly our fault. They've learned from our example in the east. But historically and culturally, it's the fault of the Roman Catholic Church and Italian fascists."

Schellenberg, who had recently returned from Italy to report to Himmler on the deteriorating fortunes of Benito Mussolini, confessed he was feeling gloomy about the Italians, too:

"Italy presents an awful warning for Germany," he said. "After twenty years of fascism, the country that produced Michelangelo, Leonardo da Vinci, and the Renaissance is in a state of total collapse. In Venice even the gondolas aren't working. Imagine that. I tried to buy an inlaid musical box for my wife and couldn't find one. Switzerland looks so much better off, as you'll see for yourself. Five hundred years of democracy and neutrality have worked very well for them. And they'll work for us, too. The country might have no natural resources other than water, but it manages to produce a lot more than just cuckoo clocks. Everything works in Switzerland. The same things that used to work in Germany, I might add. The trains, the roads, the banks. And no one in Switzerland lies awake at night and worries about what's going to happen when Ivan shows up at the front door. They worry about us invading them, it's true. But between you and me, I see it as of vital importance to keep them out of the war. So does Himmler. So does everyone, except Hitler. He still entertains hopes of bringing them into the war on our side."

We were all silent for a moment after that mention of the leader's name.

"What did you choose in the end, Herr General?" I asked politely, to break the silence. "For your doctorate."

"Oh, I decided not to bother with getting one. Originally I thought I should have a doctorate in law because half of the senior officers in the SD have one. Men like Ohlendorf, Jost, Pohl. Even some of the officers in my own department, like Martin Sandberger. Then we invaded Russia and several of those officers went off to command SD forces tasked with murdering Jews in Ukraine and Poland. And I thought, what's the point in having a law doctorate if, like Sandberger, you just end up murdering fifteen thousand Jews and communists in Estonia? What's the point of a doctorate in law if that's where it takes you?"

Eggen looked at me. "You're not a lawyer, too, are you, Gunther?"

"No," I said. "I already have a good pair of gloves at home to keep my hands warm in winter."

Eggen frowned.

"What I mean is, you won't catch me with my hands in someone else's pockets. It's a joke."

They both smiled without much amusement. Then again, they were both lawyers.

Twenty-six

The next morning I got up early, left my SD uniform at home, and went shopping.

Before the war, Rochstrasse, a few blocks away from the Alex, had been filled with Jews. I still remembered the several bakers' shops there and the delicious smell of babka, bagels, and bialys that used to fill the street. As a young beat copper I'd often gone into one of those shops for breakfast, or for a quick snack and a chat; they loved to talk, those bakers, and sometimes I think that's where I learned my sense of humor. What I wouldn't have given for a fresh bialy now—like a bagel, except that the hole was filled with caramelized onions and zucchini. There was still an early morning market on Rochstrasse where fruits and vegetables were sold, but I wasn't looking for oranges any more than I was looking for bialys. Not that I would have found any oranges there, either: these days, root vegetables were pretty much all there was to be had, even at five in the morning. I was looking for something that was almost as hard to find as a bialy or an orange. I was looking for good quality jewelery.

On Münzstrasse, at number 11, was a six-story redbrick building with a bay window at the corner of every floor. It was only a year or two since the ground-floor shop had been occupied by a Jewish-owned jewelry store. That was now closed, of course, and boarded up, but on the top floor was a man who I knew helped some Jews who were living underground somewhere in Berlin, and from whom it was possible to buy bits of decent jewelry at good prices that might help a family to survive. This man wasn't Jewish himself but an ex-communist who'd spent some time in Dachau and had learned the hard way how to hate the Nazis. Which was how I knew him, of course. His name was Manfred Buch.

After an exchange of pleasantries I gave him a cigarette and he showed me a small velvet tray of rings and let me take my time.

"Have you asked her yet?"

"No."

"Then if you don't make a sale with this little lady, you bring the *Schmuck* back to me. No questions asked."

"Thanks, Manny."

"For you this is no problem. Look, the fact is, I can sell this stuff three times over. Most of the *Schmuck* you'll find in the fancy shops like Margraf is poor quality and expensive. What you're looking at here is the last of the good stuff. At least for now. Most quality merchandise has been sold already or is being held back until after the winter, when it's generally assumed things are going to get much worse."

"From what I've heard that's a fair assessment."

"And of course you can be quite sure that whatever you buy is going to help people who are in real need. Not profiteers and gangsters. That is, if you can tell the difference between them and our beloved leaders."

"What about this one?"

"That's a nice band. Good quality gold. Eighteen carat. Nice and thick. She'll love you for the rest of her life if you give her that one. And if she doesn't, you can always get her drunk and while she's asleep, put a little soap on her finger and I guarantee you'll sell it for twice what I'm asking."

"There's an inscription inside. In Hebrew script."

"Is she anti-Semitic?"

"No."

"Then you should think of that as a guarantee of absolute quality. No Jew would put a cheap ring on her finger."

"Yes, but what does it mean?"

Manfred took the ring, put a glass to his eye, and scrutinized the inscription.

"It's from the book of Jeremiah. It says, 'For I know the thoughts that I think toward you.'"

It seemed appropriate.

That night I arranged to meet Kirsten at Kempinski's on the Kurfürstendamm. Unusually, in spite of being Aryanized and there being little on the menu, the place still managed to feel like a decent restaurant. I'd decided to ask her to marry me without mentioning anything of what Goebbels had told me; she was a nice girl and I figured she deserved to think that I was asking her for all the right reasons, instead of a desire to keep her out of the hands of the Gestapo. I was just about to put the question to her when the rise and fall of air-raid warning sirens sent us running to the nearest shelter; and it was down there I finally got around to proposing marriage.

"I know I'm not exactly a catch," I said as the walls vibrated around us and dust fell off the ceiling into our hair. "You could almost certainly find someone younger. With better prospects. But I'm honest. As far as that goes, these days. And it's just possible that I'll make you a good husband. Because I love you, Kirsten. I love you very much."

I threw that bit about love in because, generally speaking, it's what a girl wants to hear when a man asks her to marry him. But it wasn't true and we both knew it. I'm a much better liar than I am an actor.

"I assume that your proposal has something to do with this," she said.

She opened her handbag and showed me a buff-colored envelope she'd received that very morning. It had no stamp, just a postmark, and was quite obviously from the Gestapo.

I took the letter out of the envelope, noted the address on Burg-strasse, and nodded. I knew the address, of course. It was part of the old Berlin stock exchange. And the official letter was a formal summons to explain her "antisocial" comments to a commissar Hartmut Zander. My only worry now was that she might think I'd engineered the whole thing in order to persuade her to marry me. It was the kind of dirty trick that many Gestapo men were wont to pull, just to get a peek at a nice girl's underwear.

"It's very sweet of you, Bernie," she said, "but you don't have to do this. I couldn't let you."

"Listen, you have to trust me on this, angel, I knew nothing about that letter. But now that I've seen it, here's what I think. You're in a tight spot. There's no doubt about it. I'd come with you but I'm not allowed. You're not even allowed a lawyer present at the interview. But marry me and I think I can make all this go away. In fact I'm certain of it. After that you don't ever have to see me again if you don't want to. I'll forget about the ring I have in my pocket and the loud evening I had planned after we got married. We'll just call it a marriage of convenience and leave it at that. It'll be like a business arrangement. We'll meet for a coffee in a year's time and have a good laugh about it. You can divorce me quietly and everything will be like it was before."

"Why are you doing this, Bernie?"

"Let's say that lately my own lack of nobility has begun to get me down. Yes, let's say that. I have an urgent need to do something good for someone else. In recent weeks I've seen one too many bad things, and the plain fact of the matter is I like you a lot, Kirsten, and I don't want to see anything bad happen to you. It's as simple as that, really."

"Could something bad happen to me?"

"If what you told me is true, then they'll give you a rough ride. Oh, not that rough. Just a verbal battering. And you even might talk your way out of it. Some do. Maybe you're the type to give as good as you get. Don't admit anything. That's the best way to handle these Gestapo commissars. Then again it's equally possible you'll go to pieces, in which case you might end up in prison for a short spell. Say, six months. Ordinarily that's not so bad. But lately things have got much tougher in the cement. Even on the outside food is short. In Brandenburg it's several hundred calories less than that. Skinny little thing like you might find that hard going. At the very least you might lose your job. And jobs are difficult to get when you lose them on account of the Gestapo. It might be awkward getting another."

She nodded quietly. "The ring, Bernie. Could I see it, please?"

"Sure." I felt inside my vest pocket, polished it on my trouser leg, and then handed it over.

She looked at it for a moment, smiled a charming sort of smile, and then put it carefully on the finger of her left hand.

The next day we were married and, during the simple ceremony, Kirsten moved the ring onto the finger of her right hand, as if she really meant it, like a proper German wife. It was a small but important gesture and one that did not go unnoticed by me.

Twenty-seven

The S-Bahn train to Genshagen, about an hour south of Berlin, was packed with car workers and factory managers returning there from visiting relations, and officials from the German Labor Front, the SS, and the Luftwaffe. Eavesdropping on their cozy conversations, it was impossible to tell them apart, and this caused me to reflect on the long and close relationship the Nazis had enjoyed with Daimler-Benz AG. Jakob Werlin, one of the company's directors, had been a personal friend of Hitler's since before the 1923 putsch and, according to the *Munich Post*, on the leader's release from Landsberg Prison in 1924, it was Werlin who collected him from the gates and drove him away in a new Mercedes-Benz that he subsequently gave to Hitler. So perhaps it was Daimler-Benz's support for Hitler that had helped persuade the Nazis to eliminate taxes on German automobiles soon after they formed a government—a nice payback for all their support. But it wasn't just cars that Daimler-Benz supplied to the Nazis. There was a huge number of airplane engines for Germany's fighters and bombers, as well; the company was crucial to the country's war effort. One day I hoped some thoughtful historian would point out the close connection between the Mercedes-Benz motor car and Germany's favorite dictator and that the Lord would find a way to pay these bastards back for their help in bringing the Nazis to power and keeping them there.

One of the company directors, Max Wolf, met me at the train and drove me straight to the factory. He was in his late fifties—one of those very stiff, mustachioed Prussian Lutherans from Schwiebus, in Poland—and a man for whom the Daimler-Benz company was a way of life. The little gold Party badge glittering like a tiny satrap's diadem on the lapel of his tailor-made suit seemed to indicate that his particular way of life had worked out well for him so far. He couldn't have seemed more smug if he'd been a bull walrus at the end of a successful mating season.

"The director of the factory, Herr Karl Mueller, is a personal friend of General Schellenberg," he informed me. "Herr Mueller has instructed me to provide you with all the cooperation you need in the completion of your orders, Captain."

"That's awfully kind of him, and you, Herr Wolf."

"As you probably know, we're mainly aircraft engines here at Genshagen," he explained in the car. "The Mercedes-Benz automobile is made at Sindelfingen, near Stuttgart. That's where General Schellenberg's car is now. I'm to give you the export paperwork for that vehicle and then lend you another vehicle that you can drive south to Sindelfingen, where you can collect the new one, to drive to Switzerland."

I winced a little; whenever people use the word "vehicle" it always reminds me of pompous traffic policemen, which, I now realized, was what Wolf most reminded me of.

We drove into a factory compound that was as big as a decent-sized town and surrounded with the very latest 88-millimeter antiaircraft guns. These were obviously effective as there wasn't a lot of bomb damage to be seen. I also noticed the presence of several female SS troopers. Wolf saw me paying them attention.

"Given the makeup of the workforce, the SS guards are an unfortunate necessity, I'm afraid. Half of our twelve thousand car workers are foreign, many of them slave laborers—Jews, mostly, and all of them women—from the concentration camps of Sachsenhausen and Ravensbrück nearby. But they're well fed and quite happy with the conditions here, I think."

"I suppose that's why the guards are carrying whips," I said. "To keep them smiling through the day."

"We don't tolerate any ill treatment of our slave laborers," said Wolf without a trace of embarrassment. "Our German workers wouldn't stand for it. Well, you can guess what these fellows are like. Most of them are beefsteak Nazis—you know, brown on the outside and red in the middle. Our Jews work hard, and I've no complaints about any of them. Frankly, they're the best workers anyone could wish for. Sure, sometimes we catch our German workers giving the Jews extra bread and sharing their coffee but that's not so easy to stop in a factory this size."

"Easy enough, I'd have thought. You could give the Jewish workers more to eat at dinnertime."

Wolf smiled uncomfortably and shook his head. "Oh no. That's really not for me to say. The policy on slave labor is set in Berlin by Reich Minister Speer and enforced by the SS. I just do what I'm told. It's as much as I can do to supply enough interpreters to make sure the assembly line continues to move efficiently. We have Poles, Russians, French, Hungarians, Norwegians, Czechs, and Dutch working here— even a few English, I'm told. They're the laziest, you know, along with the French. Your best worker is a Russian Jewess. She'll work all day and half the night if you tell her. We're producing nearly four thousand aircraft engines a year at this plant alone. So we must be getting something right."

"You must feel very proud," I observed.

"Oh, we are. We are. If you'd care to, you're very welcome to join us for lunch in the executive dining room. You'll find we have all sorts. Labor officials, officers like yourself—"

I thought about that for about a millisecond: I was hungry, all right, but after Jasenovac I couldn't have thought of anything worse than eating lunch with men like Max Wolf, especially when German workers were sneaking bread to Jewish slave laborers. The food would have stuck in my throat.

"It's kind of you, sir, but I'd best get on my way as quickly as possible. I've a long drive ahead of me."

"That you have," he said.

He drove me straight to where my car was parked. It was a 190, with a camouflaged paint job, exactly the same as the one I'd driven in Croatia. He handed me the keys and the paperwork. I expect he was keen to be rid of me. But not as keen as I was to be rid of him.

"You'll want to take the road to Munich, of course," said Wolf. "From there you can pick up the road to Stuttgart. It looks longer on the map to do it that way, but of course it isn't. Thanks to the leader we have autobahns—the best roads in the world. In a Mercedes-Benz you can be in Munich in less than six hours from Berlin, with another two hours to Stuttgart. If you try to drive straight to Stuttgart from here it will take you at least eleven or twelve hours. Believe me, I've done it both ways and I know what I'm talking about."

"Thanks. I appreciate the advice."

And I did. I made good time on the autobahn. It just goes to show that even the most loathsome sort of pen-pushing nine-till-five Nazi can sometimes put you on the right road to exactly where you want to go.

After the roads in Croatia this one was a dream to drive on. I was almost enjoying the journey. All advertising was banned on the autobahn, which made the roads a pleasant escape from the seemingly endless propaganda posters that were such a blight in the cities. My only concern was that driving at high speed on a uniformly straight road with little to look at I might succumb to the highway-hypnosis that Fritz Todt—before Speer, Germany's leading engineer, and the man who had done most to build these autobahns—had warned about, although frankly the speed limit was much lower than of old; to save on fuel it was just eighty kilometers an hour. But with two lanes on either side of an oak-planted median strip, the autobahn still ran as straight as an aircraft runway; and this was why, here and there, sections of these medians had been converted to auxiliary airstrips, with the aircraft that sometimes used them hidden in nearby woodlands. The other traffic was mostly trucks carrying tank parts and motorboats, although once I drove past a whole U-boat, which struck me as a little surreal.

On Schellenberg's instructions I wasn't wearing a uniform and, because all nonmilitary traffic was allowed on the autobahns only in exceptional circumstances, the Orpo pulled me over a couple of times to check my papers, which at least broke the monotony of the journey. About halfway to Munich I stopped at an Alpine-style filling station to fill up, get some coffee, and stretch my legs. But then I was straight back on the road, as I was hoping to reach the Swiss border before dark.

Somewhere on the journey south I thought about my new bride and our unconsummated marriage, although that particular fact had seemed of lesser importance. After the ceremony, it had felt to me as if I would have been taking advantage of Kirsten in those circumstances, especially since these circumstances certainly included a strong intention on my part to sleep with the lady from Zagreb again, either at my hotel in Zurich or at her matrimonial home in Küsnacht. But mostly I just felt glad to have kept Kirsten out of the Gestapo's hands. Goebbels had given me his word that she wouldn't be bothered by the SD again, and while I was reluctant to trust him, I had little alternative. Of course, being alone in a car like that for hours on end means you're inside your own skull a lot and after a while you're seeing marks on a white wall that maybe aren't really there; I had the crazy idea that maybe Goebbels knew I'd slept with Dalia and that my being forced to marry Kirsten was his way of paying me back—twice over if he chose not to keep his word after all.

Another crazy idea I had was that I was followed all the way from Genshagen. Except that it wasn't crazy at all. With so little automobile traffic, it's not easy following someone unnoticed on the autobahn. Another Mercedes 190 in your rearview mirror, matching your speed for six or seven hundred kilometers, is hard to miss. Schellenberg had warned me I might get followed by the Gestapo in Switzerland. I suppose I wasn't very surprised that they decided to follow me in Germany, too.

I arrived at the factory in Sindelfingen just before six in the evening. My replacement car—another 190, with a civilian paint job, black— was awaiting collection and I was soon on my way again, although with less pleasure than before. I was running the engine in, of course, but that shouldn't have made the new car seem heavier and more sluggish than its predecessor. And soon after leaving Sindelfingen I stopped the car and opened the trunk just to make sure I wasn't carrying anything illegal. I found nothing, but this still worried me all the way until Fort Reuenthal on the southern side of the river Rhine, where Swiss customs searched the car more thoroughly and, much to my relief, they found nothing illegal, either.

The fort wasn't called that lightly. There were bunkers, tank barricades, infantry barracks, and artillery emplacements, including two 75-millimeter rapid-firing antitank guns. Seeing all of this for the first time, I realized just how seriously the Swiss took the matter of defending their borders against any foreign potential aggressor, namely Germany.

Sergeant Bleiker, a detective from the Zurich City Police, met me with my visa and some Swiss money, which I bought with the gold reichsmarks that Eggen had given me: the Swiss didn't like taking our paper money and, even with Hitler's head on them, preferred the hundred-mark coins. Gold has a jingle when you count your money, I suppose. The Swiss detective was in his forties, a tall quiet man with a small mustache. He wore a brown flannel suit and a brown felt hat with a wide brim. He had a firm handshake and looked a sporty type. But gregarious he was not. I've had longer conversations with a parrot.

"That's quite a fortress you've got back there," I said when at last we were on the road.

"Don't tell me," he said. "Tell your Nazi friends in Germany."

"When was it built? It looks modern."

"Nineteen thirty-nine. Just in time for the beginning of the war. Otherwise, who knows what might have happened?"

"Right. And by the way, for the record, now that I'm in Switzerland, I don't have any Nazi friends in Germany."

"I certainly hope that doesn't mean you're going to claim asylum here, Captain Gunther. Because the boat is full. And I'd hate you to waste your time trying to stay and then get into trouble with your own people when we had to send you home again."

"No, no. I just got married. So I have to go back. In fact, they insisted on it. The marriage, that is. You've heard of a shotgun wedding. Mine involved the threat of a falling ax."

"Congratulations."

"So you can relax, Sergeant. Our leader, Adolf Hitler, doesn't like it when his citizens choose not to come home."

Sergeant Bleiker sniffed. "I couldn't even tell you the name of our leader. Or anything about him."

He didn't talk much after that except to issue directions from the passenger seat, and this happened all the way to Zurich, for which I was grateful, as most of the roads were small and windy.

We drove through the Talstrasse entrance of the Hotel Baur au Lac after dark. Bleiker oversaw my check-in, bowed gravely, and told me that Inspector Weisendanger would come to the hotel and meet me for breakfast first thing in the morning.

Exhausted after my long drive, I ate some supper and went to bed. But not before I had telephoned the lady from Zagreb.

Twenty-eight

In the morning I got up very early and took a short walk along the shore of Lake Zurich and watched a passenger ferry landing bespectacled, quiet men wearing even quieter suits as they disembarked and headed to work in banks and offices. I wasn't sure I envied them their steady lives but there was a pleasing predictability about Swiss life in general. The water tasted sweet and the air tasted fresh, although that might only have been because Berlin's air and water were always full of bomb dust and a permanent smell of cordite. Sometimes, after a heavy night from the RAF, Berlin's famous air smelled like a sulfur mine.

I wouldn't say I loved Zurich but it's hard not to like a city that isn't being bombed day and night and where no one is going to arrest you if you make a joke about your country's leader. Not that there was anyone in Zurich who could have told you the name of the Swiss prime minister any more than there was someone who knew a joke. With government by direct democracy, the idea of having a leader simply was not important. You have to love a country like that, especially when you're a German. There was also something very reassuring about a city with so many banks, where beer and sausage still tasted like beer and sausage, where the last person who made a speech was John Calvin, where even the best-looking women didn't care enough about their appearances not to wear glasses. Another reason to feel reassured was that I had been booked into one of the best hotels in Europe. That's something else the Swiss do very well: hotels.

My room overlooked an attractive canal off the Limmat, the river that ran through Zurich and into the lake. The Baur au Lac was a little like the Adlon in Berlin in that everyone famous seemed to have stayed there, including Richard Wagner, the Kaiser, and more recently, Thomas Mann. According to Hans Eggen, the Baron von Mannerheim, Finland's head of state, was now in residence and, having recently signed an armistice with the Soviet Union after several years of war, he was trying to negotiate his country's independence of Germany, too, much to Hitler's fury.

In spite of the war, the atmosphere of the hotel remained elegant. Champagne was still in supply on the recently constructed rooftop terrace. Afternoon tea was served in the pavilion, and dinner dances took place regularly. But food was predictably scarce. The front lawn of the hotel, which had extended all the way down to the lakeside, was now a large potato field. These potatoes were protected with rolls of barbed wire that had once served to protect the hotel itself, although from whom was not obvious as it was impossible to imagine the luxury-loving German High Command treating Zurich's finest hotel with anything but the utmost respect. There was also an air-raid shelter in case Switzerland's neutrality was suddenly curtailed by the German Luftwaffe.

Inspector Weisendanger joined me in the restaurant for breakfast. He presented me with a business card using two hands, as if he had been giving me the keys to the city, and refused, ridiculously, to let it go until he had seen that I had read what was printed on it.

"My address and telephone number are here," he said gravely. "And I am at your disposal for the duration of your stay in Zurich."

Like Bleiker, he spoke German very well—at least to me—but

when he spoke to other Swiss he used a dialect of yodeling German called Alemannic that would have been difficult to comprehend at the best of times but, through a gray-black mustache that, joined to his sideburns, was as big as a tart's feather boa, seemed quite inscrutable.

"I get it. I'm to use this card if I get into trouble, right? I can get a taxi to this address. Or find a telephone and dial this number. This is going to be really useful."

"I'm not sure how things are with policemen in Berlin," he said. "But it's usually best to assume that any Swiss policeman you'll meet does not have a sense of humor."

"Thanks for the tip, Inspector. I'll try to remember that."

"Please do. My superiors require me to meet with you at this hotel once a day to make sure that you are in compliance with the terms of your visa. Should you fail to attend this meeting, you will be subject to immediate arrest and deportation back to Germany. Is this clear to you, Captain Gunther?"

"Does that mean we're having breakfast again tomorrow?"

"I'm afraid so. Shall we say eight o'clock?"

"I think nine would suit me better. I thought I might find a nice bar and have a late night."

"We might as well say eight. We're not much given to late nights in Zurich. And in the police, we like to get an early start."

"I guess that means Germany should look to invade after lights-out."

Weisendanger sighed. "Please try to remember what I said about a sense of humor, Captain. It doesn't translate from the German into Alemannic."

We finished a breakfast of boiled eggs, coffee, and toast, after which I gratefully bade him goodbye, collected my car from the hotel garage, and then drove along the north shore of Lake Zurich, toward the municipality of Küsnacht and Dalia Dresner's Swiss home. I was very much looking forward to seeing Dalia again, especially as her husband, Dr. Obrenović, was away in Geneva.

Fifteen minutes later I'd twice missed the quiet entrance to the house on Seestrasse, the number on the stone gatepost was so well hidden. It was only when I steered the Mercedes along a gravel drive that ran through a valley of high box hedge and around to the front of the house, where a long neat lawn gave onto the sparkling blue sapphire that was Lake Zurich, that I properly understood how Küsnacht hid itself from view like a reclusive oyster. Showing a keen appreciation of human psychology, the psychiatrist Carl Jung lived and worked in Küsnacht. Doubtless he understood well that the municipality's pampered inhabitants have the same neuroses and phobias as everyone else, with a lot more money to indulge them. But the only way to truly understand Küsnacht itself was to see it from the lakeside. This revealed it to be a little like Wannsee, only with much larger houses and bigger waterfronts. Even the boathouses looked like elegant mansions. Some of the boathouses had smaller houses attached where probably their boatmen lived. Most of the homes in Wannsee don't hide their size. The houses on Seestrasse hid everything except the numbers on the gatepost and the newspaper in the letter box. The little town's coat of arms was a gold cushion on a red velvet background, and after seeing the home of Dr. Obrenović, it was hard to see how this could have been anything else save perhaps a fat bag of gold coins. Like most Germans, I'm fond of home, but Dalia's husband's idea of home and mine had no more in common than Lake Zurich and a bucket of water.

I rang the doorbell and waited for someone to pay attention to it; as loud as a church bell, it was hard to imagine it being ignored by anyone. I was surprised to find it answered by Dr. Obrenović, who introduced himself to me with the alacrity of an older man in possession of a much younger wife, as if meeting all of Dalia's friends and acquaintances was necessary to his peace of mind; or not. Great wealth won't shield a man from being the victim of jealousy, only from the pain of hearing his wife's behavior discussed by a wide circle of friends. Men like Dr. Obrenović don't have a wide circle of friends, just an inner circle of trusted employees. Almost as soon as I felt him lay his keen blue eyes on me I knew that he knew—or at least suspected—that something had happened between Dalia and me, something outside the normal conventions of the professional, detective-client relationship. It was a curious sensation for me, like seeing my father again on the day I had almost failed my Abitur. But this certainly didn't make me feel guilty, or even awkward, just unreasonably young—which is to say, more than a decade younger than a man who was probably in his mid-sixties—and perhaps curious as to the reason why a woman as beautiful as Dalia had married a creaking gate like him. It couldn't have been money; as a young UFA starlet, Dalia was making a lot; then again, for some women, a lot is never quite enough. There's a French novel about that, I think.

I went inside and took off my hat and followed him through a hallway that was as wide as the Polish Corridor and lined with more old masters than Hermann Göring's cellar.

"My wife is just changing," he said, leading me into the drawing room. "She'll be down in a moment."

"I see."

"So you're the detective who's been looking for her father," he said in a way that made me think he was almost amused by the very idea.

"That's right. I just got back from Croatia."

"How was it?"

"I'm still having nightmares about the place. I keep dreaming I'm back there."

"That bad, eh?"

"Worse than bad. Awful. Like something from a horror film."

"Did she tell you that I'm a Serb? That I'm from Sarajevo?"

"She might have mentioned it," I said, uncertain if it had been Dalia or Goebbels who'd told me where Obrenović came from. "I really don't remember."

"Of course, I haven't lived there in a long time. Not since the king was assassinated."

He didn't mention which one, and I certainly didn't ask. As far as I could see, Yugoslavian kings were a bit like taxis; it couldn't be long before another one came to the head of the rank.

"If there's one thing European history proves it's that there's nothing more disposable than a king," I said.

"You think so?"

"They don't seem to be in short supply."

As tall as Leipzig's Volki monument, Obrenović had a full head of white hair, a pair of invisibly framed glasses, a bass tenor's voice, and ears as large as bicycle wheels. He walked like an old man, as if his hips were stiff—the way I walked myself first thing in the morning, before the day had lent them some greater flexibility.

"You obviously don't know who I am."

"Your name is Obrenović. Apart from the fact that you're a doctor of something and married to Fräulein Dresner, I have no idea who you are."

"Is that so?"

A little overawed by the size and luxury of the room, I nodded dumbly. It's always a surprise when I encounter people like Obrenović, who seem to own so much: good furniture, fine paintings, familiar bronzes, inlaid boxes, sparkling decanters, ornaments, chandeliers, rugs and carpets, a dog or two, and, outside the French windows, a Rolls-Royce. Not having anything very much myself is as near to feeling like a rich man as I'm ever likely to get, even if it is the kind of rich man in the gospels who actually took the advice of Jesus and sold all of his possessions to give the money to the poor. Perfection like mine never felt so shabby and, for a change, it made me more insolent. But this might just as easily have been caused by the disappointment of knowing I wasn't about to make love to Dalia—at least not for the present.

"So, Captain Gunther," he said, pouring himself a cup of coffee from a silver pot on a little tray. "Did you find him? That's what we're dying to find out."

I waited for a moment, until I was quite sure that none of the coffee was coming my way, and said, "Did I find who?"

He frowned and put the coffee cup to his lips. Even from where I was standing it smelled better than the coffee in the hotel. Just as important, it looked hot, which is the way I like it.

"Dalia's papa, of course. Father Ladislaus. Did you find him in Banja Luka?"

"Not in Banja Luka, no."

"In Zagreb, perhaps?"

"Not there, either."

"I see," he said patiently. "In Belgrade, then."

"I didn't get to Belgrade. Or Sarajevo. Or the Dalmatian Coast. Which is a pity, as I believe the beaches are very nice there at this time of year. I could probably use a holiday."

"You're not telling me very much."

"I certainly didn't intend to."

"My wife hadn't told me your manners were so bad."

"You'd best take that up with her, not me."

"I don't suppose I should be all that surprised. You Germans are not known for your courtesy."

"Being a member of the master race has some social disadvantages, it's true. But you can take my word for it, Dr. Obrenović, I'm just as rude in Germany as I am in Switzerland. I get plenty of complaints from my superiors. I could paper my walls with them. But if you'd just come all the way from Zurich to Berlin, I might at least offer you a cup of coffee."

"Help yourself," he said, and stepped away from the tray.

I didn't move except to turn the hat in my hands.

"You're not going to tell me anything, are you?"

"Now you're getting it."

"Might I ask why?"

"What I have to say is between me and your wife. I don't know you from the Swiss prime minister."

He frowned. "I thought you wanted some coffee."

"No. That's not what I said, Doctor. I had coffee at the hotel. It was the offer I was keener on."

"Well, I must say—I'm not accustomed to being spoken to in this way. Especially in my own house."

I shrugged. "I can wait in the car if you'd prefer."

"Yes, I think that might be best."

Twenty-nine

stalked back to the door and, followed by one of the dogs, went outside. I didn't much care if it got out of the house. It wasn't my dog. I lit a cigarette and sat on the shiny bonnet of the car, hardly caring if I marked the new paintwork. It wasn't my car. The morning was already a warm one; I threw my jacket into the backseat of the Mercedes next to the flask of homemade rakija I'd brought as a present for Dalia from Bosnia, and tossed some stones into an ornamental pond that was full of koi carp. It wasn't my pond. I waited awhile and when the big door opened again, I flicked the cigarette into the garden. It wasn't my garden. Dalia walked toward me and stood silently in front of the front passenger door. She wasn't my wife but I could certainly have wished she had been instead of the one I already had back in Berlin. Her golden hair was collected in a little bun at the back of her head and this added a regal touch to her Nefertiti neck, although that might as easily have been the sapphire-and-diamond necklace that was wrapped around it. She was wearing a navy blue dress; I might have said a plain navy blue dress except for the fact that nothing that was worn by the lady from Zagreb could ever have looked plain. She smiled a slight, rueful smile and then put her hand on the door handle of the car.

"Are we going somewhere?" I asked.

"No," she said. "Now that you've been banished from the house, I thought we could just sit in the car and talk awhile."

I opened the door and she got in. I went around to the other side.

"Well, this is cozy," I said, closing the door behind me.

"Shut up and give me a cigarette."

I lit her and she took a long hard drag on it.

"Sorry about that," she said. "I didn't expect Stefan back home until tomorrow. He just turned up in the middle of the night."

"I guessed as much."

"What on earth did you say to him?"

"Not much."

"He says you were rude."

"Only because he'd been rude to me."

"That doesn't sound like Stefan. His manners are usually impeccable. I'll say that for my husband."

"Are they? I watched him pour himself a coffee without offering me a cup."

"Ah, I see. So that's it. You have to understand, Stefan is an aristocrat. He could no more serve you with his own hand than he could sweep the floor."

"He answered the door, didn't he?"

"I wondered who answered it. I thought it was Agnes, my maid. I gave Albert the day off. Because you were coming. I wanted us to be alone in the house. I've thought about nothing else since you called last night."

"Albert?"

"The butler."

"Of course. I generally answer the door myself when my own butler's busy polishing the pewter, or fixing the dripping tap in my drafty garret."

"You make it sound rather romantic."

"My life in Berlin—it's *La Bohème*, right enough. Right down to the cough and the frozen hands in winter."

"All the same, I wish we were there right now, Bernie. Naked. In bed."

"My hotel room at the Baur au Lac's not much to look at. But it's still bigger than my apartment. The bathroom's bigger than my apartment. We could go there now, if you like. The front desk will very likely report us to the Swiss police but I think I can survive the scandal. In fact, I think I might rather enjoy that, as well."

"I will come," she said. "But it will have to be this afternoon. Around two o'clock?"

"I certainly can't think of anything else I'd rather do in Zurich."

"Only this time I'd like you to take more than twice as long doing what you did to me the last time we were in bed. Or, as an alternative, you could do something you've never done before. To any woman. You understand? You could do something you've only ever dreamed of, perhaps. In your *wildest* dreams. Just as long as you can make me feel like a woman is supposed to feel when a man makes love to her."

"I'd like that. And two o'clock sounds good. But there's something I have to tell you first, Dalia. It's about your father."

"Oh dear, I'd guessed it wasn't going to be good news when Stefan told me you wouldn't tell him about Papa."

"I'm sorry to have to tell you this, but I'm more or less certain that your father is dead."

I would have felt a lot more guilty about this egregious lie if Dalia's father hadn't been such a monster. Nonetheless I did feel guilty.

"Oh. I see. You went there? In person? To the monastery in Banja Luka?"

"Mm-hmm. By car. All the way from Zagreb, which is a journey I wouldn't recommend to anyone. I spent several hours in the monastery, having dinner with the monks. The Father Abbot told me that your father had left the monastery and joined the Ustaše. I'm afraid I got the impression that the Father Abbot strongly disapproved of your father, Dalia. Maybe because he left the Franciscan order, but more likely because of some of the things that the Ustaše has done. Like all civil wars, I think some cruel things have been done on both sides. After that, I went to the Ustaše headquarters in Banja Luka and it was there I learned that Father Ladislaus was now called Colonel Dragan and a bit of a local hero; and then, that he was dead. Killed by communist partisans in a skirmish in the Zelengora Mountains. This was later confirmed in Zagreb. Things are pretty rough right now in Croatia and Bosnia, what with the war and everything. I saw several people killed while I was there. The men I was traveling with—ethnic Germans in the SS—they were a bit trigger-happy. You know, the shoot-first-and-ask-questions-later type. It's chaos, quite frankly, and getting accurate information is hazardous. But I'm as certain as I can be that he's dead. And I'm sorry."

"That must have been horrible for you, Bernie. I'm sorry. But I'm grateful, too. Very grateful. It sounds like it was dangerous."

I shrugged. "A certain amount of danger is part of the job."

"Does Josef know? About my father."

"Of course. He sent me down here to tell you and bring you back to Berlin. Or at least to persuade you to turn up to work at the studio."

"Well, I had to try. Or rather, someone did. You do see that, don't you?"

"Of course I do. Believe me, nothing could be more understandable. With your mother dead, it makes perfect sense that you should have wanted to find your father again."

"After all, it was she who fell out with him, not me. A father is supposed to mean something. Even one you haven't seen in an age." She took another fierce drag at her cigarette. "I thought I'd be more upset. But I'm not. Does that strike you as a bit strange?"

"No, not really. After all, you must have suspected he was dead, given that your previous letters were never answered."

"Yes, I suppose so."

"And it strikes me that you're no worse off than you were before. At least you know now. For sure. You can put it all behind you and get on with the rest of your life."

"There is that to think about, yes."

"What will you do? About the movie, I mean."

"I don't really know. If I come back to Berlin, then perhaps I can see you, of course. That's on one side. To be quite frank with you, Bernie, you're the only good reason I have for going back to Germany now. On the other side's the fact that I don't particularly want to work on this stupid movie with Veit Harlan. I can't imagine it's going to do my career any good in the long term to make a movie with a notorious anti-Semite like him. It's bad enough that I was in *The Saint That Never Was*. I just know I'm already going to have a hard job living that one down. There's that *and* the fact that Josef Goebbels wants to make me his mistress. Believe me, he'll do his damnedest to find a way to make that happen. He's devious and unscrupulous and you've no idea the trouble I've already had keeping that little Mephisto from conjuring me out of my underwear. It's one of the reasons I came here. To escape from him."

"I've a pretty shrewd idea of what he's capable of. I've been subject to quite a bit of pressure myself, angel."

"Yes, I suppose you have."

"In fact, you don't know the half of it."

"Maybe not. But look, there's something I have to tell you. I don't know that it's very important in the scheme of things. But I've fallen for you, and in a big way. While you were away in Croatia I thought about you day and night."

"Me too."

"And it's no different now that you're back. I'm having a hard job keeping a smile on my face."

"Stefan doesn't know about us, does he?"

"No. But suspicion of every man I know is his default state of mind. Even when there's absolutely nothing in it." She wound down the window and dropped her cigarette onto the gravel. "Yes, you heard what I said. Oh, don't look so shocked, Bernie. You're not exactly my first lover. Where does it say that women must behave one way and men the other? What's sauce for the goose is sauce for the gander. Besides, according to Josef's telegram, you're the one who just got married. When were you planning to tell me? In bed this afternoon? Or did it just slip your mind?" She laughed and took my hand. "I'm not in the least bit angry, darling. After all, I'm hardly in a position to lecture you on your morals. Although I am a bit jealous, perhaps. It's true what I said about falling for you. Under the circumstances that sounds so much more of an insurable risk than saying 'I love you.' Although that would also be a tiny bit true."

"My marriage. It's not what you think." I was feeling slightly wrong-footed at the frankness of both of her admissions.

"I think it probably is, you know. Most people usually get married for the same two reasons. Stefan married me for love. That's one reason. But I married Stefan because he was rich and because it made me a baroness. That's the other. He knows that. Before we got married I told him I would take the occasional lover and he seemed quite sanguine about that. In the beginning, anyway. With the exception of arranged marriages and dynastic alliances between two royal families, that probably exhausts the explanations for most modern marriages. Wouldn't you agree?"

"I doubt that even King Henry the Eighth has ever encountered the reason I got married," I said, and told her about Kirsten, her problem with the SD, and how Goebbels had blackmailed me into marrying her.

"That's the most romantic thing I ever heard," she said plaintively. "I take it all back. I thought men like you only existed in stories that involve round tables and shining armor. You really are a saint, do you know that?"

"No, it's just that sometimes I have to do saintly things to balance things up a bit."

She made a fist and shook her head. "Christ, what a shit that man is. You know, I really don't think I will go back to Germany. Not for him and his stupid film. Someone else from UFA can do it. One of those bottle blondes in the chorus he's always screwing."

"Don't say that. The fact is I've fallen for you, too. And my chances of coming back to Switzerland before this war is over are about as slim as my chances of surviving it unscathed."

"Now it's my turn to object to your choice of words."

"It's going to get a lot worse before it gets any better. The Russians are going to make certain of that." I shrugged. "But what about your career? You're a movie star. You'd really give that up?"

"I told you before. I'm really not that interested in acting. I'd rather study mathematics. I can still take up that place at Zurich Polytechnic. And what's going to happen to anyone who's involved with the German film industry when the Russians turn up?"

"You have a point there."

"There's this to consider, too. If I go back. Which I seriously doubt I will. Goebbels wouldn't be nearly so understanding of my foibles as my husband. If I did get involved with Josef, or if he found out that you were an obstacle to his having a relationship with me, he could make your life very unpleasant, Bernie."

She seemed to have thought of everything.

"It would be worth it," I said.

"No, my love," she said. "You don't know what you're saying. But look, maybe love will find a way. And we still have Zurich and this afternoon. In your hotel room at the Baur au Lac. What could be more romantic? Now that you're here, please, Bernie, please, I beg you, let's make the most of it."

Thirty

I drove slowly away from Küsnacht feeling both elated and depressed. Elated at the idea that Dalia loved me, and depressed at the realization that seeing her in Germany was going to be so problematic, if not impossible. She was right, of course. I could hardly blame her. What woman in her right mind would have voluntarily put herself in danger of becoming Mephisto's mistress? But I certainly wondered what I was going to tell Goebbels when I was in his office once more. And it was clear to me that he was not going to be pleased when he learned that his favorite actress was refusing to return to Berlin. I could still hear his words, telling me to bring her back at all costs. Carl Jung would have had a difficult job persuading Dalia to change her mind.

I drove into Zurich thinking I would probably have to send Goebbels a telegram advising him of the outcome of my meeting with Dalia. Maybe he could think of something that would bring her back to work. More money, perhaps. That was something all movie actresses seemed to understand very well. It was said that Marlene Dietrich had been paid $450,000 by Alexander Korda to star in his film *Knight Without Armour*. Surely Dalia could have commanded just as much as Dietrich. She was certainly more beautiful. And her films were more popular, too. At least they were in Germany.

I was still thinking about this when I drove into the Baur's parking lot, immediately to the west of the hotel and on the other side of the canal. I stepped out of the car and was locking the door when a man got out of the car parked next to me and asked me for a light. Not suspecting anything, I reached for my lighter, which is when I found a big Colt automatic in my gut and another man frisking me for a gun. The next thing I knew I was being invited to get into the back of my own Mercedes and the man with the gun was sitting alongside me. The one who'd searched me had taken my passport and the car keys and was now in the driver's seat. A moment or two later we were speeding out of the hotel car park with the other car close behind.

I imagine they'd been following me all the way from Küsnacht. It wasn't like me not to spot a tail, but with so much on my mind I simply hadn't noticed it. There were four of them—two in my car and two in the car behind. I turned to take a longer look but the man seated beside me flicked the lobe of my ear meaningfully with the Colt and told me to keep my eyes to the front.

"Who are you?" I asked. "You're not Gestapo. Not with those suits and that cologne."

The man with the gun said nothing. By now all I knew was that we were driving north. That's easy when the river is to the west and on your left. Five minutes later we turned into a dull, quiet neighborhood full of tall white houses with gable roofs and stopped in front of a corner house with several stories and a steeple. One of the men in the car behind opened a garage door and we drove inside. Then I was marched upstairs and through the door of a barely furnished corner apartment on the uppermost floor—a safe house, I imagined, with a nice view of nothing very much. A man smoking a pipe and wearing a three-piece suit was seated behind a refectory table. His hair was thin and white and he had a broad gray mustache. He wore a spotted bow tie and a pair of wire-framed glasses. He continued writing something on a sheet of paper with a fountain pen while I was escorted to a chair in the middle of the room. I sat down and waited to discover who these people were. So far, their accents had led me to believe they were neither Swiss nor German, and I quickly presumed they were English or American.

Eventually the man behind the refectory table spoke in fluent German that was too good for an American.

"How are you today, General?" he asked.

"Thank you, I'm well, but I'm afraid you've obviously got the wrong man. I'm not a general. Last time I looked at my pay book it said captain."

The man with the pipe said nothing and continued writing.

"If you bother to check my passport you'll see I'm not the man you probably think I am. My name is Bernhard Gunther."

"In our profession none of us is ever really what he seems to be," said the man with the pipe. He spoke calmly, like a professor or a diplomat, as if he had been explaining a philosophical point to a dull student.

"In Nazi Germany not being who you are is a regular way of life, for everyone. Take my word for it."

The pipe smoke was sweet and actually smelled like real, unadulterated tobacco, which made me think he must be American. The English were just as badly off for tobacco as the Germans.

"Oh, I think we know who you are, all right."

"And I'm telling you that you've made a mistake. I'm guessing you think that I'm General Walter Schellenberg. I am driving his car, after all. He asked me to bring it here, from the Mercedes car factory in Sindelfingen. And now I've met you I'm beginning to understand why. I'm guessing he was expecting something like this might happen. Getting snatched off the streets by American spies. That's what you are, isn't it? I mean, you're not German. I know you're not Swiss. And you can't be English. Not with those suits."

The pipe smoker started writing again. I had nothing to lose by talking. So I talked. Maybe I could talk my way out of this.

"Look here, I've an important appointment back at my hotel at two o'clock. With a lady. So I'll tell you everything you want to know. Which isn't much. Keep the car. It isn't mine. But I'd rather not miss that appointment."

"This lady. What's her name?"

I said nothing.

"If you tell us her name we shall leave word at your hotel that you have been unavoidably detained."

"So you can snatch her, too?"

"Why would we do that when we have you, General?"

"I'd rather not say what her name is. We're lovers, all right? But the lady is married. I expect you could find out, but I'd rather not say what her name is."

"And how would your wife, Irene, feel about that?"

"I think Irene would be all right with it since I'm not married to her."

"I'm afraid you're going to be here awhile," said the man. "So you might as well get used to the idea. You won't be keeping your appointment with your lady friend. You'll be helping us with the answers to some important questions we have, General Schellenberg. And it would be unfortunate for us both if your answers were not truthful."

"Look," I said. "You know the name of General Schellenberg's wife. Congratulations. But you obviously know very little else because if you did you'd know that he's nothing like me. He's short. I'm tall. He's younger than me. Thirty-three, I think. Better-looking, too, although I agree that seems unlikely. He speaks fluent French. On account of the fact that he lived in Luxembourg. I hardly speak a word of it. And he's a snake, which is how I'm here now instead of him.

Look, there's a man—a Swiss—who'll vouch for what I say. He's an intelligence officer, too—a captain by the name of Paul Meyer-Schwertenbach. He works for military intelligence. His boss is a man named Masson. Meyer knows who I am because he's met the real General Schellenberg. And he's met me, in Berlin. Last year he came to an international crime commission conference. I got to know him reasonably well. He lives in a château in Ermatingen, called Wolfsberg Castle. Why don't you telephone him? He'll tell you what Schellenberg looks like and what I look like and we can sort this whole thing out in a few minutes. I've got nothing to hide. I'm not a spy. I'm really not in a position to tell you anything very much. I was a criminal commissar with Kripo in Berlin, and until recently I was working for the War Crimes Bureau, at army headquarters. I've been sent here on a private mission by Dr. Goebbels in his capacity as head of the UFA film studios at Babelsberg. There's an actress, living here in Zurich . . . he wants her to star in his next film. That's it, gentlemen. I'm sorry to disappoint you, but this time you got the monkey, not the organ-grinder."

"This conference. Where was it held?"

"The Villa Minoux, in Wannsee. That's a sort of guesthouse owned by the SS."

"Who else was there?"

I shrugged. "The usual suspects. Gestapo Müller, Kaltenbrunner, Himmler. General Nebe. And Schellenberg, of course. It was him who introduced me to Captain Meyer-Schwertenbach."

"You move in very elevated circles for a mere captain."

"I go where I'm told to go."

"Have you ever been in Switzerland before?"

"No. Never."

The pipe smoker smiled in a faceless sort of way, without conveying anything of his emotions, so it was impossible for me to determine if he thought what I'd said was true, or false, funny, or beneath contempt. The three other men in the room were all thugs—Gestapo types with better haircuts and nicer breath.

"Tell me, General, what plans does Germany have for the invasion of Switzerland?" he asked.

"Me? I really have no idea. You might as well ask me when Hitler is going to throw in the towel and surrender. But from the little I've heard, our dear leader still believes the idea of invading Switzerland is a possibility. Only there's no appetite for it among the German leadership. Goebbels told me that himself. The fact is, everyone in the German Army lives in fear of invading this little country because the Swiss Army enjoys a reputation for marksmanship that's second to none. That and the fact that the Alps mean that even the Luftwaffe wouldn't be able to count for much in attempting to subdue the place. It's just not worth it."

The man with the pipe spent several minutes writing this. I glanced at my watch and saw that it was already midday.

"Could I have a cigarette?" I asked.

"Give him a cigarette," said the pipe smoker, and without hesitation one of his men sprang forward with an open cigarette case. I picked one, noted the name—Viceroy—on the paper, and put it in my mouth. He lit me and sat down again. From the speed with which the man had moved I formed the conclusion that the man with the pipe was no ordinary spy; perhaps this was the American spymaster himself. He certainly fit the description given by Schellenberg.

"So you *are* American," I said. "The OSS, I suppose." I smiled at the pipe smoker. "And perhaps you're even Mr. Allen Dulles himself, of the OSS in Bern."

The pipe smoker stayed smiling, inscrutably.

"You know, Mr. Dulles, the Swiss will be very cross with you when they find out what you've done to me. They take their neutrality very seriously indeed. Your treatment of me—a German guest with a visa—might easily cause a diplomatic incident. After all, someone from the Swiss police or intelligence services must have told you I was in Zurich. That won't go down well with the people in our embassy when they find out what's happened. Which they will, of course, when I fail to report back to Berlin."

"General, this will all end more quickly if we confine ourselves to me asking the questions and you giving the answers. And when you have done so to my complete satisfaction, you will walk out of here a free man. You have my word. Neither the Abwehr, nor your boss, Heinrich Himmler, will ever be the wiser. He's the man who calls the shots in Department Six these days, isn't he? I mean, since General Heydrich's death. You're Himmler's special plenipotentiary, and answerable only to him."

"Look, I'm not even a member of the Nazi Party. How can I persuade you that I'm not General Schellenberg?"

"All right. Let's see if you can. You don't deny you're driving his car. All of the paperwork in the glove box confirms Walter Schellenberg as the car's exporting owner. And the importing company as the Swiss Wood Syndicate. Then there's the booking at your hotel. That was made by a company called Export Drives GMBH, a subsidiary of another company called Stiftung Nordhav, of which Walter Schellenberg is one of the directors and of which Reinhard Heydrich was formerly the chairman. The same company also paid the bill at the Baur au Lac for a Hans Eggen when, in February this year, he visited Zurich. He traveled to Switzerland at the same time as a Walter Schellenberg, who had also had a room at the Baur but didn't actually stay there. The two men crossed the border by car at Fort Reuenthal."

"If that's so, then the Zurich cantonal police will easily be able to confirm that I'm not Schellenberg. You could ask Sergeant Bleiker, or Police Inspector Weisendanger. I believe I have the inspector's business card in my wallet if you care to look for it."

"As I'm sure you know, General, it's only since your previous visit that Colonel Müller of the Swiss Security Service—your opposite number, so to speak—has insisted that you be kept under surveillance by the Zurich police whenever you are in Switzerland. He would like to find out what you've been up to almost as much as I do. Which is probably why you're using an alias now. Beyond the fact that you and Eggen had meetings with Meyer and Roger Masson of Swiss Military Intelligence, very little is known of your activities in Switzerland. Perhaps you'd like to take this opportunity to enlighten me. What are you doing here now? And what were you doing then? After all, you were both here for almost two weeks. What did you discuss with Masson and Meyer?"

"Would it be easier to ask them?"

"I doubt that the Swiss would want to share any intel with me. They turn a blind eye to what we're doing here in Switzerland just as they do their best to ignore what you Germans get up to. Let's face it: their surveillance of you is hardly oppressive, is it? What can you tell me about the Swiss Wood Syndicate?"

"Nothing at all."

"I find that hard to believe."

I shrugged.

"Come now, General. There's no need to be so coy about this. The SWS manufactures wooden barracks. Presumably the SS and the German Army have a use for wooden barracks."

"If you say so."

"Only, some of these barracks end up being used in concentration camps, don't they?"

"I really wouldn't know. Look, I just remembered something.

Someone else who might confirm who I say I am. Heinrich Rothmund of the police section at the Swiss Department of Justice and Police. When I was a detective working for Kripo in Berlin I had several conversations with Rothmund. A missing persons case that was never resolved. I wouldn't say we're old friends but he'll know exactly what we spoke about then."

"But as you yourself have said, the Swiss police take a dim view of any interference with the diplomatic community in their country. I can hardly ask Herr Rothmund to come here and identify you without alerting him to the fact that you're being held against your will. I'm afraid I'd soon find myself asked to leave Switzerland for good."

"I'm sure you can think of a way of checking me out without raising his suspicions. After all, it's the intelligence community you work in, not a local department store. Even your mind ought to be able to devise some means of establishing beyond all doubt that I am who I say I am." I shrugged. "Look, Mr. Dulles, I'm just trying to save us both some valuable time here."

"That reminds me, General, when is your next scheduled meeting with Police Inspector Weisendanger?"

"Tonight. At six."

"We both know that this can't be true. By the terms of your visa he's only obliged to meet with you once a day. To make sure that you keep out of trouble. Since the two of you had breakfast this morning, I have to conclude that your next meeting must be tomorrow. But it would be useful to know at what time this will be. Are you to have breakfast again tomorrow?"

"Yes."

"So, we have until then to get to know each other better."

Allen Dulles—for so I believed him to be—checked his wristwatch and stood up.

"I will see you this afternoon, General," he said. "I have a lunch appointment, here in Zurich. You will be well looked after in my absence. And you might take advantage of your time to reflect upon our conversation. In the absence of your cooperation I should hate to tell my associates here to treat you roughly, just as I should regret having to provide German intelligence with evidence of our conversations. You're no good to me if I have to burn you, General. I should much prefer it if we can establish a proper working relationship for the future."

"You mean you want me to spy for you." I smiled. "Well, why didn't you say so? I don't have to be General Schellenberg to do that. Bernie Gunther could be just as useful a spy as him. I'm not nearly as expensive as a general. And after all, as you say, I do sometimes move in elevated circles. Since I've never been a Nazi, it's my earnest wish that the war ends as soon as possible. Is that straight enough for you? As my country was hijacked by a bunch of gangsters, I have no reason not to betray it and, more particularly, them, to people like you. So, by all means let's talk about my becoming an American spy. Where do I sign?"

Allen Dulles checked the bowl of his pipe, relit it carefully, and stared at me through eyes that slowly narrowed behind his glasses.

"We'll talk again, this afternoon."

He was about to leave the room when one of his OSS men handed him a photograph, which he looked at for several seconds through ruminative clouds of pipe smoke.

"Now, this is interesting," he said. "While we've been talking, one of our more diligent desk analysts has come up with this photograph. Perhaps you'd care to comment on this."

Dulles handed me the picture. There was a caption on a label affixed to the bottom of the print that I hardly needed to read as I recognized the picture immediately. It read: *Picture taken at the Prague Circus Krone in October 1941 for local Czech newspaper. The two officers in foreground are Generals Heydrich and Frank. Also pictured are*

Heydrich's wife, Lina, Frank's wife, Karola, Heydrich's three aides-de-camp, believed to be Ploetz, Pomme, and Kluckholn, and an unknown man, but also believed to be a senior officer in the SD.

"That's you, isn't it?" said Dulles. "That 'unknown' German officer with Generals Heydrich and Frank?"

"Yes, that's me," I admitted. "I see no point in denying it. But I don't know that it tells you anything very much, Mr. Dulles. After all, none of us is wearing a uniform. It certainly doesn't tell you that I'm an SS-Obersturmbannführer, which I think is the rank that Walter Schellenberg held around that time."

"It tells me that you knew Heydrich pretty well if you went to the fucking circus with him and his wife."

Thirty-one

They locked me in a bedroom. There were no bars on the window but this was in the tower room—the one that looked like a church steeple from the outside—and the drop straight to the sloping ground was at least fifteen meters. The Three Toledos wouldn't have made a jump like that if the famous Erwingos had been there to catch them. I certainly wasn't about to try it.

There was a table with a drawer and a chair; I opened the drawer and found some sheets of Prantl, which would have been useful if I'd planned to escape from the window on a paper airplane. I lay down on a surprisingly clean bed, reached for my cigarettes, and then remembered they'd been confiscated along with everything else except my wristwatch. One o'clock became one-thirty, and then one forty-five, and I felt my spirits start to lower even further as I pictured Dalia arriving at the Baur au Lac and discovering to her surprise that I wasn't there. How would she feel? How long would she wait before concluding that I wasn't coming? Fifteen minutes? Half an hour? For a while I thought about being in bed with her and the pleasures I was surely missing, but that didn't help. It just made me want to punch the door or smash the window.

At exactly two o'clock I went to the sash window and tried to open it, but the paint on the frame had left the window sealed. I thought about smashing the glass and shouting down to the street, but for as long as I stood there looking out, I saw no one in the street. Not even a dog or a cat. Zurich was quiet at the best of times. But this neighborhood was as quiet as a Swiss watch movement. I also imagined that the minute I started shouting out the window the American who was seated on the other side of the door—I could hear his feet on the floor and smell his cigarettes—would come in and belt me in the teeth. I'd been punched before and didn't mind being punched again, but I figured I was going to need to keep all of my wits if I was ever going to persuade Dulles that I wasn't General Schellenberg.

It seemed that I had until morning to do this. And if I didn't persuade him, then what? Would they really let me go? If making a spy of the head of SD Foreign Intelligence was what this was all about, how did they intend to compromise him enough to make him turn against his Nazi masters? There was nothing that Allen Dulles had said that led me to think they had very much information about the real Schellenberg. Since they didn't know what he really looked like, it all felt like a poorly conceived fishing expedition. At least it did until you considered another, more uncomfortable possibility, which was that they intended to question me for as long as they could before they killed me, or somehow got me out of the country and back to the USA for further interrogation. Getting me out of a landlocked country— Switzerland was, after all, surrounded by Germany, fascist Italy, Vichy France, and Nazi Austria—looked like a tall order, even for the Americans. Killing me looked like a better bet. If they did suppose I was a top Nazi general, then killing me would have made perfect sense, too. In spite of Dulles's smooth assurances, a bullet in the back of my head appeared to be the real fate that lay in store for me. Assassinating the general in charge of SD Foreign Intelligence would have been no less useful to the Allied war effort than assassinating Heydrich, or Field Marshal Rommel, who had famously and narrowly escaped an attempt on his life by British commandos in November 1941.

At two-thirty I went to the door and listened carefully. The Ami on the other side seemed to be reading a newspaper. I thought I heard him fart, and a few seconds later I was sure of it.

"I wouldn't mind a cigarette," I said, retiring to a safe distance. "You're never alone with a cigarette."

"Sorry," said the man, in German. "Boss's orders. No cigarettes, in case you set the room on fire. And then where would we be? Explaining ourselves to the Zurich fire service."

"How about a cup of coffee?" I said. "Have you any orders against giving the prisoner food and drink?"

"No. As a matter of fact, I was thinking I might bring you a coffee. But before I did that I was just trying to think of the German for 'No tricks, you Nazi bastard, or I'll shoot you in the fucking leg.'"

"I think you've made yourself perfectly understood."

"How do you like your coffee?"

"Black. Plenty of sugar, if you have it. Or saccharine."

"All right. Wait there."

"You know, I think I will."

I dropped onto the wooden floor and peered under the door just in time to see a pair of stout-looking brown, wingtip shoes walk loudly away and the butt of a cigarette he had discarded, which still had plenty of good tobacco left in it—in fact it was still burning. I went quickly back to the desk drawer, fetched a sheet of notepaper, and slid it underneath the door and then the cigarette butt. A minute later I was lying happily on the bed and puffing the Ami's Viceroy back to life. No cigarette ever tasted better than that one. It felt like a small, exquisite victory—temporary but no less satisfying for all that, which is of course pleasure incarnate.

I'd hoped the Ami might come back with the coffee in time for him to see the cigarette in the corner of my mouth. But I smoked it right down to the butt, reminding myself of how much I preferred European cigarettes, and still he did not return. When I heard a muffled commotion I dropped back onto my belly and stared under the door again.

I could still see the wingtip shoes but now they were pointed at the ceiling, and while I was still trying to puzzle out why, I heard a gunshot. And then another. The Swiss police? I couldn't imagine that anyone else was trying to rescue me; then again, it seemed unlikely that the Swiss would have fired shots at foreigners and risked their very neutrality. More shots were fired. And then I heard footsteps outside my door. Seconds later I heard the key in the lock and the door was flung open to reveal a man in a gray suit who was more obviously German than Swiss or American. His hair was as yellow as corn, there was a small dueling *Schmiss* on his cheek, and there was no mistaking his accent.

"Are you Hauptsturmführer Gunther?" he barked.

"Yes."

"Come with us. Quickly."

I didn't need asking again. I walked out of the tower bedroom and followed the man to the door of the apartment, where I stopped and glanced around, looking at the room where I'd been interrogated earlier. The air of the apartment was thick with the smell of gunpowder. It hung visibly in the air like a poltergeist. Three of the Amis lay bleeding on the floor; one of them had been shot through the head and was almost certainly dead; the other had an expanding bubble of blood in one of his nostrils that seemed to indicate there was still breath in his body. Another German with a broom-handle Mauser was reloading it in case he needed to shoot someone else.

"My passport," I said. "My car keys."

"We have everything," said my rescuer. "Come on. We have to get the hell out of here before the cops show up. Even the Swiss are not about to ignore gunfire."

We ran downstairs and outside where a black Citroën was parked at the side of the road. The other man—the man I'd seen with the Mauser—was reversing my Mercedes out of the Ami safe house's garage.

"Get in," said Scarface, pointing at the Citroën. "He'll follow us in your car."

We drove west this time. I know that because we drove across the river before turning south again. A couple of times I looked around and saw the Mercedes following close behind us. There was no gun on me now.

"Here," said Scarface, and he handed me a cigarette.

"Thanks," I said. "And thanks for the rescue."

I lit it; after the Viceroy it should have tasted bad but to me it was like smoking the best hashish. I shook my head and smiled. "Who are you?" I asked. "Abwehr?"

Scarface laughed. "The Abwehr. You might as well ask a dead cat to follow a dog. We're Gestapo, of course."

"I never thought I'd be glad to see the Gestapo. Is it just the two of you?"

He nodded. "It's lucky for you that there's been a twenty-four-hour tail on you since Genshagen. You've been our beer since you checked into the hotel here in Zurich. We saw the Amis pick you up in the hotel car park this morning. At first we thought they might be Tommies but when we saw Dulles and his driver coming out of the building, we knew they were Amis. Besides, the Tommies wouldn't have the nerve to do what the Amis did to you. They're even more respectful of Swiss neutrality than the Italians, and that's saying something. We were going to wait for backup. Anyway, when Dulles and his driver came out, we still weren't sure how many that left inside. The fellow in the car behind has spent the last hour listening at the door of every apartment in that building."

"They thought I was General Schellenberg," I said.

"Not unreasonably, I'd have thought. You were driving his car, after all. You're a lucky fellow, Gunther. After interrogating you, they'd have killed you for sure. The Americans like to shoot people who they perceive to be a threat. But only after they've beaten the shit out of them first. They think Europe is like the Wild West, I expect. Last year they were behind the murder of some French Vichy admiral called Darlan."

After a while we started up a winding road and soon I could see Lake Zurich below and behind us.

"Where are we going?"

"A safe house just a few kilometers outside Zurich, in Ringlikon, near the foot of the Uetliberg. You can go back to the Baur when we're sure we're all in the clear for this. The safe house is not much of a place but the fellow who owns it is a Swiss-German dairy farmer who's owned it since before the last war."

The house in Ringlikon was a three-story, half-timbered farmhouse-style building beside a field of brown Swiss cows. What else do you expect to find in a Swiss field? In a shed beside the house, a large bull was standing by himself. He looked cross. I expect he was keen to get among the cows. It was a feeling with which I was familiar. We parked the cars and went inside the house. There was a lot of wooden furniture and pictures that looked like they'd been there a hundred years. The Swiss flag over the back door was a nice touch. But almost immediately I spied a bottle of schnapps on the kitchen shelves.

"I could use a drink," I said.

"Good idea," said Scarface, and he fetched the bottle and some glasses. "My hands are still shaking."

"I'm grateful to you both," I said. "And to our host, whoever he might be."

"He's away right now. Delivering milk to some of his customers. But you'll meet Gottlob later, perhaps. He's a good Nazi."

"I can't wait."

The Gestapo man held out his hand. "Walter Nölle," he said.

We shook hands, toasted each other with schnapps, and for a while at least, behaved like we were friends. Half an hour passed before I said, "Where's the other fellow? The one who was driving my car."

"Edouard—he'll be here in a minute. Probably sending a message on the radio." He glanced at his watch. "We usually clock in around this time." He poured some more schnapps. "So what *did* you tell the Amis?" he asked.

"Nothing," I said. "I told them it was a case of mistaken identity so I could hardly answer questions they'd set for Schellenberg. I think they were planning to get rough this afternoon. Which doesn't bear thinking of. There's nothing worse than being asked questions to which you just don't know the answers. But I'm sure you know all about something like that."

"Someone in the Swiss police obviously tipped them off," said Nölle. "About the car."

I nodded. "That's the way it looks."

"Did General Schellenberg tell you why he's exporting a car to this Swiss Wood Syndicate?"

"He's a general," I said. "He's not in the habit of explaining himself to a mere captain."

Nölle let out a deep sigh.

"Look here, Gunther," he said, "we're going to have to make a full report on what we did today, to our superiors in Bern. You're a cop. You understand how all that works. Our superiors won't be at all happy that we've shot three Americans in Zurich. The Swiss are going to make a real stink about this. Because even without any evidence, the Americans will almost certainly point the finger at us. I've got to give my boss a full explanation for why we did what we did—for rescuing you—and somehow I don't think the fact that you're a fellow German is going to satisfy him. So, anything you can tell us will be gratefully appreciated. Anything at all. But we've got to tell those bastards in Berlin something."

He paused.

"All right, perhaps you can tell us why Goebbels sent you all the way down here to see Dalia Dresner? Is he fucking her? Is that it?"

"I'm sorry. Don't think I'm not grateful, but my lips are sealed. I'd like to help you out here. Really I would. As far as I know the minister wants her to star in a new movie called *Siebenkäs,* based on some crappy novel of the same name. In his capacity as head of the UFA film studios in Babelsberg. Nothing more. Schellenberg oiled the wheels for my trip. That's all."

"Goebbels sent you all the way here, just for that? Christ, that's a nice trip. He must be fucking her."

"Your guess is as good as mine. Look, as far as I can determine, the Swiss manufacture wooden barracks for the German Army and the SS. The car was meant to sweeten some deal the SS has going with the Swiss, that's all."

"The SS, you say?"

"Yes. But I don't think it's much of a secret." I frowned. "Unless."

"What?"

For a moment I thought of the camp at Jasenovac.

"I was just thinking that some of those wooden barracks must have been used to help build German concentration camps. For the SS. Places like Dachau and Buchenwald. I mean, it stands to reason that with the German Army on the move and living under canvas or in cities it's conquered, there's less of a need for them to have wooden barracks. Concentration camps need wooden barracks, right? It just occurred to me that the Swiss might be a little embarrassed if this became public knowledge. Which would certainly help to explain the murder of Dr. Heckholz last year."

I pictured the scene in the lawyer's Wallstrasse office, in Berlin-Charlottenburg: Heckholz's body lying on the white floor, his head surrounded with a halo of blood after someone had smashed it in with a bronze bust of Hitler. No wonder I hadn't read the crime scene properly—I'd been much too concerned with being amused at the idea that Hitler had killed the man. I'd ignored the fact that instead of writing the name of his killer with his own blood, Heckholz had used it to make a cross on the white floor—a white cross in red blood.

"Of course," I said again. "It was a Swiss flag he was trying to make with his own blood. It wasn't Schellenberg's people who killed him. It was the Swiss. That's what he was trying to tell us. That Meyer, or more likely that other fellow who was with him—Leuthard—must have killed him. They went to the German Opera that night, which is just around the corner. Leuthard claimed he'd slept all the way through act three of Weber's *The Marksman*. He must have killed him then. To stop Heckholz from exposing what the Swiss had been up to in association with Stiftung Nordhav; to stop him from going to the international press."

"I'm delighted for you," said Nölle, "but none of this helps me. I'm supposed to find out what the hell you're doing down here. If Schellenberg is a traitor. If he's seeking to make a secret deal with the Allies on Himmler's personal instructions. That's what I want to know. And if Goebbels is having an affair with Dalia Dresner. So far you've told me fuck-all. That won't do, Gunther. That won't do at all." He shook his head. "I'm asking you nicely. Please. Tell me everything you know. Given the fact that I just saved your life, it's the least you can do."

"I don't know anything about Schellenberg betraying us to the

Allies. That doesn't make sense at all. Look, surely the fact that the Amis kidnapped me and were questioning me on the assumption that I was General Schellenberg confirms that they don't know anything about it, either. No, that doesn't work at all. The Swiss are in business with the SS. And more particularly, Stiftung Nordhav—a company owned by a few select members of the SS. That's a secret worth killing for."

A strong sense of relief at having escaped from the Amis and now this realization that I had most likely "solved" Heckholz's murder had perhaps blinded me to the threat that was now right in front of me; but how all of this might eventually play out was now delayed as the other Gestapo man came through the kitchen door. He wasn't wearing a jacket. His sleeves were rolled up, there was oil on his face and hands, and he looked as if he'd been working.

"You'd better come and look at this, boss," he said.

Thirty-two

We went through the kitchen door into a large garage where my car was now parked over an inspection pit lit with an electric light illuminating its underside. It was dark outside and through a high window into the farmyard, cooler air full of moths and the sweet smell of cow dung flowed into the garage. A sign above the door said *Beware of the Bull*. A few chickens wandered in and out of the garage to see what had happened to my car, which was hardly surprising. The Mercedes looked as if a small grenade had exploded inside it. The bonnet and trunk and all of the doors were wide open. The spare wheel was on the hay-strewn floor next to the flask of rakija I'd been intending to give Dalia as a present. The leather panels had been removed from the inside of the doors. Even the rocker panels under the doors had been opened up. It was now very clear what the other Gestapo man had been up to while I'd been talking to Nölle.

"What did you find, Edouard?"

"Gold," said the other man. "This car looks as if it was owned by Rumpelstiltskin."

He reached into the rocker panel and withdrew a gold bar. And then another. Within minutes eight gold bars lay shining on the garage floor. I picked one up. It was heavy.

"Must weigh at least ten kilos," I said, and gave it to Nölle.

"More like twelve," he said, hefting it in his hand. "At thirty-five dollars an ounce, each one of those bars is probably worth what—fourteen thousand dollars? Which is about two hundred and fifty thousand reichsmarks."

"Two million in gold," I said. "No wonder the car's steering felt heavy. And why I was using so much petrol. I was driving half the Reichsbank across the Swiss border."

Nölle tossed the bar onto the floor.

"Are you saying you didn't know anything about this?" Nölle asked me.

"Of course I didn't. If I'd known, I'd be in hiding by now preparing for a new life in Mexico. But it certainly explains why Schellenberg didn't want to drive this car into Switzerland himself. Why take the risk when I could do that? The question is, who does the gold belong to? Is it Schellenberg's personal supply? Stiftung Nordhav's gold? That's the company I was telling you about. Or is this Himmler's gold?"

"I'm not following you," said Nölle.

"Well, look, this is your idea, not mine," I said. "But it occurs to me that if you and your bosses are right and Himmler is using Schellenberg to try to extend peace feelers to the Allies, then that's going to need finance. This country's neutrality doesn't extend to money. The Swiss don't like our paper money. Nobody does. Very sensibly, they much prefer gold. Alternatively, the gold might be intended to make sure that the Reichsführer himself is well insured against a rainy day. If the war goes against us, he's going to need a supply of money outside Germany, wouldn't you say? I'd have thought a hefty deposit of gold in a Swiss bank will prevent a few sleepless nights for the Reichsführer."

"You're a smooth talker, Gunther," said Nölle, and he reached under his jacket. "That's what your file says. It's easy to see why Schellenberg picked you for this job. And if anyone could talk his way out of a spot, it's you, probably. The way you picked up what I said earlier—about Himmler's peace feelers—and threw it back to me, just now, with some spin on it. That was clever. Wasn't it, Edouard?"

"He's a clever bastard right enough," said the other man. "Typical Kripo. Makes a better criminal than the criminals."

The broom-handle Mauser in Nölle's hand didn't escape my attention. Not least because it was pointed at me. And there were three bodies in an apartment somewhere in Zurich that told me he was quite prepared to use it.

"I like you, Gunther. I really do. It's just a shame we've got orders to kill you." He shrugged. "But we have. Just as soon as we found out what the hell you were up to in Switzerland. Well, I reckon now we have. Or at least now we have something we can get a fix on. But I really don't think I'll mention half of all that shit you said in the house. Frankly, I couldn't remember half of it anyway. I daresay you're right about nearly everything. But my pay grade doesn't really cover me to think very much."

"Oh, I don't know. You were pretty quick with the math on those gold prices."

"Before the war I worked in a bank. But I think it's best I just tell my superiors that you were smuggling gold out of Germany and leave it at that. Frankly, anything else is likely to get me into trouble just for mentioning it. What the generals do is for them to fight about, not the likes of me. Now I can make my report and wash my hands of the whole affair."

"I know that feeling very well myself," I said. "Crime doesn't seem to matter so much when there's so much of it around. When it's completely out of control. After a while you just want to keep your head down and get by without comment. You have my sympathies."

"I'm glad you see it that way."

"Sure. I'd probably do the same myself. We're cut from the same piece of wood, Nölle. We're both of us ordinary cops just trying to get along. The way I see it, there's plenty of gold for all three of us to live out the rest of our lives in considerable luxury."

"You'd really do that? Steal the gold?"

"Why not? They stole it from someone. The Jews, probably. What's to stop us stealing it back? Two million in gold split three ways? That's seven hundred and fifty thousand for each of you and half a million for me. How about it?"

He looked at the other man, who shook his head slowly.

"Sorry," said Nölle. "But we can't do that. It's not that we don't want to. But we're not like you, Gunther. It's that we just don't have the guts, I think. Besides, there's Gottlob to consider. Our friend the farmer. He's what you might call a die-hard Nazi. He'd never agree to what you're proposing."

"So you're really going to shoot me."

He nodded. "I'm afraid so. I could shoot you here but I wouldn't like to risk the neighbors hearing the shots. Sound carries around here. Especially at night. Besides, I figure the Zurich cops have probably had enough shootings for one day. So we'll go for a drive, I think. Edouard, bring the car around. And get the bottle. We'll share a last drink before the end, Gunther. I've no wish to make this any more unpleasant than it needs to be."

"Very thoughtful of you, I'm sure."

"You've no idea. Gottlob would probably feed you to his pigs."

After Nölle had forced me to put the gold back into the Mercedes we all climbed into the black Citroën and drove out of Ringlikon, up a winding mountain road, and across an open railway line, to the top of the Uetliberg, which, at almost nine hundred meters, is the highest spot in Zurich. It took about ten minutes to reach the top from the safe house. In any other circumstances I'd have been pleased to be there. There was a hotel—the Uto Kulm—and a thirty-meter-high viewing tower, as if the mountaintop itself and its many precipitous footpaths were not enough for the Swiss. It seemed almost blasphemous to try to improve on what nature had done, but that's the Swiss for you, I suppose.

The darkness and a sudden heavy shower of rain had deterred the usual lovers and happy wanderers and it seemed we had the place to ourselves. We stepped out of the car and I looked around. For a moment my eyes caught some awful sculptures of deer that looked more like camels and I wondered how it was that the Swiss had permitted such an important beauty spot to have these ugly ornaments. Whatever Schellenberg said about the Swiss, they were still capable of the most appalling lapses of taste.

At gunpoint, the two Gestapo men forced me to climb up the tower. I didn't think it was to appreciate the spectacular night views of the city or the red rooftops of the hotel itself. I've never much liked heights and this one was already beginning to bore me.

"This is nice," I said. "I needed some air."

"There's plenty of that up here," said Nölle. "All the air anyone could want."

"I assume we're not here to enjoy the view," I said when we had reached the top of the tower.

"You're right," said Nölle, and he produced the flask of rakija he'd found in my car. "This is journey's end for you, Gunther, so drink up, there's a good fellow."

Reluctantly I took a swig. With a gun shoved in my face I could hardly do otherwise. The rakija tasted like liquid lava and was probably every bit as inflammable.

"You're not drinking?" I asked.

"Not this time. Which is good because there'll be more for you. I want you to drink all of it. All of it, you understand?"

Reluctantly I took another swig. "I get it. I'm going to get drunk and have an accident. Is that it? The way some communists used to fall in the Landwehr Canal and drown. With a little help from the Gestapo."

"Something like that," said Nölle. "As a matter of fact, this is a popular place for suicides. The Swiss have one of the highest suicide rates in Europe. Did you know that? Of course, that might have something to do with the fact that assisted suicide has been legal in this country since 1941."

"Fascinating."

"So what we're doing, you might almost say it's legal," he said. "Helping you to commit suicide. You see, the local police will like it a whole lot better if you jump instead of them finding you with a bullet in your head. That is, when they eventually find you. Drink up. That's it. You can take my word for it, the trees are rather thick down there. We'll write you a nice suicide note when we get back to the house and leave it in your hotel room tomorrow."

"That's a nice touch. The lonely German abroad. Away from home, he gets depressed and starts drinking heavily. Maybe he had something to do with the deaths of those Americans. That would tie a nice bow on everything."

"To understand all is to forgive all," said Nölle.

"Drink up," said Edouard. "You're not drinking. You know, you'll feel a whole lot better about this with a few drinks inside of you. I know I will."

He was holding the bottle to my lips and tipped some more in my mouth. I gulped at the fiery liquid and retched over the railing a little. But already I was starting to feel a little drunk. I sank onto my knees, cowering in the corner against the railing. The Mauser was pressed right under my ear. I knew if I finished the bottle I would die anyway, that they wouldn't have to push me off the tower to kill me.

"Don't throw up," said Nölle. "That will spoil everything."

A faint breath of wind stirred the hair on my head but that was nothing beside the effect that the height was having on the sinews of my heart. I glanced over the railings. Through the glass rooftop of the hotel's brightly lit winter garden I could see people enjoying drinks and cigarettes and reading newspapers with not the least clue of what was about to befall me.

"Listen," I spluttered, "if you're going to kill me, for Christ's sake give me a nail. At least let me have a last smoke with my drink. I never much liked one without the other."

"Sure. We'll all have a cigarette. And then you can finish your drink. Before you take wing, so to speak."

I stood up, fumbled a cigarette into my mouth with trembling hands, lit it, handed them the pack, and then took as large a mouthful of that filthy rakija as I could manage, only this time I didn't swallow it. Neither of the two Gestapo men was looking at me. I waited just long enough for them to get a cigarette in their mouths and then dip them to the lighter now springing into life in Nölle's hands. And then I spat the whole mouthful of rakija at the steady flame between their two bowed heads.

Even I was surprised at what happened next. I'd heard horror stories of what happened when a *Flammenwerfer* went in to clear a trench on the Western Front—horror stories of human torches and burning Frenchmen—but I'm pleased to say I'd never seen it myself. It wasn't a weapon that I could ever have used with a clear conscience. It's one thing putting a rifle bullet in a man's head, or even a bayonet through his gut, but it's something else to set him on fire. As soon as the rakija— which Geiger had said was more than eighty-proof alcohol—hit the flame from Edouard's lighter, it ignited the hands, shoulders, jackets, faces, heads, and hair of both men; in fact, it set fire to anything that the rakija from my drunken mouth had landed on, including the railing. A ruthless *Flammenwerfer* couldn't have done a better job. A strong smell of singed human hair and burning flesh filled the bright and fiery air alongside their screams. Edouard plucked at his burning hair and a piece of it came away in his burning hand. Nölle twisted one way and then the other in hideous slow motion like a living Roman candle. The next second the alcohol had burned off and the flames were gone. For a moment they stopped screaming. At the very least, I'd blinded them.

I hardly hesitated. I reached down, grabbed Nölle around the ankles, lifted him up and then tipped him over the railing like the trash from a ship at sea. Edouard guessed what had happened and lashed blindly out in front of him. I caught his wrist, twisted his arm hard around his back, bent him over the railing, and tried to get a hand under his knee. But like a stubborn mule, he splayed his feet and stayed put until I punched hard at his balls several times and then felt him relax a little. He puked some, I think, and then I lifted him off his feet.

"No, don't, please," he yelled, but it was too late. The next second he fell through the air, screaming like an injured fox, and it was only when he vanished through the treetops and hit the ground that the silence of the mountaintop was restored.

Horrified at what I had done and yet relieved still to be alive, I sat down and took another swig of the rakija. Then I threw up.

Thirty-three

Trembling violently as if I'd just touched a live electrical wire, I drove back down the mountain in the Citroën to the safe house in Ringlikon. The night was not yet over. A truckload of milk churns was parked on the edge of the field. The lights were on in the safe house and a man—the dairy farmer, I presumed—was moving between the kitchen and the farmyard. He was a tall, powerful man wearing a black, short-sleeved jacket with red piping, a white shirt, and black leather trousers. It was probably all the fashion in Zurich. I didn't want to harm him—I'd had enough violence for one evening—but I wanted my passport and my wallet and my car back more, and I couldn't see how I was going to get them unless I had a gun in my hand. So I sat in the Citroën for several minutes trying to compose myself and wondering if I could bluff him, but I wasn't able to think of anything that stood even half a chance. You didn't run a safe house for the Gestapo without being just a bit hard to fool, not to say treacherous. Nölle had described him as a die-hard Nazi and as someone who would have fed me to his pigs. Even though I hadn't actually seen any pigs, that certainly sealed his fate as far as I was concerned. I didn't think this man was going to let me go on my sweet way without a fight. At first I thought to sneak up behind him and hit him with something. But then a low bellow ripped through the Swiss night air and I asked myself if I could enlist the help of the bull in the shed. I knew nothing at all about bulls except that they were often dangerous. Especially when there was a big sign above a doorway into the yard inviting you to beware of one. There ought to have been a sign above my head, as well. Fed up with the way the day had turned out and deprived of a pleasant afternoon with a female of my own species, I was feeling kind of pissed off and dangerous myself.

I stepped out of the car and very carefully tried the handle on the front door. It was not locked. A Swiss village isn't the kind of place where people lock their doors. I walked back down the street and climbed the fence into the field so that I could enter the yard that way. Up close, the bull was even meaner than I had supposed. His horns were quite short but that didn't handicap his ability to intimidate. Clearly the farmer thought the same way because the bull had a ring through his massive pink nose and it was attached to a short chain that led up his muzzle and onto a loop around each horn. It looked like the last thing you wanted to find yourself holding when you were looking to flush the lavatory in the dark. Even as I approached his stall, the bull backed off from the gate a little, snorted, flicked his tail, lowered his hay bale of a head, and started to sweep the straw back with one hoof. After a while he realized I was safe behind the gate and, appearing to tire of this, he turned around as if to show off his balls, which were bigger than a silk stocking full of grapefruit. It all seemed designed to tell me just one thing: bulls are dangerous. I looked around for something to goad him with and caught sight of a pitchfork, which seemed ideal. So I picked it up and poked him several times with the blunt end. And when that didn't work I gave him a short jab with the sharp end, which soon had him giving me the eye again. This time he bellowed for good measure and butted his head at the gate, which shook like a cheap car on a rutted road. It was time for me to execute my improvised plan. I drew the bolt on the gate, opened it a few

centimeters, and then ran. In my haste to be away I slipped on the cobbled ground and almost fell, but once safely over the fence and into the
field, I climbed back onto the road and came around the front of
the house. I had a clear view of everything. The bull was now loose in
the dimly lit yard. He was standing there, head lowered with intent,
snorting his frustration at not finding me beside him and looking more
than a little like the Ox Fountain of Fertility in Berlin's Arnswalder
Platz where the childless sometimes went in search of miracles.

Meanwhile the farmer didn't seem to have noticed anything was
amiss. I needed to get him out of the house and into the farmyard so I
could run into the house and bolt the kitchen door behind him. So I
picked up a milk bottle off the front step and lobbed it into the yard,
where it exploded like a glass grenade. Then another. I heard a question shouted in the house and then heavy bolts on the kitchen door
being drawn. I opened the front door, waited a second, and then ran
into the house just in time to see the farmer advancing from his brightly
lit kitchen and into the near darkness of the yard. I sprinted into the
kitchen and slammed the door shut behind him. The farmer turned
around and started to hammer on the door, still unaware of just how
precarious his situation really was.

"What the hell?" he yelled. "Open this damn door. Is that you,
Edouard? Stop fucking around, will you? I've had a long day and I'm
tired and I'm not in the mood for any stupid jokes. D'you hear? Open
this fucking door."

I didn't see what happened next. For one thing I was busy looking
for my passport, the car keys, and a gun; and for another, there wasn't a
window that looked out onto the farmyard. But I heard more or less
everything that took place.

"Oh, Jesus," the farmer screamed. "For Christ's sake, open the
door. Oh Christ. Oh Jesus."

I could hardly avoid hearing it. I've heard some awful things in my life—the noise of the trenches will live with me forever—but this ran that a very close second.

I heard the bull bellow loudly, then the sound of hoofbeats on the cobbles. The farmer screamed again and the next second the kitchen door shook as if it had been struck by a panzer tank. And then again. All told, the door was battered in this way five times before it stopped and everything was silent in the yard again. I didn't like to think what had happened on the other side of that door. And I felt guilty, as if I'd stabbed the farmer with the pitchfork. Telling myself that Gottlob would certainly have shot me if he'd got the chance, I carried on looking for my things and eventually found them in the kitchen drawer, alongside a flashlight and an Arminius—a .22 caliber pistol made by Hermann Weihrauch, a company that also manufactured bicycles— and a box of ammunition. The Arminius was only a bit more threatening than a loaded bicycle but not much. I pushed the gun under the waistband of my trousers and the box of ammunition in my pocket but only until I saw the Walther P38 hanging in a shoulder holster on the back of the front door. I checked the Walther and, finding it was loaded, returned the Arminius to the drawer. A .38 always feels better in your hand than a .22. Especially when you're trying to make your point in an argument.

Feeling a little braver now that I had a decent gun in my hand, I went to the kitchen door, opened it a fraction, and shone the flashlight around the yard in the faint hope that the farmer might still be alive and that I might offer him an escape. But I could tell I was too late. The farmer called Gottlob lay curled up on the cobbles as if he'd gone to sleep on the ground. He was dead, of course. His face looked as if it had been demolished by a wrecking ball. The light caught the bull's big brown eye and he charged again. I closed the door quickly and bolted it just in time, top and bottom, even while the beast battered its head against timbers that barely held. Through planks thicker than my hand, the bull sounded as big as an elephant.

I went into the garage where we'd left the Mercedes and screwed the rocker plates on top of the gold bars and the panels back on the doors. There was a petrol pump so I filled the 190's tank with gas, too. Then I washed myself in a pantry sink in the garage, straightened my tie, brushed off my suit, and generally tried to make myself look like someone who belonged in a nice hotel in Zurich. With any luck I might have a quiet night and then meet Inspector Weisendanger for breakfast as if nothing had happened. I was hardly proud of my night's work. One way or another, six men—three Americans and three Germans—were now dead because of me. But I hadn't asked for any of this. I'd much prefer to have spent the afternoon in bed with Dalia Dresner. Any man would.

At the Baur au Lac, the antique carriage clock on the mantelpiece said it was past ten o'clock. Everything was exactly as I had left it earlier that day, and in this oasis of lakeside calm it was hard to believe that organizations like the OSS and the Gestapo even existed, or that the world was even at war. The Russian front and the bombing of Hamburg and Berlin might have been taking place on another planet. The neatly bearded desk clerk was wearing a bow tie and a matching black morning coat and he had the cool, imperturbable air of a man for whom nothing was ever a surprise. He regarded my arrival back in the hotel's elegant, wood-paneled lobby with a good show of pleasure, which is saying something for a Swiss. I suppose I just didn't seem like the kind of guest who'd probably doubled the country's annual homicide rate in just one night. And when I asked for my room key, he also handed me a note written on the hotel's expensively thick stationery. If he could smell the alcohol on my breath and clothes, he didn't let on.

"Is there anything else I can do for you this evening, Herr Gunther?"

"Yes. Please ask room service to send up a bottle of beer and some scrambled eggs, will you? Bread and cheese, some sausage and pickles. Anything at all. And as soon as possible, please. I'm ravenously hungry."

Alone in my room I read Dalia's note several times before my supper turned up. Then I had a hot bath. I thought about telephoning but it was late by Swiss standards and I decided to do it in the morning, after I'd had breakfast with Weisendanger. I went to bed thinking sweet thoughts of Dalia. In her note she apologized for her lateness—it seemed she'd been unable to escape from her husband until almost four p.m., and assumed my not being at the hotel had something to do with that—and she suggested we meet again the following day. There were lots of written kisses at the bottom of the notepaper and a real one made of lipstick. I felt like I was fifteen again. In a good way. The older you get, the more attractive that idea starts to seem. And when I saw her, it would be even sweeter than it might have been because I had survived a kidnapping and an attempted murder.

Perhaps it's true what Goethe says, that destiny grants us our wishes, but in its own way, in order to give us something beyond our wishes. It's curious, but often, just as I'm drifting off to sleep, I feel I might be Goethe. It could be his disdain for the church and the law and of course the Nazis—he would certainly have loathed Hitler; it's certainly the Nazis he has in mind when he tells us to disdain those in whom the desire to punish is strong—but I once visited the famous Auerbachs Keller in Leipzig where the poet spent most of his student years drinking wine, and felt an affinity with the man that I've felt for no other. Then again, it might just have been all those pictures on the wooden walls of Faust drinking with Mephistopheles. I've often felt an affinity with him, too. How else was I to explain my still being alive? My mind sidestepped the present once again, and for a moment I was drinking in the medieval cellar's subterranean depths; then I was astride a wine barrel as big as a bull and riding out the door and up into the marketplace where the last scene from *Jud Süss* was already under way, and poor Oppenheimer was screaming for his life to be spared as the cage carrying the gallows was raised to the top of a tower high above the citizenry's heads. I stayed to watch before oblivion took us both to its black velvet bosom. It was a very German dream.

Thirty-four

'm normally an early riser. Especially in summer when the sun gets up before anyone. But that morning neither of us was quite ready for the Zurich police at 5:30 a.m. Weisendanger was there, of course, and stood quietly by while I dressed and his men searched my room, to find nothing. When I'd got back to the Baur the previous night I'd taken the precaution of hiding my gun behind the wheel of an enormous Duesenberg that was underneath a car cover in the parking lot, so that wasn't anything to worry about.

"What's this all about, Inspector? Was I late for breakfast? Or is it an especially nice dawn sky this morning?"

"Shut up and get dressed. You'll find out."

"The last time I got woken up like this I spent a very uncomfortable day with the Gestapo."

"I told you we like to start early in the Swiss police."

"I didn't think you meant this early. Let's hope the breakfast is better where we're going now."

We went to the Zurich police headquarters in Kasernenstrasse, which was about a fifteen-minute walk northwest of the hotel, and just a stone's throw from the main railway station. I know that because I had to walk back to the Baur after they'd finished questioning me about the three Amis they'd found shot dead in the Huttenstrasse apartment. Police HQ was a disproportionately large, semi-castellated building with a big central clock and two white-painted wings, and what looked like an enormous parade ground to the rear.

"This is a hell of a shit factory for a country without much real crime," I remarked as we trudged up four flights of stairs.

"Maybe that's why we don't have much crime," said Weisendanger. "Did you ever think about that?"

We went into a top-floor room with three lateral bars across the window. I suppose they might have prevented a fat man from committing suicide by being thrown into the street—which was a favorite interrogation technique of the Gestapo—but only just. From the room where they questioned me I could see across the river to what looked like a military barracks and stables. I lit a cigarette and sat down.

"Where were you yesterday?" asked Weisendanger.

"After a very pleasant breakfast with you," I said, "I spent the morning in Küsnacht. At the home of Dr. Stefan Obrenović. I expect you can ask him. He'll certainly remember my visit. He didn't like me very much."

"I wonder why?"

"The very same thing I was asking myself. After that, I took a drive around the lake. Which was nice. It's a beautiful lake you have here. Then I went to the zoo, where I also had a late lunch. You could have asked me all this over a soft-boiled egg and a cup of coffee."

"The zoo?"

"Yes, it's on the slopes of the Allmend. And better than Berlin Zoo, I have to admit. A lot of our animals have been eaten, you know. It's a short-sighted policy for a zoo, I think."

"What animals did you see?"

"Lions and tigers. Things with fur. The usual kind."

"Then what did you do?"

"Let's see. I had a coffee at Sprüngli on Paradeplatz. No trip to

Zurich would be complete without that. Then a beer at the Kronen-halle. Maybe two or three because I fell asleep in the car. Came back here at around nine o'clock."

"The desk clerk said it was more like ten."

"Was it really that late?"

"You weren't anywhere near Huttenstrasse?"

"Not to my knowledge. What's in Huttenstrasse?"

"Right now the bodies of three dead Americans."

"And you think I had something to do with that?"

"For five hundred years we've had democracy and peace in this town. Then the day after you show up we have three shootings in one day. That's a hell of a coincidence, wouldn't you say?"

"Would you be as upset if they were Germans who'd died?"

"Try me."

"I hate to sound like the elder statesman here, but when I was a detective in Berlin, I used to look for something we quaintly called 'evidence' before bringing a suspect in for questioning. That way I could catch him out if he was lying. You might try that sometime. You'd be surprised how effective it can be in a situation like this."

"You think you're pretty smart, don't you, Gunther? A typically arrogant German."

"The last time I looked, that wasn't a crime. Even in Switzerland."

"You know, I'd be well within my rights to throw you out of the country right now."

"If you were going to do it you'd have done it already. That much is obvious. So why am I here? It can't be the view. And it's certainly not the coffee. I know the Swiss like to go fishing but it's common practice to hang your hook in water that's deeper than a couple of centimeters. You're staring into a puddle of piss and you know it."

"I warned you before, Gunther. Cops in Zurich don't have a sense of humor."

"Okay, you've got the rope under my ear for that one. Type out a confession and I'll sign it now."

"We still have the death penalty in Switzerland," said Weisendanger. "For certain crimes."

"Forget it. I didn't kill those Amis."

I glanced around the room. On the wall was a flag and a map of Switzerland just in case we forgot where we were. I didn't think that was likely. Weisendanger might have been speaking German but he still wasn't making much sense. So far, so Swiss. Unless . . .

"Shall I tell you what I think happened? Don't get your hopes up, Inspector. I'm not about to explain a smart theory about those dead Americans. I don't know anything about that. But I'll bet good Swiss money that this morning's little charade was a politician's idea. Not someone who understands how policemen work, like you and I. Am I right?"

"The government councillor in charge of security is keen for you to move on—at least from Zurich."

"I've just got here. Why should I leave? I haven't broken any laws. I don't intend to, either."

"He feels that you might be an undesirable element."

"Believe me. I'm already quite used to that back home. You see, I'm not a Nazi. I only look like one."

"A commissioner of police can make life difficult for someone."

"That doesn't sound very democratic. In fact it sounds like the sort of thing a Nazi would say."

"But you do have business in Ermatingen, do you not?"

"Yes."

"In which case I strongly suggest that you go and do it, while you can."

"Pity. I was getting to like this city."

"I wouldn't like you to owe me anything. Like your life."

"That sounds like a threat."

"You're not listening to what I'm saying, Gunther. You see, I've got a hunch that trouble is something that comes your way. And since I'm supposed to protect you while you're in Zurich, I just don't want to be the one that has to pull your chestnuts out of the fire. Maybe you had nothing to do with those three dead Americans. Maybe. But perhaps there will be others who might think differently. Americans, for example. Who might make the same stupid mistake I did. You see what I'm saying? This is a quiet town. We like it that way."

I thought of the dead man in the village of Ringlikon. At least his sudden death would look like an accident. Farmers get killed by bulls all the time. It's an occupational hazard. But the two men who'd fallen from the viewing tower at the top of the Uetliberg—you could hardly have concealed the fact that they were both wearing second-degree burns on their faces. And when they were identified as German— maybe even Gestapo—then someone might make a connection with the dead farmer, and the Swiss police would start to believe they had a tit-for-tat war on their hands between us and the Amis. So Weisendanger was probably right. If the Amis didn't try to nail me, the Swiss would almost certainly have to pick me up again and then where would my mission be? It was best I went to Ermatingen. Even if that meant I wasn't going to sleep with Dalia anytime soon. That was a pity but it couldn't be helped. Not unless her husband had gone to Geneva again.

As soon as I was back in my room at the Baur, I called her at home in Küsnacht. Agnes, the maid, answered and told me that her mistress would telephone me back in five minutes. Twenty minutes later Dalia called up.

"Darling, what happened yesterday? At the hotel?" she asked. "I know I was late, but surely you must have guessed why. Were you angry with me?"

"Not in the least. I had to go out. On business. Suffice to say it was a very long day."

"That sounds difficult."

"You could say that. Listen, I don't suppose you've changed your mind about coming back to Germany?"

"You mean to be in this film? No. I haven't. Being a movie star no longer interests me very much. I've decided to go to the polytechnic and study mathematics. I'm particularly interested in studying set theory and the continuum hypothesis. There's a theory I should like to prove by a man called Georg Cantor."

"Sure, I know. The singer. Banjo Eyes."

Dalia laughed. "That's Eddie Cantor."

"I know. But I didn't want you to think I was completely ignorant."

"I hope that my decision doesn't leave you in a difficult position with Josef."

"With Josef?" I smiled, as for a second I imagined myself on first-name terms with the minister of Truth. "No. I'm sure it will be fine."

"Are you all right, baby? You sound tired. I miss you so much."

"I'm all right. And I miss you, too. I can't believe you're so close and yet so far. Every time I see that lake I know you're looking at it, too. Why don't I just swim down there and see you? Right now. It couldn't take me more than a couple of hours. Seriously though. I don't suppose there's any chance your husband is going away on business today. Only, I have to leave Zurich."

"So soon? Oh, no. That's too bad. You're going back to Germany?"

"It might happen that way. I have to go to somewhere first. On the Swiss-German border. I'm not sure when I'll be back down this way, if at all."

"Stefan is still here, and he's very suspicious, Bernie. That's to say even more suspicious than normal. Well, you got my note at your hotel. What are we going to do? I think I'll die if I don't see you soon."

"Look, I'm going to a château in a place called Ermatingen."

"Ermatingen? That's not so far. About an hour away by car. We might meet there, perhaps. But Rapperswil would be better for me. I could easily get to Rapperswil and there are lots of hotels in Rapperswil."

"I'll call you when I get to Wolfsberg. Maybe we can meet up at Rapperswil. I don't know. But don't give up, angel. Don't give up. Like you said before. Love will find a way."

Thirty-five

Wolfsberg occupied an elevated, north-facing plateau between the Thur valley and the Untersee of Lake Constance. I parked beside an extensive pear orchard and walked toward one of several buildings and, summoned by the crunch of my car tires on his gravel, I found Paul Meyer-Schwertenbach walking toward me, taller and more handsome than I remembered, and smiling warmly. He was wearing the informal clothes of a southern German gentleman: a gray Trachten-style hunting jacket with green piping and gold deer on the lapels, a pair of matching riding pants, and short brown ankle boots. There was a hock glass in his hand. I expect there were servants around but at least for the moment I didn't see any, and Meyer struck me as the type to pretend that he and his wife were simple souls who much preferred to look after themselves. Preferring to look after yourself and doing it by necessity are very different things; especially when you have a butler and a maid and a cook and maybe a couple of gardeners to help out with a few light duties around the house.

"You made it," he said, and handed me the glass. "I'm very glad. Welcome to my house. Welcome to Wolfsberg."

"Thanks," I said, and tasted the wine, which was a delicious Riesling. "That's the most hospitality I've had since I got to Switzerland."

"We weren't expecting you until tomorrow," he said.

"I had to change my plans."

"Let me show you around," he said with justifiable pride.

"You have a beautiful home," I said redundantly.

"There's been a house on this site since 1272."

"That's nice. With a position like this, it makes you wonder why they waited that long."

"I'm pleased you think so."

The château comprised the old château and the new château—a nicety that was lost on me, save to say these were two separate buildings—a sweet little chapel, a library, a coach house, a pantile-roofed walkway, and, for all I knew, a police presidium and a dungeon that was home to the man in the iron mask. Meyer told me that the new château was in a poor state of repair—which struck me as being counterintuitive—and that I would be staying with him and his wife, Patrizia, and their other guests in the old château. With its three stories and a façade that faced south toward an attractive French garden, the old château was a compact four-square building with dormer windows and a pyramidal mansard roof, on the summit of which was an onion-topped bell-carriage that resembled the cherry on a very large white cake—the kind of cake that very rich people are wont to have. It was a spectacular house, but for my money it was the view that made it especially enviable because, in the middle of Lake Constance, you could see as far as the German island of Reichenau with its famous abbey. Meyer told me he had some powerful binoculars on a tripod and through these you could see German soldiers watering their horses in the lake. I didn't doubt this for a second. From Wolfsberg Castle you could probably have seen Abbot Berno of Reichenau eating his breakfast back in 1048.

One thing I didn't expect to see from the terrace at Wolfsberg Castle was General Schellenberg. Wearing a light summer suit, he was sitting below the terrace on the lawn at the back of the house with a woman I guessed was the wife, Patrizia, two dogs, and, in no particular order, Major Eggen. Meyer led the way down a flight of steps to greet them.

"This is the man I was telling you about, my dear," he told his wife. "The famous Berlin detective. Bernie Gunther."

"Yes, of course. Welcome to Wolfsberg, Herr Gunther."

She stood up politely to shake my hand. Patrizia was a woman of spectacular beauty who reminded me a little of Hedy Lamarr. Tall and willowy, with an easy laugh, she wore a floral summer dress and white Persol sunglasses and smoked as if her life depended on it. I might justifiably have paid her more attention but for the realization that Schellenberg and Eggen had certainly used me to smuggle gold across the Swiss border—that I'd taken all of the risk, unwittingly, while they'd traveled in complete safety.

"Everything all right, Gunther?" asked Schellenberg.

For the moment I decided not to let on I knew about the gold or to tell Schellenberg that the OSS had mistaken me for him, and with lethal consequences. The two Germans remained seated, smirking quietly and looking like they'd both been very clever. But the P38 in the shoulder holster I was wearing under my jacket was just itching to come out.

"Yes, everything's just fine, sir," I said.

"Any problems with the car?"

"None at all."

"Good. And where is it now?"

I was tempted to say I'd left it in Zurich. Instead I sat down and let Patrizia refill my glass, and after a short delay, said, "Out front." I teased him with the keys for a moment and then dropped them back into my pocket.

"How was Zurich?" she asked.

"I liked it. Especially the lake. And the hotel was lovely."

"Where did you stay?"

"The Baur au Lac."

"That's the nicest," she said.

"This is all very cozy," I said. "I certainly wasn't expecting to see both of you here. General. Major."

"It was a spur-of-the-moment sort of thing," explained Eggen. A little bead of sweat rolled off his forehead and onto the bony bridge of his nose. It was a warm day but not that warm, and I realized he was nervous—of me, perhaps.

"I could sit here all day and look at that view," I told Patrizia.

"We frequently do," she said. "The desk in Paul's study is set deliberately against a wall, so that the view doesn't stop him from writing. It's a tip he picked up from Somerset Maugham when we were on the Riviera before the war. Although Paul hasn't done anything as extreme as Maugham did. When he bought the Villa Mauresque, he had the window in his study bricked up so that the view wouldn't distract him."

"It's difficult enough to write a novel as it is without staring out of the window all day," said Meyer.

"I have the same problem at police headquarters on Berlin's Alexanderplatz," I said. "I frequently find myself staring out the window. Wondering what I'm doing there at all."

"I'm looking forward to hearing much more about that," said Meyer.

"Uh-oh," said Patrizia. "I hear a writer coming. If you'll excuse me, I'm going to see how dinner is coming along."

"I'll come and help you," said Eggen.

Schellenberg waited until they'd gone and said, "I thought I told you not to bring a gun to Switzerland." His keen eyes hadn't missed the fact that I was wearing a shoulder holster.

"This?" I patted my left breast. "I didn't bring this to Switzerland. I acquired it along the way. A souvenir of my visit, you might say."

"Get rid of it, for Christ's sake. You're making our hostess nervous."

"You know, I don't think I will, General. Not for the moment. Too much has happened since I got to Switzerland. Best it stays where it is for now. Tucked up in its little holster."

"I can assure you," said Meyer, "Patrizia is fine with guns. Like most Swiss, we keep quite a few guns around the house."

"It's too late for that," I said. "The Germans are already here."

"I thought you said there were no problems, Gunther," said Schellenberg.

"With the car. The car's just fine. It's out front. With me, things were a little more difficult."

Schellenberg looked relieved. "Such as?"

"Nothing I couldn't handle."

"That sounds a bit ominous."

"It's not at all ominous." I lit a cigarette. "Not really. You see, it already happened. To me, at any rate. I'll tell you about it sometime, General. When I'm in a more even frame of mind than I am at this moment. It will be better for you that way. Right now I just want to enjoy this very impressive view, this excellent glass of wine, and this cigarette. And to talk to Captain Meyer, of course. I haven't seen you since last July, Captain. We've got a bit of catching up to do, you and I." I smiled a sarcastic sort of smile. "With the accent on 'catching,' perhaps."

"Whatever do you mean? And, please, call me Paul."

"Thanks, but for now I'll just stick to captain, if you don't mind. And what do I mean? Well, at the risk of seeming rude, I have to ask you a formal question. A policeman's question, I'm afraid."

"What the hell are you talking about?" asked Schellenberg.

"The last time I saw you, Captain Meyer, at the German Opera in Berlin, there was a murder just around the corner. Fellow named

Heckholz. Dr. Heckholz. Someone stove his head in with a bust of Hitler. There's a joke in there somewhere but not for Dr. Heckholz. He died, you see. Not the first person killed by Hitler, and certainly not the last. There, I made it. The joke."

"No one's laughing, Gunther," said Schellenberg.

"Let me finish. Heckholz was a lawyer for the Minoux family, who used to own the villa on Lake Wannsee. Where the IKPK conference took place. Heckholz was preparing to ask some awkward questions about the Nordhav Foundation and the purchase of the villa and who received all of the money from the sale. At first I thought the general here had ordered one of his men to shut Heckholz up. After all, he is the managing director of Nordhav and rather conveniently he does command an office full of murderers."

"Really, Gunther, you're the most extraordinarily impertinent fellow I think I've ever met," said Schellenberg.

"But then—it was only yesterday, as a matter of fact—I realized who really killed him. It wasn't the general or any of his men. And I don't believe it was you, Captain Meyer. You don't strike me as the type. But I think you know who it was. Which brings me to the formal question, sir. Was it your colleague, Lieutenant Leuthard, who killed Dr. Heckholz?"

"I must say," said Schellenberg. "If that doesn't beat all. You turn up at a man's house, as a guest, and within ten minutes you virtually accuse the man to his face of cold-blooded murder. You astonish me."

"Actually, General, I don't think it was cold-blooded at all. I think the lieutenant hit him on the spur of the moment. With the first heavy object that came to hand. If he'd gone there to kill him, he certainly would have brought a more effective weapon than a bronze of Adolf Hitler. Which means I'm certain that the captain here didn't order Heckholz to be killed, either. No, I'd say Leuthard acted way beyond his brief. After all, Captain, you yourself told me that Leuthard was a difficult character, at the best of times. A bit hotheaded, I think you said."

Schellenberg stood up. "I think you should leave now, Gunther."

"In the Mercedes?" I smiled. "The one I just arrived in? I don't think so, General. You wouldn't like that."

"Sit down, Schelli," said Meyer. "Sit down and be quiet for a moment. Captain Gunther is absolutely right. Lieutenant Leuthard did murder Dr. Heckholz. Just as he described."

"That much is now certain, anyway," I said.

"Leuthard was a lot more than a hothead," said Meyer. "He was a thug. I had no idea what kind of man he was when he accompanied me to Berlin. The army insisted I take him with me, for security in the event that someone from the Gestapo decided to kidnap me from the conference. Out of fear that under torture I might reveal some state secrets."

"Would you care to tell me exactly what happened, sir?"

"My God, Gunther," complained Schellenberg, "you sound exactly like the village policeman."

"I don't think I'm going to tell you exactly what you sound like, General. It might tempt me to reach for that gun. This is a neutral country, after all."

"No, no, Schelli, Gunther's quite right. He was first on the scene of the crime, after all. Heckholz was threatening to expose a business deal between the Swiss Wood Syndicate and a subsidiary of Nordhav—Export Drives GMBH—in the Swiss newspapers."

"You mean the deal to supply wooden barracks to the SS and the German Army?"

"How do you know about that?" asked Schellenberg.

"Precisely," said Meyer. "Two thousand of them. The first five hundred were shipped last year. The whole deal is worth a lot of money to Switzerland's rather beleaguered economy. About twelve million Swiss francs, to be honest. Not that it would be the first time our two countries have done business together. Back in 1939, Major Eggen's department bought a large quantity of machine guns from us. Of course, not all Swiss are happy that their country is making business deals with yours. Especially when it's military equipment. But those who are opposed to such deals don't tell us how this country is supposed to survive economically while remaining a neutral country that's surrounded by Germany and its allies. The fact is, we have to export to survive. We need German money, and to stay neutral, we need to do business with Germany. But this is a very sensitive subject and it would not have been helpful for someone to write about it in the Swiss newspapers. It's that simple. Schelli here has been very helpful in making such deals happen. He believes very strongly in Swiss neutrality. In fact, that's why he's here, right now."

"You're telling him much more than he really needs to know," said Schellenberg. "He's really not that important."

"Get to Leuthard's role in all this," I told Meyer.

"Soon after we checked into the Adlon I received a message from Heckholz asking for a meeting. So while you and I were chatting in the sunshine outside the hotel, I sent Leuthard round to Heckholz's office to set something up. He wasn't there. So he went back again during the opera, and this time he was. All that he was supposed to do was arrange a meeting. I certainly didn't expect him to bash the man's brains in. I was horrified when he told me what had happened. As soon as I got back to Switzerland, I arranged for Leuthard to be transferred from my section."

"So you're saying that Heckholz wasn't killed to save Switzerland from any embarrassment about the end users of those wooden barracks," I said.

Meyer looked puzzled. "Aside from the fact that a wooden barracks is going to be occupied by German soldiers," he said, "I really don't see that anyone can complain very much about a bloody hut. It's not like we're selling your country machine guns. That's why we're doing it. A hut is just a hut. Much less emotive than guns, I can assure you."

"That's fair," I said. "All the same, I wonder what the Swiss people might say if they knew exactly what the SS is using some of those huts for."

"I don't understand."

"They're being sent to concentration camps. You've heard about those, I suppose."

"You don't know that for sure, Gunther," said Schellenberg. "You're just guessing."

"Two thousand of them? I should think it's a fair guess that quite a few of them have ended up in one KZ or another."

"Do shut up, Gunther," said Schellenberg, "you're in way over your head."

"I'm used to that, oddly enough."

"You haven't the first idea of what we're trying to accomplish here."

"Of course they're not for soldiers, Captain Meyer. They're for Jewish slave labor. Jews and anyone else the Third Reich has deemed subhuman and therefore expendable. I should like to tell you more about those but I'm afraid I don't know much about what happens in these places, though I can guess."

"I see." Meyer looked grimly at Schellenberg. "Did you know about this, Schelli?"

"If he didn't know, he certainly suspected as much. And if a man as intelligent and well connected as the general here suspects something, then you can bet it isn't very long before he makes it his business to know everything about it. That's Schelli's job, after all. To find out where others have hidden the truth."

"Damn it all, Gunther, how dare you walk in here in your size forty-fives and trample all of the months of good work that Major Eggen and I have done."

"But sometimes he also makes it his business not to know what he suspects," I said. "Just as he's managed very carefully to avoid the murderous work that most of his unfortunate subordinates have been obliged to carry out. Is that right, General? Your small white hands are quite clean, aren't they?"

Schellenberg looked fit to burst with anger. Like a lot of small men, it turned out that he had quite a bark.

"Do you honestly think you're any different?" he said through gritted teeth. "If I've avoided getting blood on my small white hands then that's only because I've been hiding myself away in the same lavatory as you, Gunther. We've both been crouched in the end stall, living in fear that we'll have to do something to stay alive that makes staying alive seem like a high price to pay for what we've had to do. Haven't we? So what the hell gives you the right to judge me? Do you think that the captains are any less culpable than the generals, is that it? Or is it that you think that my soul has already paid a higher price by reason of who and what I am? Well, you're wrong. If I've got where I am with a shred of self-respect left to me then that's because I'm rather better at walking the high wire than you are. Did you ever consider that? And you can't look inside my heart and know me any more than I can look inside yours. The way I see things, it's my duty to try and save this country and, as a corollary, my country from total destruction. So let me explain it very simply in a way that even you can understand, Gunther. Only if Switzerland remains neutral will anywhere exist that Germany can conduct peace negotiations with the Allies. It's as simple as that. The Americans are here. The English are here. Even the Russians are here. All we have to do is find somewhere quiet with a nice round table and then sit down and talk. It's taken me months to

persuade Reichsführer Himmler that this is the only way forward for
Germany. Do you understand? It's our duty to end this war. And to do
that we need this country."

"That's a nice speech, General. If it wasn't for all the other stupid
generals who screw things up for the ordinary Fritz, I might start to
think I'd misjudged you entirely. The generals at Verdun and Arras
and Amiens. Not to mention all those incompetent generals who've
tried and failed on many occasions to kill Adolf Hitler. You'll pardon
me if I don't kiss you on the cheek and give you the Knight's Cross
with oak leaves."

Despite what I said I was feeling a little sick that I'd perhaps set
back important negotiations that might have put a swift end to the war.

"Is it true, Schelli?" asked Meyer. "Are these barracks we're exporting to Germany being used to house Jewish slave labor?"

"Probably, yes. But that shouldn't be your concern, Paul. I really
thought it best you didn't know on the principle that what you don't
know can't hurt you. Look, everything you said remains fundamen-
tally true. If Switzerland is going to survive as a neutral it needs German money to pay its way. Listen to me, Paul. There is a greater good
here. That's what you have to remember. Trust me. What we have
planned can still be achieved."

"After what Captain Gunther just told me, how can I go on trusting
you now?" asked Meyer.

"Because I can prove my loyalty to you as a friend," insisted Schellenberg, "and as a friend to this country. Hidden inside Gunther's Mercedes is quite a lot of gold. As a sign of the Reichsführer's good faith.
And not only that. Inside the exhaust pipe is something that should put
you in very good odor with General Masson—for that matter with
everyone in the Swiss intelligence community. Even Reichsführer
Himmler doesn't know anything about this. I've brought you the crown
jewels, so to speak, Paul. Or rather more accurately, Gunther has. That

car he just drove here from the factory in Germany contains secret plans that were drawn up by the Army High Command on Hitler's orders, for the possible invasion of Switzerland. I've betrayed my country, in order to save it. That's what I've done, Gunther. Can you honestly say the same?"

Thirty-six

I had to admit Schellenberg had me there. To the best of my knowledge I'd never committed treason. But there's a first time for everything.

"For Germany and for you, General Schellenberg, I volunteer," I said. "How can I help?"

"You can start by telling me what the fuck's been going on?" He shook his neatly combed head with exasperation. "Clearly something's been going on. Your attitude. That gun. Your cryptic remarks about the car. Tell me the gold is still there."

"It's still there. I told you. The car is fine."

"But?"

Feeling slightly ashamed of having misjudged Schellenberg so profoundly, I told him everything while he and I and Meyer walked back to the car.

"Can't be helped," said Schellenberg. "Their three will cancel out our three. That's the way these diplomatic things usually work. With any luck this whole thing will blow over and we can start the tricky business of negotiating the negotiations. The plans? They're still there, too?"

"The Gestapo found the gold, but nothing else. But it's all there. Everything. Don't worry."

"And you're sure they didn't have time to send a message to Berlin telling them what they'd found?"

"Quite sure."

"Because that would be just the evidence Kaltenbrunner needs to bring down Himmler. And by extension, me. But he'd certainly settle for me if he couldn't nail Himmler."

"Somehow I just don't see the Reichsführer as a peacemaker," I said.

"Did you ever hear of an American gangster called Arnold Rothstein?" he asked.

"Vaguely, I think."

"In 1919, Rothstein made a huge bet that the Chicago White Sox, who were the overwhelming favorites, would lose the World Series. And he won that bet because he'd bribed some White Sox players to lose. A couple of years later, Rothstein bet a huge sum on a well-fancied racehorse called Sporting Blood after he made sure that the other favorite was scratched from the race at the very last minute. What I'm saying is that there was nothing sporting about Mr. Rothstein. Like any high-stakes gambler, he much preferred a sure thing. Himmler's no different. Only in this case he's betting on both horses. If Hitler wins, Himmler wins. And if Hitler loses, Himmler wins again." Schellenberg shrugged. "Of course, if Hitler does win then the Reichsführer will need to prove his loyalty to the leader. Which means I'm dead. You see? Not only am I a useful emissary in this whole affair, I'm a useful scapegoat if things go wrong. Me. Eggen. And you, Gunther, if we're ever found out."

"Point taken, sir."

"Drive the Mercedes into the garage," said Schellenberg.

Meyer didn't have an inspection pit, but he did have a garage ramp, and as soon as we'd retrieved the gold bars from underneath the rocker plates, I drove the Mercedes up the ramp. Meyer handed Schellenberg a hacksaw and he started to cut through a section of the car's exhaust pipe.

"By the way, Captain Gunther," said Meyer. "Call it professional curiosity, but before I forget, you said it was only yesterday you realized who killed Dr. Heckholz. How did you work out that it was Leuthard who killed Heckholz and not Schelli's men?"

I described how the dying Heckholz had made a Swiss flag out of a pool of his own blood on a white floor.

"That was clever of you," he said.

"Not really. You see, it took me a whole year to think of that. Which doesn't say much for my powers of detection. Sometimes a stupid man is only a couple of good guesses away from looking clever. The same is true in reverse, of course. But there's that mark against me and now this. I mean, the way I'd figured, the general here was in this whole thing for himself. I'm used to that, you see. The fact is, everyone in Germany is looking after himself these days. Me included. It's become a national pastime. Anyway, the truth is, Paul, I'm feeling about as clever as a man with the brains of a potato. So the next time you're writing a detective story, see if you can work out a way of making your hero look stupid. It'll be much more realistic that way."

"A stupid detective? That could never work. Readers wouldn't like it. That's much too like real life for the readers of detective stories. The writers, too. No one wants realism, Bernie. They get enough of that at home and when they read the newspapers. They read books to escape from real life, not to be reminded of it. Take my word for it, realism plays very badly in modern fiction."

I grinned. "I guess you know your business. But I know mine, too."

"Do you read much, Bernie?"

"Some. There's not much else to do at night in Germany, these days. Provided the electricity is working."

"What do you enjoy reading?"

"History, mostly. But not as much as I enjoy watching a general getting his hands dirty."

A few minutes later Schellenberg removed a section of the exhaust pipe from which he then extracted a carefully wrapped tube of papers that was about a meter in length.

We took the tube of papers into the house. On the desk in Meyer's study, and under the eyes of a rather severe and Flemish-looking family group portrait, we tried spreading the plans out on his narrow desk; but we soon moved them onto the floor where it was easier to keep them flat and see what was what. From time to time I glanced around at our surroundings. The house was full of rough timber ceilings, nut wood floors, Gothic cupboards, old tapestries, tiled ceramic stoves, and expensive works of fine art. Thanks to Bernard Berenson's last book on old masters, I knew they were expensive because they had gold frames that were even bigger than the paintings. That's what's called connoisseurship. But you didn't need to be a connoisseur to see that the most beautiful thing in the house was Patrizia herself. Quite possibly she was Meyer-Schwertenbach's second wife—she was certainly young enough. And that's what's called cynicism. Although I can't imagine there was a man there—myself included—who'd seen the dogs with their muzzles on her lap having their ears folded who didn't envy them just a little. She and Eggen came and found us in her husband's study and listened carefully as Schellenberg described what was in the German plans.

"I had these plans stolen to order from the Bendlerblock's Strategic Planning Section," said Schellenberg. "On the day after the building was hit by an RAF bomb. That way I didn't think they would be missed. Or at least not for long."

"So that was you, was it?" I said. "Clever. You know they asked me to investigate the theft of some plans. To avoid involving the Gestapo."

"What did you conclude?"

"That they'd been destroyed in the fire."

Schellenberg nodded. "Good."

"I was told not to worry too much because it turned out there were copies of the plans kept at the Wolf's Lair, in Rastenburg. So I dropped it."

"This plan was code-named Operation Christmas Tree," he explained, "and is dated October 1940. This was submitted for consideration by General Ritter von Leeb of Army Group C in response to a directive from General Halder of the General Staff's Operations Section. German forces—the blue arrows—would attack from occupied France in the west, from Germany in the north, and from Austria in the east. The black arrows represent Italian forces, who would attack from the south. The number of German divisions—twenty-one—is a strong indication of the expected level of resistance. Von Leeb estimated as many as four hundred and seventy thousand Swiss troops would oppose ours. But the real reason the plan was set aside was because Hitler made the decision to attack Russia in the spring of the following year. Perhaps even earlier, as a memo attached here shows Christmas Tree was canceled as early as November eleventh, 1940."

"And so," said Meyer, "but for the Russian invasion we might now be living under the Nazis."

"A Swiss invasion could still happen," said Schellenberg. "As this later plan proves. Operation Province-in-Waiting was prepared in the summer of 1941, by Colonel Adolf Heusinger, chief of the Operations Division of the Army General Staff. It was Heusinger who planned Operation Barbarossa for the invasion of the Soviet Union."

"He was a busy man in 1941," I said. "Wasn't he?"

"You can see here how Province-in-Waiting differs from Christmas Tree. For one thing, there will be a Rhine crossing, in twilight or fog. With seaplanes carrying lightly armed troops landing on the main Swiss lakes, including Zurich, Lucerne, and Geneva. The idea being that these troops would attack Swiss border defenses from the rear, rendering fortifications worthless. Himmler calls this plan the Swiss Project, and until recently it remained the one most likely to be implemented in the event that Hitler decided he needed a quick victory to restore the faith of the German people in his leadership. Himmler even named the man who will head up the Nazi police state that Switzerland will become: an SS major-general called Gottlob Berger. He's always been a very vigorous Nazi, with all that such an appellation entails."

"The man's an absolute swine," I said. "He runs the main SS office in Berlin."

"You said 'until recently,'" observed Patrizia. "Are we finally safe?"

"I regret to say no," said Schellenberg. "Recent events in Italy have made Switzerland strategically important as never before. With the collapse of Mussolini and the Italian fascists now imminent, the responsibility for defending Italy now rests with the German Army. That means Italian supply routes are critical. Which means that new plans are being formulated even as we speak. I happen to know that another SS general, Hermann Böhme, who is also the chief of the Austrian military intelligence service, has been charged by Himmler with devising a new invasion plan by the end of the year, for implementation in the summer of 1944."

"Jesus Christ," I said. "And this is the man who wants to extend peace feelers toward the Allies."

"As I said, Himmler likes a sure thing."

"But," interjected Patrizia, "you've often said, Schelli, that our forces were highly respected by the Wehrmacht. That Swiss marksmanship and our fighting spirit would help to deter them."

"That's true, Patrizia. Still, it's up to us now—to help deter them even more."

"That's a tall order for the people who weren't deterred by the sheer size of the task of invading Russia."

"Which is precisely why, Gunther, I'm here at Wolfsberg now," insisted Schellenberg. "All war relies on spies to discover information that reveals the enemy's true intentions. But that has never been enough. Deception is just as important. Bonaparte was a master of deception. Maneuvers from the rear, he called this. At the Battle of Lodi he had some of his army cross the River Po to persuade the Austrian commander de Beaulieu that he was attacking him; but in reality he had the bulk of his army cross further upriver, enabling him to attack de Beaulieu from the rear, and to defeat him. I'm the chief of SD Foreign Intelligence. It's my job to discover the enemy's true intentions. But it's also my job to devise deceptions. The Russians have a good word for this that I rather like. It's *maskirovka*, and in my opinion there is no one better at devising effective and persuasive *maskirovka* than a writer of fiction. Especially detective fiction. A man such as Paul Meyer-Schwertenbach, who possesses an imagination second to none. Between us, we've cooked up a plan that I'm going to take back to Germany and present to the High Command. It will be a complete work of fiction, of course. But as with all the best fiction, it will have a strong element of truth. The kind of truth that some of the generals in Germany, like poor Johann de Beaulieu, will simply want to believe."

Thirty-seven

n an elegant dining room a horse-faced maid served a dinner of cold
rabbit fillets with creamed horseradish, and pike and perch with a
peppercorn sauce, on Meissen tableware that was the same color as
the napkins and the blue-and-white curtains. A virtual cornucopia of
pears, red currants, and plums occupied a central spot between two
candelabra. Silver place settings glittered and crystal glasses chimed
lightly as Meyer poured a delicious Spätburgunder from an ancient-
looking and probably very valuable wine jug. Patrizia was up and down
from a mahogany Zopfstil chair with a back that was almost as straight
as hers, helping the maid to bring to the table tureens of vegetables and
more fish, bowls of radishes and pickles, bread baskets, and sauce boats.
On the wall, a picture of a lady wearing a wimple as tall as a circus tent
stared down at our simple Swiss dinner and licked her lips at seeing so
much food. She was probably German.

"Hans was telling me that you were married just before you came
to Switzerland," said Patrizia. "That you hadn't even managed to go on
your honeymoon."

I glanced at Eggen and gave him my best blue eyes.

"That's right, Frau Meyer."

"Tell me about her? Is she very pretty?"

"Her name is Kirsten and yes, she's pretty. She's younger than me. Her father owns a small hotel in Dachau. Which is where she's from, originally. But she's a schoolteacher at a girls' school in Berlin."

"Was it a sudden thing?" she asked.

"It was rather."

"Well, I wish you all the luck in the world."

"Thanks, but we won't need that much. Besides, I think the general is going to need quite a bit of luck himself if he's going to pull off this plan he was talking about. I'd like to hear some more about that, if I may."

Schellenberg nodded. "Yes, I think you deserve that." He shrugged. "The deals done by the Nordhav Foundation with the Swiss Wood Company weren't just designed to provide Switzerland with much-needed foreign currency, and to demonstrate my good faith to Swiss Army intelligence. They were also meant as a useful cover for me. So that I could work on Operation Noah with Paul without attracting too much suspicion. Although it doesn't seem to have worked where you were concerned, Gunther."

I nodded, but I was just beginning to understand the complexity of Schellenberg's existence and how carefully he was obliged to tread. By contrast my own life seemed almost carefree, not to say somewhat feckless. While the little general had been devoting himself to ensuring Switzerland's continued neutrality so that peace negotiations between the Allies and the Axis might finally get under way, I had been dallying with a beautiful actress. And it seemed the least I could do was offer him the respect he deserved.

"Yes, sir. I'm sorry about that. I can see that now."

"I'm leaving tomorrow, for Berlin and then Rastenburg," he said. "With Mussolini's overthrow imminent, I'm afraid there's not a moment to lose. While Paul is in Bern, presenting these genuine plans to his masters in Swiss Army intelligence, I'm going to be at the Wolf's

Lair, giving these fake ones to mine. Quite possibly to Hitler himself. Whatever people say about him, Hitler always listens to his generals. Even me, I have to confess. And being so much younger than the others, I am allowed a certain licence to speak freely."

"Is Hitler a monster?" asked Patrizia. "One always imagines that he must be."

"To be honest with you, Patrizia, he is the most extraordinary man I have ever met," said Schellenberg. "Had he died in 1940 he would have been the greatest German who ever lived. If only he had been more interested in diplomacy he might have been better served diplomatically and we could have avoided war altogether. It doesn't help that von Ribbentrop was Germany's foreign minister. The man is a fool. Not that this ever mattered much to Hitler, who always seems to prefer military solutions to almost every problem. That's what you have to remember about Hitler. He favors getting what he wants by violent means. Which means that speaking to him—giving him advice—is a prospect that always makes me nervous. I feel a little like that fellow Franz Reichelt, who jumped off the Eiffel Tower to demonstrate his new invention: a parachute. It didn't work, unfortunately for him, and he was killed. I can still remember as a small boy seeing the newsreel footage of Parisian newspapermen using a ruler to measure the depth of the hole in the ground made by his body."

"Please be careful," said Patrizia, touching his hand. "We've grown very fond of you, Schelli. And you, Hans. Haven't we, Paul?"

Meyer nodded. "Absolutely. Considering he's my enemy, he's also one of my best friends."

"Thank you, Paul."

"Before you throw yourself off the Eiffel Tower, General, I'd like to hear some more of these fake plans," I said.

"Good idea," said Eggen. "I think a healthy degree of Berlin skepticism is just what we need around here."

"That sounds like you're not convinced this plan will work, sir," I said. "Are you? Do you think it will work?"

"If anyone can make it work, it's Schelli," said Eggen. "In my experience there's no one better than him at the practice of *maskirovka.*"

"Oh, I don't know," said Schellenberg. "I think Captain Gunther himself does quite a job of concealing what he really is."

"That's not what I asked, sir," I told Eggen. "I asked you if you think his plan will work."

"Then let me say this. I think Hitler and his generals will believe the plans, yes. I think the Operation Noah plans are quite plausible. What Paul and Schelli have done is create a rather brilliant scenario in which it would seem like folly and madness to invade this country at all. The trouble is that folly and madness rule right now. The folly and madness of continuing this war for another week is there for all to see in the person of our leader, Adolf Hitler. Hitler doesn't live in the real world. He has an absurd faith in the German Army. He still believes that the impossible can be achieved. That's the real problem with these plans. Not that they are wrong or inadequate or even too far-fetched, but that Hitler is wrong and inadequate. He might think the destruction of this country is a price worth paying for its daring to oppose his will in the first place. I've an awful feeling that he has something similar in mind for Germany if we dare to let him down."

"Nevertheless," I said, "I would like to hear more about Operation Noah. I'm still just a little sheepish that I didn't have more faith in you, General."

"Faith has never been your strong suit, has it, Gunther?"

"Faith is for people who believe in something. I don't believe in anything very much. Not anymore. After all, look where belief has got us now."

Schellenberg and Meyer looked at each other. "Do you want to tell him?" asked the Swiss.

"You're the storyteller, Paul," said Schellenberg. "You tell him."

"All right. Well, as Napoleon himself observed—"

Schellenberg grinned. "Paul is a great student of Bonaparte."

"He said that nature had destined Switzerland to become a league of states and that no wise man would attempt to conquer it."

"That lets Hitler out, then," said Eggen. "He hasn't acted like a wise man since the summer of 1940."

"We've always had the largest percentage of soldiers in the world compared to overall population—six hundred thousand soldiers out of a population of just four million. Quite possibly we could mobilize the entire population in our defense. Everyone in this country knows how to shoot. Hitler knows to his cost just how stubborn the people of Russia have been in their country's defense. Switzerland has always maintained that we would be no less stubborn. You can see this demonstrated in the way that we have set up the defenses of our country's key mountain passes: Sargans in the east, Gotthard in the south, and Saint-Maurice in the west. Each area has a series of huge fortifications stretching across some of the most rugged and impassable mountain terrain in Europe. Any invader would be greeted by heavy artillery fire over many kilometers. In short, this is not panzer country. No more are these defenses vulnerable to Luftwaffe attacks. And as if all this were not enough, there is also the threat that we would blow up these mountain passes to deny them to the enemy. In other words, the very thing that makes this country worth invading—namely, as an easy route to Italy—would be rendered useless. Germany's would be a Pyrrhic victory of epic proportions. And having sacrificed many thousands of troops to secure Switzerland, the German Army would find itself landlocked with nowhere to go. And not just landlocked, but quite literally bogged down. You see, all of the land you can see between here and Lake Constance was once swampland and a system of canals was constructed to drain it. But these same canals can release all of that water back onto the floodplain. Three years ago—and much to the irritation of local farmers, myself included—this was actually tried as an experiment by the Swiss Army. It was very successful, too. It became clear that an invading German army would soon find itself unable to move.

"Schelli and I simply decided to take those plans a stage further. What we've done is create some fictitious but entirely feasible and convincing plans—code-named Operation Noah—which amount to nothing less than a Swiss doomsday scenario that is based on the dynamiting of Switzerland's biggest glacier lakes, including Geneva, Zurich, Neuchâtel, Maggiore, Lucerne, Lugano, and Constance. The idea is that by destroying the terminal moraines of all these glacier lakes, we would turn Switzerland's only major natural resource—water—into a weapon that would devastate the whole country, in much the same way that the RAF achieved a few months ago when they bombed and breached your Möhne and Edersee dams, causing catastrophic flooding of the Ruhr valley. A moraine is a sort of glacial bath plug that keeps all the water in the lake. There are over fifty Swiss lakes occupying an area of more than one square kilometer. We estimate that if the terminal moraine of just the biggest lake—Geneva—were destroyed, then almost ninety cubic kilometers of water would be released over the surrounding area. If the moraines of the largest ten lakes were blown at the same time as the major passes, then we could turn Switzerland into one vast European sea. No army on earth could deal with something on that kind of scale."

"The trick," added Schellenberg, "will be to convince Hitler that the Swiss really would go through with a plan like this. I don't think there's any doubt that the generals in Berlin believe that the Swiss would go ahead and blow up the passes, which is why Operation Province-in-Waiting was shelved. But with Mussolini gone, it's clear to me that we're going to need something else to dissuade them more finally—something even more determined that will convince them that any kind of lake-landing by German seaplanes would be suicide, not just for them, but for the Swiss, too. So, I shall simply tell Hitler and the generals that my bravest and most resourceful agent—code-named Tschudi—who is employed in the Technical War Unit of the Swiss General Staff, in Bern—has stolen these plans from the office of Colonel von Wattenwyl. Plans that could make the whole Russian campaign look like a stroll in the Tiergarten."

"We have compiled a feasibility study of Operation Noah," said Meyer, "as if written by Colonel von Wattenwyl himself. I've met this man. He's a member of one of Switzerland's most distinguished families; he's also a very highly gifted military tactician. We also have a memorandum from the chief of the Swiss General Staff, General Henri Guisan, which describes this operation as part of the National Redoubt or mountain fortress concept that he outlined in an address to the Swiss Officer Corps in 1940. We even have fake reports from the army's maritime branch on Lake Zurich which purport to indicate the underwater mining of the lake's terminal moraine at Zurich and plans for the partial evacuation of the city, which would of course be inundated. The report describes the previous effect of the breach of the moraine that runs between Pfäffikon and Rapperswil and which can be seen in the shallow upper part—the Obersee—and the lower part—the Untersee."

"We certainly hope we've thought of absolutely everything," said Schellenberg. "If we haven't, then I've a feeling that they won't need a ruler to measure the depth of the hole in the ground I make in the forest at Rastenburg. That swine Ernst Kaltenbrunner will dig my grave himself."

Thirty-eight

The next day Schellenberg and Eggen returned to Germany. Meyer and I drove them to a small private jetty in an extensive pear orchard on Meyer's estate. A Swiss Army motorboat was waiting to take them quietly back across Lake Constance to the island of Reichenau, where an SS staff car was ready to drive the general to an airfield in Konstanz. From Konstanz, Eggen was going by road to Stuttgart to catch a train back to Berlin, while the general had arranged to fly straight to the Wolf's Lair at Rastenburg. I didn't envy Schellenberg that journey. Quite apart from my fear of flying, which had been hardly helped by the severe electrical storm we had encountered on my trip back from Zagreb, deceiving Hitler and all his staff generals was a task that would have given any ordinary man considerable pause. Deceiving Dalia's husband, Stefan Obrenović, felt like something I was much more equal to. Him, and perhaps the minister of Propaganda, for whom, of course, I was still working; otherwise I might have chosen to accompany Eggen back to Germany. After the events at Uetliberg, I'd had enough of Switzerland. But there was still the matter of Dalia's future to consider, for, although she seemed to have given me a definitive answer to the question of her own return to Germany, I knew it was a question that I was obliged to put to her again, if only because of who my client was. Goebbels wasn't the kind of man who would have allowed me to take Dalia at her word. I could almost hear his brittle sarcasm now, wiping the floor with me like a rag in that mocking Westfalish accent of his, for not even trying to talk her out of it.

"What are your plans now, Bernie?" asked Meyer.

"I can't go back to Zurich. Not after what that stupid cop from police headquarters told me. I'm not entirely sure what I'm going to do now. It all depends on a telephone call I need to make. I have my own rather more mundane mission to complete."

"You're very welcome to use our telephone. And to stay here at Wolfsberg. For as long as you want."

"Believe me, you and your wife wouldn't want me for that long."

"Schelli spoke very highly of you to me last night, after you'd gone to bed. He says he thinks you'd be a good man to have around in a tight spot."

"Maybe. But of late the spots seem to be getting tighter."

"I'd really like you to stay so that I could ask you a few more questions about your old cases. You know? For my next book. I'm thinking of a story of a Swiss cop with a Berlin connection. Before the war, of course."

"Of course. When there was still some real crime about." I smiled thinly. Somehow the idea of helping Meyer with his book appealed a lot less to me than the possibility of seeing Dalia again. "And some real detectives, too."

"Exactly."

"It's kind of you, Paul, but I can't. I thought I'd motor down to Rapperswil and send Goebbels a telegram, then wait for further instructions. I really can't leave Switzerland until that's happened. I've heard Rapperswil is very pretty. With a castle and everything."

"Oh, it is. Very picturesque. But you know, I could drive you down there myself. It so happens that there's an unsolved murder that took place in Rapperswil. The local police inspector is a friend of mine. Perhaps you might even remember me mentioning it when I was in Berlin last year."

I didn't, and of course I certainly wasn't remotely interested in some old murder case but it occurred to me that if I did go to Rapperswil it might be useful to have a Swiss police inspector on my side, especially if I was going to be meeting in secret with the wife of a prominent local businessman. Besides, with the OSS probably still convinced that I was Walter Schellenberg, it couldn't do any harm to have a cop to help me out if they again tried to kidnap me, or worse.

"I'll be straight with you, Paul. I like you. I'm grateful for your hospitality and I wouldn't like to embarrass you. But there's a lady I have to see when I'm down there."

"This actress who Dr. Goebbels is interested in. The one he wants to go back to work at UFA studios. Sure, I get it."

"No, you don't. The fact of the matter is, he's not the only one who's interested in her. You know what I mean? She and I—it's complicated. She has a husband. In Küsnacht. Which is just up the lakeshore from Rapperswil, right?"

Meyer nodded.

"She and I had sort of planned that we might find a nice hotel. Just for the afternoon."

"Bernie, I'm a detective writer, not a monk."

"You'd be surprised what monks are capable of. Believe me, you could write a hell of a book about one particular monk that I met down in Croatia."

"Look, I know just the place for you both. In Rapperswil. The Pension du Lac. I'll check into the Schwanen Hotel, next door, so there won't be any possibility of embarrassment for either one of you. We'll drive down this afternoon. Have dinner with Inspector Leuenberger tonight. Chat about the case. You can see your lady friend tomorrow. And then we'll drive back. What could be simpler?"

"Let me call her first."

Thirty-nine

Rapperswil was a charming, cuckoo-clock town on the north shore of Lake Zurich and dominated by a William Tell sort of castle with a watchman's tower and probably some crossbows for hire. I certainly wouldn't have put it past the Swiss to have defended their country against a German invasion with crossbows.

It was a warm afternoon and the water looked as cool and inviting as an enormous gin and tonic. The sun shining on the calm blue water had encouraged a flock of sparrows to take a bath. I wouldn't have minded a swim myself. A causeway about a kilometer long, including a swing bridge, connected Rapperswil with Hurden on the lake's south shore, and separated Lake Zurich proper from the Obersee. Meyer explained that this causeway was built on an old moraine that had been breached many centuries before.

"Until then," he added, "Zurich probably wasn't on a lake at all."

Being a metropolitan sort of fellow, I normally find places like Rapperswil just a little bit too quaint for my taste, but after Zagreb and Zurich, I liked the place just fine. I continued liking the place even when a wasp dropped out of a lime tree and stung me on the nose as I tried to brush it off my face. After all I'd been through in Croatia, it seemed almost laughable for anyone to take an injury like that at all seriously but, at Meyer's insistence, we went to the nearby Schwanen

Hotel to find some vinegar to dab on my reddening nose. That lessened the pain, but for the rest of my stay in Switzerland I looked like Grock the Clown. Quite what Dalia was going to think of me now I didn't know. I was going to have to allow her a laugh or two at my expense. Then again, it might have been worse; the wasp could have crawled up a trouser leg and done some damage elsewhere. In the great economy of the universe—even when you're planning to make love to a beautiful woman—a red nose isn't such a hardship.

Having sent a message to Goebbels from the local telegraph office on Bahnhofplatz and received my new orders in his swift reply, I joined Meyer at the uncut sapphire that was the lakeside where he told me about the little town's unsolved murder. But while he spoke, my mind wandered a little for a second and I got to wondering why a man like Meyer was so interested in murder in the first place. With me, it was just a job. Living in a beautiful place like Wolfsberg Castle with a wife as lovely as Patrizia—I think I'd have left the subject of murder well alone. Real murder is sticky under your shoes, and gets ugly in your nostrils and your stomach. And I prefer the smell of lime blossom in summer—unless there's a wasp in it. What was more, I'd killed enough people myself to know that there's nothing entertaining about it. So what was it about murder mysteries that made them so fascinating to people like Meyer? Maybe in the end it was because, in fiction, justice is always served. Which is the very essence of fiction, of course, and nothing at all to do with real life. Life doesn't have neatly tied-up endings. And even when it does, it often takes several years to tie the bow; I had the evidence of the Kuhlo killings to support that point of view. But what kind of a neatly tied ending that served justice was ever going to satisfy the Russians, the British, the Americans, and the French? Not to mention the Jews, homosexuals, Jehovah's Witnesses, Gypsies, and Serbs? I'd like to have seen the detective who was going to assemble all of Germany's suspects in the library and tell them who was guilty and who was not. I thought that was going to need a bit more than just one chapter. Maybe the neatly tied ending was going to involve a gallows or two.

Meyer broke into my reverie. "As I was telling you, a couple of years ago some divers for a Swiss engineering firm were exploring the shallow upper part of the lake, which is called the Obersee. That's the part to the right of the Seedamm that you see here. It was a routine safety check but it was their work that gave me the idea for Operation Noah. Anyway, on a submerged ledge they found a sunken boat—a gentleman's day launch, I think you'd call it—and, the body of a woman. The body tied by the neck to the anchor. At its deepest part, the lake is almost one hundred and fifty meters deep but the boat had come to rest on a ledge that was less than fifty meters down. But for the ledge, they would probably never have found it. The local pike perch had eaten most of her face. The pathologist said he believed the body had been in the water for at least a year. To this day the woman has never been identified. But it's clear that the woman had been murdered because, according to a local boatbuilder, the seacocks were open and there were several holes drilled in the boat's planking, all consistent with the boat having been scuttled. There was even a drill left on the cabin floor. The woman had suffered a skull fracture, as if someone had hit her on the head, and it's quite possible she was dead before the boat was deliberately sunk. Also, the name of the boat had been removed fore and aft with a blowtorch. No woman in the area was ever reported missing. Nor is there any report of a boat having been sunk or stolen. This sort of thing just doesn't happen in Rapperswil."

I lit a cigarette, flicked the match into the lake, and almost immediately regretted it when an old Swiss woman tutted loudly and gave me a look of disgust. It was only then that I noticed how clean the water was. Probably that was why the sparrows were having a wash in it.

"What do you think, Bernie?"

"About what?"

"About this murder."

"I'll admit, it doesn't sound much like suicide," I said. "But without seeing the boat or the body, I'm not sure there's much I can say. It sounds like the perfect murder. I'll be sure to think of this if ever I want to murder my wife."

"The body was buried long ago," said Meyer. "But we can still see the boat, if you like."

I stifled a yawn. "All right. I'll take a look. But in my experience, with a cold case like this, there's really very little to go on. It was an absolute fluke that I caught Gormann. I couldn't say it at the conference last summer, for obvious reasons. But it was. I might have said more about that but my bosses in the RSHA wouldn't have liked it. They're wedded to the idea of German efficiency and police omniscience. Now, that's what I call fiction."

We walked along the Strandweg to a ramshackle boatyard with the word RAPPERSWIL painted in large letters on a sliding yard door, in case there was any doubt about where we were. A sign advertising boat-hire lay propped half-forgotten against the wall; looking around the yard, it was hard to see a boat that could have kept your feet dry. A diminutive bearded man as brown as an oven-baked nut with a briar pipe in his face was carefully craning a polished motorboat out of the lake and into the yard. There was a hole in its hull. Most of the other boats in the yard were in similar stages of disrepair. Across the yard, another man with an oxyacetylene torch was welding a rudder back together. A small dog lay asleep inside the rim of a large car tire and a radio was playing some German band music. The bearded man seemed to recognize Meyer and left off craning the boat for a moment to chat in the weird German that people spoke in and around Lake Zurich. I'd long given up trying to understand it. We followed the man into the corner of the yard, picking our way carefully between boats, trailers, tool kits,

coils of rope, fenders and buoys, oil drums, planks of wood, and out-
board engines. Puffing his pipe and possibly himself back into life, he
pulled away a tarpaulin to reveal a boat that was about nine meters
long, with a beam of about two meters, and a little cabin at the back.
The boatman found us some steps and we stood on these and peered
into the boat's dilapidated interior, which told me absolutely nothing.
Not that I expected the boat to tell me anything. It was beginning to
feel embarrassing the way Meyer seemed to regard me as some kind of
great detective, one of these other omniscient sleuths from popular fiction. I wanted to tell him that these detectives were no more real than
the gods they seemed to imitate and perhaps even just as false in the
devotion they seemed to inspire.

"The lady was found in a fetal position on the floor," said Meyer.
"Which suggested that she'd been killed and placed there before rigor
mortis could set in. The knot on the rope around her neck was a bit
unusual. A bit like the knot in a cravat. And the lady was wearing a
pink pinafore-style dress, expensive shoes, silk stockings, and—most
interesting of all—a good diamond ring. And I mean a good diamond.
At least three carats in size and worth a lot of anyone's money. I mean,
it's hard to imagine someone not taking that ring before disposing of
the body. That's what made the newspapers take notice. The size of the
diamond. What else? Red-and-white cushion covers on the seats of the
boat. Nothing unusual about that. Swiss people are fond of red and
white, the colors of our national flag. That's about all, I think."

"I don't understand," I told Meyer. "A woman's body was found in
the lake. So what? Why does this interest you? Paul, this is 1943. If it's
dead bodies you want, I'll take you to the Ukraine and show you
thousands."

"This is Switzerland, Bernie. Murders like this just don't happen
here. In peacetime we have one of the lowest homicide rates in Europe.
Most murder is domestic, and in half of these cases a firearm is

involved. Less than ten percent of our murder cases remain unsolved. But it was the ring that awoke the public's interest. I mean, a three-carat ring is the size of a bird's egg. So she had to be somebody, right? That's what interests me. One day I want to write a book about this case. I thought I might call it *The Lady in the Lake*. It's a good title, don't you think?"

"Oh, sure. But look, Paul, everyone is somebody. Even when they're nobody. That's the first thing you tell yourself when you join the Murder Commission. Doesn't matter if it's a homeless old man, a ten-year-old child, Walther Rathenau, or the king of Yugoslavia. They all rate investigation. At least they used to before our government started doing most of the killing."

It sounded good but the truth was that after what I'd seen in the Katyn Forest earlier that year, I was hardly inclined to think of one woman's death as in any way important. Death had undone so many since the beginning of the war that one more murder seemed irrelevant.

"Of course, of course, I just thought that something might occur to you, that's all," said Meyer. "In your speech last year you said that a cold case is nothing but all of the false and misleading evidence that, over a period of years, has come to be accepted as true. In other words, you start by patiently challenging almost everything you think you know."

I nodded. I didn't want to be rude to Meyer after his kind hospitality but it was all I could do to stop myself from telling him he was wasting his time and mine. From what I'd seen so far, this case was as cold as the Ypres Salient. And it wasn't his fault that he'd managed to get through the war without seeing a single body. I envied him that, just as much as I envied him his lovely château at Wolfsberg and his beautiful wife. Besides, my nose was hurting and I really only had room for one thing in my mind and that was seeing Dalia once more.

Especially now that I had a telegram from Goebbels. At least after our hotel tryst I'd be able to tell him that I'd seen her again. Maybe I could walk her up to the telegraph office in Rapperswil and get her to send him a telegram; that way I'd be off the hook.

Dinner at the Schwanen Hotel with Meyer and Police Inspector Leuenberger wasn't any more interesting than my afternoon trip to the Rapperswil boatyard. Very thoughtfully, the Swiss cop brought some color photographs to the table but I didn't look at them and there are better after-dinner subjects to talk about than a woman who's been half-eaten by some pike perch, especially when that's what's on the menu. In spite of everything I now knew about their diet, I'm fond of pike perch. But the Riesling was a good Trocken and I drank a little too much of it, or at least enough to ask some questions about the lady in the lake; and from these I gathered only that the Rapperswil police were utterly clueless. It seemed that even a top detective from Bern had turned up and pronounced himself completely baffled.

"Maybe she had it coming," I suggested when we finished the wine and started on the schnapps. "Maybe nobody came forward because people were glad to see this lady dead. That happens, you know. It's not just nice, innocent people who get murdered. Not so innocent ones do, too. Perhaps someone bashed her head in because she deserved it. Did you think about that for a motive? That someone did the world a favor?"

Inspector Leuenberger frowned. "I don't believe that for a second. No one should die that way. And it's a very cruel thing to say about a woman you don't know."

I almost laughed. "Cruel? Yes, I suppose I have become cruel. Which isn't a surprise, really. I've learned from the experts. But what I say still stands. If no one reported this lady missing, then it can only be because no one missed her. And if no one missed her, then it might be because people were glad to see the back of her. Look, forget about the lady in the lake, think about that diamond ring. No one missed that, either. That ought to tell you something. It takes a lot of hate to over-come the love of a good diamond, especially one as big as a bird's egg. Either that, or a lot of money. From what you've told me, you've been looking for a murderer among the kind of people who commit murder. Crooks and gangsters. The usual suspects. But that's all wrong. You want to know something? I think I can already give you a perfect description of the person who killed this woman. In fact, I'm sure of it. Believe me, it's easy to spot a murderer. They're nearly always decent people, Inspector. You'd better look for someone who's law-abiding."

"He's right," Meyer told Leuenberger. "Gormann worked in a bank, didn't he, Bernie? He was respectable."

I nodded and lit a cigarette.

"So maybe we should look elsewhere for a suspect. Someone respectable."

"Of course it's someone respectable," I said. "This murderer has been living right under your nose all this time and you didn't notice. It's your next-door neighbor. Your boss. Your dentist. Your doctor. The local banker. That's how they got away with it. That's how they all get away with it. That's why when the police finally do carry a fellow off to the local shit house, the rest of the neighbors will all stand around in the street looking bemused and say, 'Who would have thought old so-and-so was a murderer? To look at him you'd have thought he wouldn't have harmed a fly.'"

Meyer was taking notes now and as well oiled as I now was, I had warmed to my subject at last.

"Maybe you couldn't identify your lady. So maybe you should try to identify the *Schmuck*—I mean the ring on her finger. Did you show it to some dealers? Did you ever put a picture of it in the newspaper?"

"No."

"Why the hell not?"

Leuenberger colored. "Because we didn't want to have to deal with a lot of time-wasters claiming it was theirs, when it wasn't. That's why not."

I laughed again. "Dealing with time-wasters is what this job is all about, Inspector. That's why they pay us. To waste our time. I'm perfectly serious. That's what police work mostly is. A waste of time. Whenever I hear a copper say, 'They don't pay me to waste my time,' I say, 'That's exactly what they do pay you for.' Inspector, if I were you I'd take that ring to every diamond dealer in this canton. And then the next canton. Ninety-nine percent of your effort will be wasted, of course. But it's quite possible that one percent of it will be useful. Just see if I'm wrong. It strikes me that you've only ever carried out half of this investigation. Most of the real police work has yet to be done. The body and the boat are probably the least important parts of this whole case."

"Maybe you should reopen the case," said Meyer.

"Maybe," said Leuenberger. "I'd have to ask the commissioner. I'm not sure he'd agree. Reopening a case is not something we very often do in Switzerland. People here prefer a quiet life. To reopen a case I would need some real evidence. And to get that, I'd need to justify a budget to my boss. Which I can't do, right now. Money's tight here."

I poured myself another glass of schnapps and laughed again, enjoying the inspector's very obvious discomfort. Sometimes the only fun of coming from a big city is to make people who come from somewhere small feel even smaller.

"I don't blame you. And honestly, Inspector. What does it matter? In almost any country outside of Switzerland murder has ceased to be very shocking. And you can take my word for that. From what I've heard, murder's a way of life in Poland. The person who murdered your lady in the lake was a rank amateur by comparison with some of the people I work for."

"That's wartime for you, I suppose," he said.

"Yes," I said. "That's wartime." It was clear he had no idea what I was talking about; and I wasn't much inclined to tell him. I felt ashamed enough of being German as it was.

"All the same," said Leuenberger, "to say what you say, Captain Gunther, and indeed the way you say it, is to believe in nothing. What about Christianity? What about love your neighbor? What about forgiving our enemies?"

"Oh, I fully intend to forgive them. Just as soon as I've kicked them around the room and shot them in the head."

"You sound like a nihilist."

"No, I just don't think that life has very much meaning."

"To be a nihilist," he continued, "well—I think a man must feel very alone to believe in absolutely nothing, as you seem to."

"I don't mind being alone. Being solitary—that's an occupational hazard. Men in our profession need to be alone so that we can ignore the roar of our colleagues' ignorance and stupidity and think for ourselves. But I'm not so crazy about being *lonely*. There's a difference between that and solitude. Being lonely makes me feel sorry for myself and I can't stand that. I end up doing things I shouldn't do. Like drinking a little too much. Stealing other men's wives. Trying to stay alive at all costs. And looking for just a little happiness in this life. You know, I often think if I hadn't been a policeman, I might have been a really good man."

"Come now, Bernie, you are a good man," said Meyer. "You're just trying to shock us."

"Am I? I wonder, although mostly I wonder about the lady I'm going to see tomorrow. The lady *on* the lake. Perhaps if she wasn't made to look so very like temptation I might find that kind of thing easier to resist. Then again, I guess that's why women are shaped that way. If they were shaped any differently, I guess the human race would be much less successful."

"There's a sting in the tail of nearly everything you say, Captain," observed the inspector.

"I come by it naturally. My own mother was a scorpion. Look, I'll tell you one more thing about human nature and then I'll go to bed before I drink too much and say something really cynical. The lady I'm seeing tomorrow certainly won't thank me if I can't stand up. She's keen on good manners. Then again, maybe if I drink enough she won't notice my nose being red. So, listen. This is some real wisdom for your next book, Paul. Good people are never as good as you probably think they are, and the bad ones aren't as bad. Not half as bad. On different days we're all good. And on other days, we're evil. That's the story of my life. That's the story of everyone's life."

Forty

Dalia started to undress the minute she came through the door. It was almost as if she didn't trust herself not to change her mind, or perhaps me not to start talking about Goebbels and the film role that was waiting for her back in Berlin. It worked, too. As soon as she threw off her Borsalino straw hat and her blue linen blazer and started to unbutton the white cotton blouse she was wearing, I felt obliged to come to her immediate assistance; her fingers were just too slow at pushing the buttons through their heavily starched holes. In just a matter of a few minutes I had her bare breasts balanced in my hands, after which it was impossible to think about anything else but her. Time passed quickly after that, as it always does under those circumstances. Anything compressed by desire shrinks a little. Goethe once compiled a list of what you needed to do in order to complement the sense of the beautiful that God had implanted in the human soul; and, to a list that included hearing a little music, reading a little poetry, and seeing a fine picture every day of your life, I would only have added contemplating the naked body of a beautiful woman like Dalia Dresner for a long half hour before making love to her. In fact, I think I might have placed that at the very top of the list.

"Don't stop," she whispered as my mouth and fingers took their cue from her very visible pleasure.

I had no intention of stopping, not even when, long behind her, I had finished and was little more than a pelvis pushing spasmodically at the space between her thighs like the last pumps of a dying heart as it attempted to delay the inevitability of our separation.

We lay awhile without moving at all. And finally she said, "Your face looks like a stoplight. What happened to your nose?"

"A wasp stung me."

Dalia did her best to suppress a giggle. "Does it hurt?"

"Now you're here, I don't feel any pain at all."

"Good. I thought maybe someone had hit you."

"Who would want to do a thing like that?"

"I can think of someone."

"Your husband, I suppose. I was afraid he was going to stop you from coming."

"You were right to worry. I nearly didn't get here at all. Stefan took my car. His Rolls-Royce is in the shop. Or so he says."

"How did you get here?"

"I have a motorboat moored to the jetty right outside."

"I never thought of that."

"Everyone in and around Zurich has a boat somewhere. That's the main point of living here. I love boats. As a matter of fact, I'm rather glad that I had to take the boat today. There is roadwork on Seestrasse and the boat was certainly quicker than the car. Less than half an hour. Besides, the lake is lovely at this time of year. The water is a lot smoother than the road right now."

She kissed me fondly on the head, pushed me firmly back on the bed, and then kissed me on the chest and the belly before taking me in her mouth to "clean me up," as she put it. I've never enjoyed feeling I needed cleaning quite so much.

"I missed you," she said when she'd finished.

"I missed you, too, angel."

"I would have come last night, too, but I couldn't get away. Someone from the polytechnic came to dinner. To talk about my mathematics course. It seems that I can start in September, just as long as I pass the entrance exam. Although to see if I was equal to that he did ask me if I could add together all of the numbers between one and one hundred in my head. It's actually quite simple. All you have to do is add the numbers in pairs—the first and the last, the second and the second to last, and so on, and what you quickly realize is that you just get fifty lots of one hundred and one, which is five thousand and fifty."

"There's no need to explain. I mean about you staying here in Switzerland. Not the maths. I get a headache just listening to all that. It's as much as I can do to add two plus two and make five."

"I hate to tell you, but two plus two makes four."

"Not in Germany. Two plus two makes five is simple Nazi arithmetic as described by your friend Josef. Which reminds me. No one gets handed brains and beauty these days. He certainly didn't. So which line were you in when you were born?"

"Two plus two equals five isn't a sum. It's a prayer for a miracle. Dear Lord, grant that this be so. It's a little like you and me, don't you think?" She smiled, without artifice, and kissed my shoulder. "So. What did you do last night? Without me."

"I met up with the local police inspector. A fellow named Leuenberger. And the man who owns Wolfsberg Castle—the fellow I told you about."

"The detective writer."

"Yes. Paul Meyer-Schwertenbach. He's a friend of the inspector's."

"Good gracious, has there been a crime in Rapperswil? You astound me."

"Not exactly. No, we had dinner at the Schwanen Hotel, next door."

"I think I prefer this place. In fact, I never want to leave this room. We'll stay here forever, shall we? And you can make love to me every day."

"I'd like that, too."

"What did you talk about? You and your two friends?"

"I think Meyer wants me to help him write a book about an old murder case. *The Lady in the Lake*, he calls it. A couple of years ago, some woman was found murdered in a boat that was deliberately sunk in the Obersee not very far from here. As a matter of fact, he was a real bore about it."

"Deliberately? How could they tell something like that? I mean, boats sink, don't they? I should know, I've sunk a few myself."

"From the fact that the planks in the hull looked like Swiss cheese. The murderer even left his drill in there."

"I do remember that case," she said. "It was in all the Swiss newspapers, wasn't it?"

I nodded. "Anyway, the police are thinking of reopening it."

"Has there been some new evidence?"

"No." I sighed.

"Why the long face?"

"Because I behaved badly, last night—the way I taunted that policeman. I don't think he's the complete idiot I tried to make him feel he was. I don't know, maybe I drank too much. These days, back in Berlin, I don't often get the chance. To drink, I mean. Anyway, it's all a waste of time, if you ask me. They still don't even know who she was. Although she was wearing a big diamond, which is obviously the key to everything. They may not know who she was but I'm damned sure they could identify that *Schmuck* on her finger."

Dalia nodded. "I love you," she said. "I suppose you do know that."

"And I love you, angel."

"Can you please stay here in Switzerland? Forever?"

"I would but I don't think the Swiss would like it. In fact, I'm sure of it. And there's another thing. If I don't go back, the Nazis will probably make things very difficult for my wife. That's the only reason anyone ever goes back to Germany these days. If someone else is likely to suffer for it if they don't."

"Oh, yes. I'd forgotten about her. The wife you say you had to marry to keep her out of the clutches of the Gestapo. Kirsten, wasn't it? I'm very jealous of her."

"There's no need to be. I'm not in love with her. You might almost say it was a marriage of convenience."

"That's not what I'm jealous about, dear love. I'm jealous that you couldn't do something as noble as that for me. Nobody has ever done something as noble as that for me. Someone should knight you for it. Or give you a medal. An Iron Cross on a nice ribbon. Or whatever it is they give you for acts as selfless as that."

"I don't know that it was quite as selfless as you seem to think," I admitted. "If I hadn't married her, Goebbels would never have let me come to Switzerland to see you."

"Yes, I see what you mean." She hit me on the arm. "You've spoiled it now."

"How?"

"By telling me that. I much prefer to think of you as doing something noble."

"I'm not much good at being noble," I said. "Frankly, there's not a lot of call for it these days. Not in Germany."

"There is as far as I'm concerned. And I really think you're selling yourself short. I think you're every bit as noble as one of those crusading Teutonic knights of medieval history. What was their motto again? 'Help, Defend, Heal.' That's you in a nutshell, Gunther. You'll have your work cut out doing all that when I come back to Berlin again."

"I thought you were staying here to learn how to be Carl Friedrich Gauss."

"Oh, I expect you'll think me terribly capricious but I have a strong sense that if I stay here, Stefan is going to get even more difficult than he is already. Lately he's become much more possessive. Not to say unconscionably jealous. Which wasn't our arrangement at all. I'm sure there's absolutely nothing wrong with his damn car. I think he was just looking for an excuse to take mine so I couldn't go anywhere today. The fact is, I'm beginning to think that Goebbels might be easier to handle. After all, he's a lot smaller. And at least he's got other things on his plate. Like winning an unwinnable war. Besides, there's bound to be another actress before very long. One he likes better than me. With any luck I can even procure one for him. In fact, I think I know just the girl."

"You mean it?"

She thought for a minute. "I think so."

"This is good news. I thought I was going to have to kidnap you and drive you back to Germany in the trunk of my car. Which is what Goebbels wants me to do. He sent me a telegram yesterday. I'm to use every argument I can think of to persuade you to come back. Including money. He's offering you double what you were offered before. And more than Zarah Leander got last year for *The Great Love*. Whatever that was. And in whatever currency you want, as well."

"More than Zarah Leander," said Dalia. "That is interesting. Me, paid more than her. The Diva of the Third Reich. I heard a rumor that Zarah got paid in Swedish kronor. Maybe I could get paid in American dollars. Hey, perhaps I could even share some of it with you."

"And if that fails, I'm to put you across my knee and spank your bare bottom very hard until you agree."

"You're making that up."

"About the spanking, yes. But not the money. Not only that, but you get to keep the house in Griebnitzsee." I shrugged. "Even Faust wasn't offered a house like that one."

"He is a devil, isn't he?"

"If you make a deal with him, just make sure you have a couple of angels to intervene on your behalf when he comes to collect on the bargain."

"That's where you come in, surely."

"My earthly powers are weak compared with his."

She smiled. "I wouldn't say so. Not on the evidence of what just happened in this hotel room."

With that she climbed on top of me like a Valkyrie mounting Odin's eight-legged horse and we made love again. I ought to have been paying more attention to the Mephisto story, of course, but in my own defense, it's difficult to think clearly when the girl immolating herself on top of you is a nude movie star. It's not every devil that will do absolutely everything in bed you ever dreamed of and make you feel like a god.

Later on she asked me if I would drive her back to Berlin.

"What about the motorboat outside?" I asked.

"I didn't mean right now, darling, I meant tonight. In your car. No, wait, first thing in the morning would be better. Like six a.m. Stefan won't be out of bed. Agnes can pack me an overnight bag and then come on to Berlin by train in a few days with the rest of my luggage."

"I have to go back to Wolfsberg Castle and collect some things myself. But I can do what you're asking, yes."

"Perhaps we could even find a hotel halfway. In Munich. The Bayerischer Hof. They know me there and they won't ask too many questions as long as we take separate rooms. It'll be blissful, don't you think? We'll be able to spend the whole night together. I can wake up in your arms. Wouldn't you like that, too?"

"You really want to do this? I can see you managing to keep

Goebbels at bay. Just about. For obvious reasons, the doctor's not as fast on his feet as you are. If anyone can do it, you can. But what happened to hating the whole stupid industry? What happened to not wanting to work with an anti-Semite like Veit Harlan? And what will you tell Stefan?"

"If I'm as powerful as Zarah Leander, my love, then I can certainly get Veit Harlan taken off the picture," she said. "I'll have Joey appoint another film director. Someone a little less controversial. Rolf Hansen, perhaps. He directed *The Great Love*. He can direct me. In fact, I think he'd do a good job. Anyone that can make Zarah Leander look ladylike has got to be good. That woman's a giant. They had to use SS men in drag on that picture because they couldn't find any chorus girls who were as tall as her. I'm not joking." She shrugged. "As for Stefan, I shall just tell him that the money was too good to refuse. That's something he can certainly understand."

"Then it's settled. I'll pick you up in the morning. At six."

A couple of hours later, we went onto the lakeshore where the citizens of Rapperswil were strolling around in the late afternoon sunshine, eating ice cream and studying the water almost as if they expected something to come out of it: a woman's arm holding a sword, perhaps. At the café in front of the Schwanen Hotel, people were drinking coffee and watching a procession of ducks make its stately way toward the water. If a French painter of the rarer kind who was more interested in light than brandy had been on the scene, he'd have unfolded an easel and started work right away, and I wouldn't have blamed him at all if he'd turned out one of those mottled masterpieces that make you think you need a better pair of glasses. A big bell was tolling in the church clock tower and everything felt like it was just another ordinary summer's day. It didn't feel that way to me. It's never an ordinary day when a beautiful woman allows you the run of her naked body.

Dalia led me a short distance from where the local steam ferries and the island water taxis plied their trade, to an L-shaped pontoon on which a selection of small runabouts were moored, including a smartly polished, mahogany speedboat with a little red-and-white Croatian flag on the stern. It looked like a floating sports car. Dalia kissed me fondly, lifted the hem of her skirt a little, and I held her hand while she stepped into the boat.

"Could you untie me, darling?" she said, and pulled in the fenders.

"Sure."

"I'll see you tomorrow morning at six a.m.," she said.

I nodded and sniffed my fingers ostentatiously. She knew I hadn't washed—I wanted to smell her on me long after she was gone—and she blushed.

"Stop it," she said. "You're making me feel shy."

"I like that. It reminds me that you're really human and not something that just stepped down from Olympus for the day."

"Don't come up the drive, tomorrow. Stay on the road and I'll come and find you. All right?"

I nodded again.

"You won't let me down, will you, Gunther? I don't much like movies when the girl gets stood up."

"I'll be there, all right. Never doubt it. Teutonic knights are always on time. Especially when there's a damsel involved."

Dalia sat down behind the white leather steering wheel, lit a cigarette, put on some sunglasses, and adjusted her shapely behind on a seat cushion that matched the flag on the stern. She turned a key on the dashboard, a big engine coughed into life, and water spluttered out of the twin chrome exhausts that were on either side of the boat's name in gold paint: *The Gretchen.* I coiled the wet ropes neatly and then dropped them onto the boat's rubberized floor. By now several people were watching her, and I have to admit that Dalia couldn't have looked more like a movie star if she'd been walking down a red carpet with Emil Jannings on one arm and Leni Riefenstahl on the other. And if that was all that she'd looked like I might have felt a surge of pride, given what had just taken place between us. I'd have said, "Gunther, old man, if you told some of these people what you and she have just been doing up in that hotel bedroom, they wouldn't believe you." I could hardly believe it myself, any more than I could accept the current evidence of my own eyes, which was that she—or someone very close to her—had very probably murdered Meyer-Schwertenbach's lady in the lake. It wasn't just the cushion cover with checkerboard red-and-white squares that seemed to match exactly the one found in the sunken wreck, or the knowledge that her big mansion in Küsnacht was possessed of a very convenient boathouse from which an expedition to scuttle a boat in the lake could easily have been launched; it wasn't the large diamond ring I'd seen on Dalia's own finger, which served to remind me that only someone who owned a ring as big as the one found on the dead woman's hand—and very likely several others besides—could ever have afforded not to take it before sinking the boat; it wasn't even the expert way she handled her own motorboat as she left the pontoon. Clearly she knew a great deal about boats. No, it was the way she had turned on a five-pfennig piece about returning to Germany almost the minute I'd told her that Inspector Leuenberger was planning to reopen the lady in the lake case. She'd been so adamant she didn't want to work for Goebbels again when we'd talked about it earlier; and now she was preparing to come back to Berlin with me in the morning. Just like that. It didn't make any sense, unless she'd had something to do with the murder and was now keen to leave Switzerland before Inspector Leuenberger found something incriminating to Dalia and her husband.

I watched the motorboat until it was a silver speck racing across the navy blue thread that was the horizon. My eyes might have been narrowed against the dazzling sun but they could still see that she was probably using me. Not that I minded very much about that. Sometimes being used is fine if you know that this is what's happening. You go along with it. Especially when you're a man and it's a beautiful woman who's doing the using. Exploitation can feel a lot worse than something as human as that. That's certainly how I felt about it. We're all using someone else for something if we're really honest about that. Some sort of deal or transaction lies at the heart of most human relationships. Karl Marx knew all about that. He wrote a very large book about the subject. Of course, the part of me that was still a cop wanted to go to the Schwanen Hotel, find Paul Meyer-Schwertenbach, take him around the corner to the police station in Rapperswil where I would describe the seat cushion in Dalia's boat to Inspector Leuenberger, and then suggest that he mount a search of her house in Küsnacht. At the very least, she and Stefan Obrenović had some serious explaining to do. That's certainly what I might have done before the war, when things like murder and being a cop, like law and justice, seemed to matter. How naïve we were to imagine that such things were always going to be important. Perhaps one day they would matter again, but right now, the part of me that was a man said something very different about how I should handle this latest discovery and, even as that antique part—the cop part—was still speaking, I put my fingers to my nostrils and inhaled the most precious, intimate scent of Dalia's pleasure, and straightaway I was certain I was never going to talk her up for a murder that everyone else in Switzerland seemed to have forgotten about anyway. I knew as surely as Heinrich Steinweg knew how to make a good piano that I was going to be waiting in a car outside the house in Küsnacht at six the following morning. Short of Inspector Weisendanger turning up at Wolfsberg Castle or a whole truckload of OSS agents kidnapping me again, there wasn't a snowball's chance in hell of me not being there.

Forty-one

The Kon Tiki Bar in the basement of the Hotel Bayerischer Hof was supposed to look like something on an exotic Polynesian island but it seemed a little gloomy to convince anyone that we were in the South Pacific instead of Munich's city center. I don't know if the totem poles and tribal masks that lined the walls and the puffer fish hanging from the bamboo ceilings were the real thing, but the cocktails tasted real enough (even though they were mostly sugar), especially after Dalia produced a bottle of rum from a hornback alligator handbag to put some extra snap in them. She was full of surprises like that. We were certainly in the mood for a few drinks following the long drive from Küsnacht and, with several under our belts, we probably wouldn't have noticed if the whole of the RAF had come calling while we were in there, especially as the bar doubled as the hotel's bomb shelter. But for once it was a quiet night—rare for a full moon—and we decided to take a walk to get some Munich air and generally try to sober up a little before going to bed. Just outside the hotel—which was Munich's best—on Promenadestrasse was the street where Kurt Eisner, Bavaria's first prime minister after the abolition of the monarchy, was murdered by an anti-Semite, in 1919. It was the first of many similar, politically motivated murders. And perhaps it was the combination of this and several rum cocktails that prompted me to mention the delicate subject of the murder while we walked through the cobbled streets all the way to the infamous Hofbräuhaus. We didn't go inside the beer hall where Hitler had proclaimed the program of the Nazi Party in 1920, which was why the place was treated like a shrine, with Nazi flags and a policeman to guard them. Rum and the watered-down beer they were probably serving don't mix any more than a jolly brass band in your ear and a whispered half-accusation of murder. Instead we stood under the arches of the entrance, peered through the glass door for a moment at some of the men in their lederhosen and extraordinary Tyrolean hats, and then retired to a safer distance.

"You know, it's really none of my business, and frankly I can't bring myself to give a damn about it one way or the other. I'm sure you had your reasons for what happened—good reasons, too—but yesterday, when we were in Rapperswil, I had the strange idea that it was you or someone close to you who killed that girl who was found at the bottom of Lake Zurich."

"Whatever makes you say a thing like that, Gunther?" She took a cigarette from the case in my pocket and lit it so calmly she might have been playing a scene in a movie. "Frankly, I'm a little bewildered that you could even say such a thing."

"I certainly wouldn't tell anyone in the Swiss police, angel. You needn't worry on that score. Real police work has long ceased to inter-est me very much. And I'm only mentioning this now because I want you to think highly of me. I know what I'm saying sounds strange, but the fact is your opinion of me suddenly matters more than it did yester-day. So wait until I'm through and then you can talk.

"When you told me how you did that mental arithmetic for your friend from the polytechnic the other night, I was impressed. After-wards I sat down with a pencil and paper and worked it out for myself and saw it was just as you'd said it was—that each first and last number made one hundred and one, and that there were fifty lots of them.

Then I got to thinking that I wasn't smart enough for you. It's not that I mind about that, particularly. I've met plenty of women who were smarter than me. Usually I like it that way. It keeps me on my toes to be around clever women. It saves having to explain myself. But I realized that it's important to me that you understand that, in my own crude way I'm smart, too. Maybe not quite as smart as you, angel, but still smart enough to have worked out in my head that you had something to do with the lady in the lake. I'm not sure I can explain how and that it all adds up as neatly as the way you explained those numbers yesterday. I can't even tell you if it makes a nice number like five thousand and fifty, but everything under my hairline tells me you knew her and that only you can tell me how she ended up searching the bottom of Lake Zurich for someone's surplus sword."

"You'll forgive me if I ask to hear how you worked this out," she said, still looking skeptical.

"Oh, sure. Here, let me show you."

I took her small but surprisingly strong hand, opened it and, like a gypsy reading a palm, I took each finger, starting with her pinkie, and gave it a reason for why I thought what I did. But the real clincher was her forefinger. I held on to that for quite a while as I explained how a cushion cover in the sunken boat was the red-and-white Croatian flag and identical to one on her own motorboat—*The Gretchen*—that I'd seen underneath her own behind the previous day and how, if they really paid attention to what they were doing, even the Swiss police could probably match the one to the other.

"Red and white," she said. "That's not such an unusual color combination in Switzerland, Gunther. They even make little pocketknives that are red and white. I'll buy you one for your birthday if you can remember when that is."

"No, that's quite true. Red and white. I get that. But the cushion on *The Gretchen*—like the one on the sunken boat—is curved at the front and straight at the back, with twenty-five red-and-silver squares. They look white but the heraldic boys like to describe them as silver. Thirteen red and twelve silver. I counted them. The chessboard—that's what they call it, isn't it?"

"A *Šahovnica*," she muttered. "Yes."

"Right. So, there's no doubt about it, angel. That's the Croatian flag, all right. I spent enough time in Zagreb and in several hellholes south of there, seeing that damn flag every day, to know it like the back of my hand, and wishing frankly that I'd never see it again. Like Pavlov's dog, I don't think I'll ever see Croatia's flag again *without* associating it with murder. So when I saw it under your beautiful behind, angel— the behind I'd not long finished kissing so fondly at the Pension du Lac—well, it kind of caught my attention."

She smiled as the door of the beer hall opened and we heard the band in the Hofbräuhaus strike up with "So Long Old Peter," which was enough to put a smile on anyone's face.

"All right, I'm impressed," she said. "Let's agree that you're not as dumb as you look. What of it?"

I took her by the arm and led her farther away from the beer hall and down a quiet alley.

"If I'm going to perform dressage for you, angel, I need to know what happened. That's all. You see, when you're a detective and you find out that someone killed someone else, it says on page one of the police manual that you're supposed to do something about it. It's just good professional conduct. Like I said, that was then. But I still have to look at myself in the shaving mirror every morning. And it wouldn't do for me to lose all my self-respect about this. Not that there's much of that left, you understand, but maybe there's still enough that I need to be able to meet my own eye. Any detective would tell you the same thing. Finding out things, cracking a case open, solving crimes—even if that doesn't amount to much more than solving the crossword in today's newspaper—it's what detectives do, angel, even when we choose never to do anything about it afterward. That's all I'm saying. I've got an itch and I want you to help me scratch it. After that we can forget all about it. Honest. But I need to know, see?"

She sighed, snatched a drag on the cigarette, and then shot me a sulky look.

"Talk to me," I said, taking hold of her elbow. "You knew her. Tell me what happened."

"All right," she said, pulling her elbow away again. "But it wasn't murder, Gunther. You're wrong about that. I promise you, I didn't mean to kill her. It was an accident."

"Who was she? The woman in the boat."

"Does it matter now?"

"I think so."

"All right. She was an old girlfriend of mine. Someone who lived in Zurich. She came to the house in Küsnacht one night, got stinking drunk, and we had an argument. Maybe I was a bit drunk, too, I don't know. We argued about a man. What else? She was planning to go and see this man and I said that she shouldn't. Maybe I was a little more forceful than that. Anyway, the argument grew a bit heated and I'm not sure why but she took a swing at me and missed, and then I hit her back. I slapped her, hoping to bring her back to her senses. It didn't. I slapped her a little too hard and caught her right on the chin and she went down like Schmeling in the first. Hit her head on a big cast-iron firedog and that was it. She was dead. Agnes used to be a nurse and checked her pulse, but it was no good. There was blood all over the carpet and it was obvious to anyone that she was dead. Have you ever killed your best friend? It has its low points. I sat around for a long time, crying and wondering what to do. Feeling sorry for her but sorrier for myself, I guess. Well, I wasn't married to Stefan at the time—we were just sort of living in the same house. The Swiss could have deported me at any time. Anyway, when he came home he took charge of every-thing. It was Stefan who suggested that we should dispose of the body. That it certainly wouldn't help my movie career or him if we involved the police. By then I was a little calmer. So, in the middle of the night, we carried her down to the boathouse and took her out in this old boat that was moored in there. Stefan drove that boat while I followed in *The Gretchen*. We sailed down the lakeshore for a bit and then scuttled her. That's it. Before you ask, I married Stefan the following week. She stayed down in the water for almost a year before they found her, but by then it was almost impossible to identify her, of course. So, I figured I was in the clear. At least I did until yesterday, Gunther." She tossed her cigarette away and stamped her foot. "Why did you have to—" She sighed. "Be so damned clever? I hate you knowing this. I could kill you, Gunther. Really I could."

"This is a nice quiet place. Nobody's around. Maybe now's your chance."

"What? What are you talking about?"

I took the Walther out of its shoulder holster, worked the slide to put one in the chamber, put it in her hand, and lifted her arm so that the gun was pointed straight at my heart.

"You said yourself that nobody has ever done something noble for you. Well, now I'm doing it. Sacrificing myself to your happiness. Just like one of those Teutonic knights."

"Be careful. I'll do it. You just watch me."

"Go ahead," I said. "Be my guest. That's a P38 you're holding. It fires eight rounds of nine-millimeter Luger ammunition. But at this kind of range one's more than enough to put a decent-sized hole in me."

"Don't be so sure I won't do it, you big stupid ape."

"That's really the point of the whole exercise, my love. A month or two ago I'd have said you'd be doing me a favor or something like that. But since I met you, I've changed my opinion."

"You're drunk."

"Not so drunk that I don't know exactly what I'm doing. All you've got to do is pull the trigger, drop the gun, and walk quickly away. That's right. Think about it. With me gone, there's no one in Germany who's ever going to know that you killed that girl. You can go on being a movie star without a care in the world. No one will ever figure a beautiful woman like you for a shooter. Especially not in Munich. Unlike Prussians, Bavarians are a little old-fashioned like that. Go ahead and shoot."

"Stop it, Gunther."

"You can do it if you want to do it. You said you wanted to kill me. Believe me, on a dark night, in a quiet street, with a loaded gun in your hand, you'll never get a better chance than this."

"Stop it," she said. "Of course I don't want to kill you, Gunther. I was just saying that. Why would I want you dead, you idiot? I told you I love you, didn't I? Well, I do."

She lowered the gun and turned her face to the wall. I took the gun away from her and let the hammer down gently. The safety was still on—had been all along—but she wasn't to know that. It's the good thing about the P38—it's always been very safe, for a gun. You can keep one quite safely in the chamber all the time without worrying that you're going to blow your ear off. I returned the P38 to my shoulder holster, took her in my arms and then kissed her face, which was now wet with tears.

"Only now I'm sure of that," I said quietly. "And that's really all that matters, isn't it?"

"You're crazy," she said. "Suppose I'd shot you?"

"You didn't. And if you had shot me, it wouldn't have mattered anyway. The fact is, I really don't like the idea of carrying on without you in my life. You'd have been doing me a favor, angel."

"I don't believe that," she said.

I kissed her again. "Sure you do."

"What happens now? About the other thing?"

"The lady in the lake?"

She nodded.

"Nothing. Maybe you weren't listening. These days murder isn't a crime, it's a map of Germany's so-called protectorates and puppet states with the numbers of dead proudly delivered and announced as birthday presents for the leader. There's no reason why you should understand what I mean by that, or why anyone should tell you. Maybe one day I'll explain it, but not now. So forget about all that and we'll make it just this: whatever happened, whatever you did, I don't give a damn. All that matters now is today. And that's all that will matter tomorrow. And the day after. Your secret is safe with me. And anytime you bid me to go and throw someone or something into a lake for you, angel, I'm your man."

Forty-two

W hat the hell happened to your nose?"

"I blew it a little too loudly, I think. Either that or it's a lot colder in Berlin than I thought."

Goebbels smiled. "You really brought her back from Switzerland?"

"I left her drinking coffee at the house, in Griebnitzsee, an hour ago. She's fine. Reading her script. Looking forward to starting work on Monday."

"But, I don't understand, why hasn't she called me?"

"I don't know, sir."

"Perhaps I should go down to the house, with a bunch of flowers. With a piece of jewelry, perhaps. I wonder if Margraf on Kanonier-strasse might have something."

"I think she said she was going to take a bath. It is a long drive from Munich, sir. And it is a hot day. Perhaps she intends to call you later. After she's freshened up a bit."

"Yes, I expect you're right. Gunther, I'm amazed. What with the bombing and that unfortunate business with her papa, I thought she'd never come back to Berlin. The last time we spoke on the telephone she virtually told me to go to hell. I'd even started to look for another actress to replace her. In the picture, I mean." He smiled. "She's really there now? In Griebnitzsee?"

"As soon as I saw that she was safely through the front door, I came straight over here to tell you. I would have telephoned but I thought I should tell you in person."

"I just knew it was going to be a great day," said Goebbels. "Yesterday, on my way here from Tempelhof Airport, I was reflecting on the folly of human beings who wage war when nature is so very beautiful. It's hard to imagine anything like that happening on a day as beautiful as this, isn't it? And now this. Your fantastic news. Really, I couldn't be more delighted."

Goebbels grinned, flipped open the silver cigarette box, and bounced a little on the sofa cushion. "Help yourself to a cigarette, Captain. Fill your case."

I smiled thinly, unbuttoned the breast pocket in my tunic, and took out my case. I was back in uniform now. My suit was still on the floor of Dalia's bedroom at the house in Griebnitzsee, where she had hurriedly thrown it before we'd gone to bed. I'd forgotten to hang it up and now a small part of me was worried that the suit would still be there if on the spur of the moment the minister for Truth decided to dash round there to welcome his favorite actress back to Berlin. Good housekeeping wasn't Dalia's strongest suit and without Agnes there to remember these things, I'd not much confidence that the suit wouldn't still be lying there when Goebbels walked in. And not just my suit, but also my dirty underwear and the shoulder holster with the P38 I'd borrowed from the farmer in Ringlikon. The gun I might have been able to explain, but not the underwear.

In his own white summer suit Goebbels looked exactly like a male nurse in an insane asylum, which was perhaps not so very far from the truth. Waging war—total war—was one of the Mahatma's most famous mantras, and to hear him waxing lyrical about the follies of war took me by surprise. What could he possibly know about peace and nature?

I was also surprised he'd seen me without an appointment. The ministry was full of state secretaries and stenographers running around the palace like lunatics. Clearly something very serious was up but no one I asked felt at all inclined to say what this was. For a few glorious moments I thought that the whole government was fleeing Berlin, which had been the rumor on the streets ever since the RAF bombing had intensified. Hamburg had been hit again and was supposed to be in ruins. And there was no doubt that certain Berlin public offices had been evacuated. The minister of the interior, Wilhelm Frick, was reputed to have taken his entire department to the country. Every real Berliner I knew was anxious to see the back of them all. But Goebbels certainly didn't look like a man who was about to run away from Hitler's capital. In fact he looked so pleased with the news I'd given him and so relaxed that he crossed his legs, giving me a clean view of his deformed right foot dangled in front of my face, something I'd never known him to do; I'd become aware he usually crossed them left over right.

"However did you do it?" he asked. "You have to tell me everything because I certainly won't get the truth from Dalia herself. She'll give me some nonsense about how she didn't want to let everyone down. Me, Veit Harlan. The rest of the cast. The woman is an expert liar. Take it from one who has a nose for the truth. What on earth did you tell her?"

I took a cigarette from my refilled case, rolled it under my nose to savor the sweet scent of good tobacco—which, unlike most German cigarettes, stayed tight in the paper and didn't fall out in your pocket—and lit it with the table lighter. "The money, sir." I aimed the smoke at the high ceiling and shrugged. "I told her about the money and the house you were offering to give her, for doing the picture. You mentioned it in your telegram."

"She always knew that more money was in the cards," he said, shaking his head. "That's how these people work, you know. Actors.

The women are especially ruthless. They wait until they have you between the jaws of their pliers before they start to squeeze you for the last penny. But money was never the issue with her. She has a rich husband. Houses and money are not that important to Dalia. No, there has to be something else, Gunther. Something you're not telling me. She's back in Berlin for something other than money. But what?"

I didn't think he wanted to hear about the lady in the lake or that maybe her presence in Berlin had just a little to do with me, so I took a long haul on the cigarette, swallowed the smoke whole this time, and then said: "I told her she was going to be getting even more money for this movie than Zarah Leander got when she made *The Big Love.*"

"*The Great Love.*" Goebbels frowned. "The film was called *The Great Love.* But now I come to think of it, *The Big Love* sounds much more modern. More American. Anyway, the point is, there was nothing in my telegram about Zarah Leander. All I said was that I would double what Fräulein Dresner had been offered before. Which is already a hell of a lot, I don't mind telling you, Gunther. You've no idea what these people call a day's pay."

"No, sir. That's true. I'm afraid I took the liberty of adding that bit about Zarah Leander, just to help sweeten your offer. And, as it happened, Fräulein Dresner was pleased when I pointed out that she was going to be making more money than Leander. She seemed especially delighted when I suggested that she'll be the highest paid actress in German cinema. Ever. I suppose you might even call that politics. As a result I think I might have given you a problem with Zarah Leander. You might have to arbitrate a power struggle between those two."

"Brilliant," said Goebbels, and he clapped his hands loudly. "Brilliant. Why the hell didn't I think of that? Yes, of course. All of these actresses are pathologically jealous of each other. Dalia hates Zarah, who hates Marika Roekk. And everyone hates Marlene. How did you know that?"

"I didn't. But when I did physics at school I learned about something called Coulomb's law, which says that highly charged particles whose charges have the same sign repel one another. Sometimes violently. The same is often true with women. When there's one woman who's attracting all of the men in a room, then some of the other women might very well be repelled by that. At least that's been my own experience. Sometimes I think that women pay more attention to each other than they do to men."

"Isn't that so true?" said Goebbels. "But not just of women, let me tell you. Male actors are just the same. Heinz Rühmann can't be in the same room as Ferdinand Marian. Mind you, no one else can stand to be in the same room as Ferdinand Marian, either. His ex-wife is a Jewess, you know. They even have a half-Jewish daughter. His second wife used to be married to a Jew, as well. Incredible, isn't it? Not being a Jew himself—you'd think he'd be a little more careful about that kind of thing, wouldn't you? I mean, him of all people."

I nodded vaguely; Ferdinand Marian was the actor who'd played the Jew Süss, in the film of the same name.

"But it's exactly the same on Wilhelmstrasse. Everyone scrabbling to get the leader's attention. Yes, they're just like actresses, some of these people, with Bormann and Speer the very worst of them all. You've done well, Gunther. Very well indeed. I can't tell you how pleased I am."

"Thank you, sir." I was already looking at the exit, wondering when I might finally escape the doctor's pleasure and go home to my own apartment. After driving all morning from Munich, I was tired. Especially following a sleepless night in bed with Dalia. As a lover she was proving to be quite insatiable.

"You're wasted in the War Crimes Bureau, Gunther. You should come and work for me here. I need someone resourceful. Someone who can think for himself. I suppose that's what's held you back in your chosen career. I mean, it's very difficult to get on when you're so independently minded as you are. But I can use that. And now I come to think of it, there's one more job I need you to do for me. Yes, I'm afraid you can't go and see your new wife quite yet. Sorry about that, but this is much more urgent. You might even say that this is your fault—the result of your earlier good work. That might well be unfair. But really it can't be helped. Yes, this has to be sorted out as soon as possible." He looked at his watch. "The sooner the better.

"Now that Mussolini has gone—yes, I'm afraid so, Gunther, the Duce has resigned and Badoglio has taken over in Italy. That's what all the fuss is about. Out there. In the corridors of power, so to speak. Why everyone is running around like headless turkeys. The whole situation is still very obscure. I've just got back from the leader's GHQ in Rastenburg, where I spent hours in conference with him. Anyway, everything is in a state of flux here, in Italy of course, and in Croatia. The Croatian Poglavnik, Ante Pavelić, is already here in Berlin to seek assurances from von Ribbentrop. Not that von Ribbentrop could give anyone an assurance about anything very much. I'm afraid that our illustrious foreign minister is diplomatically illiterate and couldn't manage to reassure a simple schoolboy if his pockets were full of lollipops."

I took a deep breath before prompting him. All I really wanted to do now was go home. "So, what's this job you want me to do for you, sir?"

"Oh, yes. Well, this is our problem, do you see? The one we created just a few days ago in this very office, you and I. Yes, I freely admit, this is my fault, too. But in my own defense, Gunther, I should say that this was your idea. Correct me if I'm wrong, but you did come up with the idea. The Poglavnik has brought some of his people with him. His head of internal security, Eugen Kvaternik; Lorković, his German liaison minister; Perić, his foreign minister; and various bodyguards and

Ustaše officers. And here's the real hair in the soup. It seems that one of these officers is none other than our old friend Colonel Dragan. Yes, that's right. Dalia's father. Father—what's his name?"

"Father Ladislaus. He's here in Berlin? Christ, how did that happen?"

"It's all von Ribbentrop's fault. He just went ahead and issued everyone in the Poglavnik's delegation with a visa without consulting anyone in this ministry, or even the Ministry of the Interior. Well, you'd have to find someone in the Ministry of the Interior, I suppose. Anyway, he's here now and it seems more than likely he'll try and make contact with Dalia, if he can, don't you think? I've already called security down at the film studios to make sure he's not allowed through the gate."

"He won't go to the studio," I said. "He won't need to. Her address in Griebnitzsee was on the letter I gave to the colonel when I met him, at Jasenovac. I can't imagine he'd have lost it. When I gave him the letter he put it in his breast pocket, over his heart."

"That is unfortunate."

"The house has got to be his first port of call."

"I can see you understand the problem. I knew you would. So it's up to you now to make sure he doesn't ever see her. After all, he is supposed to be dead. At least that's what you've told her, isn't it? That the Father Abbot from the monastery in Banja Luka told you that he was killed in the war by Serbs, or something? It wouldn't do at all if they met now. Not after all the effort we've been to in bringing her back to Berlin. Chances are she'd go straight back to Switzerland. And then we'd be back to square one."

I nodded. I could already hear the way that Goebbels would spin this if ever Dalia came to demand an explanation of him:

"*I can understand why you're upset about this, Dalia. But you mustn't blame me. And you mustn't even think of going back to Switzerland. The fact is, that awful fellow Bernhard Gunther has lied to us both. He told me your father was dead, too. I've no idea why he did that. It's inexcusable, I agree, but I had nothing to do with it, you must believe me."*

"Drive over to the house in Griebnitzsee, for a start, and make damn sure Colonel Dragan doesn't get through the fucking door. Tell Dalia he's an impostor, tell her he's an assassin—tell her anything you damn well like and shoot him if you have to, but just make sure the two of them never meet. If they do, she'll know we've both lied to her. You and me. And no amount of special pleading will fix that, Gunther. He is her father, after all, even if he is a psychopath."

"Where is the Croatian delegation staying?"

"All over the city. Pavelić and Kvaternik are at the Adlon with some of the bodyguards. Perić is at the embassy. Most of the Ustaše officers are at the Villa Minoux, in Wannsee. But a few, including Dalia's papa, are staying with the Grand Mufti at his villa in Goethestrasse."

"Jesus, that's halfway to Babelsberg."

"No doubt he and the mufti are comparing notes on this SS regiment of Bosnian Muslims that Haj Amin has persuaded Himmler to set up so they can go and murder some more Jews. What are they called?"

"The Handschar," I said.

"Crazy, if you ask me, but when did something like common sense ever stop Himmler? Well? Have you any bright ideas? About what to do about this unconscionable mess we've managed to make?"

"I think the best thing would be if I got her out of town for a few days. Until the delegation from Croatia has left Berlin."

"That's an excellent idea. But not Switzerland, eh? We've only just got her back. Somewhere in Germany would be best. But where would you suggest?"

"It had better not be in Berlin. Dalia's too famous to put up in any Berlin hotel. Why can't you take her to Rastenburg?"

"You are joking, aren't you?"

"Sorry." I thought for a minute. "Look, don't you have a safe house? Somewhere you go when you don't want to be found?"

"I'm a married man, with six children. Seven if you count my wife's son, Harald. What kind of man do you take me for, Gunther?"

"I could always take her to my own flat."

"No, I don't think that would be appropriate, do you?" He thought for a minute. "Actually I do know a place. There's a small cottage I own, near the Potsdam Forest in Wirtshaus Moorlake, a little way southwest of Pfaueninsel. You could take her there, I suppose. Tell her—tell her that the Aviation Ministry have given us some intelligence that there's going to be a bombing raid on the film studio, to destroy German morale."

"Does it have a telephone?" I asked. "This cottage."

"Yes, of course. Or you might tell her that the Jew who once owned that house in Griebnitzsee has escaped and is believed to be on his way back to Berlin. That he might try to attack whoever is living there. Yes, that might work. It does happen, you know. Not all Jews take the process of Aryanization lying down."

"Then I'll bring her to the cottage. You can call me again when it's safe."

"Or just say that there's been a threat to my own life and the lives of those who I'm close to. That would work, too, don't you think?"

I was beginning to wonder just how close the two of them actually were. I only had Dalia's word for the fact that she and Goebbels weren't lovers. But his talk of flowers and buying her jewelry from Margraf was beginning to persuade me otherwise.

"You'd better tell me where this cottage is, sir. And give me the telephone number."

He told me the address and showed me where it was on a map he retrieved from his desk.

"I know the area well," I told him. "I had lunch with General Nebe there once. It's nice down there, at this time of year. Really beautiful on the lake. And very discreet, I imagine. And very romantic, of course." I smiled. "Do you go there often, sir?"

Goebbels gave me an icy look, which made me feel much more comfortable. I knew exactly where I was with him that way. "I'll find the key for you," he said. "Telephone me as soon as you get there."

Forty-three

I rang the house in Griebnitzsee from a cream-colored private telephone in the ministry but there was no reply. That didn't worry me. Dalia probably was taking a bath. I never knew a woman who took so long in the bathroom. Washing and drying her hair could take more than an hour. At the Bayerischer Hof in Munich, where she had taken a suite almost as big as the Tiergarten, she'd used six large towels in the course of just one evening, which would have shocked many Germans who managed to make one towel last a whole week, but somehow this struck me as amusing. Most of the time Dalia managed to live as if the war only existed for other people. I admired her for that. What was the point of pretending to be as miserable as everyone else when you already had everything anyone could ever have dreamed of in peacetime? Me, I just wanted to be near someone like that for as long as that was possible and to enjoy that carefree existence, albeit vicariously. It felt like a very welcome intermission in the black-and-white horror movie that was my life. Of course, both of us were living in the moment, although for entirely opposite reasons: Dalia because she could see no reason to deny herself whatever earthly pleasure she wanted; as for me, because all earthly pleasures seemed as if they might be denied me at any time. In my world, heads were usually removed at

Brandenburg Prison, or at Jasenovac. But in hers, the only heads that needed cutting off were the ones on the roses.

At least that's what I'd told myself.

I was heading toward the marble stairs when I spied the screening room where State Secretary Leopold Gutterer had had me read the speech I would make later at the Wannsee IKPK conference. Maybe it was my clown's red nose, but even though I was worried about Dalia I was in the mood for some minor sabotage after that meeting with Goebbels. I went into the room, closed the door behind me, and walked over to the big Telefunken radio that stood up against one wall. From the size of it you might have thought that these were the controls to a cruise ship you could have steered up Wilhelmstrasse all the way north, to the Baltic Sea. As with all radios in Germany, this one carried a little warning sign over the plastic tuning knob to remind you that listening to forbidden radio stations was an offense punishable by death. With the radio not yet switched on, it took only a few seconds for me to quickly tune it to the BBC. I adjusted the volume to maximum before finally switching it on and then swiftly leaving the room. Like most radios—even one like this, which looked like it had ten or twelve tubes—the Telefunken would take almost a minute to warm up, by which time I would be safely away from the scene of the crime. As acts of resistance go, this wasn't much, but at least it made me laugh. Where the Nazis are concerned, sometimes humor is the best weapon there is.

I left the ministry and walked quickly back to the Mercedes. I was going to miss having that car when the time came to return it to Schellenberg. I put my foot down and started driving fast, through the Tiergarten, past the Victory Column, and into the west end of the city before turning south on the AVUS speedway. Goethestrasse was on my way to Griebnitzsee and it made sense to stop there first. If I found Colonel Dragan, I'd spin him some squelch about us going to the film studio in Babelsberg so that he could speak to his long-lost daughter. Instead I'd drive him deep into the Potsdam Forest and then just leave him there, abandoned like Snow White, miles from anywhere, while I went back to the house on Kaiser-Strasse and then took Dalia to the cottage near Pfaueninsel. We could probably hole up there for at least a week, or until Goebbels gave me the all-clear siren.

Goethestrasse was a Gold Coast cobbled street with big cars and expensive houses; it certainly looked as though the Grand Mufti had landed on his leather sandals. The elegant mandarin-colored villa on the corner of Schillerstrasse wasn't one of the biggest but it might just have been the nicest. It was the kind of place I'd have chosen to live myself if I'd had a good friend like Adolf Hitler. I parked the car in the shade of a tall birch tree, switched off the engine, and stepped onto the cobbled sidewalk. It was all a long away from Jerusalem. Six years ago—it must have been September 1937—the SD's Jewish Department had sent me to Palestine and Egypt in the company of two SD NCOs as part of a fact-finding mission. In Cairo, I'd been present in a hotel room at the National Hotel when the two Germans I was with met the Grand Mufti, whose hatred of Jews was nothing short of pathological, and my most earnest hope now was that I could avoid meeting this mad mullah again. Not that I thought he'd remember me. And I didn't think I'd like him any better now that he was living in Berlin.

I gave a false name to the sullen Handschar guarding the gate just in case the colonel ever tried to find me again. I certainly wasn't about to forget his fondness for cutting throats and severing heads. I still had bad dreams about his front garden at Jasenovac. The Handschar was wearing what looked like a field gray fez, with a Nazi eagle and an SS death's head on the front. A black tassel dangled off the top like a hellish bellpull. He didn't seem particularly Ottoman—for one thing he spoke goodish German. And he couldn't have looked more bored if he'd been the life model in a class of blind draftsmen.

"Good morning, sir," he said politely as I presented myself at the gate. "How can I help you?"

"I'm hoping to see Colonel Dragan," I said. "He's part of the Pog's delegation from Croatia. I believe he's a guest of the Grand Mufti. I need to speak with him on an urgent personal matter."

"I see."

"Is he here now?"

"I don't know. People come and go from this place all the time. Nobody tells me anything. I'm just the dog on the gate."

The gate remained closed and time was beginning to feel short. But I hardly wanted to start barking orders at him. He had the look of someone who wanted to bark back.

"You're a long way from home, aren't you, sonny? Bosnia, isn't it? Where you boys in the Muslim SS are from?"

The Handschar nodded wistfully, as if he missed his country.

"I was there a few weeks ago," I said. "Place called Banja Luka."

"You were in Banja Luka?" He made it sound like I'd spent a wild weekend in Paris.

"That's right."

"I wish I was in Banja Luka," he said. "My home is in Omarska. Which is near there." He shook his head sadly. "I don't know why I'm here. But I am. Next week we have to go on a training course in France. But I really don't want to go on a training course in France. I just want to go home, sir."

"You'll be back home before you know it," I said. "With a story to tell. Not to mention a nice pair of boots that you can sell."

He smiled and opened the gate for me. "There are Ustaše staying here," he confirmed. "But I think maybe some of them went out. You'd best ask at the house."

I walked along a short gravel path, between neatly clipped lawns, past a circular fountain, and up a flight of stairs to a portico with four

Doric columns, where I knocked loudly on a big mahogany door and then turned to look back at the garden. To the right of the house was a public footpath that led across a small lake. In the big white house opposite, several dozen windows shone with an eye-catching glamor. Somewhere behind the trees I could hear the grass growing quickly and the squirrels breathing loudly and I felt the silence as strongly as if it had boxed my ears. Nature looked respectable enough, but it offended me that a fanatic like the mufti should have been living in such a nice part of Berlin as Zehlendorf. If I had been living across the road from such a beast I'd have held a party every night, with lots of alcohol and half-naked girls, just to annoy him. But now that I'd thought about it, I couldn't see why a party like that wasn't a good idea anyway.

Unlike the guard on the gate, the man who answered the door was an Arab. He was wearing a white *jalabiyah* and a red tarboosh. In his hand was a set of prayer beads and he smelled lightly of cardamom seeds and Turkish cigarettes. His face was badly pitted, and poking out from under his long shirt was a colony of ugly brown toenails that looked as if it should have been kept in the insect house at Berlin Zoo. Behind him I could see a large round hall and a mosaic table with a glazed earthenware Persian-style vase of lilies. On one wall was a large black flag with some Arabic writing in silver-white that might have been designed for the SS by Hugo Boss. Then again, maybe it was supposed to be a picture of a snake pit. With modern art these days, it's a little hard to tell. On another wall was a portrait of Adolf Hitler, which prompted me to wonder why he hated Jews but not Arabs. After all, some Jews are just Muslims with a better tailor.

"I'm looking for Colonel Dragan," I explained. "I believe he's staying here?"

"Yes, he's staying here," said the doorman. "But he has gone out, I believe. About twenty minutes ago."

"Did he say where he was going?"

"He did not tell me, sir."

"Was he on foot? Or in a car?"

"He borrowed a bicycle, sir."

"A bicycle?"

"And a map of Berlin."

"What kind of map? Pharus, or Schaffmann?"

"I don't know. It was just a map."

"A Pharus goes further south," I said. "Makes a difference."

The doorman shrugged. "Shall I inform the colonel who called, sir?"

"Captain Geiger," I said. "We both served in Croatia."

I turned to go back down the steps and then stopped. In a back room I could hear a man's voice searching for the right musical note and never quite finding it. Then again, it might have been some kind of prayer.

"What does it mean?" I asked, pointing over the doorman's shoulder at the black flag on the wall. "The Arabic writing on your flag. What does it mean? I'm interested."

The doorman glanced at it for a second. "That's the *Shahada*. It says, 'I bear witness that there is no god but Allah, and I bear witness that Muhammed is the Messenger of Allah.'"

I nodded. "And how does that translate into 'Kill all the Jews'?"

"I don't understand."

"Sure you do. What have you people got against the Jews? I mean, is it in your book to hate them? The way it is in ours?"

"Your book?"

"Hitler's book. *My Struggle*. You know?"

"To my knowledge you are the first German who ever asked this question."

I shrugged. "Well, I'm a very nosy sort of fellow."

"I knew that just by looking at you, sir."

I touched my nose and smiled. It didn't hurt anymore, but I kept forgetting how comical it made me look. But I didn't feel very comical. If I'd been worried before I was even more worried now. It was just twelve kilometers from Goethestrasse to where Dalia was living on Griebnitzsee. A twenty-minute drive. A bit longer on a bicycle, but probably not much longer. Berlin is a very flat city, and excellent for cyclists. It's possible to go from the Brandenburg Gate all the way to Potsdam—a distance of almost thirty kilometers—and not encounter a single hill. The fact was, the colonel might already be sitting in the drawing room with his daughter.

"Yes, it's in our holy Quran to kill all unbelievers, including Jews."

I nodded. "I just wanted to know. For future reference, you understand."

I ran back to the car and started her up.

Forty-four

While I drove the car I rehearsed some of the explanations I might give to Dalia for lying to her so egregiously. "I was only obeying orders" wasn't going to do me any good, that was obvious. It was also obvious that Goebbels was right: if the colonel was already with Dalia, then no amount of special pleading was going to change her opinion, which was that I had deceived her, cruelly. Trying to justify what I had done in the name of her feelings simply wasn't going to alter things for the better. Perhaps later on I might get a chance to offer an excuse for my behavior, but the nearer I got to the house on Griebnitzsee, the more I realized that if Dragan was there already, then the best thing I could probably do would be to withdraw quietly and leave them to their reunion. It was also becoming clear to me that, while I might have had the best of intentions, it had been very wrong of me to lie to her. Dalia was an adult, after all, not a child; she ought to have been given the opportunity to make up her own mind about what kind of man her father was. Protecting a grown woman from the truth was no kind of solution in a world that was already ruled by lies. That's the thing about breathing the same air as the minister of Truth; after a while, truth is just another Paschal holy day you can move to suit the calendar. I felt disgusted with myself.

I parked the car on Kaiser-Strasse and walked along to the big creamy house. There was no sign of a bicycle in the garden or leaning by the front door. It looked as if I had succeeded in getting there before Colonel Dragan. Dalia's bedroom window was open and a net curtain was spilling out of the castellated turret as if a damsel were in there, signaling to her knight with a handkerchief to come and rescue her. Everything looked exactly as it did when I'd left the place a couple of hours earlier. I breathed a sigh of relief and looked up the street to see if I could see an approaching bicyclist but there was no one in sight, not even a gardener.

I went around the back of the house to the kitchen door, which was rarely ever locked. Dalia preferred to leave it open to get a current of cool air through the house. There wasn't a lot of crime in that part of Berlin and I couldn't blame her for wanting some fresh air. It was almost thirty degrees and, at the bottom of the garden, I could see several boats moving up and down the river in the sunshine. It was a perfect day. Goebbels was right about that, too. The sky felt so big and blue and the few clouds looked so shapely I half expected to see the edge of a gilt frame over my head. Instead I saw a bicycle lying on the lawn under the lowest leaves of a weeping willow tree.

I moved quickly to the kitchen door and went inside. White plates and saucers occupied the slots on a wooden draining board like the skeleton of some fossilized animal. A coffeepot stood on the cooker. It was cold to the touch. The tap was dripping cold water into the butler's pantry sink. I started slowly up the creaking wooden stairs. For a few seconds I heard raised voices in a room above my head and then the sound of a single shot. The shot brought me up short; then I heard seven more.

Gun in hand, I bounded up the rest of the kitchen stairs and into the hall. An officer's peaked cap with a letter U around the Croatian flag lay next to Dalia's unopened post on the table. A strong smell of gunpowder was drifting through the house. After eight shots, someone was dead. But who? I caught sight of my own reflection in the big mirror on the hall tree where the hat she'd been wearing in Munich was hanging next to some of her many handbags. I was wearing an anxious, puzzled look. Where was she? Was she all right?

"Dalia?" I yelled. "It's me, Gunther. Where are you?"

I heard something hard fall on the floor. It might have been a gun. I ran into the drawing room.

The black lyre-shaped clock on the mantelpiece was ticking loudly, as if to remind me that time could not be turned around and that in the ten seconds it took to fire eight pistol shots everything had changed forever. I hadn't minded the paintings by Emil Nolde before, but there was one in particular that now seemed sinister: grinning, garishly colored grotesque masks that looked more Halloween than African. And it struck me now that they were laughing at me. What were you thinking? How could you have been so foolish? This is where your carelessness gets you. How did you think that this could end well?

Wearing a plain white summer dress that accentuated her tan, Dalia was sitting on the piano stool with her back to the piano and facing the white leather Swan Biedermeier sofa where she and I had first kissed. She was lighting a cigarette with a fireside match. The P38 I'd left in her bedroom now lay empty but still smoking on the floor about a meter away from Colonel Dragan's dead body. His light gray dress uniform was covered in blood from the several shots she'd fired at his body, although the one through his right eye would by itself certainly have killed him. The whole eyeball was hanging off his cheek like a carelessly served poached egg.

She saw me look at the picture and smiled a sad smile. "I'm not so sure that Hitler wasn't right when he told Joey to get rid of these paintings," she said. "It's not that they're degenerate. I don't know what that means in the context of something like art. It's that the artist's colors feel like they're a part of the human soul. They feel as if they're so much more than just colors. You know what I mean? But for that picture, I don't know that I would have shot him. You see, it reminded me of who and what he was. I know that doesn't sound like much of an explanation to a man like you. To a policeman. It's not very logical, I'll admit that. But looking at that picture now, that's how I feel. Somewhere on the color spectrum between heaven and hell."

Her approach to art appreciation was more convincing than mine.

"I'm sorry I lied to you," I said. "About your father. When I told you he was dead I only meant to spare you the knowledge of who and what he was. To protect you from the truth."

"He's dead now," she said. "At least, I hope he is. I mean, that was certainly my intention. To kill this evil bastard."

I supposed she had shot him because she'd believed exactly what I'd told her, which was that her father was dead, and that she'd assumed the man in her house was an impostor. He must have scared her. Something like that. I don't know. People have been murdered for a lot less than that. I knelt to the side of the body with the least amount of blood on the carpet and pressed my fingers against the dead man's neck, which was still warm to the touch. The hot metal grouped in his chest was making the shirt under his tunic smolder a little. Dark arterial blood was spreading quickly underneath him, like he was an animal lying on the floor of an abattoir.

"He's dead all right," I said, standing up again.

I had to admit that she'd made an excellent job of it. Colonel Dragan had cut his last throat and placed the last human head on his rockery at Jasenovac. If I was at all sad about what had happened it was only because no one should ever find themselves in a position where they end up killing their own father, no matter how terrible he might have been. You don't ever get over something like that. And if that wasn't bad enough, I could see that I now had the awful task of telling the woman I loved the unpalatable truth: that the man she had just shot and killed really was her own papa.

Forty-five

Life moves at the speed of light when there's gun smoke still hanging in the air over a dead body. In just a few seconds a gun changes time forever and everything else that follows. Why had I left it there? It was all my fault. And I could see no way on earth of making this better now.

"Good," she said. "And you needn't worry. He's certainly not my father."

"You don't understand," I said. "I'm sorry. Look, I know I told you that your father was dead, but he's not. Or at least he wasn't. This is Father Ladislaus. This is the man I gave your letter to, in Jasenovac."

"It's *you* who doesn't understand," she said. "Oh, I don't doubt that he's who you say he is. That this man—Antun Djurkovic—was Father Ladislaus, better known now as Colonel Dragan. But I can assure you he was not my father. I know that because I also know that this is the man who killed my father. Not to mention God knows how many others in Yugoslavia since."

"Thousands," I muttered, still uncomprehending.

"So you have met him," she said.

"Yes. When I was in Croatia I went to a concentration camp where he and another priest were killing Serbs for the pleasure of it. I told you he was dead because I thought it best you didn't need to know what a monster he was. No one should have to know something like that."

"That was kind of you. Kinder to me than I've been to you, perhaps. Fetch me a drink, will you, Gunther? A brandy, I think. I owe the truth to you, at least."

I poured us both a drink and then sat down on the sofa and waited patiently for the truth to come out of her. She swallowed the brandy in one gulp, wiped a tear from her eye, and then lit another cigarette. I noticed a tiny fleck of blood on the hem of her dress.

"Believe me, Gunther, I've wanted to kill this man for a long, long time. Dreamed of killing him. Many times and in many different ways. But now that he's dead, I'm surprised to find that I'm not nearly as happy about it as I'd imagined I would be. Why is that, do you think?"

"It's a hell of a thing killing a man," I said. "It always seems like the bullets go through two people: the person who gets shot and the person who does the shooting. I know what you're feeling. But if you're in any doubt about what you did, angel, then let me assure you that this person badly needed to be shot, like a rabid dog or a crazy pig. You can't hear them yet but there are ten thousand bells ringing in heaven for the death of this man and lamentations only in the darkest corner of hell that one of theirs got what he richly deserved."

"I'm just sorry it was so quick. I always wanted him to suffer more for what he did. I mean, I think he was dead after the first shot, but I kept on firing. I'm not sure how."

"That's an automatic pistol for you. It seems to have a mind of its own, and no mistake. Sometimes God or the devil just takes over a trigger and there's nothing you can do about it. The number of times I wanted to fire just the one shot and ended up firing two or three. It's the difference between life and death."

I sipped the brandy and let her walk up to the explanation in her own way.

"Have you got a handkerchief?" she asked.

I handed her mine. She blew her nose and, laughing nervously, apologized for the loud noise it made. "Sorry."

"Forget about it. And take your time, angel."

"He wasn't my father."

"I understand that. Although I'm not sure how."

"Last night, in Munich, you asked me if I'd had anything to do with the death of the lady in the lake and I told you everything about her except for one thing. Her name. You remember when we sat in this room and I told you my real name was Dragica Djurkovic? Well, it's not, it's Sofia Brankovic. Dragica Djurkovic is the lady who was in the lake. You understand? Everything I told you about how she came to be there is true. I mean about it being an accident. It was. Dragica and I were friends. Good friends, for a while. But the fact is that Dragica Djurkovic was this man's daughter."

"I see."

"No, you don't. Not yet. In 1930 my real father, Vladimir Brankovic, was assassinated by the man you see lying on the floor—Antun Dragan Djurkovic. My father was murdered because he was a prominent Serb politician. Almost no one but my mother knew who'd done this and, fearing for our lives, my mother and I fled Croatia to Switzerland, where I became Dalia Dresner. We started a new life and tried not to pay too much attention to what was happening back in Yugoslavia. Which was easy enough in Zurich. Swiss neutrality isn't just political, it's temperamental, too. After a while, news reached us that Djurkovic had repented what he'd done and become a Franciscan monk in Banja Luka, but since he'd been an army chaplain during the Great War, my mother said that his repentance wouldn't last longer than a short summer and that the leopard couldn't change his spots. She was right, of course.

"About eight years later I was at a party given by my future husband in Zurich, and it was there I met Djurkovic's real daughter, Dragica. We'd been friends at school in Zagreb, but for a while we didn't even recognize each other. She was living under the name Stepinac, and it turned out that she'd come to live in Geneva with her grandmother to get away from her father, whom she hated because he used to beat her mother and had tried to rape her. With my own acting career taking off, I made the decision that I would befriend her again and try to help her. And we had a great deal in common; we liked the same books, the same music, the same movies, we shared the same taste in clothes—we even looked a bit like each other. Then her grandmother died and Dragica started drinking heavily. Several times I paid for her to go to a clinic and dry out. But when news of her father's activities in the Ustaše started to reach Switzerland, her drinking got worse. I could hardly blame her for that. He'd left his monastery and was rumored to be part of a murder squad that was now killing thousands of Jews and Serbs. Which is how our argument came about. Dragica had arranged to travel back to Yugoslavia, and the night before she was to leave she came to the house in Küsnacht and explained that she was going back to try to persuade him to change his ways. I'm not sure how she thought she was going to do this, but anyway we argued about it and because she was drunk, she tried to hit me, but I hit her instead and she fell and hit her head and was killed. And Stefan and I hid her body in the lake.

"Time passed and eventually the body was found, of course. Stefan and I held our breath for a while and waited but it was soon clear that no one was ever going to find out who she was. Everyone in Zurich thought Dragica had gone back to Yugoslavia, and because of the war, it was impossible to prove that she hadn't. No one had even supposed she was missing. Meanwhile we started to hear some more about Colonel Dragan's atrocities in Croatia and, being good Yugoslavs, we— Stefan and I—we decided to try to do something about it. Stefan is a Serb and quite a patriot, you know, and has long wanted to do something to help his country. But with me, it was always just revenge. I'm a Serb, too, and vengeance runs deep with us.

"The plan was that I would take advantage of my new friendship with Goebbels, who was clearly obsessed with me. It seemed there was nothing he wouldn't do for his latest starlet. Hardly anyone in Berlin knew my real name was Sofia Brankovic. All they seemed to care about was that I wasn't Jewish. Goebbels took my word for it and organized my Lesser Aryan certificate himself. And then I asked him if he could help me find my father. Which is where you come in. I'm sorry about that. I'm not sorry that I met you, Bernie, but that I lied to you. The plan was that I would pretend to be Dragica. We were the same age. Both from Zagreb. And Dragica was just as pretty as me—I mean she could easily have been a film star herself. After you had found the colonel, we would get Goebbels to organize an invitation from the foreign office for him to come to Berlin in the hope that he might be reconciled to his long-lost daughter, Dragica. The letter encouraged him to do just that. And the plan was that when he did turn up in Berlin, we'd meet somewhere nice and private—the kind of place where you might organize a private reunion—and while we were talking there, Stefan would kill him.

"But then you came back from Croatia and told us that Colonel Dragan had been killed. The detail you provided seemed to be quite convincing. There's not much news coming out of Yugoslavia right now to contradict what you said. Either way it was clear that Dragan wasn't going to be arriving in Berlin for some kind of family reunion anytime soon. I was relieved, frankly. If Dragica's death taught me one thing, it was that I can't stand to have that kind of thing on my conscience. And now this.

"When the doorbell rang I thought it was you, of course. But it was him. For a minute he just stood there and then he started crying. I let him embrace me, which was loathsome. It seems he really did think I might be Dragica. After all, she'd been just a child when last he'd seen her so he really wasn't to know I wasn't her. But there was no time to give it very much thought. I knew that if I didn't kill him right away, then I'd never do it. Not just that, but I might never get a better chance to do it. I remembered you'd left your gun on the back of the chair in my bedroom. So I asked him to wait down here in the drawing room and then went upstairs to fetch it. And the minute I came back into the drawing room, I saw that picture and started shooting. Then you turned up."

"So I see. You did a good job. From the look of the body, every one of the bullets in the magazine must have hit him. If I had a goldfish, I'd give it to you, little girl."

I felt a tremendous sense of relief that I'd not been part of something as awful as a daughter killing her own father. I almost felt decent again. And it was now clear to me where the true path to my own future lay. Perhaps I could do something noble for a change.

"Would you have stopped me?" she asked.

"Probably not. He had it coming with a trumpet fanfare and a red carpet."

"Oh, dear," she sighed. "They chop people's heads off in Germany, don't they? For murder?"

I didn't answer. For a brief second I remembered Gormann the strangler and the awful moment when the men with black top hats had slid him, kicking and screaming, under the blade of the falling ax. If I never did anything else with my life, I was going to prevent that from happening to Dalia. Even if that meant putting my own neck under the blade. What else was a Teutonic knight supposed to do, anyway? If I'd had a sword I'd have knelt and given her an oath of loyalty.

"Will they chop off my little head for it, do you think? Like that poor girl in February? Sophie Scholl, wasn't it? I can't imagine the Pog is going to be very pleased. Or Hitler. Or von Ribbentrop. Or

Goebbels, for that matter. They're going to put me to death for this, aren't they?"

"Nothing is going to happen to your little head, do you hear? I'm not going to let anything like that happen. Trust me, angel. You're going to be fine. But if you're to keep your head on your shoulders you're going to have to make sure you don't lose it, first. That means you're going to have to do exactly what I tell you. Without argument."

She smiled. "My Teutonic knight to the rescue." She shook her head. "Help, Defend, Heal. But I think he's a little beyond healing, don't you think?"

"Yes, he is."

Then she began to cry. I sat beside her on the piano stool and put my arm around her.

"But I can still help and defend you, can't I?"

"I'm scared," she said.

"No need to be. Everything is going to be fine. I promise."

"Even you can't help me now, Bernie Gunther."

"Yes, I can, if you'll listen. When Goebbels told me that Dragan was in Berlin, we agreed that I should take you to a safe house. Somewhere that only he knew about, and that he would call me there, when things were safe—when we'd had time to get Dragan out of the way. That's why I came here. To tell you. That's where I'm going to go when we've finished our conversation."

"Am I coming with you?"

"No, angel. You can't come with me this time. What I want you to do is get in that lovely big Mercedes and drive all the way home to Switzerland. Right now. You know the road. You know how long it will take. Maybe ten or twelve hours. Only this time you're not going to stop in Munich. You're going to keep going until you're safely across the border. And you're never coming back. Never, do you hear? Not while the Nazis are still in power. You're going to go to Zurich

Polytechnic and you're going to study mathematics, just like you'd planned. Don't worry about the cops in Zurich. I seriously doubt they'll reopen the lady in the lake case. And even if they do, they couldn't find their hands in their coat pockets."

"What about you?"

"I'm staying here, in Berlin, like I said."

"Why don't you come with me?"

"Because someone has to stay here in Berlin and lie to our diminutive minister of Truth. I have to call him up from his cottage and say you're there. If I don't, he's liable to send someone around here. And we don't want that. Not until tomorrow, anyway."

"Suppose he wants to speak to me? On the telephone?"

"I'll tell him you're asleep. Don't worry, since I started working for him I'm getting to be quite an accomplished liar. Besides, the Swiss aren't about to let me back in your country. Not after the way I behaved last time."

"No, Bernie, no."

"You've got to listen to me, Dalia. Once I've spoken to Goebbels, I figure I can stall him until tomorrow morning. By which time, you'll be safely home. As soon as you're there in Küsnacht, I want you to call this number." I handed her the business card that Goebbels had given me with the cottage's number written on the back. "Ring the number just twice and then hang up. That way I'll know you're safe." I grinned. "After that I can relax."

"What about us?"

"Us? Look, angel, I thought I told you before. I'm a married man. Or had you forgotten? It's time I went back to my beloved wife. She'll be wondering where I am."

I could see she didn't believe that; I was having a hard job believing it myself.

"Bernie, they'll send you to a concentration camp. Or worse."

"I'll be all right. I'm a survivor. Look, I'll just tell Goebbels the truth. You shot the colonel and that you took off. I'll tell him that I assumed he'd be just as glad as I was to see you get away with it. He won't be pleased, it's true. And he'll have to recast his stupid movie. But once he's thought about it, he'll see that it's best for everyone that you don't stand trial for this. Him, most of all. The last thing the minister of Truth wants is for the truth to be told about what happened here. My guess is that he'll want this whole affair hushed up as quickly as possible. The colonel shot himself eight times. That's certainly been my experience with sudden death and the Nazis. This was a clear case of suicide."

I hoped all of that was true. But I had a feeling that things were going to get a lot worse for me before they got better.

She put her arms around me. "Take me to bed," she said. "Take me to bed one last time and tell me you love me the way I love you."

I took hold of Dalia's arms and pulled her up onto her feet.

"There's no time for that. Not now. You have to leave. And you have to leave right away. Someone's bound to miss the colonel before very long. For all I know, your letter is lying on his bedside table. Or maybe he told another officer in the Ustaše he was coming here. It won't be long before someone turns up and they find him dead. I would take him down to the lake and dump him in the water but there are so many people out there, enjoying the sun, that I might be seen. And they'd certainly soon see him. Besides, I think one body in a lake is enough where you're concerned."

I moved her out of the drawing room to the bottom of the stairs. "Pack a bag," I told her. "Do it quickly. And change that dress. There's blood on it."

Fifteen minutes later I was opening the garage door and Dalia was steering her own Mercedes along the drive and onto the street. I leaned in the window and kissed her briefly.

"Will I see you again?" she asked tearfully.

"Sure you will."

"When?"

"I don't know. I'm sorry, angel, I haven't got a better answer for you right now. At least not one you want to hear. Look, you'd better get going. Before this car of yours starts to attract attention. With any luck when it's seen on the road people will assume it's just Faust flying out of Auerbach's Cellar on a wine barrel."

"Goodbye," she whispered. "And thank you."

Forty-six

When I got to the cottage near Pfaueninsel, I telephoned Goebbels and told him that everything was fine. He sounded
relieved. Then I found a bottle of Korn in a cabinet and a box
of cigarettes, made some coffee, and waited. Thirteen hours later the
telephone rang twice. I wanted to answer it, of course, but didn't. I
knew that would only make things harder for the both of us. Then I
called Goebbels again. I hadn't heard him shout like that since his
total war speech at the Sportpalast, in February. I think if I'd been with
him he'd have ordered someone to shoot me.

They arrested me, of course, and took me to the police station in
Babelsberg, just outside Potsdam, but I didn't care because I knew that
Dalia was safe in Switzerland. For two days they held me in a cell
before they took me to the Linden Hotel. It wasn't really a hotel. That's
just what the people of Potsdam called the place because it was on
Lindenstrasse. In reality this large creamy white building with redbrick
windows was a Gestapo prison. There they locked me in a cell with
more locks on the door than a bank vault and left me alone, but with
meals and cigarettes. I had lots to read. The walls of my cell were covered with graffiti. One stayed with me for a very long time afterward: it
read "Long Live our Sacred Germany." Now, that was something

noble, to give a man hope, as opposed to the dirty little secularist tyranny that Hitler had imposed on my beautiful country.

Five days after Dalia left Germany for good I received a visitor. A little to my surprise it was State Secretary Gutterer, from the Ministry of Truth. He'd put on a little more weight since the last time I'd seen him but he was just as supercilious as ever; all the same I was pleased to see him. I'd have been pleased to see anyone after spending almost a week by myself. Even a man wearing a black top hat.

"You're very fortunate you're not going to stay in here for a lot longer," he said. "It's lucky for you you've got some friends with influence."

I nodded. "That sounds promising."

"As soon as it can be arranged, you're leaving Berlin," he said. "You can spend a couple of weeks on Rügen Island with your wife and then you're to join army intelligence on the Panther-Wotan line. It's an insignificant section of the defensive line that runs between Lake Peipus and the Baltic Sea on our Eastern Front. You'll be a lieutenant in the 132nd Infantry Division, part of Army Group North, where a man of your negligible talents can be properly appreciated. Right now, I believe it's uncomfortably hot there. Lots of mosquitoes. But you won't be surprised to learn that it gets very cold in winter. Which is only a couple of months away. And of course let's not forget the Russians are coming. They should keep you occupied for as long as you manage to stay alive."

I nodded. "Fresh air, sounds good," I said. "And Rügen Island with my wife. That will be nice. Thank you. She'll like that."

Gutterer paused. "What? No jokes, Lieutenant Gunther?"

"No, not this time."

"I'm disappointed in you. No, really."

"Lately—I'm not quite sure why—I've lost my sense of humor, Herr State Secretary. I suppose it weighs a bit heavily on me, being in the

Linden Hotel, of course. This isn't a place for mirth. That and the fact that I've just come down to earth with a loud bump and realized that I am no longer a god. The fact is, I've suddenly stopped feeling as if I were painted with gold and lived on Mount Olympus."

"I could have told you that, Gunther."

"For a short while she made me feel that way. I walked as tall as the tallest man, breathed the purest air, and took an absurd delight in myself. I even managed to face myself in the shaving mirror. I thought, if she can look at me with pleasure, then perhaps I can, too. But now I shall have to get used to being ordinary again. I am, in short, exactly like you, Gutterer: ignoble, inhuman, small-minded, sterile, ugly, with a mind like a paper knife."

"You're making no sense at all, you know that, don't you?"

"I daresay that a man with your great wordsmith's skills could have written that speech better for me, Herr State Secretary. But you'll forgive me if I say you couldn't ever have felt any of those things. Not in a thousand years. You were never a Teutonic knight of the Holy Roman Empire. You've never fought and defeated a troll or a dragon. You've never sacrificed yourself for a noble cause. You've never pledged a woman loyalty on your sword. Which is really what's important in life."

Gutterer sneered.

"Let me tell you something," he said. "And you can take this from the Ministry of Truth. She's going to forget all about you, Gunther. Maybe not today, and maybe not tomorrow, but as time goes by, I can absolutely guarantee it. You'll certainly never hear from her again. My ministry is going to make absolutely sure of that. Any letters sent to or received from her house in Switzerland won't ever arrive. Telegrams will be ignored. Nothing. You mark my words, by the time Christmas comes she won't even remember your name. You'll just be a sentimental little adventure she had one summer when she played Lili Marlene to your soon-to-be-dead soldier. A footnote in the life of a minor film actress of insignificant talent. Think about that when you're sitting in a cold foxhole on the Dnieper River and waiting for an ignominious death. Think about her, wrapped in a fox fur, and in some other man's arms, her husband, perhaps, or some other fool like you who thinks he's more than just her favorite toy."

Gutterer got up to leave.

"Oh, I nearly forgot something important." He tossed an official-looking envelope onto the table in front of us and smiled unpleasantly. "Those are two tickets to the cinema for you. A last gift from Dr. Goebbels. *The Saint That Never Was* starring Dalia Dresner is playing at the Kammerlichtspiele in the Café Vaterland. The minister thought that you might like them so you can see her and know that you're never going to see her again."

"Kind of him. But that makes two of us, doesn't it?"

As Gutterer walked out of my cell, I remembered the graffiti on my cell and for no reason I can think of, I said it out loud.

"Long live our sacred Germany."

I don't expect he understood what it meant. In fact, I'm fairly certain of it.

Epilogue

I'm not sure the ending of my story would ever have satisfied a proper writer like Paul Meyer-Schwertenbach. There was no restoration of moral order—at least none that I could see; such a thing seemed impossible while the Nazis remained in power. Not to mention the fact that the detective had helped the murderer to escape. Twice. This would have been bad enough, but in my story the cop had been so slow on the uptake he'd needed the help of the killer to understand what had happened in front of his own eyes. And I'd nearly forgotten the fact that the detective himself had killed two people. Three, if you count death by farmer's bull. That wasn't good, either. Detectives are supposed to solve murders, not commit them. All in all I thought it was a pretty poor excuse for a detective story. In fact, the only murder that was properly solved—that of Dr. Heckholz, and even that was little more than a good guess—was promptly ignored. Perhaps that was why only the detective himself was punished. At least that's what it felt like. I don't know how else to describe it when you meet a girl, fall for her in a big way, and never get to see her again, except on the cinema screen, which, as I think I said before, is itself a very subtle kind of punishment. It's a bit like what happened to that demigod Tantalus, for whom food and water were placed forever and tantalizingly out of reach.

These days I read a lot. In the winter there's not much else to do on the Côte d'Azur. The Greek and the German philosophers—I love that crap. I can't see the point of reading a book by someone who's dumber than you are, which accounts for most modern fiction, in my humble opinion. Plato talks about something called *anamnesis*, which is when something long forgotten comes to the surface of a man's consciousness. Now, I'll admit that just sounds like a fancy word for remembering something, but actually it's more than that because, with remembering, it's not necessary to have forgotten anything, which makes for a subtle distinction. That's what cinema does. It brings long-forgotten things to the surface. When you're least expecting it, too— which is how you come to walk out of a pretty bad film in La Ciotat with tears streaming down your face. Goebbels had been a very subtle torturer when he'd had Gutterer hand me those cinema tickets at the Linden Hotel in Potsdam. Ever since then I'd avoided seeing Dalia's movies; the pain had been too much. But after more than a decade I thought I was over that and it came as a bit of a shock to discover that I could still cry like a baby when I saw her up on the screen. Fortunately, it was a matinee and there was no one else to see me. Not that I think there's anything wrong with anyone crying in a movie. If a movie can't make you cry, then nothing can. When I saw *Dumbo*, I thought I'd never stop crying.

I walked out of the Eden and along the seafront to a bar I often went to in the summer after finishing my work at the Miramar Hotel. But right now it was winter and the hotel was closing and I was wondering how I was going to survive until spring. It was only the serious yachtsmen who came to La Ciotat in November, although some of the bars stayed open all year around to get their trade. It could be worth it, too. If you can afford a yacht, you can afford a lot. While I drank my coffee and schnapps I borrowed the bar owner's binoculars and watched a very serious-looking yacht as it docked. If you have a peculiar sense of humor like mine you can get a lot of laughs watching some fellow scrape his very expensive toy and then bawl someone out for it, usually his wife. But with this one, they knew what they were doing. It was a wooden-hulled, schooner-rigged boat about thirty-five meters long and maybe a hundred or more tons with a French flag on the stern. The owner and his crew came ashore and walked straight by my table in a haze of cigarettes, expensive perfumes, and a variety of accents.

To my surprise, one of them stopped and stared at me. I stared back. I never forget a face and I wished I'd forgotten this one, but his name still eluded me. He spoke to me in German.

"Gunther, isn't it?"

"Not me," I said, in German. "My name is Wolf, Walter Wolf."

The man turned to his friends. "I'll catch you up," he said, and sat down.

After they'd gone away, he offered me a cigarette, which I declined, and waved the bar owner over. "What are you drinking, Herr Wolf?"

"Schnapps," I said.

"Two schnapps," he said. "Better bring the bottle. Make it the good stuff, if you have any." He lit a cigarette and smiled. "I seem to remember you have a taste for schnapps."

"Your memory is better than mine, I'm afraid. You have the advantage of me, Herr—"

"Leuthard. Ueli Leuthard."

I nodded.

The bar owner came back with a bottle of good Korn and two glasses and left them on the table.

"The last time we did this was in July 1942." Leuthard poured two glasses. "In the Tiergarten. Don't you remember, now? You'd stolen the bottle and the glasses from the Villa Minoux in Wannsee. I was impressed with your enterprise. But I was young then."

"Now I come to think of it, I do kind of remember. That was the night you smashed a man's head in with a bust of Hitler, wasn't it? Heckholz. Dr. Heckholz. That was his name."

"I knew you'd remember."

"What was it made you kill him anyway?"

"Does it really matter now?"

"No. I suppose not."

Leuthard looked somber for a moment. "Believe me, I'm not proud of killing him. Frankly, it's bothered me ever since. But it had to be done. I had my orders. My general told me to shut Heckholz up for good and so that's what I did. I'd have shot him if I'd been allowed to carry a gun in Germany, but I wasn't, so I was forced to improvise. And look here, it was wartime, after all. Even for Switzerland. We may not have been at war but it wasn't for want of Germany's desire to take over our country. So, I had to kill him. It would have been embarrassing for the Swiss government if it had been generally known how much business we did with the German government and, in particular, the SS. Not to say compromising, diplomatically. Our neutrality was at stake."

"I'm sure I don't care. No, really. It's none of my business. It was the war. Really, that's all that needs to be said about it."

"Did you change your name because you were SS? I mean, let's be honest, Gunther. I bet you have a past, too, right?"

"No, that wasn't the reason. But you're right. I have a past. There's quite a bit of it, actually. And each year it seems there's just a little bit more of that than there is a future, perhaps."

"I heard how you figured it was me who killed that lawyer. Paul Meyer told me. That was clever of you."

"Not really. How is he? Your friend Meyer."

"Still writing books. But we were never really friends. He was pretty pissed about what happened that night."

"I liked him."

"He liked you. And your friend—that dyed-in-the-wool Nazi, General Schellenberg."

"That Nazi helped to save Switzerland, too."

"Really?" Leuthard looked less than convinced by this argument but I didn't feel much inclined to argue Schellenberg's case. "I read somewhere that he was dead, didn't I?"

"That's right. Four years ago."

"He couldn't have been much more than forty."

"Forty-two. He had a liver condition. The same one I've got, I imagine. It's the one you get when you keep using your liver to process very large quantities of alcohol."

"Talking of which." Leuthard raised his glass. "What shall we drink to?"

"How about absent friends?"

"Absent friends."

We drank and then Leuthard poured two more.

"What are you doing these days?" he asked.

"I work at a hotel round here."

"Is it a good one? I speak as someone who would prefer to sleep on land tonight."

"Not really. Fortunately for you it's just closed for the winter, which saves us both the trouble of my recommendation, which would be untruthful."

"That's my yacht on the pontoon."

"Yes, I saw it dock. Very impressive. I didn't see the name."

"*The Zaca.* It's very nice but the beds are a little hard. I'm going to have to have them replaced. Either that or get myself a new yacht. You used to work at another hotel, didn't you? The Hotel Adlon, wasn't it? In Berlin?"

I nodded. "That's right. I was the house detective. I tried running a hotel myself after the war but it didn't work out."

"Oh? What went wrong?"

"It was in the wrong place. For a hotel that's always more important than you think it is."

"It's a tough business. Especially in winter. I should know, I run a hotel myself. It belongs to someone else. But I help to run the place. The Grand Hôtel du Saint-Jean-Cap-Ferrat. Perhaps you've heard of it."

I smiled. "Everyone on the Riviera has heard of the Grand Hôtel du Saint-Jean-Cap-Ferrat. That's like asking a German if they've heard of Konrad Adenauer."

"As a matter of fact, he stayed with us, last summer."

"I wouldn't expect anything else of a good Christian Democrat."

"What else have you heard? About the hotel, I mean?"

"That it's the best on the Côte d'Azur."

"You don't rate the Pavillon Eden-Roc in Cap d'Antibes as highly? Or any of the others as much?"

"The Pavillon has a bigger swimming pool, but the service lets it down and the décor is a little tired. And maybe they're a little inflexible with credit. The Grand in Cap Martin isn't doing so well right now; rumor has it that the whole hotel is going to close and become apartments before very long. The rumor's true, by the way. Being right on the main road, the Carlton in Cannes is too noisy, and so is the Majestic. Not only that but people can see into the rooms with a sea view when guests leave the French windows open, which isn't very private for more famous guests. The Negresco in Nice has the best barman on the Riviera but the new chef isn't working out. I hear he drinks. The Hôtel de Paris in Monaco is full of crooks and Americans— the crooks follow the Americans, so you'd better watch your purse— and much too expensive for what it is. It's no accident that Alfred Hitchcock chose to base much of his very colorful film in that hotel. You'll find more thieves working in the restaurant than in the casino. Fifty francs for an omelette is pushing it, even for the Riviera. No, if it was my money and I had enough of it, I'd stay at your hotel. But I'd still ask for a winter rate."

Leuthard smiled. "And here? Where would you stay round here?"

I shrugged. "Like I say, it's out of season right now. But if you really wanted to sleep on land, I'd pick the Rose Thé, on the Avenue Wilson. It's not the fanciest hotel, but it's clean and comfortable and for one night, it should be fine. Good restaurant, too. Better than most. You should eat the red mullet. And drink the local Bandol rosé. Oh, and by the way, I'd leave someone to watch your boat. Some of the locals can be a little light-fingered at this time of year when their employment prospects dry up. You can't blame them for that."

"I'm impressed."

"Don't be. After you've been a Berlin cop for twenty years, information just sort of sticks to your hands like white lint to a pair of black trousers. There was a time when I could tell you if an informer was to be relied upon. Or if a man was armed just by the way he buttoned his coat. Now I can tell you only which taxi service is the most reliable. Or if a girl is on the make or not."

"How do you tell that? I'm interested."

"Down here? They're all on the make."

"You're not including the wives, I hope."

"Especially the wives."

Leuthard smiled. "Tell me, Gunther—"

"Wolf, Walter Wolf."

"Apart from German, what languages do you speak?"

"French. Spanish. Russian. My English is getting better."

"Well, there's not much call for Russian on the Riviera and, thanks to their socialist government, the English have no money. But it seems to me I could use a man like you. A man with particular skills."

"I'll be sixty quite soon. My detective days are over, Herr Leuthard. I couldn't find a missing person in a phone booth."

"I need a good concierge, not a detective. Someone who speaks languages, who's good with information. A good concierge has to be a little bit like a detective, I think. He's expected to know things. How to fix things. Sometimes he even has to know things he's not supposed to know. And do things that others wouldn't want to do. Pleasing guests can be a tricky business. Especially the ones with a lot of money. Handling guests who've had too much to drink, or who've just smacked their wives—I'm certain you could do this in your sleep. I had to let the last concierge go. Actually we have three. But Armand was our head concierge."

"Tell me about him."

"Frankly, he was lazy. More interested in playing the slots at Monaco. And there was a woman."

"There's always a woman."

"How about you?"

"There was a woman, yes. Elisabeth. She went back to Berlin."

"What went wrong?"

"Nothing very much. Let's just say my conversation has ceased to be as stimulating as it used to be. Keeping my mouth shut was once a necessity. Now it's my defining characteristic. She was bored, poor woman. And she never managed to learn French. She felt isolated down here, I think. So she went back home. Me, I like to read. Play chess—it's the only game I play. No, that's not true. I play backgammon and I've learned bridge. I like to go to the cinema. Generally I just keep out of trouble. Avoid the police and criminals, although they're often one and the same on the Riviera."

"You've noticed that, too." He sat back. "You know, they say that the Swiss make the best hoteliers but that's only partly true. The best hoteliers are Swiss-Germans. I think it's the German part which is important. Hotels in Bern and Zurich are much better than those in Geneva. The French are lazy. Even in Switzerland. That's why I got rid of my concierge. The Adlon is closed for good now. But while it was there it was probably the best hotel in Europe. Maybe I could use some of that German excellence in my hotel."

I smiled.

"I'm perfectly serious."

"I don't doubt it. I've seen what you can do with a bronze bust of Hitler."

"The pay's good. The tips are excellent. And it's a beautiful place to work. Of course, you'll have to wear a tailcoat. But after an SS uniform you can get used to wearing anything, right?"

I smiled patiently. "Right."

"Come on, Gunther. What do you say? You'd be helping me out of a spot. I'm about to go on holiday and I really need a man to take the job. As soon as possible would be good."

"Ah, well, there's the thing you never want to hear. A man who asks you to help him out of a spot. As soon as possible."

"What are you going to do in La Ciotat until next season starts? Go to the cinema every day?"

"This week I just might."

"Come on. Say yes."

"Tell me, I bet you get all sorts of movie stars at your hotel."

"Oh, for sure. Charles Boyer is a regular. And so's Charlie Chaplin. Discretion forbids me from naming any other famous names. We guard our privacy very carefully."

I shrugged. "Well, why not? You wouldn't be the first killer I've worked for, Herr Leuthard. And you may not be the last." I thought of the lady from Zagreb for a moment and smiled. "It would seem that some of the nicest people in the world are capable of just about anything."

Author's Note and Acknowledgments

Friedrich Minoux was starving to death when he was released by the Allies from Brandenburg Prison in April 1945. He never recovered his health and died in Berlin-Lichterfelde on October 16, 1945. He was buried in the Alter Friedhof, in Wannsee's Lindenstrasse.

Walter Schellenberg testified against other Nazis at the Nuremberg trials. In 1949 he was sentenced to six years' imprisonment, and wrote his memoirs, entitled *The Labyrinth*. He was released in 1951 because of a worsening liver condition and moved to Switzerland, where he turned to Roger Masson for help. The Swiss intelligence chief tried to help his old friend but was prevented from doing so by Swiss national authorities. After receiving financial aid from no less a figure than Coco Chanel, Schellenberg settled in Turin, Italy, where he died in 1952.

Hans Eggen performed several heroic services for Switzerland at the end of the war, helping to evacuate many Swiss from Germany. Roger Masson invited Eggen to Bern in order to thank him personally. Eggen did not have a visa and was arrested by Swiss police. He was imprisoned in Switzerland until September 1945 and then expelled from the country. Roger Masson was forced to resign as chief of intelligence because of his connections to Schellenberg and the German RSHA. He retired at the age of fifty-three.

Paul Meyer-Schwertenbach continued to write novels as Wolf Schwertenbach. In the 1960s Eggen tried and failed to extort 250,000 Swiss francs from him. Meyer died in 1966. Wolfsberg Castle was sold in 1970 to the UBS Bank of Switzerland, which developed the castle into what it remains today: an executive training and conference center.

I am indebted to Dr. Toni Schönenberger, CEO, Wolfsberg, and Rea Reichen, head of Cultural Affairs at Wolfsberg, for their help with my research, not to mention a delicious lunch in the beautiful castle itself. Walking around what had been the home of another writer, I felt a great affinity with this intensely patriotic and in my opinion quite admirable man. I tried to trace copies of his novels but failed.

The Swiss really did plan to blow up the major mountain passes in order to deny their country to Hitler, who, as late as 1944, still entertained plans to invade Switzerland.

The character of Dalia Dresner is based on two UFA stars: **Pola Negri** and **Hedy Lamarr**. Anyone who doubts that a UFA starlet might also have been a talented mathematician should read Lamarr's biography. She was the coinventor of a technology that has become a key component of all modern wireless data systems. At the time, the U.S. government deemed Lamarr's invention to be so vital to the national defense that scientific publication was forbidden her. She tried to join the National Inventors Council but was told that she could better use her celebrity status to sell War Bonds.

The character of **Colonel Dragan/Father Ladislaus** is based on two or three real figures in the Ustaše. Peter Brzica was a student at a Franciscan college in Herzegovina and one of the guards at Jasenovac; he won a contest there for being the person who could dispatch the highest number of victims in one day with a *Srbosjek*, the curved reaping blade described in the book. His fate is unknown. Miroslav Filipović was a Roman Catholic military chaplain of the Franciscan order and was a monk at the monastery described in the book. He excelled in sadism and was also known by inmates as "the devil of Jasenovac"; Croatian troops called him "the glorious one." He was hanged wearing the robes of the Franciscan order after his conviction by a Yugoslavian civil court, in 1946. Though he was expelled from the Franciscan order, he was never excommunicated. Another Franciscan priest, Zvonimir Brekalo, helped Filipović with the killings; on one occasion these two Catholic priests set about the murders of fifty-two young children. Between eighty thousand and one hundred thousand Jews, Serbs, and Gypsies were brutally murdered at Jasenovac. It was not a concentration camp, or a death camp like Auschwitz, but a murder camp where sadists like these three priests could refine their cruelty. Jasenovac is now a memorial open to the public with a visitor center. Of the camp there is nothing to see except the train that brought these poor people to their deaths. However, close to the border of Croatia and Bosnia Herzegovina is the site of the Stara Gradiška sub-camp where many people died, and which provides a much more atmospheric place of contemplation. I'm not sure if I should want to live in the block of flats that also exists there.

In Croatia I was patiently and bravely assisted by the indefatigable Zdenka Ivkovcić of whom I cannot speak highly enough as a guide and as a translator. The site of Zagreb's mosque can still be seen today; it's a Croatian cultural center. You can also visit the Petrićevac Monastery of the Most Holy Trinity, in Banja Luka, although when I turned up they didn't come out.

Kurt Waldheim became the United Nations secretary-general.

The Grand Mufti of Jerusalem was a nasty piece of work. In February 1943, when an initiative of the Red Cross made possible the evacuation of five thousand Jewish children to Palestine, Haj Amin al-Husseini strongly advised Himmler against this; the children were taken to Auschwitz and gassed. The Grand Mufti held the rank of SS-Gruppenführer.

Regarding **the Handschar**—the 13th Mountain Division of the Waffen SS—I should like to mention the fact that most of these young men were from poor homes and were reluctant "volunteers," and that many of them were not in the least anti-Semitic. In September 1943, at Villefranche-de-Rouergue in France, a group of Muslim officers and NCOs staged a mutiny against their German SS masters; the revolt was suppressed and as many as 150 shot or executed afterward. Eventually more than eight hundred Bosnians were removed from the division and sent to Germany as slave labor. Two hundred and sixty-five of these refused to work and were sent to the Neuengamme concentration camp, where many of them died. Not all Muslims hate Jews.

There really was an international crime commission conference held at the villa in the summer of 1942—just a few months after the more famous conference presided over by Heydrich to decide the fate of Europe's Jews.

Anyone wishing to visit the villa should take the S-Bahn to Wannsee Station. Better still, hire a bicycle and carry it onto the S-Bahn. From the villa I easily cycled to the house of the Grand Mufti on Goethestrasse, and to the studios at UFA-Babelsberg, which are still making excellent films. As always I stayed in Berlin at the superb Hotel Adlon and would like to take this opportunity to thank the wonderful Sabina Held from the Kempinski Hotel Group for all her continued kindness.

I also need to thank Ivan Held at Penguin Putnam for actively encouraging me to write *The Lady from Zagreb*. After ten "Bernies" I sometimes think that maybe people have had enough of this character, but Ivan was adamant that this is not the case and strongly persuaded me to pick up my pen once more. To him this book is dedicated for that reason. I should also like to thank my editors Marian Wood and Jane Wood (no relation), my resourceful and always genial publicist Michael Barson, my agents Caradoc King, Robert Bookman, and Linda Shaughnessy, and my excellent lawyer in Munich, Martin Diesbach. I should also like to thank my wife, the author Jane Thynne, for her help with the research.

For anyone who cares about such things, Bernie Gunther will return in 2016, with *The Other Side of Silence.*

Philip Kerr, London, October 2014